dying wishes
A SHELBY NICHOLS ADVENTURE

Colleen Helme

Book Cover Art by Damonza.com Copyright ©2020 by Colleen Helme
Book Layout & Design ©2017 - BookDesignTemplates.com

Dying Wishes/ Colleen Helme. -- 1st ed.
ISBN 9798674499565

Dedication

To my sweet dog
Sally
For your love and devotion,
happy greetings, and wet doggy kisses.
You will always have a special place in my heart.

ACKNOWLEDGEMENTS

This book wouldn't be possible without all of my readers and fans who love Shelby almost as much as I do! Thanks for your support, encouragement, friendship, and love of Shelby Nichols and the gang! You keep me writing.

Also a shout-out to a couple of you who let me use your names in this book—mainly, Bob Spicer and Clue, or should I say Cluella? He-he. I hope I did you proud!

A big, huge thanks goes to my daughter, Melissa, for your encouragement and amazing support. You are always willing to listen to my plot ideas and your input is invaluable. You've helped me more than you'll ever know!

Thanks to my wonderful husband, Tom, for proofing the manuscript and your great input – and also for believing in me, even when I struggle. To my awesome family for your continued encouragement and support. I love you all!

A big thanks to Kristin Monson for editing this book and making it better. You are the best!

I am so grateful to the talented Wendy Tremont King for bringing Shelby and the gang to life on audio. You rock!

And last but not least, to all of my furry and not-so-furry pets, for your devotion and love throughout the years.

Shelby Nichols Adventure Series

NEWSLETTER SIGNUP

For news, updates, and special offers, please sign up for my newsletter at www.colleenhelme.com. To thank you for subscribing you will receive a **FREE** ebook: *Behind Blue Eyes: A Shelby Nichols Novella.*

Contents

CHAPTER 1

Two days ago, I returned home from my vacation to New York City—the city that never sleeps. While there, I'd been threatened, shot at, and kidnapped, so I didn't get much sleep either. In fact, I still hadn't recovered.

What was that saying? It's never a good thing when you need a vacation from your vacation. That was me in a nutshell. My arm ached from a knife wound resulting in twenty-two stitches, but at least it was healing. I couldn't say that about my state of mind. Those jitters I'd been experiencing, along with the nightmares that haunted my waking hours, hinted that it was time to talk to someone.

Good thing that was already on my agenda. It happened to be a condition of my return to my paid consulting job for the police department. After I'd killed someone—in self-defense—talking to a counselor was standard procedure if I wanted to keep my job.

I knew putting it off would give me a chance to have a much-needed break. But, after the horrible nightmare I'd had last night, I was ready to make the appointment.

Naturally, I put a call through to my partner on the police force, Detective Drew Harris, aka Dimples. I'd missed him and his dimples, and I knew it would do me good to talk to someone who was naturally upbeat and positive.

In fact, Dimples had been there from the beginning, when I got shot in the head at the grocery store during a robbery, and I'd gained my mind-reading ability. With so much going on recently, I hadn't seen a lot of him, so I looked forward to catching up.

"Shelby!" he answered. "Are you back?"

"Yes I am. How's it going?"

"Good. Everything's good. I heard about your investigation in New York. Let me tell you, Chief Winder was real happy that you solved the case for his friend. He was even bragging you up."

"I'll bet." Chief Winder had basically coerced me into helping the NYPD while I'd been on vacation in New York. His friend, Chief Wallace, had a difficult murder case that he'd needed my special help to solve.

Unfortunately, it had nearly gotten me killed. That's what had given me the nightmares. Well... maybe not just that... having a hit put out on me by a vengeful mob boss was the main reason for my jitters, but, in the end, it was all tied together anyway.

"You'll have to tell me all about it the next time you come in," Dimples said. "When do you think that will be?"

"Uh... that's partly why I'm calling. I need to set up an appointment for counseling. It's a condition of returning to work."

"That's right," he said, sounding distracted. I heard papers shuffling in the background before he spoke again. "So... you should do that, and maybe give yourself a few weeks before you come back to work. No need to hurry right back, you know?"

The back of my neck tingled. That didn't sound like the detective I knew. He usually begged me to come in any time I would. "Why? Is something going on?"

"What? No. Not a thing. Just normal stuff. I mean... sure, there's plenty of work to do, but we're okay without you for now. I mean... after everything that happened to you in New York, I'm sure you could use a break, right? So you should take your time. There's no need to hurry back."

Now I knew something was up. "Okay. Cut the crap. What's happened?"

Dimples let out a big sigh. "Fine. I guess you were bound to find out sooner or later."

"Find out what?" My heart skipped a beat. This sounded bad, and I worried that I'd start twitching uncontrollably if he didn't spit it out. "Do I have to come down there?"

"No. No... sorry. Let me explain. A few weeks ago, a child wandered off from a playground up near the woods. Searchers did everything they could to find her, but came up empty. Daylight was running out, so the little girl's grandmother brought in an outside expert to help. Within a few hours, the expert told them where to look, and the child was found, safe and sound."

"Okay... so what does that have to do with anything?"

"Well... that's the weird part. This expert person... well... she claims to be a psychic, and that's how she found the little girl. So... since you've been gone... and you need to be cleared to work again, she's uh... kind of taken your place."

My mind went blank. Of all the things I'd thought he'd say... that was not one of them.

"Shelby? You there?"

"What the hell? Are you serious? Is this some kind of a joke?"

Dimples sighed. "I wish it were. But now that you know, maybe it's a good thing. You can come in and tell me if she's the real deal. I have my suspicions about her... but... after knowing you, I guess it's easier for everyone in the precinct to believe her. I mean... I'm not sold, but she's got something going on."

Dimples knew my secret that I could actually read minds. I'd told everyone else in the department that I had premonitions... a psychic ability. Now he was telling me there was another psychic helping the police?

"Okay... but... I don't get it. First you don't want me to come in, then you do. So which is it? Is she there now... like on a daily basis?"

"Uh... well... kind of. We got a phone call this morning from a bus driver who stopped for a woman sitting on a bench. When she didn't move, he realized that she had blood all over her. He thought she was dead, so he called nine-one-one.

"It turned out she wasn't hurt, but she also wasn't talking. They took her to the hospital, and she's been there ever since. The verdict is that she has amnesia. The doctors think it was brought on by whatever she witnessed. The chief called Willow in to see if she could get a reading on the woman. So she's here helping with the case."

"Willow? Her name's Willow?" I shook my head. "Is she some kind of flower child or something?"

"Uh... I don't know. But if you came in, you'd figure it out pretty fast, right? It's been kind of strange with her here doing all the stuff you normally do. I have to say, I don't relate to her very well. She's nothing like you."

"So she seems suspicious?" Was that what he meant? Now I couldn't wait to go in and find out what the heck was going on. Then what he'd said clicked. "Wait a minute... you're working with her? Like... she's your partner?" Pain tightened my chest. Had I been replaced?

"Oh... no. Well... not exactly. No one's been assigned to work with her, but I'm the one who caught the case, so... in a way, I'm working with her. But it's not at all how you and I work together."

"Uh-huh." Now there was no question about it. If she was messing with my partner, she was dead meat. "Listen, I'll call Leslie Gilman and see if she's got my counseling approved. If she does, I'll set up a time and come down. I can meet this Willow person while I'm there."

"That sounds great." From the relief in his voice, I knew he meant it. After the shock, it warmed my heart. I told him I'd let him know when I was coming in, and we disconnected.

In a daze, I shook my head and let out a heavy sigh. What the hell? Another psychic? How could this be happening?

I found Leslie's card and put the call through. She sounded happy to hear from me and even happier that I was ready to meet with a professional. "Our counselor is here today. Let me give you his number." I jotted it down and called him. His name was Bob Spicer, and he had an opening at two-thirty this afternoon, so I told him I'd be there.

Now that the appointment was set, relief washed over me. I'd taken that first hard step to getting some help. I didn't know how it would work out exactly, since I'd know what he thought of me. And there was no way I'd divulge my secret, but it couldn't hurt to talk to a professional. Whatever happened, I'd been through a lot worse. I could take it, and it might actually help.

My worry now centered on this other psychic person and what she was doing at the department. Was she for real? Did she have some sort of scheme going? Maybe she had some psychic ability, but seriously, this was just odd.

On top of that, I felt betrayed. It was like they'd replaced me. Me—the only real mind reader around, and ten times more valuable than some psychic. I'm gone for a couple of weeks, and this happens? Sheesh! This was the worst.

"Mom," Savannah called, coming down the stairs and rushing into the kitchen.

My daughter was barely thirteen, but she was growing up way too fast for my taste. We'd just come back from New York, where we'd had a sample of the good life from Uncle Joey. He was the mob boss for whom I worked, on account of him knowing my secret.

Recently, he'd claimed my family as part of the Manetto clan, even though we weren't really related. I'd worked for him for just over a year now and, in that time, things had changed between us. Now I worked for him willingly because... well... he was like an uncle to me, and now the whole family part was basically official.

Then there was his eighteen-year-old son, Miguel, and the fact that Savannah had a huge crush on him. Could my life get any more complicated?

"Did you call him?" she asked.

"Call who?"

She rolled her eyes. "Angel. You said you'd call him today, remember?"

"Right. Sure. I haven't yet, but... I'll call him now." Her eyes brightened. I'd promised her that we'd get a dog after our vacation, and she wasn't about to let me forget it.

I looked through my contacts list and found Angel Molina's name. He'd been accused of murdering his girlfriend. While he'd been in jail, we'd taken care of his dog. Because of my mind-reading ability, I knew Angel was innocent right off the bat. Then I'd found out who'd really killed his girlfriend, and now we were friends.

Taking care of Angel's dog had convinced my kids that we needed a dog. After discussing it with my husband, Chris, we had given in to their pleas. Now it was time to follow through. Since I didn't want to make a mistake, I figured Angel could give us some pointers.

His dog, Pepper, had been rescued from an animal shelter, and I knew he'd be happy to tell us about the process. Plus, I could check up on him and see how he was doing. He greeted me enthusiastically, and it was nice to hear he was doing so well. After exchanging pleasantries, I told him we were ready to adopt a dog.

"That's great," he said. He filled me in on the details and told me which shelter he'd gone to. "Good luck. Let me know how it goes. I'd love to stop by once you have your dog."

"Okay. Thanks Angel. That sounds great. I'll be sure to give you a call."

After relaying the details to Savannah, she practically jumped up and down. "Can we go now?"

I tried to come up with a reason to put it off, but there wasn't one. The truth hit me that I wasn't ready for this change in our lives. On the other hand, would I ever be ready to get a dog? Right now, it seemed like just one more responsibility. But we'd made a promise, and there was no going back.

On the bright side, my kids were old enough to take care of a pet. And part of me wanted a dog, too. Maybe it would be a good thing. I could sure use something like that in my life right now.

Since it was barely past eight-thirty in the morning, I had plenty of time to fit in a visit to the shelter before my appointment with Bob Spicer. I nodded. "Sure, but only if Josh can come."

"Sweet!" Savannah ran down the basement stairs to pound on Josh's bedroom door. I wasn't sure he'd be too happy about that, since it was his day off from his life-guard job at the country club, and he was sleeping in. If it wasn't for my nightmare, I'd still be in bed, too.

I heard Savannah telling Josh to get up already. After several tense rounds of negotiation, she ran up the stairs. "Okay. He's coming."

"Uh... I've got to take a shower, but I won't be long." Savannah threw her hands in the air. How could I do this to her? At least she didn't say it out loud, so I just smiled and hurried upstairs to get ready.

We arrived at the shelter an hour later. The workers were all excited to see us. They loved these animals and wanted them all to find a forever home. One of them, Krista, volunteered to help us. She didn't seem old enough to be working there, but I caught enough to know she was seventeen and would be a senior at her high school in the fall.

I also picked up that she thought Josh was cute. She wondered how old he was and where he went to high school. I almost told her that he was fifteen and way too young for her, but I kept my mouth shut. Still, I took a moment to study Josh.

Within the last year, he had changed dramatically. He'd shot up to about five foot ten, and he was still growing. But even more obvious was the facial hair. I guess some boys matured earlier than others, but it began to bother me that he looked the same age as Krista. This was not good.

"I'll take you back to the kennel, and you can see the dogs we have ready for adoption," Krista said, opening a door and motioning us to follow.

We entered a tile-and-concrete room with floor-to-ceiling cages on both sides that held all different kinds of dogs. As we went down the aisle, Krista spoke to each of the animals and told us a little about them. Every dog came over to us, some jumping up on the wire to sniff and greet us. A few barked with excitement, while others whined for attention.

I listened real close to see if I could pick up anything. When we'd taken care of Angel's dog, I'd actually managed to understand what some of her barks meant. It was a side effect of reading minds, and it had totally floored me. I'd told Chris, but no one else.

Even Josh and Savannah didn't have a clue about my limited ability to understand dogs. Of course, they didn't know I could read minds either, and I planned to keep it that way. Like everyone else, I'd told them I had premonitions. After all the close calls I'd had, they believed me. I was pretty sure they knew there was more to it, since I'd messed up a few times, but they took it in stride, which suited me just fine.

So between Chris, Dimples, Uncle Joey, and his hitman, Ramos, that pretty much covered everyone who knew my secret. Well... there were a couple of others, but Gabriel lived in France, and Kate lived in Seattle, and they had both sworn to keep my secret. So it was mostly safe, and I'd do everything in my power to make sure it didn't get out.

The dogs all seemed adorable, and I knew this was going to be hard. How could we pick the right one when they all seemed so sweet? While Savannah spoke to one of the smaller dogs, a dog sitting in the last cage caught my attention.

The tan-and-black dog lay in the corner with his head resting on his paws. He didn't look up at us like the other dogs, and I got the feeling he was sad. Krista noticed me looking his way and came to my side. "We don't know much about that dog. Someone dropped him off a few days ago, said his name was Coco, and left."

"He seems depressed. Is that possible?"

"Sure. I don't know what happened to him, but he hasn't shown much interest in anyone or anything since he got here."

"He's a beautiful dog. He's a German Shepherd, right?"

"Yeah, that's definitely his breed. I just wish the person who brought him in would have given us more information." She thought the dog was probably worth a lot of money, so it didn't make sense he'd been dropped off here. "He's a beautiful animal. I've tried to make friends with him, but he's not very responsive."

She was thinking that all of the staff had tried to engage him, but none of them had succeeded. It was a shame, since that meant he'd be hard to place with a family, and the longer he stayed, the worse his chances of adoption became. Lately, he'd hardly touched his food. It was so sad, like he'd given up on life.

Hearing that broke my heart. I wandered over to his cage and crouched down on his level to peer at him. "Hey Coco. What's going on?"

His head jerked up, and his ears straightened. He studied me for a few seconds, then rose to his feet and trotted over to me. He sat down on his haunches, right next to where I crouched, and looked me straight in the eyes. Surprised, I smiled and reached out my fingers for him to sniff.

"Hey buddy. What's up? Are you sad?"

After sniffing my fingers, he gave them a lick before nuzzling them with his nose. Then he placed his paw on the cage, right next to my hand, and let out a low woof that sounded just like *help*. Surprised, I lost my balance and fell on my butt.

He stood, peering my way like he was concerned that I'd fallen over, then woofed deep in his throat asking if I was all right.

"I'm fine," I told him. "I'm just surprised, that's all." Oops. Did I just say that out loud? I glanced behind me, noticing that Krista, Josh, and Savannah were all watching me with fascination.

Needing a distraction, I smiled at my kids and looked back at the dog. "Coco, this is Josh and Savannah." They came close to the cage and knelt beside me.

He looked from me to them, then he moved to where they knelt and sniffed their fingers in greeting. They both spoke to him, and he seemed to enjoy the attention. After they stopped admiring him, he sat down and placed his paw on the cage and woofed.

I heard *help* again, and both my kids seemed to understand that he wanted something as well. Krista shook her head in wonder. "Wow. He's never done anything like that before. Do you want to take him outside? We've got an area all set up where you can play with him."

"Yes," Savannah said.

"Okay, good." Krista grabbed a leash and opened the cage door. She snapped the leash to his collar and led him out. "From what we've observed, he's well-trained and responds to most of our commands. If you decide you want to take him, I'll show you what they are and how to talk to him."

I had a feeling that wasn't going to be necessary, since I could understand him just fine. He let her lead him out of the cage, but he stopped next to me and wouldn't budge. She shrugged and handed the leash to me and we followed her outside.

As soon as I started walking, he stayed right beside me. I took him through a door to a fenced lawn area with trees and a bench. Krista explained some of the commands to me, and I walked him around the enclosure. He was so well-trained that I wondered if he'd been a service dog, or even a police dog.

"Now let's take him off his leash," Krista said, handing a rope toy to Josh. "That signals to him that it's okay to play, and you can see how he interacts with you."

She unhooked his leash, and he ran over to Josh and Savannah. He played tug-of-war with Josh and the rope. Soon, both of the kids were talking to him and petting him like they were best friends. Coco followed their commands with attentive intelligence, and we were all impressed by how smart he was.

As we watched them interact, Krista shook her head. "This is unbelievable. He's never taken to anyone like this." She wondered what made us so special. She'd heard that animals had a sixth sense about people. Maybe he knew we'd be a good match for him? But what if we didn't take him? She didn't even want to think about that. We had to take him. We just had to.

I wanted to assure her that he was my choice, but I had to talk to my kids first. Still, the way they were enjoying his company, I didn't think I had anything to worry about. Coco nuzzled Josh's hand, then trotted over to the toy box. He picked up a Frisbee and brought it back, dropping it at Josh's feet.

Josh threw it, and Coco made some amazing catches. He always brought it back and dropped it for Josh to throw. After the third time, Coco surprised everyone by giving it to Savannah. He looked at her with his tongue hanging out like he was grinning, and she couldn't resist his charm.

Savannah could throw just as well as Josh, and Coco had a great time. They switched to a ball, then a few other toys Coco found in the box. While the kids continued to play with Coco, Krista went back inside, giving us some privacy to make our decision.

Several minutes later, both Josh and Savannah sat on the lawn in the shade. Coco sat down right beside them. After a moment, he laid his chin on Savannah's knee and gazed up at her with his big brown eyes. She was totally smitten and stroked his silky head with abandon.

"Well, what do you think?" I asked, sitting beside them.

"He's great," Josh said, thinking Coco was perfect. Almost too perfect. "I can't believe someone let him go."

"Yeah, I know," I agreed. "I wonder what happened."

"We have to keep him," Savannah said. "It's almost like he picked us, you know?" She couldn't bear the thought of leaving him there in that cage where he'd seemed so lonely.

"So you're both good with him?" I asked, just to make sure. They both agreed, so I patted Coco's head and looked him in the eyes. "You want to come home with us?"

He jumped to his feet and woofed, then he nuzzled Josh and Savannah, who both responded with lots of enthusiastic petting. Last, he approached me, sat on his haunches, and let out a woof that sounded just like *home* to me.

I was better prepared this time, so I didn't fall over. Still, it was a shock to understand what he meant. "Okay, Coco. You're coming home with us." He woofed again, wagging his tail back and forth and doing a little dance like he was happy.

"Wow," Josh said. "It's like he understands exactly what we're saying."

"I think he does," Savannah said, giving his head a loving pat. She clipped the leash onto his collar, and we headed into the shelter.

It didn't take long to fill out all the paperwork and pay the fee. All of the staff members couldn't get over the change in Coco, telling us he was a totally different dog. Krista even got a little emotional and gushed that she was so happy for him... and us... but I knew her tears were mostly for Coco.

On the way home, we stopped at a pet store and picked out a nice collar and leash. We made a name tag with our information to add to the collar. Then we grabbed a bag of dog food, some bowls, and a bed, along with everything else we could think of, including a Frisbee and some other toys Coco helped us pick out.

Coco was so well-behaved that I almost felt guilty. Almost... but mostly I just thanked my lucky stars to find such an amazing animal. On the way home, I picked up some of the same sentiments from Josh. He wondered where Coco had been and what had happened to him.

The shelter had said there were no signs of abuse, so that was good. He was most likely between two and four years old. I hoped the vet we'd decided on could tell us more about his age. Other than that, there just wasn't a lot of information to go on.

I had heard one of staff members thinking that his owner might have died, and no one else had wanted him. That made sense to me, especially since he'd seemed depressed. Too bad he couldn't tell us. Hmmm... but maybe I could pick up something about his past from him? Who knew? On the other hand, maybe it didn't matter. He was with us now, and we'd take good care of him.

At home, the kids took Coco through each room in our house. After that, they took him outside to explore the yard, and I called Chris to tell him the news. "Wow. That was fast," he said. "But he sounds pretty great."

"He is. And I think he picked us." I began to explain the circumstances, but didn't get far before Chris had to go.

"Sorry. But I have a client who just arrived. Can you tell me the details when I get home?"

"You bet." We said our goodbyes, and I went to the window that looked over the backyard and watched the kids play with Coco. Several minutes later, they all came inside, and the kids decided to take him for a walk.

After getting his leash, I made sure they took some bags along. I'd always hated it when dog owners let their dogs poop on my lawn without cleaning it up. Now that we were dog owners, there was no way we would ever do that.

My kids weren't too excited about that part, but I knew they'd do it anyway. As they left, Coco turned back to look at me. He woofed, *come.* The kids tried to pull him along, but he wouldn't budge. It was after one-thirty, and I had my appointment soon, so I couldn't go. Would Coco understand? Now was a good time to find out.

I knelt beside him. "I can't come right now, but Josh and Savannah will take care of you. Go on... you'll be fine."

"Come on Coco," Savannah said. "Let's go for a walk."

Coco woofed his enthusiasm and let them lead him away. I leaned against the doorframe and watched them walk up the street. When I couldn't see them anymore, I went back inside, amazed. Savannah and Josh going on a walk together? And actually speaking to each other? I couldn't remember the last time the two of them had done anything like that.

So far, getting a dog was working out great.

CHAPTER 2

I arrived at the police station and pulled on my special ID badge. I'd changed my clothes from this morning, going with my black jeans and new ankle boots. I wore a soft, periwinkle blue v-neck shirt topped by a silver necklace and matching earrings. With my blouse tucked into my jeans, I looked pretty hot. Not that I was trying to impress anyone, but I couldn't help hoping I looked better than my competition.

Since I didn't want to run into Willow-the-Psychic before my appointment, I took the elevator straight to the third floor. I found the door with Bob Spicer's name stenciled on the glass and knocked. A thin man with a receding hairline opened the door and smiled. "You must be Shelby. Come on in."

He motioned me inside and shut the door. "Have a seat," he said, pointing to a soft, plush chair sitting in front of his desk. "I'm Bob. It's nice to meet you." He shook my hand and moved to take his seat behind the desk.

"I've been looking over your file. From what I've read, you've been a huge asset to the police."

I nodded, listening real close to his mind. I picked up that he was genuinely impressed. I couldn't tell if he believed in my abilities, but he was willing to go with it since that's what I believed. Helping me was important to him, especially after what I'd been through. Plus, talking to someone like me could prove to be exciting and completely different from anything he'd ever done before.

"You've helped them out with a number of high-profile cases," he continued, "all because of your psychic ability. I have to say I was skeptical at first, but, after reading through your file, it's obvious you know what you're doing."

"Uh... thanks." What was I supposed to say? Thanks for believing I'm not nuts?

He smiled, picking up my reticence. "I'm not here to judge your ability. I'm just really glad you came in to see me." He thought it was a good move to tell me to get counseling, after everything I'd been through. Killing someone was the main reason, but he knew there was probably more to discover.

When had my premonitions started? From what he'd read, I'd claimed it was a recent development. How had I coped with this sudden notoriety? Had my relationships with my family and friends changed? How did my husband feel about it? Had it changed our relationship? Had I tried to hide it from others so people wouldn't think I was crazy? There were probably issues I dealt with on an ongoing basis that I wasn't even aware I had.

Yikes. He was right about that, but I didn't want him concentrating on my psychic ability. I mean... sure it was a part of who I was now, but there had to be more to talk about than that.

"So... how are you doing?" he asked.

I shrugged. "I'm doing okay. I mean... I've been better, but I'm managing."

He nodded, knowing I was evading the question. "Was there something that prompted you to come in to see me today?"

Telling him about the new psychic downstairs didn't seem like a good idea, so I went with the other reason I was there. "I've had some bad dreams lately. And... things tend to upset me more than usual."

He nodded. "Bad dreams can manifest for many different reasons, but one is because we're not dealing well with a traumatic experience, or because we have unfinished business. You say you seem more stressed than normal. Why do you think you feel that way?"

"Oh, I don't know." He made a go-on gesture, so I figured I'd better keep talking. "I guess it's because I've had a lot on my plate lately. I mean, first I'm working for the police, then I also do work for a... uh... family member." I swallowed, glad I hadn't spilled the beans about Uncle Joey, and calling him a family member was almost true.

"Then I have my own consulting agency. Although, I have to say, I haven't done a lot of that lately, at least not since the stalker. That's how he got to me in the first place. He was a client... but then he used that to set me up."

"How did that make you feel?" Bob asked.

"Pretty angry. I mean, how would you feel if some crazy stalker person used you to hurt others, just to make a point?"

He nodded. "I see what you mean. That would be upsetting. What was the point he wanted to make?"

"He wanted me to fail... you know... with my psychic abilities. I think he wanted to prove that I was a fraud."

"But that didn't happen, did it?" Bob asked.

"No." Tension radiated across my shoulders and neck. "But it was close. It put a lot of pressure on me. I mean... he planted a bomb to see if I could stop him. How sick is that?

Then... he grabbed me and shot someone who was trying to save me. He would have killed him, and probably me too, if I hadn't shot him first."

Bob nodded. "How do you feel about shooting him?"

"I guess I'm angry, but... I don't feel too bad about it. I mean... I didn't have a choice. It was him or us, and, to be honest, I'm not freaked out that I pulled the trigger and killed him. Is that normal?"

"It's good that you don't blame yourself for his death. He targeted you, not the other way around." Bob thought that this guy had really done a number on me. Not only had he stalked me, but he'd focused on proving my psychic skills didn't exist. Proving their existence was something I'd probably had to do over and over again, and it could leave me with a lot of anger. No wonder I had issues.

Issues? He thought I had issues? I may be a little angry, but it wasn't that bad. In fact, I was doing pretty well after what I'd been through. Maybe he needed to talk to someone about his issues. He said he didn't judge, but he was certainly judging me.

"Shelby? Is something wrong?" He'd noticed me tense up, and my brows had drawn together like I was angry at him. What had brought that on? It was almost like I'd sensed his thoughts and it had made me mad.

Crap. He was way too perceptive... and he was right. I was upset because of his thoughts, but I couldn't tell him that. Knowing what he thought, along with basically everyone else I ever met, was probably the biggest cause of my stress. It came down to the fact that I couldn't talk about my abilities.

All the lies I'd told, and the deceit I'd used to keep my secret safe, might be giving me a complex. All at once, I wanted to tell him my secret. It would be such a relief to talk to a professional about everything. I could just let it all out. Wouldn't that be great?

I swallowed. No. I couldn't talk to him. He wasn't on my side. He worked for the police, and I couldn't forget that.

"Sorry," I said, shaking my head. "I guess talking about that whole experience is upsetting. Can we talk about something else?"

His lips turned up in a tiny smile, and he thought *isn't that the point of talking to me?* Instead, he said, "I know it's upsetting, so sure, let's change the subject. You were on a vacation recently. How did that go?"

It was all I could do not to roll my eyes. "Uh... maybe we shouldn't talk about that either."

His brows rose. "That bad, huh?"

"Just more of the same. Chief Winder talked me into helping the NYPD while I was in New York City, and I nearly got killed, so talking about that might not help me so much."

"Oh." He nodded with comprehension. "Were you in a rough spot, or did someone target you specifically?"

"Uh... yeah, they wanted me dead."

His brows rose. "I take it that happens a lot?"

"Pretty much."

He nodded, thinking I was like a walking trouble-magnet, and it had everything to do with my psychic ability. Good thing I was talking to him. Still, he knew I was holding something back. Every time I spoke about my ability, I glanced away and wouldn't look him in the eyes.

Intuitively, he knew that being psychic—or whatever it was I did—was the basis of all my troubles. He'd have to recommend more sessions so he could get to the bottom of it and give me the help I needed. Maybe we could talk about the first time I realized I was a psychic and how it had changed my life.

Oh great. That was that last thing I needed. Maybe talking to him hadn't been such a good idea after all.

As the silence continued, he changed tactics. "Let's talk about something else." He rubbed his hands together and leaned forward. "How about this? Is there anything positive that's happened lately? Something that's made you smile?"

I brightened. "Actually yes, there is. We... my kids and I... adopted a dog this morning. He's smart and well-behaved, and my kids love him."

"Oh, that's wonderful. Pets can really have a soothing effect on people. That might be just what you need."

I hadn't considered that, but he was right. Petting Coco, and talking to him, had helped lighten my load. I looked forward to seeing him once I got home, so it was already working.

"We're almost out of time," Bob said. "But this is a good start. I want to give you some tools that might help relieve some of your stress. Considering your bad dreams, I'd like to recommend doing some meditation before you go to bed." He explained why and how it worked, and gave me a list with some apps and websites on meditation to choose from.

"Also, you might find it useful to keep a journal. At the end of each day you could write down what happened that day and how you felt about it. One of my officers calls it a "barf journal." He smiled. "It's just a way to put it all out there, so you're not internalizing or denying those feelings. I think it could help with your stress."

"Okay. I'll try it out."

"Good. As I'm sure you know, it's my job to determine how you're doing, and it's up to me to decide when you can return to work. Right now, I think you're fine to get back on the job, as long as you keep coming to see me."

"Really?"

"Sure. I think what you've done, and how you've handled it, is remarkable. I want to see you again day after tomorrow, and then we'll figure out how many more times you need to come in. Sound good?"

"Yeah, sure."

"Great. Day after tomorrow, I'll expect to see you again at two-thirty." He stood and held out his hand. After I shook it, he handed me his business card. "And feel free to call me anytime—day or night, whatever you need."

"Okay. Thanks."

He came around his desk and opened the door for me. I thanked him again and walked out, feeling relieved. That wasn't so bad. And the fact that he thought I was doing well, in spite of it all, made me feel even better.

With a light step, I took the stairs down to the detectives' offices. Entering, I glanced over the room, looking forward to seeing Dimples. He sat at his desk, studying something on his computer. My gaze wandered the room for a glimpse of the psychic, but I didn't find a new person anywhere. Did she go home already?

Dimples caught sight of me, and his lips turned up into a big grin that sent his dimples swirling. From here, they looked like little tornadoes in his cheeks. Naturally, I smiled back and made my way to his desk. He jumped to his feet and gave me a big hug. Unfortunately, he squeezed my injured arm, and I flinched.

He noticed and quickly pulled away. "Are you hurt?" I'd automatically covered my arm with my hand, so he focused on it. "What happened? Let me see."

I pulled my hand away and lifted my short-sleeved shirt, so he could see my wound. "Just a few stitches from a knife wound."

He examined it, thinking it looked worse than a few stitches, especially with the yellow color of bruising all around it. Had someone squeezed my injury on purpose? His questioning gaze caught mine. Is that what had happened?

I nodded. "Yeah, pretty much. The cut is the result of the first time the guy tried to kill me. After he was ordered to kidnap me instead, he liked to squeeze my arm to keep me in line."

Dimples's face hardened, and his jaw tightened with anger.

"It's okay," I said, wanting to calm him. "The guy's dead, so it's all good."

He shook his head, and a few choice swear words ripped through his mind. His gaze caught mine and his eyes widened. "Uh... sorry. But what the hell?"

He wondered if it had happened because of the police case or because of Manetto. Had the mob boss nearly gotten me killed again? Knowing I'd heard that, he heaved out a breath, then spoke softly so only I could hear him. "I can help you take him down. You know that, right?"

I sighed. Not this again. It was an ongoing argument between us, and I did not want to go there right now... or ever. It was just too late for that. I pushed my initial anger away to placate him. He only had my best interests at heart. How could I be mad about that? "I know, and I appreciate it."

"So what happened?"

I sighed. "It's a long story, and I promise to tell you all about it another time. Right now, I think there's someone you wanted me to meet?"

"Oh... right." He glanced around the office, thinking that she'd left to get coffee in the break room and should have been back by now.

"Maybe she left the building and went to a coffee shop? The coffee around here isn't the best, right?"

"Uh… that's true." He was thinking that getting a cappuccino with whipped cream and sprinkles was more Willow's style. She wouldn't think twice about leaving, but how did I know that? Did I get a premonition?

I laughed and he smiled. "That must be it," I agreed. "So tell me about your case."

His smile dropped. "We still haven't found a body, and Willow didn't pick up much from the woman at the hospital. It would help if we had the woman's name, but she doesn't remember anything, and her purse is missing."

"Wow. That's nuts. So Willow hasn't helped much, huh?" Deep down, I was happy she'd failed; how crazy was that? Dimples pursed his lips and gave me a knowing smile. I just shrugged. "Maybe I should talk to the victim?"

"Yeah… maybe. But are you cleared for that? How did your counselling session go anyway?"

"It was good. Bob Spicer is great, and he cleared me to get back to work."

"Good to hear. Maybe we should—"

"Harris," Chief Winder said, coming out of his office. "We found a body. I need you to head down there— Shelby?" He caught sight of me, and a guilty flush stained his cheeks. "Uh… you're back. That's great."

Before I could respond, a woman stepped out of his office behind him. Tall and thin, she had long, brown hair with blond streaks and bangs. Her hair lay in wispy tendrils that framed her square jaw. Heavy makeup accented her large eyes and red lips, and she wore a white, v-neck, bohemian-style peasant dress that hit her legs several inches above the knee. With wedge-style sandals on her feet, she was nearly as tall as the chief.

Keeping with the peasant style, she wore several beaded necklaces that dipped toward her cleavage, with matching beads that jangled on her wrists and ankles. If she was going for the fortune-teller look, all that she lacked was a scarf around her head.

She caught sight of me, and her brow wrinkled. She was thinking, uh-oh, I must be Shelby Nichols, and I was staring at her like I wanted to kill her. This was bad karma. She'd thought she'd have more time. Now she'd just have to pretend she didn't know anything about me.

Noticing my pursed lips, the chief hurried toward me with a smile and an outstretched hand. "I can't tell you enough how much your help meant to Martin. You really came through with the case. It's still hard to believe how much you were able to do."

He dropped my hand and turned to Willow, who'd followed him to my side. "Shelby was instrumental in taking down a drug ring, and the mob family behind it, just last week in New York City. It was huge."

Willow sent a reserved smile my way, while the chief quickly introduced us. "Shelby, this is Willow Maguire. She's been helping us while you were gone."

This close, I could see that the blond streaks were mostly to cover the gray in her hair. Black eyeliner framed dark, long eyelashes that could only be fake, and she smelled like smoky incense and flowers, or some kind of patchouli. I'd say she was in her late forties or early fifties. Without all the heavy makeup, she would have looked more wholesome. Instead, she looked like she was playing a part.

I strained to listen to her thoughts, but she guarded them well, easily slipping into her persona with the talent of a skilled actor. I even picked up a sense of superiority from her, like she was looking down her nose at me.

"Oh, is that right?" I asked, acting like Dimples hadn't told me. "How exactly does she help you?" I wasn't about to let the chief off that easily, and I wanted him to squirm. He flushed a deep red and couldn't quite look me in the eyes.

Before he could answer, Willow spoke up. "I'm a psychic." The perkiness in her voice sounded forced, and she smiled like it was a joke. "I know it's hard to believe, but it's true, and I'm glad I've been able to help. Did you hear about the little girl who went missing? I'm the reason we found her."

"Oh," I said. "Well... then Brian was lucky you showed up." I used the chief's name to let her know we were on a first-name basis. She didn't seem to know who I was talking about, so I continued. "I mean... Chief Winder."

"Oh... right," she said, waving her hand in a dismissive gesture. "Anyway, he..." she glanced at the chief. "Brian... asked me to come back in and help with another case. So... here I am. We were just coming out to tell Drew about the body. In fact... we should get going, right Drew?" She said his name like they were a couple, and I nearly gagged. "It was so nice to meet you, Shelby." To Dimples, she said, "Ready to go?"

Dimples had that deer-in-the-headlights look, and I could totally see how much he disliked her. He didn't want to go with her, but he was stuck. He looked at me and thought *what should I do? I don't want to go with her. Can you come too? Please?*

The chief was thinking that he'd like me in on this, but he couldn't send two psychics. "Uh... Shelby, do you have a minute to talk?"

I looked between them and shrugged. "Sure." To Dimples, I said, "Call me when you have a minute. I'd be happy to help."

Willow wanted to tell me that they didn't need my help, but she wisely kept her mouth shut. She'd speak up if she needed to, but it wasn't necessary now. This was her investigation, and she'd worked too hard to be replaced. She'd have to pepper Drew about me once they'd left. The more she knew about me, the better prepared she'd be. Still, she'd hoped to have more time before I showed up.

Dimples sighed with defeat and nodded. Then he ushered Willow to the stairs. She sent me a wary smile before turning away. That smile, along with the intent behind it, told me more than I got from her thoughts. She wanted my job. It was that plain and simple. But why go the psychic route?

That was about the hardest way to get a job as a consultant for the police, especially if she had no skills. Of course, because of me, more people, including the chief of police, believed in that sort of thing. But, if that was her reasoning, that just made her seem even more manipulative and downright evil.

Chief Winder led the way to his office, and I sat down in front of his desk. "I'm glad you're back," he began. "But I have to say that I was surprised to see you so soon. I thought you might need some time off after everything that happened in New York."

"Oh... well, I came in today because I had an appointment with Bob Spicer. After we were done, I thought I'd come by and say hello."

The chief's face brightened. "That's great. So what did Bob say? Did he clear you to come back to work?"

"He said I was good to go, but not to take on too much, you know?" I hoped that was enough to keep me on the sidelines. "I could probably help Detective Harris if you need me, but it looks like you've already got someone else on the case." At his pained expression, I continued. "I have to admit that it was a shock to find out you'd replaced me."

His eyes widened. "Replaced? Oh no... not at all. You could never be replaced."

"Well, that's nice to know." I stood, suddenly too angry to stay. "If that's all, I've got to go."

"Uh… sure." He knew he was in hot water, but he didn't know how to fix it. "I'm glad you're seeing Bob."

"Yeah, me too. He's great."

"Good. Hey… uh… take as much time as you need. When you're up to working again, let me know."

He thought that would be the ticket to smooth things over between us, but that was the last thing I wanted to hear. He should be telling me how much they needed me, and that Willow was a fake and nowhere near as good as me. Geez.

I nodded, but I couldn't keep the icy smile off my lips. As far as I was concerned, he was in the dog house, and I wasn't sure I ever wanted to come back. Willow could just help him out from now on. Then he'd find out how much he really needed me.

After a curt goodbye to the chief, I left the precinct with a heavy heart. It was discouraging to know I was replaceable, even though I knew it wasn't completely true. What I needed was a friendly face and maybe a ride on a motorcycle to help me feel better. With that in mind, I drove to Thrasher Development.

I pulled into the parking garage and headed to the elevator, taking a quick peek around the cement column where Ramos kept his motorcycle. Yup, there it was. Just looking at all that magnificent chrome and leather unfurled something in my heart.

The song, "Devil Rider," by Jodie McAllister, started up in my head and brought a smile to my lips. She'd written that hit song about Ramos and his motorcycle. With it on my mind, I sang the chorus out loud in the elevator on the way up to the twenty-sixth floor. By the time the doors opened, I was in a much better mood.

I walked into Thrasher Development with a smile on my face. I hadn't spoken to Uncle Joey or Jackie, his secretary and wife, since we'd come home, and I was pretty sure they'd be surprised to see me so soon.

In fact, it even surprised me that I'd voluntarily show up at the office of a mob boss. After everything I'd been through, I should know better, but, here I was with a smile on my face. What would Bob Spicer think about that? He'd probably want to commit me.

"Shelby!" Jackie exclaimed. "I didn't expect to see you today. How are you doing? How's the arm?"

"It still hurts a little, but it's healing. How's Uncle Joey's shoulder? Did he ever get it looked at?" He'd gotten shot coming to my rescue... well... I guess it was more like a flesh wound. But a bullet's a bullet, right?

"Yes, but only because I made him go in." She shook her head. "That man can be so stubborn."

"Yeah, no kidding." Uncle Joey may be a mob boss, but he'd changed in the past year or so, mostly because of me... or at least that's what I liked to think.

Since I'd met him, he'd made several discoveries. He'd found out Jackie was in love with him. They'd secretly married, but now everyone knew. He'd also found out he had a son, Miguel, who, at eighteen, had enough talent to become the lead singer in a Broadway musical in New York City. That musical was the main reason we'd all been in New York, but it had turned into so much more, and we were lucky to be alive.

"Joe's in his office with Ramos," Jackie said. "And I'm sure they wouldn't mind if you interrupted them." She knew Joe would be happy to see me, especially since I'd come in all on my own. Ramos was half in love with me, so she knew he wouldn't complain.

That was a sore spot for her, and she wished he'd get over it. I was a married woman, and she didn't want him to destroy my life. But the way he looked at me even made her hot all over. If he kept it up, she worried that I wouldn't be able to resist his charms. Of course, I'd kept my distance for over a year; maybe I was stronger than she thought.

As I walked down the hall, I fought the urge to turn around and tell her that she didn't need to worry. Ramos and I had an agreement. He may tease me, but he didn't want to ruin my life, so it was all good. Besides, even if I wasn't happily married, he was a hitman and not relationship material... at least that's what I told myself.

Uncle Joey's office door was open, so I gave a slight tap on the door and stepped inside. Uncle Joey glanced up, and his eyes widened. "Shelby. This is a pleasant surprise. Come on in."

"I was in the neighborhood and thought I'd stop by."

Uncle Joey smiled broadly and came around his desk for a quick hug. "I'm glad you came. It's good to see you." I met him halfway, surprised at the warmth I felt to see him again.

"You too."

While he returned to his seat, Ramos stood from his chair and looked me over with a wicked gleam in his eyes, thinking that he liked what he saw, especially the tight, black jeans and soft blue shirt that made my blue eyes sparkle like gems. "How's the arm?" he asked, wondering if I was going to give him a hug, too.

Crap. Jackie was right. The intense way he looked me over sent tremors from my head to my toes. Of course, he'd do that to anyone, right? It didn't help that he was dressed in his black hitman attire, and danger rolled off him like he was ready to kill someone. Why was that so attractive? Hmmm... what would Bob think about that?

Ramos's lips quirked up in that sexy smile of his, and I picked up his satisfaction that he'd made me forget why I was even there. With a huff, I pulled up my sleeve and stepped close enough for him to examine it. "I think it's getting better all the time, see? The bruises are even fading, and it's not as swollen."

Just looking at the damage to my arm made Ramos mad all over again. Satisfaction that he'd killed the bastard calmed him down. "Yeah, you're right. It does look better."

Standing so close, I couldn't help taking a long whiff of his clean, woodsy scent. His dark, knowing gaze jerked to mine. Chagrined, I stepped away and quickly took a seat in the chair next to his, in front of Uncle Joey's desk. With a smirk, Ramos sat back down.

"So, what brought you downtown?" Uncle Joey asked, picking up on our interaction and thinking that Ramos and I would never learn. It was like a game we played. As long as it stayed that way, he wouldn't interfere, but if Ramos stepped over the line—

"Oh look," I said, pointing at a photo framed on Uncle Joey's desk. "It's the photo of all of us at Miguel's opening night in New York."

"Yes," he agreed, not missing my attempt at distraction. "I think it turned out pretty well."

"It did." We were all smiling, and everyone looked great, just like one big happy family. "I'd love a copy."

Uncle Joey grinned, happy that I'd finally accepted that we were part of the Manetto clan. "Jackie thought you'd like one, so she had an extra copy made for you. It's in your office on your desk."

"Oh... that's great. Thanks."

"Of course. Now... as I was saying... what brought you downtown?" He was thinking about the task he'd given Chris this morning. Had I been to his office? Had Chris spoken to me?

What did he mean by that? My husband, Chris, had recently made partner at his law firm, mostly because of Uncle Joey's influence. He was now Uncle Joey's lawyer.

"What's up? Does Chris need my help?" Since I didn't want to tell him I'd been to the police department, I focused on his thoughts about Chris. Uncle Joey didn't like that I helped the police, so the less he knew, the better for me.

He narrowed his eyes, since I'd picked that up from his mind. Knowing I heard his thoughts was like a two-edged sword. It was useful when he wanted me to know something without actually having to say it, but there were times he didn't like it.

But... while it irritated him, he had to remember that it came with the territory, and he shouldn't get too upset with me. In New York, he'd done a great job of blocking his thoughts, but it wasn't something he needed to do all the time.

Ramos had no idea what we were talking about. It didn't bother him too much, but he was thinking that I should at least try not to blurt out everything I picked up.

He was right, but I was tired of being so careful all the time. Uncle Joey and Ramos knew my secret, and it was such a relief to let it all out. I glanced at Ramos. "Don't worry, he's okay that I listen to his mind." I glanced at Uncle Joey. "Well, most of the time you are... right?"

Uncle Joey snorted, then waved it off. "I'm sure I can manage. In fact, now that you're here..." he glanced at Ramos. "What do you think? You want her to go with you? It might make things easier."

"Yeah, it would, but only if she wants to."

"I'm right here."

Uncle Joey chuckled. "I've asked Ramos to run an errand for me. One of my tenants is behind on his payments. His excuses don't make a lot of sense, so I'm sending Ramos to sort it out. You know how I hate being taken advantage of. So if you go, it would help me out. What do you say?"

I turned to Ramos. "You taking the Harley?" At his nod, I smiled. "I'm in." They already knew riding on the back of the motorcycle with Ramos was a deal I couldn't resist.

"All right, let's go."

Before I stood to leave, I flashed Uncle Joey a big smile. He just shook his head, but I picked up his underlying satisfaction that his offer to accompany Ramos had made me happy. It was the least he could do after everything I'd been through in New York. Plus, as much as he didn't like the whole flirty thing going on between us, he wasn't worried that someone would try to kill me if Ramos was there.

I caught that last part as I walked into the hallway, and my heart swelled that he cared. Then I had a moment of fear that he'd just jinxed me, and now something bad was going to happen. With a shake of my head, I pushed that worry away. It was probably just a product of the jitters I'd been experiencing lately, and nothing like a premonition. Besides, I didn't have premonitions.

While we rode in the elevator to the parking garage, I told Ramos about Coco. "I can't believe we have a dog now."

"I think it's great, especially if he's as well-trained as you say. It's an extra layer of protection for you and your family."

"You're right. I didn't even think about that." Not too long ago, an escaped prisoner had come to my house looking for me. He had a gun and had threatened my kids. Wow. The pluses of getting a dog like Coco were really adding up, and some of the constant stress I felt seemed to drift away.

Ramos opened the trunk of his car and got out my helmet. After slipping it on, I waited until he was on the bike before I climbed on behind him. With anticipation sending butterflies through my stomach, I wrapped my arms around his waist, and off we flew. I wasn't sure of our destination, but that hardly mattered. I just held on and enjoyed the ride.

It ended all too soon at the strip mall a few blocks away. I recognized it immediately. There were several shops, including a jewelry store I'd visited quite a few times. It had originally belonged to a man named Hodges, but he'd had the misfortune of trying to double-cross Uncle Joey. Now he was dead, and the new owners were much better tenants. Were we here to talk to them?

Ramos found an empty parking spot in front of the health-and-nutrition store next door to the jewelers, explaining we were here to talk to the health store manager. After clipping our helmets to the bike, I followed him inside. Three aisles of shelves in the middle of the store were filled with all kinds of vitamins, protein bars and protein supplements, along with products for weight management.

A man in a tight shirt that showed off his muscles stood at the back counter. He had the look of a body-builder-surfer-dude with his blond hair and tanned skin. He hurried to greet us, then slowed when he recognized Ramos.

"Hello Aaron," Ramos said.

"What are you doing here?" Aaron asked, backing up. "I explained everything to Manetto."

Ramos stalked toward him, shaking his head. "That's the problem. You're not making a lot of sense, so he sent me to clear things up." Aaron backed up against the counter and stopped with nowhere to go. Ramos stepped into his personal space and spoke in a low voice. "Manetto's always been clear about what you owe him, and you're late."

Aaron swallowed. "But I thought—"

Ramos held up his hand, cutting him off. "Nobody asked what you thought. Do you have the money or not?"

He was thinking that he had the money, but, after all the risks he took, it just wasn't fair. Still, having Ramos breathing down his neck took all the bluster out of him. "Fine. It's in my safe. I'll have to get it."

He thought about the gun in the safe. He could shoot Ramos and take off with the money. He'd get out from under Manetto once and for all. But... he'd most likely end up dead if he went that route, and he wasn't quite that desperate yet. But he was getting close.

"I'll come with you," Ramos told him.

"Uh... Ramos," I said. "You should probably know that he has a gun in the safe... and he might be tempted to use it."

Ramos's brows rose, and he turned back to Aaron. The shock on Aaron's face quickly turned to fear. "I would never do that."

Ramos grunted and grabbed Aaron by the shirt. He shoved him around the counter and marched him into the back of the store. As they disappeared through the door, I decided to stay right where I was. Ramos had everything under control, and I had no desire to interfere with that. Besides, someone needed to mind the store.

I stepped toward one of the shelves and glanced over the supplements. They ranged from body building and weight loss to increasing your sex drive. Another shelf sported women's ultra-super supplements that included essential wellness oils and antioxidants. Hmmm... if I wanted to be healthy and keep from aging, I should probably get some of those.

I heard the creak of the door opening, but the bell never jingled over the door. Not too worried, I finished reading about the amazing benefits of Biotin before I stepped into the center aisle to take a look.

A young man wearing a hoodie nearly mowed me down. He jerked in surprise at the last second and swore under his breath. The kid had a big neck and the broad shoulders of a football player, and he wasn't happy to see me.

"Uh... can I help you?" I asked him.

He'd watched the store manager leave through the back and thought the store was empty, yet there I was complicating things. He glanced back at the entrance, and I caught sight of another guy standing guard in front. I noticed the sign on the door had been turned from open to closed, and a chill of dread ran down my spine.

Before I could pick up his intent, he shoved me into the shelves and ran to the back counter. I hit the shelves hard, knocking a bunch of plastic pill bottles onto the floor. Off-balance, I grabbed a shelf to keep from falling and knocked several more items onto the ground before I landed on the floor beside them.

As I climbed to my feet, the guy stepped around the counter and shoved several boxes to the ground, clearly looking for something he wanted. He froze, then grabbed a small shoe-sized box and glanced inside before placing it under his arm like a football.

He came my way, rushing back down the aisle. Since he didn't expect it, I tried to stop him. That probably wasn't the best idea, and he shoved past me. I tumbled to the ground, but managed to grab one of his legs and held on for dear life. I tightened my hold while he dragged me halfway to the door.

Surprised that I wasn't letting go, he thought he'd have to kick me in the face. Since I didn't want that to happen, I let go just as he pulled his leg off the ground to kick me. Without my weight, he tilted back on one foot. Taking advantage of his unsteadiness, I gave his raised foot an extra shove. He crashed into the shelves, knocking the contents to the ground and dropping his precious cargo.

Seeing my chance, I lunged for the box and picked it up. As I scrambled to my feet, the guy grunted with anger and lunged toward me. With a powerful tug, he wrestled the box out of my arms, causing me to pitch forward. I slipped on some pill bottles and grabbed his shirt so I wouldn't land on my face.

He tried to shake me off, but he'd had enough and raised his fist to punch me in the face. I quickly let go of him and fell onto my side. He contemplated hitting me anyway, and raised his fist.

The back door crashed open, startling him.

"What the hell?" Ramos rushed toward us with murder in his eyes. The guy took one look at him and took off out the door. Ramos would have followed, but, with me flat on the floor, sudden worry tightened his throat. "Are you all right?"

"Yeah." I swallowed. "I'm a little rattled, but I'm okay." My voice shook, and Ramos helped me up. My legs were a little shaky too, so I was grateful for his strong arms.

Aaron had followed Ramos from the back and stood there with his mouth hanging open. Ramos turned to him. "What the hell is going on here?"

Aaron shook his head. "Those stupid kids. Did they take the box?"

"Uh... you mean the shoe-sized box under the counter?" I asked. "Yeah, he did."

Aaron's shoulders slumped, and he rubbed his hands through his hair. "I'm so screwed." As he took in the condition of his shop, an idea occurred to him. "You have to tell Manetto that it's not my fault. In fact, I should get compensated for this. He should pay me more, and I shouldn't have to pay him at all."

"What?" Ramos asked. "What are you talking about?"

Aaron didn't answer, but I picked it up from his mind. I met Ramos's gaze. "He sells steroids... and other drugs... mostly to high school kids, but other people too... and he thinks he's doing it for Uncle Joey."

CHAPTER 3

R amos's eyes widened. "What?" He turned his gaze to Aaron. "Is she right?"

Aaron glanced between us, not sure what was going on. If I already knew what he was doing, how come Ramos didn't know? "Yeah. But if she knows, why don't you?" It was hard for him to believe that Manetto had kept something like this from Ramos. Why would he do that? And who was I anyway? Was I Manetto's niece?

Oops. I glanced at Ramos and motioned him to lower his head toward mine, so I could whisper in his ear. "Since I read his mind, he's thinking that I know what's going on and you don't, so it's confusing him."

I started to pull away, but Ramos held onto my shoulder and began to whisper into my ear. "I got that. So what should we do about it?"

His warm breath on my neck sent shivers up my spine. With his face right next to mine, and his lips close enough to kiss, I found it hard to breathe. His scent wafted over me and I froze. "Uh... what?" I couldn't think straight. What were we whispering about? Oh yeah. "I... I don't know... wait... are you..." I sucked in a breath and pulled away. His brows rose, but it was hard not to miss that wicked gleam in his eyes.

"You... ugh."

With satisfaction rolling off him, he turned back to Aaron. "I think you'd better tell us what's going on." Aaron glanced my way, and Ramos continued. "Pretend she doesn't know."

Aaron shrugged. "Fine. Whatever. Your guy came in couple of months ago and set it up."

When he didn't continue, Ramos shook his head, clearly losing patience. "Set what up?"

"I can't believe this. Why don't you know about it? She does."

I struggled to keep from grimacing. "Aaron. Just explain it to us. Okay? Who came in to see you?"

"The guy said his name was Slasher, and Manetto sent him. He told me Manetto wanted to set up a delivery system here at the store because it was the perfect front for getting certain drugs to the athletes at the high schools and gyms. You know... since they come in here a lot for protein shakes and whatnot."

"Go on," Ramos said.

Aaron shrugged. "Slasher supplies the drugs, and the kids come by and pick them up. I don't know anything else... except that Slasher told me I didn't have a choice, and he'd break both my legs if I told anyone about it."

"Do the kids pay you directly?"

"Yes, of course they do." He gestured at the mess. "Except for those kids. I've seen them a few times with buying customers. I guess they decided to risk Slasher's wrath and not pay. Slasher's gonna throw a fit."

Unease crept over him. Could our visit be about Slasher's deal to give him twenty percent of the profits? He wasn't sure Manetto knew about that. Maybe that's what this was all about, and Ramos was shaking him down and playing dumb, so he'd confess.

Ramos glared at him, and Aaron braced himself for the worst. When Ramos didn't speak, Aaron got nervous. "What? I didn't do anything wrong."

"That's not it. Whoever this Slasher person is, he doesn't work for Manetto."

"What the..."He glanced my way, thinking I wouldn't appreciate his foul mouth, especially if I was the boss's niece. "What are you talking about? He set it up. It's Manetto. Who else runs drugs around here?"

Ramos shook his head, thinking Manetto's plan to go straight always seemed to backfire. After the fiasco with Dusty McAllister, he'd decided to get out of the illegal drug business. But he just couldn't catch a break.

"He is?" I asked, shocked and excited. "That's amazing. I never thought... I mean... He kept saying he'd changed but—"

"Shelby," Ramos said, interrupting me. He nodded his head toward Aaron, thinking now was not the time to talk about Manetto's change of heart.

"Oh... right."

Aaron couldn't figure out what the heck I was talking about. It didn't make a lick of sense. Who'd changed? Manetto?

Before he could ask, Ramos spoke. "Does this Slasher person have a real name?"

"Not that I know of, but he's one of Manetto's guys."

Ramos shook his head. "Like I said, Slasher doesn't work for Manetto."

"Son of a bitch." A string of profanity rushed through his mind, so I tried to block him out.

Ramos leaned against the counter and folded his muscled arms. "We need to turn the tables on this guy. I have an idea. Why don't you tell him some kids came in and stole the box? That should get his attention. You can set up a meeting to discuss it with him, and I'll be happy to back you up. Then I can take him off your hands and figure out what's going on."

Aaron nodded, thinking he'd hate to be Slasher. "Okay. I'll call him right now."

Aaron picked up his phone and placed the call, sounding frantic about the stolen drugs. If nothing else, he was a darn good actor.

"What should I do?" He listened for a minute, then suggested that Slasher bring more drugs to replace them, since this left him short. "Those items were for tonight. Unless you bring more, I won't be able to make the deal."

Aaron listened to Slasher's tirade and shook his head. "Fine, whatever man. Just be here by nine-thirty. The kids usually show up at ten. I'll meet you behind the store."

They disconnected, and he slipped his phone into his pocket before glancing at us. "I think he'll come through for tonight, but he said he's taking it out of my pay. He even said that Manetto might kill me for this." Aaron shook his head. "I can't believe this is happening to me."

"I feel your pain," I said. After the day I'd had, this was par for the course. Aaron looked at me sideways, thinking I had no idea what I was talking about. "Hey... stuff like this happens to me all the time. It's rough." He wasn't convinced, but he didn't want to argue with the boss's niece.

"So he's coming between nine-thirty and ten?" Ramos asked, thinking we were getting sidetracked with all our complaining.

"Yeah. The kids usually come between ten and ten-thirty."

"Okay. I'll be back here by nine to wait for him. Does Slasher usually come alone?"

"Yeah. At least, I've never seen him with anyone else."

"All right. Call me if anything changes."

"Sure. See you tonight." He almost added that Ramos should bring a gun, but stopped himself, knowing that was a stupid thing to tell a hitman.

Ramos and I left him to clean up the mess. I was hoping to buy some of those anti-aging pills, but decided now might not be the best time with Ramos watching.

Ramos handed me my helmet. "That was strange."

"I know. Has anything like that ever happened before?"

"No. Manetto won't be happy, but I'm sure we can take care of it."

I snorted. "Yeah. After New York, this should be a piece of cake."

He grinned, liking my sassy attitude. "Do you want to take the long way back?"

"Yes!" I couldn't contain my enthusiasm. Ramos grinned. He liked the way my eyes lit up, thinking it was a beautiful thing. I chuckled and slipped on my helmet. A minute later, with my arms holding him tight, we were off.

The next twenty minutes went by way too fast. As we parked in the garage, I got off and sighed. Maybe I should volunteer to help Ramos tonight? That way I could get another ride. "Do you need some help tonight?"

"What?" Ramos's brows rose. Was I turning to the dark side? What about my responsibilities at home with my husband and kids? Did this mean I was choosing him over them?

"What? Uh... No... I mean... uh, I just like riding your bike, that's all."

"Uh-huh." He nodded. "So it's all about the bike."

"Well... yeah. Geez." I playfully swatted his arm and turned to go. "I guess I'd better get home. Tell Uncle Joey goodbye for me. And... uh... good luck tonight. Don't get killed or anything."

He did that little head nod thingy, thinking that he sure liked pushing my buttons.

I shook my head and started toward my car. Instead of heading for the elevator, Ramos stood there and watched me go. I didn't catch any words from his mind, but I definitely felt his admiration for my backside, and I nearly tripped over my own two feet.

I could have turned around and scolded him, but I figured it was better to make him think it didn't bother me. Still, getting to my car without falling on my face became a monumental task.

I opened my door and glanced back at him. Since he hadn't moved, I just shook my head and waved. He sent me that lopsided, sexy grin of his, and entered the elevator. I climbed inside my car and let out my breath.

I knew I should probably put up my shields and not listen to all of Ramos's teasing thoughts. That would solve my discomfort, but, deep down, I knew I wasn't about to do that. A part of me liked it way too much to stop. I was going to hell for sure.

After pulling into the garage at home, I came through the back door, and a soft, furry body rushed to greet me. Coco wiggled against me, shoving his nose into my hands, with his tail wagging so hard I thought for sure it might break. He seemed so relieved I'd come back that it broke my heart.

"It's okay, Coco. I'm back."

He barked, *home*. I nodded. "Yes. I'm home now. Did you have a nice walk?" He barked, *yup*, and I smiled, ruffling his fur. "Let's go sit down for a minute." He barked *yup* again, and followed me to the living room, where I sat on the floor in front of the couch.

He sat beside me and rested his head on my knee, looking up at me with those big, adoring eyes. Naturally, I lavished him with love and praise while petting his beautiful face. I even kissed him. Who would have thought I'd ever kiss a dog? Sheesh.

Savannah came downstairs from her room and told me all about their walk. "After we got home, I tried to get him to sit on the couch with me, but I guess he wasn't allowed on the furniture before, because he wouldn't do it. Should we tell him it's okay?"

"You know, I think if he's not used to it, we shouldn't change his training. It's nice not to have dog fur all over the furniture, and we can always sit on the floor like this if we want."

"Yeah, and he's got his new bed. Where should we put it?"

"I'm sure we can figure it out." As we spoke, I felt the tension of the day drain away. It amazed me how much better I felt petting a dog who seemed to adore me. After speaking a little longer, we got up to get dinner ready.

With our meal in the oven, I set the dishes on the table, and Chris walked in the door. Coco barked to sound the alarm, but settled down after I introduced him to Chris. It wasn't too much of a stretch to understand that Coco had already picked up Chris's scent, and, after one sniff, he accepted Chris pretty fast.

It wasn't until later in the evening that I told Chris how I'd understood Coco's barks. We sat out on the deck swing in the late glow of the sunset, enjoying the cooler temperature. "He's one smart dog," Chris agreed, watching him catch the Frisbee with Josh and Savannah. "I wonder what happened to him. I don't think his owner would have given him up so easily."

"I know, we've all been wondering the same thing. Maybe I'll pick it up at some point, but I'm not sure how much he can tell me. I mean, I usually just get one-word responses, you know?"

"Yeah, that makes sense." After watching Coco make another great catch, Chris pulled me against him, careful of my arm. "So, how was your day?" Naturally, I told him all about the new psychic at the police station.

"So you went in just to meet her?"

"Of course. When I talked to Dimples, he wanted to know if she was for real. But, after I got there, I didn't have much time to find out because they had to leave. I did pick up that she wants my job though. I just don't understand why she's pretending to be a psychic to do it."

"That's insane," he agreed. "But... have you considered that she might have some psychic abilities? If she's after your job, that's the only reason that makes sense, even if it seems crazy. Besides that, she sounds like trouble. Are you sure you want to get involved?"

"No. But I told Dimples I'd help him. Still... maybe he won't need me. In fact... maybe none of them will need me anymore."

Chris's brows rose. "You sound disappointed. But look at it this way; now that the police have another psychic, you can finally take some time off."

He thought I'd been through a lot lately and it was taking a toll. Besides, I'd hardly had any vacation time on our vacation, so this was a good excuse to lay low and hopefully not get shot at, kidnapped, or stabbed.

In fact, staying away from the police might be the best thing that's happened to me lately, especially with Uncle Joey's request. He still didn't know what to make of it. Should he tell me or wait for a better time?

What the hell? I caught his gaze and raised my brows. He swore, realizing I'd picked that up from his mind before he could squash it. "It's nothing to be worried about."

"Then why don't you want to tell me?"

He tamped down his concern, thinking that we needed to be calm and level-headed about this. It could be really good... or maybe really bad. Still, no one was going to make me do anything I didn't want to, so we could handle it.

"What's he done now? Is he in trouble?" Worry tightened my stomach.

"No. Not at all." Chris wished he had more time to think it through, but I wasn't about to let it go. Plus, there was the meeting tomorrow—

"Chris—what's going on?" I needed him to spit it out before I had a full-fledged panic attack.

"He's just changing a few things in his trust. You know... in case anything happens to him or Jackie... or... uh... when they die of old age? So it's probably fine."

"What's he done?"

"He's added you to his trust as the executor of his estate."

"What?" Shock rolled over me. "What does that mean?"

"It just means that you have to carry out his wishes. It shouldn't be a big deal, but I guess after what happened in New York, he wants to be prepared in case something happens to him."

I snorted. "Sorry, but that's kind of funny. I mean... if anything happens to anyone, it will probably be me, not him."

"You have a point," Chris agreed, thinking I was a bona fide trouble magnet. "I don't think you have to worry about it too much, I mean Jackie will probably outlive him, and it falls to her first."

"Then why put me in it at all?"

Chris shrugged. "I guess because it's better to be prepared for all circumstances."

"But surely Miguel could take care of it." I thought he'd probably outlive us both, but I didn't want to say that part out loud. Did that mean I was becoming cynical? Hmm... maybe I should talk to Bob about that.

"Yeah, but I don't think Manetto wants to put that on Miguel. He trusts you, Shelby, and I think he'd rather have you take care of things."

I shook my head. "But couldn't you do a better job than me? Why doesn't he just leave it to you?"

"Because I think he's got something else in mind." Chris knew this was the part that might upset me. "I could be wrong, and he certainly hasn't told me this, but I think he wants to name you as a beneficiary."

"Really? Huh... does that mean he's leaving me some of his money?"

"I think so. I'm just starting up the paperwork. We're meeting tomorrow, and he wants both of us there. So I guess we'll find out then."

"He wants me there—in a meeting with you—and you're just telling me this now?"

"Uh... yeah." His brows drew together. Why was I getting so upset? He hadn't had a chance to tell me before now.

"What time and where?"

"In his office at ten. Will that work?"

He may have asked me now, but it griped me that he'd gone ahead and set up a meeting with a time and place before asking me if that would work. He should have called me first to make sure it would work for me too, but no... he'd just gone ahead without asking. What if I was busy?

I caught confusion coming from Chris. He wondered what was going on with me. He could have called to make sure the time would work, but he knew I wasn't busy with anything at the moment, and it was Uncle Joey. Since I always jumped to do his bidding, why was I sitting there like I was angry with him?

I heaved out a breath to calm down. "Uh... sure, ten should be fine, but next time, can you call and ask me before you set something up? I mean... it's true that I'm not busy with anything at the moment, but things can change. I could be helping the police... or a client... you never know."

"Right," he quickly agreed. "Of course. I can do that. I just thought... never mind. I get it, and I should have spoken to you when we set it up."

He rubbed his chin, thinking that I seemed more stressed than normal. Was there something else going on that I'd kept to myself? Had Chief Winder coerced me into doing something for him again, and I hadn't told him? "Don't you have to be cleared before you can go back to work for the police?"

I pursed my lips. Why did Chris always think the worst? Sure, I kept things from him, but not so much anymore. "Yes. But don't worry, the chief hasn't asked for my help on anything." I didn't want to mention that he'd told me to take some time off, since it still rankled.

"But I forgot to mention the other reason I went in to the precinct. I met with a counselor. His name's Bob Spicer, and he's really nice. He basically cleared me to return to work."

Chris's brows rose. "Wow... that was fast... but... I guess that's good." He couldn't tell how I felt since I wasn't smiling about it. "So what did he tell you?" He was hoping he'd given me something to help with my short temper, because being in the hot seat was not fun. I'd always been a little dramatic, but lately, it had gotten worse. Of course, after everything I'd been through—

He glanced my way, knowing I'd just heard that. Frustration mounted that he was never going to get this right. He should know better, but damn it... how was he supposed to function if he couldn't think? And why did I have to pick up every little thing that went through his mind.

He remembered how hard it was when I'd first discovered my mind-reading ability, and how he'd asked me to put up my shields around him. He'd learned that wasn't the answer, because it just made him look like a tyrant.

So what was he supposed to do about it? He hated hurting my feelings, but some of his thoughts were deeply personal. He'd never say any of those things out loud... but I knew it all, and it made life difficult for him... and for me.

"Chris... don't get too upset. You're right. It's difficult, but not insurmountable. Most of the time, it doesn't bother me, but I'm struggling a little. Just like you said... er... thought... I've been through a lot lately, and I'm a little uptight. But now that I'm seeing a counselor it's bound to help. Maybe I can bring up how hard it is for you in one of my sessions, and see if he has some good suggestions?"

"He knows you can read minds?" Shock rippled through him. He didn't think I'd ever tell anyone that.

"No... of course not," I said, keeping my voice low. "He thinks I have premonitions... but it's basically the same thing, and it would be nice to hear what he has to say about it, right?"

He didn't think it was the same thing at all, but what did he know? "I guess it doesn't hurt to talk about it."

"I agree. I'm meeting with him again day after tomorrow, so I'll ask him about it then."

"Okay, sure."

I glanced up, noticing that both Savannah and Josh were sitting with Coco on the grass, but they'd each picked up a few snippets of our conversation. Savannah wondered if something bad was going on between Uncle Joey and me. But Josh's thoughts nearly gave me a heart attack. He wondered if he'd heard Chris correctly. Had he said something about reading minds? Was he talking about me?

As the blood drained from my brain, a voice called from the side of the house, and we all turned to find Angel Molina and his dog, Pepper, standing by the gate. Both Josh and Savannah hurried over to the pair, and I sighed, grateful for the reprieve.

I'd called Angel earlier about Coco, and he'd said he'd come by sometime tonight to meet him. Was I saved by the bell, or what? Of course that didn't change the fact that Josh might ask me about it later.

Coco took to Angel and Pepper right away, and we spent the next hour admiring the dogs and catching up. After his brush with the law, Angel was thinking about becoming a cop, and then hopefully a detective, so he could help people the same way I'd helped him, especially the innocent ones.

I thought that was a noble thing to do, but it worried me, since he'd be on the front lines with all the risks it entailed. But, wasn't that what I did, without going through the ranks? Maybe we could even work together sometime? I could definitely go for that.

We had a pleasant visit, and it was late when Angel left. Before we could discuss where Coco would sleep, Josh said goodnight and called Coco to follow him down the stairs. Savannah didn't like that and told Josh she wanted Coco to sleep in her room.

It was like a dam breaking, and Josh let out all his pent-up frustration, arguing that he was sick and tired of Savannah always getting her way, and Coco was just as much his dog as hers. Savannah began to yell back, and both of them got louder and louder with each word.

Before Chris or I could intervene, Coco barked, his tone more menacing than anything we'd ever heard before. I heard *stop*, and it seemed as though the kids did too. In the sudden silence, we all glanced at the dog. His head was lowered, almost like he was ready to attack.

"You're upsetting Coco," I said, even though it was obvious to everyone. "Why don't you take turns? He can sleep in Josh's room tonight and in Savannah's tomorrow."

"But mom..." Savannah moaned.

"No buts. This is the fair thing to do, and Coco doesn't need more upheaval in his life."

Savannah's thoughts turned to Coco and everything he'd been through. With a pout, she gave in. "Fine."

As soon as the words left her mouth, Coco moved to her side and snuffled his nose against her hand. She petted him and knelt down to give him a hug. While petting and talking to him, she secretly hoped he'd choose to go with her if she kept it up.

Josh worried about the same thing, and he let out a pent-up breath of frustration. Coco tipped his head toward Josh and, after a quick lick at Savannah's face, he followed Josh down the stairs. Savannah wiped the moisture off her face and hurried up the stairs to her room.

After her door shut, Chris and I just stared at each other. "That was interesting," Chris said.

"Yeah. Do you think Savannah will get over it? I mean... she's the one who's been pushing so hard to get a dog."

He shrugged. "True. But I have to agree with Josh that Savannah tends to get her way a lot more often than he does."

"Yeah, maybe, but that was interesting. Coco was like a referee between them. Have you ever seen anything like that before?"

"No. It makes me wonder what kind of training he's had."

"Yeah, me too." I agreed.

After checking on Savannah, and locking up the house, we got ready for bed. I'd been holding my worry at bay, but, once we slipped under the covers, I let it all out.

"While we sat on the deck swing, Josh heard us talking."

Catching my agitation, Chris's brows drew together. "What did he hear?"

"He overheard you asking me if I'd told Bob that I could read minds. You said that part pretty loud. I think Josh got distracted when Angel came over, so he didn't say anything. But now he's wondering if that's what I do. This is terrible."

Chris's lips twisted with the irony. He could hardly believe he was the one who'd messed up this time. It was usually me.

I sucked in a breath. "I heard that."

He shrugged his shoulders. "Well, it's true. You've answered their thoughts more than once, but somehow you've always managed to get away with it. To be honest, I'm surprised they haven't figured it out yet."

I frowned. He was right. Did that mean I was fighting a losing battle, and it was only a matter of time before they'd know the whole, horrible truth? I didn't want that to happen. Ever.

Chris wrapped his arms around my waist and pulled me to him. "Maybe it won't be so bad if they find out. At least it would make things easier for you."

"You can't believe that. It would make them worse. Just think about how much you hate it. In fact, you were just complaining about how hard it was. Remember?"

His teasing grin turned into a grimace. "Yeah... I guess you're right."

"Promise me you'll be more careful, and if they figure it out, we can just deny it."

"Okay." He nodded. "So, when Josh asks about it, what should we tell him?"

"We tell him that part of having premonitions is like reading minds, because I can sense if someone's lying to me, and I can pick up what they're feeling. How about that? That would be better than the truth, don't you think?"

"Yeah... that should work." It sounded like a simple solution, and he hoped Josh bought it.

I nodded, hopeful it would work, but it was just one more thing to worry about, and right now my nightmares were bad enough. Maybe I should talk to Bob about that, too? It seemed that the things I needed to mention to Bob were getting longer by the minute. I should probably make a list before my next visit.

But right now, I just wanted to go to sleep and forget all about it. Too bad I had nightmares to look forward to. Remembering the meditation app Bob had suggested, I took out my phone and downloaded it.

After explaining the app to Chris, I got started. Curious, he watched me sit cross-legged on the bed, with my hands palm up on my knees. As I tried to concentrate on my breathing, I kept hearing his thoughts about me, and how tempting it was to poke me in the side. Or tickle my neck while my eyes were shut. I'd probably jump right out of my skin.

"Would you stop that?"

"You mean this?" He began to tickle me, and I fought back. With his arms around me, it turned into a wrestling match, ending up with me on top of him, pinning him down. Score one for me. Not wanting to be bested, he took advantage of my inattention and rolled me onto my back. With a glint in his eyes, he soundly kissed away my protests.

I have to say... even though it wasn't meditation therapy, his kind of therapy worked pretty well, and I went to sleep exhausted, but with a smile on my face.

CHAPTER 4

The next morning, Coco was up early wanting to be let out. With Josh and Savannah still asleep, I fed Coco and decided to take him for a walk. Chris left for work at the same time. "See you at ten." He gave me a quick kiss and hurried out the door.

After attaching Coco's leash, we started up the street, and my thoughts turned to the meeting with Chris and Uncle Joey today. What exactly did Uncle Joey want, anyway? Making me a beneficiary might not be so bad, but executor of his estate? How big was his estate? From what I already knew, it could be huge. That seemed like more responsibility than I wanted.

I gave Coco free rein and we wandered out of our neighborhood and into another subdivision that I didn't know as well. I didn't mind the diversion and enjoyed the walk. After forty-five minutes, it was time to get back.

"Let's go home," I said to Coco. He glanced up at me, but whined and kept pulling forward. That's when I realized he'd been leading me along the last few blocks. "What is it?" He whined again and pulled harder. "Is there something you want to show me?"

He barked. *Yup.*

"Okay, but I don't have a lot of time. I've got to get back home."

This time he barked with urgency. *Come. We go.*

Wow. That was almost like a complete sentence. "Okay, okay. I'm coming."

He led the way down a small side street that I hadn't seen before. It rounded a bend into another subdivision, with homes a little older than those in my neighborhood. I could feel Coco's excitement, and I began to jog along to keep up with him.

Halfway down the street, he turned a corner into another street that wound nearly back to the first street we'd been walking along. Another street crisscrossed this one, and Coco pulled against his leash so hard that I nearly lost hold.

I pulled back, but couldn't get him to slow down, and it worried me that he was so frantic. Then he let out a bark and pulled hard enough that the leash jerked right out of my grasp. "Coco, stop!"

He bolted to a house a short distance away, running right up to the door and scratching on it with his front paws. What the heck? Did he know this place? My heart sank. Was this his owner's house? Had someone stolen him and he wasn't really ours, and now we'd have to give him back?

I kept running after him, finally making my way onto the property. Before I could reach the porch, someone pulled the door open, and Coco barreled past him and ran inside the house. "Coco? What are you doing here? What's going on?" He glanced my way and his gaze narrowed. "Did you bring him here?"

His unfriendly tone put me on the defense. "No. We were just out on a walk."

Confused, he hurried inside to find the dog, leaving the door wide open. I followed behind, wanting to make sure Coco didn't get into trouble. I passed through the living room, finding it cluttered with stacked boxes, and the furniture in disarray.

I continued toward a back bedroom, finding Coco sniffing the boxes in the stripped-down room. He circled the room several times, like he was looking for something. Then he sat down on his haunches in the middle of the floor and howled. He kept it up, and it got more and more mournful, like he was in pain, or crying, and it broke my heart.

The man stood just inside the room and watched Coco with dismay. Soon, tears began to run unchecked down his cheeks. He couldn't believe Coco was back. He thought he'd done the right thing by leaving him at the shelter, but it hadn't worked. Now what was he going to do? The man's grief echoed Coco's, and tears filled my eyes.

"I'm so sorry," I said, wiping them from my cheeks. "I adopted Coco from the shelter yesterday. We were out on a walk, and somehow we ended up here."

Lost in his grief, the man didn't answer, so I hurried to Coco and began to speak while I ran my hands over his head and around his neck. "It's okay buddy, I know you're sad, but I'm here. We'll figure it out, okay? You and me. We'll do it together. All right?"

He stopped howling and snuffled my face, licking my cheek. "That's right. It's going to be all right. I promise." He let out a small yip, and I heard *help*. "Yes. Of course. I'll help you." With that, he lay down on the carpet and rested his head on his paws. His mournful gaze locked on the man who stood in the doorway.

The man's brows rose, and he turned my way. "That was... you calmed him down. I couldn't... I tried so hard...

but there wasn't anything I could do for him. But you... you helped him."

I smiled and held out my hand. "I'm Shelby Nichols."

"Oh. I'm Austin... Austin Haywood."

I nodded. "So was Coco your dog?"

"No... no he's not. He's my dad's... he... was... my dad's dog." Austin swallowed and shook his head. "A little over a week ago, my dad was... killed. He was murdered. Right here in this house."

"Oh no. I'm so sorry."

"Yeah. It was... a huge shock. I guess someone hit him in the head pretty hard from behind. More than once. The blows killed him. From what the police told me, it wasn't a break-in, so they think he was killed by someone he knew. The funeral was yesterday, and now I'm just trying to sort things out."

He glanced at Coco. "That poor dog... you must think I'm heartless to take him to the shelter, but... he was... it was just too hard, you know?"

"Sure, I get it."

Austin was thinking it was too much. His own grief was so raw, and Coco just wouldn't stop whining. He couldn't take it anymore, so he'd put him in the shelter. Underneath that, I picked up his disappointment that the dog hadn't saved his dad. That sort of shocked me. From what I knew of Coco, he would have died trying to save his master.

"So Coco was here? When it happened?"

"Yeah." He wiped his eyes. "I guess my dad put Coco in the back room and closed the door. He must have been trying to keep the dog safe or something." He couldn't get over the fact that his dad was more concerned for his dog's life than his own.

Now I understood why having Coco around was so difficult for Austin. He held the dog partly responsible for his father's death. But there had to be more to it.

"Have the police made any progress in finding the killer?"

He sucked in a breath, then shook his head. "Not that they've told me."

I nodded. "I'm sorry we barged in on you like this, but now that I know why Coco dragged me here, I'd like to help. I'm a special consultant for the police, and I have my own consulting agency. Would you mind if I looked into the case? At no charge to you, of course. I think Coco... well... let's just say, I kind of promised him that I'd help."

We both glanced at the dog, and he sat up with his ears forward and barked. *Yup.* He came to my side and nuzzled my hand until I patted him on the head. He sat down and looked at Austin with a steady gaze of expectance.

Austin caved and shrugged. "Sure. Between you and the dog, how can I say no?"

I nodded. "I'll do everything I can to find out what happened here, but, right now, I have to go. Can we exchange numbers?"

"Yeah, sure." We both pulled out our phones and exchanged texts with our numbers and addresses. "What is your dad's name?"

"I'll text it to you, along with the address to this house."

A second later, the name, Mack Haywood, along with the address to the house, appeared on my screen. "Got it. Thanks." I slipped my phone into my pocket. "By the way... did your dad train Coco? He's pretty amazing."

"Yes, he did. After he retired, he volunteered for a search-and-rescue group. He got Coco and trained him for that group. He's always loved the outdoors, so it was like a second career for him. Coco's just two years old, but he's been involved in several searches already."

"It sounds rewarding."

"Yeah, at least my dad thought so, but there were times it didn't turn out right." An unbidden memory of heartbreak surfaced, but he abruptly shoved it away. "Anyway... it's good to know that Coco ended up with someone like you. I knew he'd be happier in a new home."

Guilt that he'd dropped Coco off at the shelter still gnawed at him, especially since the dog meant so much to his dad. But he just couldn't handle the fact that the dog was alive and his father wasn't.

"My kids love him, so I think you made the right choice. We'll take good care of him; you can count on it."

Relief washed over him. "Thanks."

"You bet. I'll get started on my investigation, and I'll keep you in the loop." At his nod, I glanced at Coco. "All right, buddy. Let's go home." Coco yipped *home* and followed me out the door. Grateful that he followed so easily after his earlier agitation, I told him what a sweet, wonderful dog he was. He barked *yup*, and I grinned, totally convinced he knew he belonged with me now.

We backtracked out of the neighborhood and began the long trek home. It surprised me that we'd gone so far, but at least now I understood why. Had Coco known where he was going all along, or was it just a coincidence? Whatever it was, this dog seemed to have freaky skills. Maybe that's why we got along so well. Of course, if he was a search-and-rescue dog, it made sense.

By the time we got home, I'd already texted Chris to tell him I'd be late. We rescheduled for eleven, which gave me enough time to take a shower and get ready. The kids were eating breakfast when I got home, so I told them all about Coco and his previous owner.

"Poor Coco," Savannah said, smothering him with all kinds of affection. He seemed to enjoy it with his tail thumping so hard.

"So, do you think he saw the killer?" Josh asked, thinking Coco was smart enough to identify the killer if he got close enough.

"It doesn't sound like it," I said. "Austin said his dad put Coco in a room and shut the door, but I wouldn't rule it out. Who knows? He might have seen the killer first, or, at the very least, heard him. Anyways, I told Austin that I'm a private investigator and I'm going to look into it."

"Cool. Was he okay with that?" Savannah asked. At my nod, she continued. "Then I'm sure you'll figure it out, and maybe Coco can help you. Right Coco?"

He woofed *yup*, and Savannah grinned. "See—he's ready to help. Maybe we could help you, too?" she widened her eyes with a hopeful look.

I chuckled. "We'll see. Right now I've got a meeting with Uncle Joey, and I'm already late."

We discussed all our schedules for the day, and I hurried upstairs to get ready. With any luck, the meeting would be quick, and I could head over to the precinct and take a look at the case files for Mack Haywood.

My outing with Coco, and finding out his former owner had been murdered, helped put my worry about the meeting with Uncle Joey into perspective. Meeting with him wasn't a life-or-death situation, and being the executor of his estate wasn't anything to worry about. I could handle it.

I pulled into the parking garage at Thrasher Development and rushed to the elevator with only five minutes to spare. Jackie waved me toward Uncle Joey's office, telling me Chris was already there. I stepped inside, and Chris let out a relieved breath.

"There she is," Uncle Joey said, standing to greet me. "Come in and sit down; we've got a lot to talk about."

At his no-nonsense tone, my stomach twisted, sending unease down my spine. His mind was shuttered up tight, so I couldn't get a read on him, but I could tell it was a grave matter.

Chris was an open book, but the pages were empty, since he had no idea what Uncle Joey ultimately wanted with us either. I sat beside him and glanced at Uncle Joey.

"I'm sure you're wondering what's going on," Uncle Joey began. "But I've put a lot of thought into this, and I think it's the right thing to do."

His gaze caught mine. "A lot of things have happened in the past year, and I've done some... soul-searching. I've decided that I need to make some changes in my organization. After evaluating several of my operations, I've seen that I can still come out ahead without some of the... shall we say... shadier aspects of the business.

"To that end, I'm working to consolidate my business dealings into a more legal, but still highly profitable organization. It might take some time, but I have some serious plans to make it happen. That's where you come in, Shelby."

He clasped his fingers together before catching my gaze. "I want to make you my successor."

My eyes widened in horror, and I felt the blood drain from my head. "What?" Similar panic came from Chris, but Uncle Joey just waved his hand and smiled.

"It's not as bad as you think. It's generally in name only." He frowned, thinking that most people would jump up and down with excitement for such an honor, but then, we weren't most people. That's why it only made sense to put me in that position.

"What brought this on?" I asked, hoping to stall for time before I had to give him an answer.

He shrugged. "I suppose after the last few months, I realized that I needed to get my affairs in order... so to speak. You both know that Miguel has chosen a different path, and you're part of the family now. I know I'm not going to live forever, so if anything were to happen to me, I need to plan for the future.

"More important, I need someone on the inside I can trust. And that's you, Shelby. With your special talents, you'll be in a perfect position to know the truth about people and make the best decisions about the direction I want the company to take." He thought it would also take care of me and my family financially.

I swallowed and tried to smile, but couldn't seem to get my face to cooperate. "Oh... yeah... I can see that... it makes sense that you'd want to name someone... but... are you sure you want it to be me? I mean... I know you've had some close calls lately, but I have too. In fact... with all the trouble I get into, you could still outlive me."

"That's not going to happen," he scoffed. "We have both survived because of your mind-reading ability. That gives you an edge, and also makes you the perfect choice as my successor."

I nodded, but I just didn't have it in me to accept, no matter what he wanted. What about what I wanted? I kind of liked my life the way it was. "I get that, but I'm not sure it's something I can do. I have no experience running a business. I'd probably make a mess of it and lose everything you've worked so hard for. Maybe you should consider someone else... someone who knows what they're doing."

Uncle Joey's lips thinned. He'd figured I'd hesitate, but this wasn't something he'd taken lightly. Hadn't he just told me he was going straight? He thought I'd be pleased.

Oops. "But... I applaud the changes you're making with the business. I mean... that's huge, right Chris?" I elbowed my husband, who still sat there in shock.

"Uh... yes. Yes, of course."

"This isn't going quite how I expected." Uncle Joey sighed. "There's something you both need to understand. I'm not turning the company over to Shelby anytime soon. I just want to have it in place for later, that's all."

Hope flooded my heart. "Really? How much later are we talking about?"

"Years... at least nine or ten. Even then, I'm not sure I'll give it up completely." Seeing my relief, he continued. "It's mostly a formality. Chris and I can work out the details, and you can think it over once it's all spelled out." That was a concession he'd hoped to avoid, but my reluctance made sense.

"Uh... okay. Sure. That seems fair." I knew the minute the words were out of my mouth that it was as good as a done deal for Uncle Joey.

His relieved smile lit up his face like he'd just won the jackpot. "Good. And let me just add that you don't need to worry about your business experience. You wouldn't be in charge of the day-to-day running of things. You'd only need to check in on the board meetings every once in a while, just to make sure no one had any nefarious activities planned. Basically what you do for me already."

"Oh... that's good." So why was he bringing this up now? Was he really thinking about retiring, even though he said he wasn't? "But... you're not going to retire anytime soon, right? I mean... it just wouldn't be the same without you."

My declaration softened his heart. Not many people who knew him felt that way. "Thank you, Shelby. That means a lot. But don't worry, like I said, it's only a formality." He waited for my nod before continuing. "There's also the change to my estate. I don't know if Chris told you about that?"

"Uh... yes. I thought that was the main reason we were here."

"So he told you that I want you to be the executor?" I nodded and he continued. "Are you okay with that?"

I shrugged. "I guess. As long as everything's spelled out in your will, I'll follow your wishes to the letter." He nodded, and I caught a hint of underlying worry that sent my heart sputtering. "You're okay, right? I mean... health-wise?"

That caught him off-guard, and he inhaled sharply. "Of course. Fit as a fiddle."

"Okay... that's good." I tried to pick up if he was hiding something, but his thoughts had shut up tight. What did that mean? He obviously didn't want me to learn anything, but, did that mean something was wrong? Did he have a health issue he'd just found out about?

"I guess that's all for now," he said, glancing at Chris. "Shall we set up a time to go over the paperwork?"

"Yes. I can have the estate plan ready for you, including the business side of it if you want to leave it to Shelby. But I will need more details from you to finish it up."

"Let's meet again in a few days. Just let me know when you're ready."

"Sure," he said. "I'll get started right away."

"Good." Uncle Joey glanced my way. "And you can join us." I nodded, and he turned to Chris. "I guess that's all for now."

Chris stood to leave and shook hands with Uncle Joey. "I'll be in touch."

I stood to go with him, but Uncle Joey stopped me. "Can you to stay for a minute longer?" He was thinking about

Ramos's adventure last night, and that he wanted to fill me in.

"Uh... yeah, sure. I can stay."

Chris had hoped to talk to me about this huge revelation. Now he'd have to wait. But what the hell? Uncle Joey's successor? This was nuts. "I'll see you later then." He gave me a quick kiss on the cheek, and hurried out the door.

After he left, Uncle Joey took pity on me, thinking that I looked a little shell-shocked. "Don't worry, Shelby. Like I said, naming you as my successor is just a formality. Nothing's going to change."

"Are you sure about that?"

He let out a breath. Now that Chris was gone, he could open up a little. "Yes. I know you don't want it, and I don't want to burden you. I just need to know that, if anything were to happen to me, I wouldn't leave a mess for Miguel to clean up."

"Of course. I understand that."

"Good. It will just give me some peace of mind, you know?"

"Yeah. I totally get that. But what about Ramos? He would be lots better at it than me."

Uncle Joey smiled. "Yes. He would. That's why I'll ask him to run the business. He knows it better than anyone."

"Then why not name him as your successor?"

"I don't know." He caught my gaze. "It just seems right to name you. You're part of the family now. I guess that's the main reason. Be it right or wrong, I can't do it any other way." He was going with his gut, and it hadn't steered him wrong yet.

I couldn't get over the fact that he thought of me as his real niece, even though I wasn't. It seemed a little ironic that pretending it was true had made it true in his mind.

Was that some kind of a syndrome or something? Maybe Bob would know more about it? It probably had a name, and he'd know exactly how it came about. Maybe I could ask him at my next appointment... hypothetically speaking, of course.

I met Uncle Joey's gaze. "So does Ramos know you want to put him in charge of everything?"

His brows drew together. "Not exactly. I wanted to talk to you about it first. Once you've made your decision, then I'll talk to him. Either way, I think he'd be fine running the business, especially if you're involved. I mean... he's always been protective of you, so it only makes sense that he'd want to be there to help you out, in whatever capacity you need."

My eyes narrowed. "Oh... so I see how it is."

"What?" He didn't like my tone.

Was it okay to tell a mob boss he was a manipulative son of a... gun? Probably not. "Sounds like you know what you're doing."

"Of course I do. And if it will benefit everyone I love, I don't have a problem with it." His direct gaze caught mine in an unspoken challenge. Since I had no idea how to argue with that, I nodded instead, and he relaxed. "Now we need to talk about this unfortunate incident with my tenant."

"Right. So what happened last night? Did Ramos talk to Slasher?"

Uncle Joey snorted, since he wouldn't call it talking. "Yes. But he didn't get the answer we wanted. Slasher told Ramos he was working for me, just like always."

"So he really didn't know?"

"It doesn't sound like it. Of course Ramos knew there was more to it, and he convinced Slasher it was in his best interests to tell him everything about the operation. It sounds like Slasher is a pusher, but he gets the drugs from

Vinny who just happens to be Victor's cousin. You remember Victor?"

"Oh yeah... he was number three on my chart." I'd met Victor the first time I worked for Uncle Joey. It wasn't until later that I'd learned his name. Still, I didn't know him well. "Does he still work for you?"

He nodded. "Yeah. Victor ran the drug side of the business, and now it looks like he's turned it over to his cousin Vinny."

I snorted. "That's hilarious." Uncle Joey's brows dipped. He wasn't amused. "I mean... the cousin Vinny part. You know? My cousin Vinny?"

Uncle Joey rolled his eyes. "The point is—it means that Victor has gone against my wishes to stop running the drug business. Even worse, he's still using my name." He shook his head. "Did he think I wouldn't find out about it? What an idiot. I thought he was smarter than that."

"Yeah... that's rough."

"And here I thought I was turning over a new leaf and getting out of the drug business. Why do these things always happen?"

"Isn't that the truth? It's like that saying... no good deed goes unpunished. I thought it only applied to me, but now it looks like you can't catch a break either."

He smiled, seeing the irony. "I know... the perils of being a mob boss. I could write a book about it."

I chuckled. "Yeah. It could be one of those self-help books, and you could call it *The Reluctant Mob Boss*, or how about *The Hazards of Being a Mob Boss*. Or maybe, *Things You Should Know Before Becoming a Mob Boss*."

His lips turned up in a polite smile, and he shook his head, thinking I was getting carried away. It might have been funny at first, but I should probably stop now.

I shrugged, not nearly as intimidated as I might have been a few months ago. "So what's next?"

"I'm going to invite Victor into the office for a meeting. I need you to be in attendance, since I'm not sure I can trust anything he says. Can you come back a little later today? Ramos should be back by then."

"Of course. Where is Ramos anyway?"

"I sent him to check on the other members of my organization. After hearing about Victor, I intend to find out if anyone else is going against my wishes."

I nodded. "That's a good idea. Ramos is good at getting people to talk, but if you need my help, just let me know."

"You know I will."

I grinned. "Okay. Well... I'd better get going. I'll see you in a bit." I made my way to the door and pulled it open.

"Shelby... wait... I just want to say... thanks for standing by me. It means a lot."

Surprised that he'd voiced his feelings... out loud... I nodded and sent him a smile. "How could I not? You're my uncle, right?"

He flashed me a grin, and I hurried out the door.

CHAPTER 5

On the way to the precinct, I couldn't get over the fact that I'd basically agreed to be Uncle Joey's successor. What was wrong with me? That was the absolute last thing I'd ever want. But he thought of me as family, and I'd even given in to the whole family thing.

After what had happened in New York, it was an undeniable part of my life now, along with Chris and my kids. We were part of the Manetto clan whether I liked it or not. That gave Uncle Joey every right to name me as his successor, but I never thought he'd actually do it.

Crap. Why did this have to happen now? And, to top it off, it was most likely my fault. I'd been calling him Uncle Joey since the beginning, mostly to bug him. But now I realized there was a reason behind it. I'd counted on that family designation to keep him from killing me. Well... it had certainly worked... and backfired in a big way.

Of course, how could I complain? Being involved with a mob boss had consequences. Good or bad, it was time to pay up. Still, it wasn't all gloom and doom. Hadn't he just said he was giving up the mob boss part? That was huge, so maybe things weren't all that bad, right?

I pulled into the precinct parking lot and slipped my lanyard over my head. Inside, I glanced over the detectives' offices, looking for Dimples. Not finding him, I decided that maybe it was a good thing. Now I could look up the information I needed on my computer without those pesky explanations.

In fact, most of the desks were empty, and the blinds were shut in the chief's office. Maybe they were all in there for a briefing?

With no time to lose, I hurried to my desk in the far corner, noticing a stack of files sitting on my desktop. Because it had been nearly two weeks since I'd been there, I could understand that someone had used my empty desk for storage. Still, I couldn't shake the suspicion that crawled through my mind. Had Willow taken over my desk, too? If she had...

Letting out a breath, I shoved down my anger and pulled out the chair, checking to make sure it wasn't the broken one Bates had saddled me with earlier. Finding it in good condition, I sat down and turned on my computer, glancing at the files while I waited for it to boot up.

The top file had "Jane Doe" on the front. I opened it to find a photo of a woman with a vacant stare on her face and her clothes covered in blood. This had to be the amnesia case Dimples had told me about.

The second file had the name "Sophie Blackwell" on the tab. I opened it to see the same woman, only this photo was from her driver's license. The intake form listed all of her pertinent information, along with a summary of the incident.

The third folder had the name "Brock Blackwell" on the cover. Inside, I found a crime scene photo, with the man lying on a bed, covered in blood. Unsurprisingly, the report listed Sophie Blackwell as the deceased's wife, along with the place, time, and date of his death, including that he'd been stabbed multiple times.

Oh man... this looked bad. Had she killed her husband? Did she still have amnesia?

"Shelby."

I glanced up to see Dimples coming toward me. Behind him, most of the detectives were leaving the chief's office. Willow followed them out. Seeing me, her brows drew together, and she wondered why I was sitting at her desk.

Anger rushed over me. My instincts were spot on. Dimples stopped beside me, and I raised my brows. Instant guilt came off him in waves. Holy hell! It was him? He'd put her here at my desk? How could he do that to me?

"I didn't expect you back today," he said, scrambling for an excuse. The hurt accusation in my eyes cut him to the quick. After a few heated swear words came to his mind, he mentally apologized, thinking *sorry*, over and over.

Swallowing an angry retort, I glanced between him and Willow, who now stood at his side. "This must be the case you guys are working on." I leaned back in my chair and folded my arms. "Made any progress?"

"Some," Dimples said. "But I'm actually glad you're here. Maybe you could help us out." Dread churned his stomach, just like that of a cheating husband who'd been caught, and he wasn't sure what to do, or how to make it up to me. "We haven't had any luck with Sophie, but maybe if you spoke with her, we could learn more. It might be worth a try."

Not ready to let him off the hook yet, I focused on Willow. She furrowed her brow, knowing that Drew usually worked with me, but this was her case now. Why was he so intent on including me? There was more than enough work to go around. Still, she easily picked up on Drew's guilt, and getting on his bad side, or mine, wasn't something she wanted to do. She decided a little damage control was in order.

"Hi Shelby." She tilted her lips in a friendly smile. "Drew didn't think you'd be coming into work for a while, so he told me I could use your desk. But now that you're here, I'm happy to move my stuff."

She reached for the files, so I handed them over, not about to give up my chair or my desk. I still had work to do on my computer, and, since it was mine, she would just have to find someplace else to work.

Dimples was suddenly grateful Willow had tried to smooth things over, and he hoped I'd accept her explanation, since it was the truth. Not liking that he took her side, I spoke up. "I take it Sophie still doesn't remember anything?"

"Unfortunately, no," Dimples answered before Willow could open her mouth. "We don't have any proof of what happened either."

"We know what happened," Willow said. "She killed him and ran, leaving her sanity behind."

"How do you know that?" I asked, speaking Dimples's thoughts out loud. He may think it likely, but he wasn't convinced, and they'd found no proof.

She shrugged. "I can't prove it, but it only makes sense that she must have caught him with another woman and snapped. If we can just find the other woman, we'll have our proof."

"So, rather than facts, this is your psychic ability speaking?" I put her on the spot, wanting to hear her explanation.

That question surprised her, since most people didn't like talking about psychic abilities. "Not exactly. I couldn't get a read on her yesterday at the hospital, so my intuition and common sense put it together." She was thinking that they had just received the video feed from the hotel, and they just needed to take a look at it to know she was right.

"Uh-huh," I said, raising my brow at Dimples, wanting him to acknowledge that she was manipulating him and the whole police department. "So you're looking at the video feed from the hotel where the victim died?"

Her breath caught. She hadn't mentioned that, so how did I know? Her eyes narrowed, and she studied me, thinking about the research she'd done after meeting me in person yesterday. She knew everyone thought I was the real deal... or at least I'd tricked everyone into believing it.

But she wasn't so sure. From her study of the paranormal, she believed most of a psychic's ability could be explained by a highly talented skillset of observation and deduction. It was exactly how Sherlock Holmes had operated, and he could have been labeled a psychic, if he hadn't explained his methods. No one, not even a psychic like her who understood tarot cards and astrology, could do the things I did without it.

Hmmm... being compared to Sherlock Holmes was a definite compliment, but didn't she know he was a fictional character? So what did that say about her psychic ability? It sounded like she believed she was a psychic because of her devotion to mysticism, and that I might be one based on my talents of observation and deduction.

I needed more time with her to figure it out, but it would have to wait, since I had my own investigation to deal with.

"That's right," she agreed, answering my question. "We've got the security feed, and we're hoping it will show us the killer."

Dimples wasn't sure what to do or say that would keep him from getting into trouble with either one of us.

I took pity on him and nodded. "Well, good luck." Glancing at Willow, I added. "I've got a couple of things to do at my desk while I'm here, but you can have it back as soon as I'm done."

"Oh... thanks." Her brow wrinkled. She hadn't expected me to be nice to her. What game was I playing? The fact that I wasn't as enthusiastic as she was about working for the police gave her hope. Maybe she could take my place after all. She never thought I'd want to quit working for the police, but maybe the last few months had changed me, and my position was up for grabs. The timing couldn't be better.

What the heck did that mean? She headed back to Dimples's desk, so I turned my gaze to him and whispered, "she's after my job."

"Shit," he said... out loud. His fierce gaze held mine. "Well, it's not up for grabs." He thought about asking for my help with the case again, but decided against it. Once it was clear that Willow had failed with her psychic abilities, he'd bring me in on it. Then I could solve the case and show her up at the same time. It would be poetic justice, and he could hardly wait.

"I won't work with her again... that's a promise." With a determined nod at me, he followed Willow to his desk and plugged in the thumb-drive with the video feed from the hotel.

I hated to admit it, but his plan put me in a good mood. I hoped it worked out just how he thought, but if not, it's the thought that counts, right?

Settling back in my chair, I logged into my account, holding my breath that my password still worked. The program opened up, and I sighed with relief. At least something was going right. The chief had given me full access to all the detectives' cases, and I typed Mack Haywood's name into this treasure trove, hoping everything was up to date.

The case file opened to his information, listing his driver's license and address with all his personal information. I scrolled to the next page and found a picture of him kneeling beside Coco. My breath hitched to see them together. He looked so happy, and Coco sat at attention beside him. Green trees surrounded them, and Coco had a special rescue-dog vest attached to his chest. They looked like a perfect team, and sorrow filled my heart.

Knowing the crime scene photos came next, I closed my eyes and swallowed. Not sure I'd ever be ready, I hesitated another second, then scrolled down to get it over with. The first photo showed Mack lying on his stomach with a pool of blood around his head.

He had fallen between the living room door and the hallway to the kitchen. I read through the report, noting that he'd been struck several times on the back of the head with a hard, blunt object. From his position, it was determined that he never saw it coming.

I glanced through the report, finding that it had happened between nine and nine-thirty that night and he'd been discovered by a neighbor who had heard Coco barking his head off. By the time the police arrived, Coco's barks were so frantic they had called animal control before letting him out, afraid the dog might attack them.

It was noted that the dog had ripped up the carpet in front of the door trying to get out of the back room. The report didn't include anything else about Coco or what had happened to him, but I knew it had been traumatic. No wonder Coco had been so despondent at the shelter.

I read through the remaining information and discovered that Detective Williams, along with Clue Ventanilla, a new detective I didn't know, had been assigned to the case. That it wasn't Detective Bates was a small miracle, since he didn't like me much.

So far, they'd interviewed the neighbors and most of the search-and-rescue people Mack worked with, along with his son and a few friends. But they didn't have a suspect. They'd also checked the neighborhood for security cameras that might have picked up something, but found nothing from them either.

I shook my head. It didn't look like the investigation was going well. But maybe I'd know more after I spoke to Detective Williams. I jotted down the names of the neighbors, and a few from the search-and-rescue team, so I could talk to them myself, hoping I could pick up something that Williams had missed.

"What are you doing?"

I jerked in surprise, quickly glancing over my shoulder to find Bates looking down at my computer. He was thinking that I'd been gone for days, and he wondered why I was looking at Williams's case.

"Did he ask you for help with that?" Moving to perch on the side of my desk, he continued, "I didn't think you were cleared to come back to work."

He knew all about my visit to the Big Apple, and the help I'd given the NYPD, mostly because the chief wouldn't stop talking about it. Now here I was... back to work already and sticking my nose into a case. What was up with that?

Willow's wildly gesturing arms caught his attention, and we both watched as she nearly hit Dimples in the head. Bates narrowed his eyes, thinking that maybe having me around wasn't so bad if that meant the new psychic would leave.

There was something about her that he didn't like, and it bothered him that the chief had called her in while I'd been gone. Between her and me, he'd go with me any day. Hell, I had more mojo than ten of the other gal, and I was a lot nicer to look at.

Wow. Would wonders never cease? Bates... on my side? "Hey Bates. To answer your question, yes... I'm cleared to work, but the chief said to take it easy, so I'm just looking through a few cases to see if anything pops out at me."

"Oh... so... Harris didn't want you to help him?" He glanced at Dimples, feeling a little sorry for the guy, but grateful it was Dimples and not him.

"Well... he did ask me, but I guess the chief can only have one psychic on a case at a time." A chuckle bubbled out of me. "Who would have thought that would ever happen... right?"

"Hell yeah. One psychic is bad enough."

"Damn straight," I agreed. It caught him off-guard, and we both laughed.

"Well, if you're looking for a case to help with, I caught one this morning that might be right up your alley. It looks like a drug deal gone wrong, so it's probably gang related."

Since that was the last thing I wanted to do, I did my best to appear indifferent. "Maybe, but I like this case better." I pointed to my computer screen. "I mean... I'm sure both cases are important but... finding a gang member's killer wouldn't be as rewarding as helping out on this case. Just look at this guy. He was a good person who didn't deserve to die. There's a real mystery here."

"Yeah, I can see that." Bates was wishing he'd gotten the call for that case, but he'd already had a full load when that one happened. "So that's a no?"

Not wanting him on my bad side, I shrugged. "I can take a look at it. Who knows? Maybe I'll pick up something."

His brows rose in surprise. "That's real nice of you. Come on over to my desk and I'll show you what I've got so far."

I followed him to his desk, a little dazed that we were working together for a change. He sat down at his computer and explained that the victim had been shot several times, but there wasn't a weapon at the scene.

"Like I said, it looks like a gang shooting in an old building on the south side. We didn't find any money or drugs, but it's practically a given that it was a drug deal gone wrong. So far, no one's talking, but you might be able to help us out with that."

He pulled up a crime scene photo, along with an arrest photo of the same person. "We just identified the victim. His name is Tommy Demarco, and he has a rap sheet a mile long. He's been in and out of the system since he was a teen, mostly dealing drugs. None of the recent arrests have stuck though. He always seemed to get off on a technicality." Bates thought it pointed to organized crime, and he'd give his right arm to tie it to the Manettos. Maybe, with my help, he could.

Yikes! I didn't want Uncle Joey tied to this, so maybe it was a good thing Bates had asked for my help. "Oh... yeah... I bet that's frustrating. Maybe when you're interviewing some of the gang members, I could listen in and pick something up? I mean... I can't guarantee anything, but I'd be happy to try."

"Yeah? That would be great." He thought it couldn't hurt to ask the cop who worked the gang unit to watch as well, in case he had anything to add.

"Okay. Just let me know when you're ready to question them, and we'll work something out."

"Thanks Shelby. I owe you one."

My brows rose. "Really? Wow... I won't forget that." He almost regretted his words, but, from my grin, he knew I was mostly teasing. "Guess I'd better see if Williams can use my help. I mean... if I'm helping you, I might as well help him, right?"

I glanced at Williams, who sat at his desk with his shoulders hunched. "He doesn't look too happy."

Bates huffed out a breath. "I guess. Just remember you're helping me first."

"I will." I sent Bates a smile and made my way to Williams's desk. From the discouragement that hung over him, it was obvious that he wasn't happy.

His partner sat at the desk across from him, glancing at her computer screen and thinking they had spoken to just about everyone, and nothing had come of it. Now she was checking his financial records for any kind of discrepancies, like a big deposit or withdrawal, but she hadn't found anything.

"Hey Williams," I said, sitting down in the chair beside his desk. "You'll never believe this, but I have a connection to the case you're working on."

His eyes widened. I'd never worked closely with him before, but he was interested in anything I could give him. "What's that?"

"I adopted a dog yesterday. His name is Coco, and his late owner was Mack Haywood."

"Oh wow. That's crazy. How did that happen?"

I explained the whole story about taking my kids to the shelter to adopt a dog and finding Coco there. "They didn't know anything about him except his name, but he responded so well to me and my kids that we adopted him. Then, this morning, I took him on a walk."

I told him that I had a premonition to walk the dog in a certain direction, and that's how we ended up at Mack's house. "I know it's hard to believe, but there it is. His son, Austin, was there, and he filled me in."

"That's nuts." Williams could hardly believe it, but then... it was me, so it had to be real. He glanced in Dimples's direction and shook his head. Having another psychic here was weird, and he was glad he wasn't the one working with her. At least I wasn't some pretender like she seemed to be.

Oh... that was so nice. Too bad I couldn't thank him. Still, it lightened my heart just the same. "I told his son, Austin, that I'd see if you'd made any progress."

Williams snapped his attention back to me, then glanced at his partner. "Shelby, this is Clue Ventenilla, my new partner." To Clue, he continued. "Shelby is the psychic that the chief keeps talking about."

"Yeah... I got that." She sat in the adjacent desk and had listened to my story about Coco. She wore the standard detective jacket over dress slacks with a white shirt, and had dark-brown, shoulder-length hair.

Her brown eyes held a hint of wariness, like she expected the worst. The coincidence didn't seem possible to her, and her brows drew together with suspicion. Another psychic? Was there something in the water around here?

I extended my hand for a quick shake, which she returned half-heartedly, waiting for the inevitable question about her name. Yes, she was named after her aunt, but where it originated, she had no idea. She just knew that most people liked to give her a hard time about the unusual name.

"Hi Clue, it's nice to meet you." Not liking her distrust, I decided to use my psychic powers about her name to convince her I was the real deal. "I think Clue is a great name for a detective. I'll bet you're named after someone, right? An aunt maybe?"

Clue's eyes widened, and she sputtered. "How... How did you know that?"

"Well... I'm the resident psychic... or I used to be." I glanced over at Willow and shrugged. "Anyway, it's nice to meet you."

Williams saw his chance to ask her about her name, since he'd always wondered about it, and jumped into the conversation. "So it's not short for anything?"

"No. It's just Clue. Besides, what could Clue be short for anyway?"

Williams thought for a moment, then shrugged. "Uh... Cluella?"

"What? Ugh... that's terrible. No... absolutely not."

Williams hid a smile, thinking that if he ever wanted to rub it in, he'd call her Cluella. Cluella Ventenilla. That had a nice ring to it.

I tried not to smile, and kind of felt sorry for her. On the other hand, maybe I should feel sorry for him if he followed through on that thought, since she was thinking of punching him in the face if he ever did.

"So... about the case." I interrupted. "Any ideas on what happened?"

Williams sighed. "There's not a lot to go on. We've checked Mack's phone records, and now we're looking into his financial records to see if he made any big deposits or payments. So far, nothing looks out of the ordinary."

"But you think he was murdered by someone he knew?"

"Yeah. He'd obviously invited them in and put the dog in the other room. We think he must have been headed toward the kitchen when he was struck on the head. The forensic results indicate the person was probably shorter than the victim, and used something like a hammer, but we haven't identified the murder weapon."

I nodded. "Well, I hope you don't mind if I look into it, too. I feel a connection since I own the guy's dog now."

"What do you have in mind?" Clue asked.

I shrugged. "I'll probably just talk to his neighbors and maybe the search-and-rescue people he worked with."

"We already did that. There was nothing there." Clue thought she was a darn good detective, and she didn't want me to waste my time. Plus, it rankled that I was stepping into her case, like I thought I could do a better job.

"I'm sure you've done a great job so far, but maybe I'll pick up something with my psychic ability. I think it's worth a shot, and I don't mind spending the time. It's worth it to me."

Her eyes widened. I'd picked up her intentions like a pro. Had I been trained to read micro expressions? That had to be it... unless it really was a psychic ability. But she didn't believe in that stuff. Still, she'd woefully underestimated me. "Whatever... I suppose we could use all the help we can get, right Williams?"

"Yeah, sure." He didn't mind at all, thinking they certainly had nothing to lose.

Clue pulled a card from her jacket and handed it to me. "Call me if you find anything."

I took it and nodded. "Sure. Thanks Clue... I'll let you know." I'd almost said Cluella, and thanked my lucky stars I'd held it back. She might not punch me in the face, but I didn't want to risk it.

As I slipped her card into my purse, I glanced Dimples's way. He and Willow were still hard at work watching the surveillance video. Since I didn't want to interrupt, I passed them with my head held high and kept going.

"Shelby, wait," Dimples called. "Are you leaving?"

"Yeah."

"I'll walk you out."

I shrugged, but waited for him to join me. Willow glanced up, not happy he was leaving. As we walked out, I felt her staring daggers into my back. She wondered what Dimples was up to. He'd better not ask me to help with the case again. She was doing a great job. They didn't need me.

It was a relief to leave her unwelcome thoughts behind. Dimples was glad to get away from her, too. Her perfume was giving him a headache. Plus, she tended to be overbearing, and it was starting to get on his nerves. But beneath all of that came a wave of unhappiness... he'd missed me.

"Uh... that's too bad she's such a... witch," I told him. "If it helps, I miss you too. How soon can you ditch her?"

His surprised gaze caught mine. Did that mean I'd forgiven him?

I smiled, and he chuckled, causing his dimples to appear. I'd missed them, too. "She probably doesn't even appreciate your dimples. Otherwise, she'd try to get you to smile more often."

This time his smile reached his eyes, showing off his boyish handsomeness. He was inordinately pleased, and grateful that I cared.

"So how's Billie doing? I haven't had a chance to chat with her since I got back." Dimples was married to Billie Jo Payne... a newspaper reporter. She still used her own name for the paper, which pleased me to no end since it fit her so well, mostly because she'd been a big *pain* in the butt when we first met.

"She's doing great. In fact, she was happy to hear you'd made it back. I told her you were taking some time off though, and that you needed a break."

"What? Why?"

"Well... you know she's still hoping to get an interview with you for the paper, right?"

"Oh... yeah. I was hoping she'd forgotten about that."

"Nope." His grin widened, and he hoped the sight of his dimples would soften me up.

I chuckled. "So... I guess I should thank you?"

He nodded. "Damn straight. You can thank me by helping me with this case."

I let out a huff. "Not fair. Besides... you didn't hear how much Willow dislikes me. She's kind of scary. Are you sure she doesn't have something to do with the case? Like... could she be the killer?"

He snorted and shook his head. "Of course not. But, if you're worried about that, why don't you and I go talk to Sophie? They released her from the hospital, and she's staying with her mom. You might pick up something."

I hated to let him down, but I didn't see how that would help. "You know, if she's got amnesia, it's not going to help me, right? Her mind will be just a big blob of nothing."

"Yeah... I know... but what if she's faking it? You'd know right off the bat."

"Oh... I hadn't thought of that. Yeah, I guess I would."

"Then it's worth a quick visit. We can go right now. I'll text Willow that something came up." He pulled out his phone and started a text before I had a chance to answer. Finishing, he sent me a big smile, making sure his dimples wobbled like little tornadoes. "Okay... let's go."

I shook my head. "It's a darn good thing you've got those crazy dimples going for you."

CHAPTER 6

Dimples drove us to the house, asking me all sorts of questions about my vacation in New York. I told him most of it, but left a lot out. Still, it was enough for him to know that Uncle Joey and Ramos worked with the NYPD to put a notorious mob boss out of commission.

"Wow. That's nuts. And you were right in the middle of it all." Not that it surprised him, but it sounded intense.

"Yeah... it was intense, especially right at the end."

"I'll bet. No wonder you're seeing Bob Spicer. I heard he's pretty good."

"Yeah... he is, but he's also fascinated by my psychic abilities. He wants to know all about them and how they work, so I have to be careful, which, in some ways, just adds to my stress. You know you're screwed when the help you need makes your stress worse, right?"

He nodded. "I can't imagine."

"I've thought about telling him the truth." Dimples's head jerked my way. It shocked him that I'd even think about it. "I know... it's a bad idea. But it would be nice to get help from a real professional, you know?"

"Yeah... sure, I get it, but I don't think you should do that. If it was someone who didn't work for the department, then maybe you could risk it, but I'd say no." He was thinking *hell no,* with an exclamation mark.

"Okay then... I'll keep it to myself."

"You can always talk to me... I mean... I'm no professional, but I'm your friend, and I might have a different perspective on some things that could help."

I sent him a grateful smile. "Thanks... I'll keep that in mind."

"We're here." Dimples pulled up in front of a small home in a nice neighborhood. At the door, he rang the bell, and we waited. A woman in her fifties, with sorrowful eyes, recognized Dimples from the hospital and opened the screen door.

"Hi Mrs. Sanchez, this is my colleague, Shelby Nichols. Could we talk to Sophie?"

"Do you have any news?"

"We're working on it, but nothing yet."

Her shoulders slumped. "Come in. She's still not responsive, so I don't know how much help it will be, but you can try."

We followed her inside to a small living room, where Sophie sat on the couch, wrapped in a blanket. Her eyes held that vacant stare, like no one was home. It chilled me to find her like that, and I knew she wasn't faking it. Her mom gestured toward a couple of chairs facing the couch, and we sat down while she sat beside her daughter.

"Has she spoken at all?" I asked.

"No. She responds to my commands, but it's like she's not all there. The doctor at the hospital thought her catatonic state was brought on from witnessing... Brock's... murder." She was thinking that whatever Sophie had seen, it must have been horrific, and, as much as she wanted her back, she knew it would be a painful reckoning.

"So bringing her here didn't help?"

"No. But she hasn't lived here for about five years. She and Brock have their own place."

As she said his name a second time, the back of my neck tingled. A slight breeze ruffled my hair, and the scent of Armani cologne tickled my nose. I knew Dimples didn't wear it, so I swallowed and glanced around the room. The windows were closed, so where had the breeze with that scent come from?

"Maybe taking her to her own house would help her wake up," Dimples said, trying to be helpful.

Mrs. Sanchez nodded. "I suppose, but it was all I could do to bring her here. I'd hoped coming home to someplace where she felt safe would bring her out of it, and taking her to her own house just seemed cruel. But... maybe that would have been best."

The smell of Armani came again, bringing with it a sense of urgency. I pulled away from the conversation and concentrated on the scent. The room grew cold, and a heavy presence settled by my side. *Tell her I'm here. Tell her she's safe and I'm okay.*

Chills ran down my spine, and I jumped a little. Holy hell. Brock was right here beside me? Grateful I hadn't yelped, I glanced at Mrs. Sanchez and licked my lips. "I'm going to try talking to her. Is that all right?" So far, I hadn't picked up anything from Sophie's mind, but, with Brock sitting right next to me, I had to try.

"Of course," she agreed.

I moved to sit beside Sophie on the couch, feeling Brock's presence follow me. "Sophie. Can you hear me?" I listened real close and felt a stirring of awareness.

Reassured that I was on the right track, I said her name again, using a no-nonsense tone of command. "Sophie. You're safe now. It's okay to come back. I know you don't want to, but it's time. We need you to help us. Brock needs you to help him."

Both Dimples and Mrs. Sanchez jerked a little, but I ignored them.

"Brock liked to wear Armani cologne. Can you smell it? He... Brock wants you to know that he's here, watching over you. Remember that song he liked to sing to you?"

In the back of my mind, he'd been singing something familiar, so I listened real close until I heard it clearly. "*Love Me Like You Do*. Remember that song?"

I waited, hoping for a response. "Sophie, Brock's okay, and he wants you to wake up. He loves you. He will always love you. Now... wake up."

Her eyes blinked several times, and she took in a few deep breaths, like she'd been drowning in a sea of dark water, and she'd suddenly come up for air.

Mrs. Sanchez moved to a kneeling position in front of Sophie and clasped both of her hands. Sophie blinked a few more times, then focused on her mother's face.

"Mom?"

"Sophie!" Her mom's voice shook, and she hugged Sophie tight before pulling away. "You're back. Oh thank God. I've been so worried about you. You've been through so much, and I'm so sorry, but it's going to be all right now. I promise."

"What... happened? Why am I here?" She glanced at Dimples and then me. "Who are you?"

"What's the last thing you remember?" Dimples asked

Sophie shook her head, and I picked up her sudden dread. Deep down; she knew it was bad, and her heart began to race. Did she really want to remember?

"Something bad happened, didn't it?" Her breathing turned shallow, and she closed her eyes, shaking her head. She couldn't think straight. What had happened? Her gaze turned toward her mother. "Where's Brock? Mom... where is he?"

Mrs. Sanchez shook her head, and her eyes filled with tears. "Sophie—honey, I'm so sorry."

"But—" She turned her frantic gaze my way, then to Dimples, and her wild eyes flashed with sudden clarity. "No. He can't be dead."

"Sophie." Mrs. Sanchez wrapped her arms around her daughter and sat beside her on the couch. "I'm here, sweetheart. We'll get through this."

As she stroked Sophie's back, she whispered soft words of comfort. All at once, Sophie crumpled against her mother in aching sobs. They clung to each other and cried. Their pain and grief brought tears to my eyes. Crap. This was horrible. Listening to their sobs tore at my heart, and tears ran down my cheeks. I dashed them away, but they kept coming.

The scent of Armani tickled my nose again, and I swallowed. Brock was here, but I had no idea how that was going to help. What was I supposed to do? The scent grew, nearly overpowering me, and I glanced at Dimples. "Do you smell anything?" I whispered.

He shook his head. "Like what?"

Before I could answer, Sophie's shoulders stopped shaking. She pulled away from her mother and glanced around the room. "Can you smell that?" Dimples and Mrs. Sanchez both frowned, each unable to smell anything.

I nodded. "Yes. Armani cologne, right?"

"Yes," she said, her gaze catching mine. "He wore it... a lot. It was my favorite."

"I know this sounds strange, but, maybe he's trying to tell you something." I waited a few seconds before continuing. "Maybe he wants you to know that he's okay. And... he's watching over you."

Sophie's contorted face relaxed, and she sat back on the couch. Tears still ran unchecked down her cheeks, but she felt Brock's presence. He was in the room, and a calm wave of peace settled over her. Pain lanced through her heart, but it was more bearable now. She knew something terrible had happened. But she didn't remember. What was it? More than anything, she needed to know why Brock was dead.

Focusing back to that night, she began to speak. "We were meeting at the hotel. It was our anniversary, and Brock said he had something special planned. But something came up at work, and he was running late, so I checked in and waited for him at the bar. He didn't want me to go to our room before he got there, because he had a surprise for me."

She shook her head, and her brows crinkled. "I'm not sure what happened after that. I think I went to our room, but it's fuzzy, like a dream..."

"Did you order a drink?" Dimples asked.

"Yeah... I'm pretty sure I did."

Dimples waited for her to continue, but she had nothing more to add. "So... you think you went to your room, but you're not sure?" At her nod, he continued. "Do you remember leaving the hotel?"

"I... I'm not sure." Her thoughts were jumbled, but I managed to pick up her growing anxiety that something had terrified her. Even now, her heart began to pound with fear. "I know something terrible happened, but I don't remember what it was." She let out a helpless breath. "What's going on? Why can't I remember?"

"It must have been the shock," her mother said. "The doctor said that a terrible experience can trigger this kind of response. That must be it."

Sophie's brows drew together, and she closed her eyes for a moment. "But I remember going to the hotel, and the bar. Why can't I remember the rest?" She glanced at Dimples. "Tell me what happened. How did I get here?"

Dimples explained that she was spotted at a nearby bus stop. "You were sitting on the bench, covered with blood, and the driver thought you were dead. He called nine-one-one, and you were taken to the hospital.

"We think that you must have left the hotel after Brock was killed. It was his blood on your clothes. You've been in a trance-like state ever since... well, until now." He studied her face. "Are you sure you don't remember anything else?"

"No. I don't. I'm sorry. I wish I did, but it's a complete blank."

"That's okay," I said, hoping to reassure her. "You've remembered a lot. Maybe it will just take more time for it to all come back."

Sophie nodded, then darted her gaze to mine. "So... what happened? You said I was covered in Brock's blood. What happened to him?"

"He was attacked in your room and stabbed." I didn't tell her how many times he'd been stabbed, since it was bad enough already.

She inhaled sharply. "So... I must have been there? But why didn't they kill me too?"

"We don't know," Dimples said. "And nothing was taken. All your things were still there."

"But I don't understand." Her voice shook with panic. "Why would someone kill Brock?"

"That's what we're trying to figure out." Dimples caught my gaze. Was she faking it? Had she killed her husband?

I shook my head. If she had, she didn't remember. I turned her way and spoke slowly. "I believe you. I believe that you don't remember what happened. But it looks... bad... and we have to look at everything and everyone. That's why we were hoping you'd remember something that would help us catch the person who killed Brock. You were the last person to see him alive... so..."

Her face went white. "Wait. You think it was me? I would never—he was my husband. We loved each other. It was our anniversary."

Dimples raised his hands in a calming gesture. "Sophie. We know you'd never mean to kill him, but somehow he ended up dead, and, as far as we can tell, you were the only one there. Can you see how that looks? That's why we were hoping you'd remember something... anything."

Mrs. Sanchez huffed out a breath, filled with indignation. "My daughter is the victim here. You need to find the person who killed Brock."

"Please," Sophie said, her eyes filling with tears. "I don't remember, but I would never kill my husband. I loved him, and he loved me. Someone must have come into our room and killed him. Please... find the person who did this. I need to know what happened."

"We will," I said. "We'll figure this out, I promise."

With anguished eyes, Sophie glanced between the two of us and nodded. "Thank you."

"If you remember anything... anything at all, please call me." Dimples handed Sophie his card. He opened his mouth to tell her not to leave the city, but I spoke before he could.

"We'll be in touch."

With a broken heart, Sophie could only nod, too caught up in her grief to speak. "We'll let ourselves out," Dimples said, and I followed him out the door.

In the car, we slipped on our seatbelts, and Dimples started the engine. "That was rough. So... she really doesn't remember anything?"

"No. After leaving the bar, everything was murky. I only picked up that she was terrified, but not why. Did the hospital do any bloodwork on her?"

"Yes. But I haven't seen the results yet." He glanced over his shoulder and pulled out onto the street. "Do you think she was drugged?"

"Yes... it's the only thing that makes sense. But what drug would make her forget everything?"

"I don't know. Rohypnol, or "roofies" are the usual suspect in this kind of case, but they wouldn't make her forget everything. So it must be something else. If she got a drink at the bar and someone spiked it, that could explain a lot. At least it's a place to start."

"True. You should see if you can get the video of the bar to go along with the others you already have. Oh... and you need to make sure Willow knows that Sophie's not our killer." I knew that Brock wouldn't have been there trying to help her if she'd killed him... at least I didn't think so.

Dimples sent me a sideways glance. "You sure about that? I mean... if she doesn't remember, and you couldn't pick it up, then why are you so sure she didn't do it?"

"I don't know. It's just a gut feeling."

Dimples smirked, thinking that line was right out of Willow's playbook.

"Hey... not fair."

"I know... sorry. Okay... I'm going to back you up on this. We'll go on the assumption that Sophie didn't do it. Willow's not going to be happy, but I will defer to your gut feeling over hers any time."

He sent me a smile. "When she finds out you got Sophie to talk, she'll be doubly upset." He was thinking that he could hardly wait to see the look on Willow's face.

It would be gratifying to see, but I wasn't so sure I wanted to be around when it happened.

We drove in silence for a few miles, then Dimples glanced my way. "Thanks Shelby. I knew bringing you in on this would help." He shook his head. "But what was with that Armani cologne thing? Did you pick it up from Sophie's mind? That Brock wore Armani? And what about the song? I think that's what brought her out of it... and I have to tell you—it was pretty freakin' weird. I felt chills on the back of my neck."

"Yeah. It kind of freaked me out too."

"So, he wasn't really there like you said, right?"

He didn't look at me, hoping I'd tell him I'd done it to trick her into talking. Since I kept my mouth shut, he continued. "What? You saying he was really there?"

I didn't want to lie to him, since he's my friend and all, but I picked up plain as day that he really didn't want to know I could hear dead people. With that attitude, what was I supposed to tell him? On the other hand, he couldn't seem to let it go; must be the detective side of him.

"I know you get a little spooked sometimes, but... you didn't see him or anything, right?"

"No. I didn't see him, that's silly. But I may have smelled the Armani." I blew out a breath. "Let's just leave it at that, all right?"

"Sure." He kept his gaze on the road, but I picked up that he was a little shocked. All this time we'd worked together, and I had kept this from him? He'd thought we were close. Partners didn't keep huge secrets like that. If I could see ghosts, I should have told him.

"I can't see ghosts," I said, throwing up my arms. "But sometimes I can hear them... in my mind. It must be part of the whole mind-reading thing. And before you get all upset that I didn't tell you, I've hinted at it... you know I have. It's just not something I've wanted to talk about... mostly because it doesn't happen very often and it freaks me out."

His brows drew together. Thinking back, he knew I was right. How could he forget those times when I'd been freaked out at the precinct when I'd worked on cases from the dead files? As that popped into his mind, it all made sense.

It also reminded him of those two skeletons they'd found under that house I'd wanted to buy. At the time, I'd claimed that I was just extra-sensitive, but I must have heard those kids. Deep down, he'd suspected that, but since I hadn't admitted it, he'd brushed it off as being a little too creepy.

"So if you heard Brock, what did he say?"

I shrugged. "Basically what I told Sophie. I only heard a few words, mostly that he was there and he loved her."

Dimples shook his head. "Wow... that's... insane."

"Yeah... it always creeps me out. But it doesn't happen often, even when I think it might, so it's not something I can predict."

"Hmm... but if you could actually talk to the murder victim... couldn't he tell you who killed him? That would sure make things a lot easier."

Oh hell. It was a good question. One I'd considered myself. But it just didn't work that way. At least not for me. "That would be nice, but it's not like that. Sometimes I hear a song... and other times it's a word or two. But what I picked up from Brock today was the most I'd ever heard at once. I think it was because of Sophie's condition and the intense feelings going on in the room. After this, I doubt that I'll hear him again."

"That's too bad. I mean... maybe not for you, but for finding the killer."

"Oh, I don't know about that. I think those small things I picked up could help immensely."

"Oh yeah... right... of course they could." He hoped he hadn't offended me. He hadn't meant to. Then his thoughts turned to Willow, and he wondered if her abilities included sensing ghosts. It seemed like she may have mentioned something like that... hadn't she said she was into mysticism? He'd dismissed it, but if she went to the house, would she sense Brock there?

"So you think she could do a better job?" That came out a little louder than I'd intended.

"Oh hell. No. Not at all. I shouldn't have been thinking about her. It's just the way my mind works, but I didn't mean it." Mortified, he rubbed a hand over his face, knowing he'd messed up big time. What kind of a friend did that?

Wretched and miserable, he hurried to make it up to me. "She's not even a fraction as good as you. In fact... I never should have brought it up. I don't know why I did that." He glanced my way. "Can you forgive me?"

Sure, he'd hurt my feelings, but he hadn't brought it up. It was all in his mind, and I only knew because I'd been invading his privacy. If anyone should apologize, it was me. "This reality I live in is a little crazy. I used to tell myself that I shouldn't get upset about what people were thinking... mostly because if I couldn't read minds, I'd never know.

"But... on the other hand... I've learned that what people think is who they really are inside. And usually, if they're thinking something, I need to take it at face value." I glanced his way. "So it puts me in a bind with my family and friends, but I've learned that it's more important to cut them a little slack, even if my feelings get hurt. In other words, it's fine."

He let out a sigh. "Okay. So... we're good?"

"Yes, we're good."

"Thanks, Shelby. This whole thing with Willow has got to stop. I don't like her coming between us, so once this case is over, I'm telling the chief that I won't work with her again."

I sent him a big smile. "Thanks... Drew." He smiled back, showing off his dimples in all their glory, and suddenly, all was right with the world.

We arrived at the precinct, and Dimples headed toward the door. I hung back. Noticing, he turned to look at me. "What? You're not coming in?"

"I've got other things to do, and you've got Willow to deal with. Why don't you call me if you discover anything new?"

"But I thought you'd want to gloat." Disappointment washed over him.

"Yeah... not really my thing. I'll gloat when we find the real killer, how's that?"

He huffed out a breath. "Sure. But will you still help me out?"

"Of course. I have to come in tomorrow for my next counseling appointment, so I'll check in with you then."

"I guess that's better than nothing. Okay, I'll see you tomorrow."

"Sure... or you can call if you get something before then."

"Thanks Shelby." With a grateful nod, he headed into the precinct.

As I walked to my car, I wished things were different. Why did this Willow person have to come along and mess everything up? Now that Dimples had her to work with, it left me on the outside. I wanted to solve Brock's murder, but my hands were tied. Stupid psychic.

It would have been nice to have Dimples's help with Mack Haywood's investigation too, but that was out of the question. I checked my watch, finding it much later than I'd thought.

I might as well head over to Thrasher Development and see if Ramos was back. Then, tomorrow morning, I could talk to all of Mack Haywood's neighbors and friends.

With that settled, I drove to Thrasher Development and headed up to the twenty-sixth floor. After a quick greeting, Jackie sent me to Uncle Joey's office, and I knocked before entering. He waved me in, finishing up his phone call.

Glancing my way, he rubbed his hands together, thinking that deal had gone well, and now that I was back he could take care of this drug business once and for all. "Have a seat and I'll get Ramos. He just got back, so this is perfect timing."

As I sat down, Uncle Joey called Ramos, summoning him to his office. He hung up and smiled at me. "Ramos checked everyone out, and didn't find any of my people in the business cheating me, so that's good news."

"Uh... yeah... for sure."

Ramos opened the door, wearing all black and looking sexy as hell. Life was so not fair. He sent me that sensual smile of his and sat down beside me. Naturally, I caught a whiff of his scent and tried not to let it go to my head.

"All right, let's do this," Uncle Joey said, pulling me out of my reverie. "Ramos, why don't you make the call to Victor? I'm afraid my anger might get the best of me, and I don't want to scare him off." He was thinking that anyone who double-crossed him was worthy of death, and he wouldn't hesitate to kill Victor if he'd made that mistake.

Ramos nodded and put the call through. It surprised me that Uncle Joey was so open about killing him. He usually blocked those sorts of thoughts from his mind. But he just waited with anticipation to see if Victor answered his phone, openly looking forward to the upcoming confrontation.

I thought if Victor was smart, he'd get out of town fast, but he picked up instead, and Ramos began talking. "Vic, Manetto wants to see you. How soon can you get here?" Ramos listened to the answer. "Good. See you in a few minutes." He disconnected. "He'll be here in about twenty minutes."

"Did he sound worried?" Uncle Joey asked.

"No. But once he sees Shelby, I think that'll change."

I was starting to get nervous. "What if it's true? What are you going to do about him?"

Instead of answering the question, Uncle Joey turned the tables on me. "What do you think we should do?" He thought that, since I was going to be his successor, this would be a good learning experience and a great time for me to voice my opinion.

Ramos's brows drew together. Why did he ask me that? What was going on? This wasn't like Manetto. He usually didn't want me around for this side of the business. Had something changed?

"Uh... well. I guess if he's double-crossing you, he's got to go." That surprised them both. Was I actually saying he should be killed? "But it might just be a misunderstanding, so I think we should wait and see."

"Good idea," Uncle Joey answered.

"Uh... since we've got some time, I think I'll put my purse away in my office and maybe grab a Diet Coke." At Uncle Joey's nod, I stood to leave.

"I'll come with you," Ramos said, eager to find out what was going on between me and Manetto. He followed me down the hall and opened my office door. I stepped inside while he waited in the hall, slipping my purse in the bottom drawer of my desk.

Before leaving, I caught sight of the photo of our family taken with Miguel after his show in New York. It sat right next to the photo of me, Chris, and the kids. The phrase, "In for a penny, in for a pound," hit me like a ton of bricks. Boy, was I ever in over my head now. Who would have thought?

I joined Ramos and followed him to his swanky apartment, situated at the end of the hall. Ramos stayed there most of the time, and his fridge was always stocked with diet soda... mostly for me. Since it was my duty to drink it, I tried to stop by as often as I could. Plus... it was a great place to take a breather from the stress of working for a mob boss.

Ramos pulled the door open and followed me inside. I went straight to the fridge, grabbed a can, and popped the lid. After taking a couple of swallows, I found a glass, filled it with ice, and poured in the rest. "You want one?"

Ramos came to my side and grabbed a cold bottle of beer from the fridge instead. "No way. This is better." After taking a swig, he glanced my way. "So what's going on?"

"I am in so much trouble."

His lips twisted into a wry grin. "Tell me something I don't know."

"Ha-ha." I took a deep breath for courage and let it out. "Okay. Here goes. This morning, Uncle Joey asked me to be his successor."

Ramos's brows rose right up into his hairline. "What the hell? You told him you'd do it?" He could hardly believe I'd agree. What was I thinking?

"I didn't tell him yes... exactly. He gave me time to think about it, but you know him. Since I didn't tell him no, he's taking it as a yes. What am I going to do?"

Ramos could hardly believe it. Why would Manetto saddle me with this now? Even more puzzling was why Manetto hadn't spoken to him about it. Somewhere in the back of his mind, he'd always thought Manetto would turn the business over to him. Not that he wanted it... but it made a hell of a lot more sense than giving it to me.

"Yeah... I agree with you, but he told me it was in name only. He wants you to run the business, not me. Sort of like we'd be partners or something."

Ramos narrowed his eyes. "That conniving son of a bitch." It made sense to him now. Manetto knew Ramos wouldn't agree to take over the business, but he had to know Ramos would do it for me. "What else did he tell you?"

I shrugged. "Just that it's for his peace of mind, and he's not ready to retire anytime soon. Like, he wants to get his affairs in order and all that. Chris is working on the trust for Uncle Joey's estate. But I guess that's a normal thing people do once they get into their sixties, right?"

Ramos nodded, but a cold chill flooded over him, and he hoped that was the only reason Manetto was making changes to his will.

CHAPTER 7

"You think there's something wrong with him?" I asked, panic catching my breath.

"I don't know. He hasn't said anything, but... he's been gone a lot lately, and he's been kind of secretive about it. Did you pick up anything from him... like if he's sick or something?"

"No. I even asked him about that, but he denied it, and I didn't hear anything from his mind to tell me otherwise."

"Okay. Good." Ramos couldn't help the worry that curdled his stomach. He'd never considered his life without Manetto, but now... what if something was wrong with the boss? He didn't like it. Not one bit.

"Now you know why I needed a soda, right?"

"Yeah." He thought I probably needed something a lot stronger than that. He was right, but I was afraid if I got started down that path, I'd never come back.

We both tipped back our drinks, swallowing a few big gulps before coming up for air. "He's going to know we talked about this," I said. "I'm a little worried about that, since I don't think he wanted you to know until I'd agreed."

Ramos shook his head. "I don't know. This might be just what he wanted. If you're unwilling to do it, and he knows you told me, he knows I'd be more inclined to accept the position to keep you out of it. On the other hand, if you did agree, he knows I'd agree to whatever he wanted, just to help you out. Either way, he gets what he wants."

"Wow. He's a genius at this, isn't he?"

Ramos snorted, thinking, *no shit*, and finished off his drink.

Since there was more to the story, I figured now was a good time to discuss it. I turned around and leaned back against the counter. "So... did he tell you the rest?"

"The rest? What do you mean?"

"That he's getting out of the mob-boss part of the business? You must suspect it, since you knew he'd stopped the drug side, right?"

"Yeah. He mentioned it, and I figured he'd had a change of heart, but it's not going to be easy." He thought Manetto would have a harder time letting go than he was willing to admit. It meant giving up power and control. Since it was in Manetto's blood to control everything, he didn't think a lifetime of conditioning would be easy to end.

Relief washed over me. "Really? That's good news. Well... not that it will be hard for him to stop being a mob boss... but it must mean that there's nothing physically wrong with him, right?" At Ramos's nod, I continued. "So... he's looking at this in the long-term."

Ramos threw his empty bottle in the trash. "Yes. You know him well. I guess we'll figure it all out at some point, but, for now, we'd better get back. What's your plan for Vic anyway?"

"I have no idea."

He chuckled. "Come on."

I followed him out of the apartment. As we passed Jackie, she glanced up with a raised brow. She hoped we were being good, but she didn't trust Ramos... or me. With a frown, I stopped beside her, and Ramos continued down the hall.

"So Jackie, how's Uncle Joey doing? Is his shoulder all better?" Short of asking if Uncle Joey had any health issues; that was the best I could do. Maybe she'd tell me if something was going on.

Her brows rose. Where had that come from? "Like I told you yesterday, his shoulder's fine."

Oops, I'd forgotten about that. "Oh... that's right. So... how about Miguel? Have you heard from him lately?"

"Yes. He's coming home for a few days in a couple of weeks, so we're looking forward to seeing him."

"That's great."

"Yeah. We'll have to get the family together."

"Sounds good." Of course we'd get together. Savannah would kill me if we didn't. But it also cemented the fact that we were part of the family, and being Uncle Joey's successor was basically a given. But, as long as he got out of the business, it should be okay, right?

Victor entered the office doors. His dark, curly hair showed signs of gray at the temples, and I pegged his age around forty-three. His clean-shaven face had an olive complexion, and his eyes were deep set and dark. He wore business casual, with blue jeans and a dark jacket over a gray, button-up shirt.

He smiled at us, but the worry of being summoned to Uncle Joey's office kept him from speaking. Upon seeing Ramos opening Uncle Joey's door, his step faltered, but he hurried on.

"He looks a little nervous," I whispered to Jackie.

"That happens a lot." She caught my gaze and we giggled.

"I'd better go." I followed Victor down the hall and entered the office right behind him.

Uncle Joey waved me in, and I took the seat next to Victor in front of his desk. Ramos closed the door and took his position standing in front of it. Victor's heart picked up speed, and his brow began to sweat. He knew something was wrong, but he had no idea what it could be.

Despite my worry about what would become of Victor, it hit me that I enjoyed this part of the job. Finding out if someone was cheating or lying brought me a sense of justice that seemed sorely lacking in today's world.

Of course, I didn't want him dead, but I did want the truth, and if he was cheating, he needed to pay the consequences. Hmm... if he knew, would Bob Spicer think I'd lost it and turned to the dark side? Maybe I'd be a better successor than I thought?

"Victor," Uncle Joey said, leaning back in his chair and looking down at him. "You've been part of my family organization now for a long time, about twelve years, if I'm remembering correctly. I've appreciated your service, and I hope you feel you've been fairly compensated."

"Yes," Victor said. "I believe so, sir."

"Good. Are you happy with your position in the business?"

"Yes."

"Do you have any plans to leave?"

"Absolutely not, sir."

"That's good to know." Uncle Joey studied Victor with narrowed eyes. In response, Victor rubbed his sweaty palms on his pants. "I'm hoping you can help me out with something."

"Of course... whatever you need."

"As you know, I've terminated my involvement in the drug business. That used to be your area of expertise, and I wondered if you've had contact with our partner since then."

He shook his head. "No. After I told him we didn't need his services anymore, that was the end of it, and I haven't spoken with him since."

"Did he seem upset?"

"Well... yes. He asked me if we had a better deal with someone else. I assured him that wasn't the case and explained that we were stepping away from that part of the business for a time. I may have mentioned that it was because you needed to lay low for a while. I think it helped. I also may have promised him that he'd be our first contact once we got back in."

"How did he take it? Did that explanation satisfy him?"

"Yeah. I haven't heard from him since." Victor's brows rose. "Are you ready to get back in?"

"No." Uncle Joey tapped his fingers against the desktop, and studied Victor until the man shrank back in his seat. "But, unfortunately, someone else has been buying and selling drugs under the Manetto name. Do you know anything about that?"

Victor's eyes widened. He opened his mouth to deny it, but Uncle Joey cut him off. "Be careful how you answer me. I'll know if you're lying, and it will be much worse for you."

Victor glanced my way out of the corner of his eyes. He knew about my premonitions, and his heart began to pound. Having me there didn't bode well for him, and he'd have to be careful. "I'm not sure, but if I were to guess, I'd think that one of the people who used to work for me... uh... you... may have stepped in to fill the vacuum."

Uncle Joey nodded, expecting this. "And which one of my former employees would do that?"

Victor thought of his cousin, Vinny, and my heart sank. Of course, that didn't mean Victor was running the show, right? It could be all Vinny's doing, and Victor wouldn't have to die for it. There was still hope.

"Uh... let me think." Victor scratched his head, wanting to spare his cousin by giving Uncle Joey a different person's name. The guy still worked with Vinny, so it wasn't a stretch to name him. "Oh yeah... the guy went by Slasher. He could have taken over. He's been dealing drugs for a long time. Maybe it was him."

Ramos stepped to Uncle Joey's side, folded his arms, and faced Victor with narrowed eyes. "Funny you should mention a guy named Slasher, because I spoke with him just last night. He's been selling drugs through our tenants and telling them that it's on Manetto's orders. You know what he said?"

Ramos paused for dramatic effect. "That your cousin Vinny is running the show for Manetto. Are you sure you still don't know anything about this?"

Victor's face went white, and his breath caught. Rubbing his sweaty palms on his pants, he swallowed and took a couple of quick breaths. "I can explain—"

"Victor." Uncle Joey's penetrating gaze pierced Victor like a knife to the heart. "I'm so disappointed in you. I thought you were loyal to me. You're part of the family. You should have known better."

If anything, Victor's face paled even more, and his eyes widened with desperation. "Look. It's not what you think. I had no idea taking over the drug business would cause any problems. But I'm positive that Vinny didn't use your name. He's not that stupid. You have to believe me."

"But you're still selling drugs through the same channels?"

"You have to understand. When you got out of the business, it was an opportunity that Vinny and I couldn't resist, and you can hardly blame us for taking advantage of the situation. If our roles were reversed, you would have done the same thing. But I swear to you that everyone in the business knows you're out of it. Vinny's running things now, not you, everyone knows that."

"Then why did Slasher tell Ramos that I was behind it? Slasher made it quite clear to Ramos that Vinny was selling drugs for me, and that's why Vinny was using my resources."

Victor shook his head. "Slasher was lying. That's the only thing that makes sense. Look, let me take care of this. I can straighten things out. I'll make it right. Just give me a chance. I'll kill Tommy myself. It's obvious he's been doing this on his own."

"Wait a minute." Alarm skittered down my back. "Tommy? Who's Tommy?"

"Uh... I meant Slasher. That's Tommy's street name."

"Uh-oh."

"What is it?" Uncle Joey asked.

"Well... I was over at the precinct a little earlier today. A drug dealer was murdered last night, and his name was Tommy Demarco."

"Shit," Victor said. "That's him... that's Slasher."

"What happened to him?" Ramos asked me.

"He was shot in some building on the south side. The police think it was drug-related, like a drug deal gone wrong. There are no witnesses, and no murder weapon was found." I turned my gaze to Victor. "Was Tommy in a gang?"

"I don't know. You'd have to ask Vinny."

"I think talking to Vinny is a foregone conclusion." Uncle Joey sucked in a breath and glanced my way. "What else do you know about this?"

"The police think it's gang-related, but there's more..." I swallowed, hating to break the news to them like this. "The detective on the case is pretty sure the murder is tied to organized crime." I shrugged. "At least he's hoping to find a link. If Tommy... I mean... Slasher was telling everyone he was selling drugs for Uncle Joey, that might be bad."

"Yes it would," Uncle Joey agreed. "But you said there were no witnesses."

"Yeah, but they're still going to talk to the gang members in the area. And... uh... they might want me there during the interviews... you know... to see if I can pick up anything with my premonitions."

I half expected Uncle Joey to blow up over this, but, after thinking it through, he nodded instead. "That could be helpful for us. If they try to pin this on me, you can point them in Vinny's direction and he can take the fall." His hard gaze landed on Victor. "It's the least he can do for selling drugs under my name. And if he doesn't like it... then he's a dead man... and you can take his place."

Victor swallowed his protest. If he didn't agree, his life was over, along with Vinny's. He'd just have to convince Vinny that taking the fall was better than death, because he wasn't about to get blamed for this. He still couldn't believe Vinny could have been so stupid. "Look. I'll make sure Vinny knows what's at stake here, but first, you have to give Vinny a chance to explain. I mean... if it wasn't him—"

"It won't matter," Uncle Joey said. "If this even remotely looks like I had something to do with it, believe me, one of you will take the fall. For your sake, I hope it's Vinny, but either way, this is not coming back to me."

He waited for Victor's nod before continuing, "Good. I'm glad you understand. And... look at it this way, you might get lucky and it won't come to that, especially with Shelby on the case. She helps the police a lot, and they trust her. She might be able to solve the murder without involving any of us, especially if it's gang-related, or if he was killed for some other stupid reason."

"That's true," Ramos agreed, thinking I was getting off lightly for helping the police this time. But, since it would help Manetto too, it was a win-win.

Crap. Was I in the middle of this mess, or what? I guess it shouldn't surprise me, but what the hell? Now it looked like I had to point the police to Vinny to save Uncle Joey, even if Vinny was innocent. It also meant that, if I wanted a clear conscience, I had to find Tommy's real killer. Still, on the bright side, maybe Vinny had killed Tommy, and solving it would be a cinch? Ha... who was I kidding? Nothing was ever that easy.

"Victor, why don't you take Ramos and Shelby to pay Vinny a visit," Uncle Joey said. "Then we can take it from there. You know where he is?"

"He should be at home. Let me text him and make sure, then we can head over there now."

"Fine. Just be sure not to mention that Ramos is coming with you."

As Victor nodded and sent the text, Uncle Joey glanced my way, thinking this was working out better than he thought. Naturally, he didn't like that I helped the police. But this time, I could actually help him without feeling guilty about it, since he was totally innocent.

I guess he had a point. I just hoped no one at the police department would find out that I was passing along sensitive information, otherwise, it wouldn't matter that

Uncle Joey was innocent. They'd kick me to the curb, and I'd never be able to help them again.

"Okay, he's home." Victor stood, resigned. "Let's get this over with."

Uncle Joey nodded at Ramos, giving him the okay to do what he had to do, even if it meant death, and we filed out of the office. With a heavy heart, I quickly retrieved my purse from my desk and followed Ramos and Victor to the elevator.

A few seconds after pushing the button, the elevator doors swished open, and Ricky, one of Uncle Joey's loyal employees, along with a couple of other men, exited. After a quick greeting, I picked up that they were there to see Uncle Joey about some important business, but the elevator doors shut before I could pick up what it was.

I suddenly realized how little I knew about Thrasher Development, or any of Uncle Joey's business dealings. And he wanted me to be his successor? This was just plain nuts. A heavy weight filled my chest, and the sudden urge to run came over me. I didn't want this. But how was I going to get out of it now?

Ramos told Victor to text him Vinny's address, thinking that he and I would get there on his bike. He thought it was the least he could do, since I looked a little sick, and he wanted to put a smile back on my face. I caught his gaze and grinned. Even in such dire circumstances, a motorcycle ride with him would always make me smile.

Without a word between us, we stepped to the bike, snapped on our helmets, and took off. Slipping my arms around Ramos's waist did wonders for my mood. I knew it wasn't the best thing for a married woman to do, but since this... and maybe Diet Coke... were my only weaknesses, it wasn't too bad. Besides, I needed some perks for doing this job, or I might go crazy.

We followed Victor to a small subdivision just off the freeway, and I realized it wasn't too far from the area where Tommy was shot. Maybe Vinny had more to do with Tommy's demise than Victor thought.

Still, I didn't look forward to confronting him. Good thing Ramos was here. I just hoped this visit didn't end up with Ramos killing Vinny. I was pretty sure Ramos wouldn't kill him in front of me, but, with my new status as Uncle Joey's successor, I'd know all about it, and it kind of made me sick.

Victor pulled up in front of a small, brick house, and we parked behind him. As Victor knocked on the door, Ramos and I held back, waiting for Vinny to open it. He wore a graphic t-shirt over a pair of jeans, and his arms were covered in tattoos. His swarthy features pegged him as a younger version of Victor, but without the class.

As Victor stepped through the door, he held it open for us to follow, and I picked up Vinny's surprise to see Ramos. Not knowing who I was, he dismissed me and focused his attention on the biggest threat to his continued health. Just looking at Ramos sent tremors of fear down his spine.

"What's going on Vic? Why are they here?" Vinny shifted on his feet with nervous anxiety. He knew something was wrong, and tension curdled his stomach.

"We need to talk," Victor said, his voice ringing with authority. "Did you hear about Tommy?"

"No... why, what's up?"

"He's dead... they found him this morning."

"Shit."

"But that's not the worst of it." Victor glanced at Ramos, nodding for him to finish the story.

"I spoke with Tommy last night," Ramos said. "He told me he sold drugs for you, and you sold drugs for Manetto.

Since Manetto's out of the business, why do you suppose he thought that?"

"What? No way. He knows we don't sell for Manetto anymore. He was lying." Vinny's shock wasn't hard to pick up. This was news to him, and he paled to realize just how much trouble he was in with Ramos and the big boss. "I swear it's the truth."

"Did you know Tommy had an arrangement with Aaron at the health-and-nutrition store?"

Vinny's brows drew together, and he shook his head. "I don't know anything about it."

Starting with our visit to the store, Ramos explained the whole story, watching Vinny grow more and more agitated. "Are you sure you don't know anything about this?"

"No, I swear I don't. This is all Tommy's doing. It has nothing to do with me."

"That's where you're wrong," Ramos said, and explained the consequences to Vinny. "If the police trace this back to Manetto, you're taking the fall."

"No way. It's not my fault. I didn't do anything wrong."

"Vinny," Victor said, shoving Vinny against the wall. "This is serious. You either agree to this or you die. Tommy was one of your guys... and he crossed Manetto. No one crosses the boss and lives to tell about it. No one. Don't you get it?"

Victor kind of skipped the part where his life was on the line too, but I couldn't really blame him for that.

"But... but..." Vinny searched his cousin's eyes and found the truth.

"It doesn't matter," Victor continued. "It's the price you pay. Tommy was out of line, and now he's dead. The police are looking into it, and they want to tie it to Manetto. If they do, you're taking the fall."

It finally sank in, and Vinny swore a blue streak in his mind, muttering under his breath. The fight went out of him, and he slumped against the wall. "Whatever man. But it won't come back to me. Whatever Tommy was doing, he did it on his own. I had no idea."

Since Vinny was telling the truth, I threw him a bone. "Maybe we can work with that. We met some of the kids Tommy sold to at the Health Store. If they come back looking to buy some drugs, maybe you can find out what Tommy had going on."

"That's true," Ramos said. "Even if they know Tommy's dead, you can take his place selling drugs to them. Once word gets out, and they come to you for their drugs, we'll make sure someone talks and get to the bottom of it. Are you willing to do that?"

"Hell yeah," Vinny said.

"Good. That will help your case with Manetto, because I've got to tell you, he's ready to kill you right now. Your cooperation will go a long way in appeasing him. But you're not out of the woods yet. Not until this is solved. Got it?"

"Yeah, sure man. I got this." He was thinking that he used to do business with Aaron back in the day, so it wasn't a problem to get back in. That must have been what Tommy thought too, and now the guy was dead. What the hell was going on? "I'll get the word out and head over there tonight. You want me to call you if one of the buyers shows up?"

"Yes," Ramos agreed. He glanced my way, thinking that I might need to come with him. I nodded. In for a penny, in for a pound, right? That was my life now.

As Ramos and I left, Ramos told both of them not to screw this up, and I nodded to show my solidarity, although I don't think either of them noticed. Soon, we were back on the bike and headed to Thrasher. The ride was way too short for my taste, but it was better than nothing.

"You coming up?" Ramos asked.

"Uh... you know, it's getting late, I think I'll call it a day."

He nodded. "Sure. I'll text you if I need you tonight, but I wouldn't count on it. With Tommy's death, I don't imagine the word will get out for another day or two."

"That makes sense." We spoke for another minute before I hurried to my car, eager to get home and put my feet up. Talk about stress. It just didn't let up, with one thing happening right after another; I was kidding myself to think I'd ever shed my trouble-magnet status.

Would things ever settle down? I had so much on my plate that I didn't know what I should do first. Mack Haywood's murder seemed the most important, so I put that at the top of my list. Next, I'd promised Dimples I'd show up his new psychic partner by solving their case.

And now I had Tommy's murder to solve. At least Vinny was taking the lead, but I still needed to work with the police on the case for Uncle Joey's sake. We certainly couldn't have it tied to him when he was innocent. Then there was the big question of being Uncle Joey's successor.

I drove home in a daze, mostly on automatic. Out of all the things I faced, being Uncle Joey's successor scared me the most. Of course, I had to remember that Uncle Joey's plans were for the future. None of it was happening right now. I wasn't in charge of a darn thing. I hadn't said I'd do it either, so I still had plenty of wiggle-room, right?

For now, I'd put the rest of my troubles off until morning... unless Ramos called me later. Sheesh! Maybe it was a good thing I had my appointment with Bob Spicer tomorrow. Hopefully, he had some coping mechanisms he could share that would help me with the stress. Not that I could tell him about the mob stuff, but the police stuff was probably more than enough.

Making it home, I walked into the house, and Coco rushed to greet me. I'd forgotten all about him, but the minute he appeared, a big smile crossed my face, and my worries lightened. I knelt on one knee and threw my arms around him. He licked my face, and I didn't even mind.

"What are you up to, big guy? Keeping an eye on the place?"

He let out a woof. *Yup.*

"Good boy. Where is everyone?"

Another woof. *Gone.*

"Oh, that's right. Josh had to work, and Savannah's at Ash's house. Do you need to go out?"

Yup. Yup. Yup. Coco ran to the back patio door, anxious and prancing a little. I opened it and he took off. Whoa, we should probably get a doggy-door installed.

Heading upstairs to my room, I kicked off my shoes and changed into a pair of shorts. Coming back down, I stepped out on the patio and sat back on the swing. Sitting in the shade with a cool breeze blowing across my face, I closed my eyes and let the cares of the day flow away. Coco joined me, and, with a little coaxing, he jumped onto the swing and laid his head on my lap.

Sitting together, with his undivided attention, I began to tell him about my day, which soon morphed into a conversation about how much my life had changed the day I'd gone to the grocery store for carrots. I told him all about the close calls I'd had with death recently, including that I'd killed a man and didn't even feel bad about it.

Coco listened attentively and didn't interrupt me once. By the time I was done talking, he was sprawled over my lap and snuggled against me. We sat like that until the kids came home, and it was time to get dinner started. Heading into the house, I realized that was the best therapy session I'd ever had.

Chris got home in time to eat, and the kids filled him in on Coco's former owner. "So you're going to look into it?" he asked me.

"Yes." I explained what I'd discovered at the precinct, and that I was planning to question the neighbors and the people from the search-and-rescue team. "The detectives have already done that, but maybe I'll pick up something they missed." I shrugged. "It's the least I can do."

"You should take Coco with you," Josh said. "He probably knows who the killer is, and he can tell you."

"Don't be stupid," Savannah said. "Coco can't talk."

"I know that, dummy, but if he starts barking at them, don't you think that's a good clue?"

"I guess… but that doesn't mean that person is the killer, maybe there are some people Coco doesn't like. You never know."

"I think I'll take him with me." I broke in, hoping to diffuse the situation. "I'm sure the neighbors and the rescue people could tell me more about Coco, and they might be more open to talk if he's there."

"That makes sense," Chris agreed. "Could you pass the salad?"

Later that night, I asked Chris how the estate planning for Uncle Joey was going. He shrugged. "There's a lot to go over. Let's just say that Manetto's got a ton of assets, and it's going to take me a while to make sure everything is included."

"So it's a big job?"

"Yeah. Once I have everything put together, I'll go over it with him so he can tell me who gets what after his death.

Legally, I'm not supposed to tell you what his assets are, but I'm a little blown away by all of his holdings. He's loaded."

I nodded. "Yeah, I figured."

"And I was shocked that he wants you to be his successor. Did you know?"

"No... it blew me away, too."

"What are you thinking? You don't want to do it, do you?" Chris didn't want me tied up in Uncle Joey's business. My involvement was bad enough already, and I had no idea how to run such a large enterprise. "I mean... being the executor of his estate is fine. You can't get a lot wrong because it's all spelled out. But running his business, even in name only, is asking for trouble."

Besides having no training in business, being tied to a mob boss would leave me vulnerable to all sorts of undesirable things. And what about the kids? This was a big deal.

All the earlier tension of the day tightened my chest until I could hardly breathe. "I know, but... weren't you there when he said it was in name only, and someone else would run the business?"

At his nod, I continued. "So it won't be that bad. Otherwise, I'll tell him no. Can we write that condition into his will or something?" Hope blossomed in my chest. "I know... you can write up a contract between me and Uncle Joey with that stipulation. That would work, right?"

"Maybe so." Chris thought about it for a few seconds, and his mood lightened. I was on to something, and it could be the perfect solution. "I'll see what I can come up with."

I didn't want to ruin that happy thought by telling Chris about Uncle Joey's drug dealer problem, and that I might have to go chasing off to help Ramos and Vinny tonight. Instead, I told him about Dimples's case with Willow-the-

Psychic, and how I'd helped bring Sophie out of it because I'd heard her dead husband.

By the time I got finished, it was late, and Chris's eyes were drooping. Luckily, I got a text from Ramos that nothing had happened, and, for now, I was off the hook. Relieved, I climbed into bed, grateful I didn't have to explain it to Chris just yet. But that didn't mean I could quit thinking about it, and worry kept me awake long into the early morning hours.

CHAPTER 8

Wide awake at seven-thirty a.m., I decided to get up. Chris was just leaving for work, so I gave him a quick kiss before he walked out the door.

After pulling on some clothes and eating a bowl of cereal, I made a couple of phone calls to the people from Mack's search-and-rescue unit. One of them was available to talk with me later in the morning, especially after I explained that I was Coco's new owner. That gave me plenty of time to take Coco on a walk back to Mack Haywood's home, where I hoped to speak with his neighbors.

With Josh and Savannah still asleep, I wrote them a note and left the house with Coco. We took the same route as yesterday, and Coco seemed to know exactly where we were going. As we neared his former house, Coco pulled on the leash a bit, but he wasn't as excited as yesterday.

He seemed to know that Mack was gone, and he wasn't coming back. There was no sign of Austin today, but boxes and furniture were visible through the window, so I knew he wasn't finished cleaning out the house.

I stepped to the neighbor's house on the right and rang the doorbell. A woman came to the door, but eyed Coco warily. I picked up her fear that someone had killed her next door neighbor, and she wasn't about to talk to a stranger. After I explained who I was, she told me she wasn't home that night, and she couldn't help me.

Discouraged, I trudged to the house on the other side of Mack's home. I rang the bell, and Coco obediently sat beside me. A man came to the door, and Coco jumped to his feet. The man was probably in his mid-sixties, with thin, silver hair, and wearing a short-sleeved shirt tucked into a pair of jeans. He spotted the dog, and his face lit up.

"Coco!" Happiness rolled off him, and Coco woofed with enthusiasm. The man threw the door open and stepped onto the porch, crouching beside the dog. "What a surprise. I never thought I'd see you again. How ya doing?" After receiving several doggy licks, and giving Coco lots of love, he turned his attention to me. His eyes were kind and gleamed with curiosity

"Hi, I'm Shelby Nichols. I'm a private investigator. I adopted Coco."

"Oh... lucky you. He's a great dog."

"Yeah, he sure is. I'm here because I met Austin yesterday. After speaking with him, I told him I'd look into his father's death. Do you have a few minutes to answer some questions?"

"Uh... sure. Please sit down." He motioned me toward a couple of cushioned chairs, with a small, round table between them, on the big front porch. "I'd invite you inside, but my wife's allergic to animals." After sitting down, he continued. "I already told the police everything I know. Do they have any suspects?"

"Not that I know of. Are you the neighbor who called the police?"

"Yes, I'm Reed Gardner."

"Can you tell me what happened?"

"Sure, but first I want to know how you ended up with Coco."

I gladly told him the story, making sure to include how Coco basically picked us. "He seemed depressed, but he warmed up to us pretty fast. Yesterday, I took him on a walk, and we ended up here. I have to admit, it was mostly Coco's doing. He pulled me the last few blocks. Austin was there in the house, and he told me what happened. Since I'm a private investigator, I told him I'd look into it."

"Wow. That's quite the story."

"I know. So... what can you tell me about that night?"

He let out a big sigh. "I heard Coco barking sometime after nine. It was loud and continuous. He doesn't usually bark like that, so I wondered what was going on. I called Mack's number, but he didn't answer, and I got worried. So I went over to the house and knocked. When no one answered, I walked in and found him lying on the floor."

"So the door wasn't locked?"

"No." Reed shook his head. "I thought he might have had a heart attack at first, but, once I got closer, I saw all the blood and the big gash on the back of his head. I felt his neck for a pulse, but he was gone. Maybe if I'd come sooner, he might have had a chance." Guilt and sorrow washed over him. It still shook him up, just thinking about it.

"When you first heard Coco barking, did you happen to look outside?"

"No. I was downstairs watching TV. At first, it didn't register that he was barking, but then his bark changed; it sounded more frantic. That's when I called Mack, but it was too late."

"What about your wife? Did she see anything?"

His brow furrowed. "No. She took a sleeping pill earlier and slept through the whole thing. She gets migraines, and sleep is about the only thing that works on them."

"Oh, that's too bad." It was hard for me to believe she slept through everything, but what did I know? From his thoughts, I picked up that his wife's condition weighed him down, and it was a little more complicated than he wanted to share.

"So what did you do after you found Mack?"

"I ran home to call nine-one-one. It occurred to me that the house was a crime scene, and I didn't want to disturb anything by staying. I gave Austin a call too, thinking he needed to know something bad had happened to his dad. But after he answered, I couldn't tell him Mack was dead. That might have been a mistake, but I wasn't thinking straight."

"So was Austin at his place when you called him?"

He shrugged. "I think so. The police showed up before Austin did, and they made me wait out here on my porch." He leaned over to pet Coco. "Poor dog was going crazy in there, but they wouldn't let me back in. I told them Coco wouldn't hurt me, but they insisted on leaving him there until animal control came to let him out."

"That must have been awful."

"It was." He swallowed. "They got him in one of those long-handled noose ropes to keep him from attacking anyone... as if he would."

Reed was thinking that Coco had to be taken out through the back door, because Mack's body was still lying in the doorway between the living room and the kitchen, blocking the front door.

"The poor dog must have seen Mack. The animal control guy told me that Coco hadn't wanted to leave Mack's side, and he'd ended up carrying him out. They were going to put him in the back of the animal control truck, but I couldn't let them do that.

"I stopped the man carrying him and convinced him to let me take the dog. Coco was whining and shivering by then, but he licked my face, and the guy finally relented. I brought him up here on the porch, and he stayed with me until Austin got here."

He closed his eyes, remembering Austin's anguish at finding his father dead. He'd hoped that having Coco would have helped Austin cope with his loss, but that hadn't turned out so well.

Reed patted Coco's head. "I wanted to keep him, but, with my wife's allergies, it wasn't possible. Austin took him home that night, but he was devastated. When he came back a few days later, he told me he'd taken Coco to the shelter."

Reed stopped and swallowed. "It broke my heart. I think it would have broken his dad's heart, too. Why would Austin do that when Coco meant so much to his dad? It makes no sense to me. I know Mack would have wanted Austin to keep Coco and continue his work with the search-and-rescue team. Austin had to know how much it meant to his dad." He glanced at me. "But maybe it turned out all right after all."

"I think it did," I said. "Our whole family loves him, especially my kids. He's a special dog, and I promise you we'll take good care of him."

Reed nodded, grateful I understood how much he needed to hear that.

"Do you have any idea why someone would kill Mack? The police think he let the person in, so he must have known them. Did you see anyone strange stop by the house before that night?"

"No. That's the thing I don't understand. Everyone liked Mack. If it was someone he knew, he must not have known them for long."

"How long have you known the family?"

"We've been neighbors for nearly five years. Mack moved in after Austin left for college. His wife had died right before that—cancer, I think—and he wanted to downsize with everyone gone. When Mack retired from his job a couple of years ago, he got interested in the search-and-rescue program. That's when he bought Coco and trained him for the job. He told me Coco's a great rescue dog."

Reed was thinking it was too bad one of the people from the rescue team hadn't had a chance to adopt Coco. But maybe he was better off with us.

"Thanks Reed... you've been helpful. I need to get going, but, if you think of anything else, would you mind giving me a call? Here's my card."

He took my card and slipped it into his front shirt pocket. "Not at all. I hope you find the person who did this."

"I'll do my best."

"And... if you're ever in the neighborhood again, be sure to stop by and say hello." He ruffled Coco's fur. "Come see me again, okay buddy?"

Coco woofed, and I heard *yup*. I smiled and told Reed we would. After thanking him, we began the long walk home. Although I hadn't learned much to help with the case, I was happy I'd met Reed, and even happier that he'd seen Coco and knew he was all right.

I'd hoped for a better clue, but at least I knew more about that night, and it could still be helpful. We hurried back home, arriving just as Savannah and Josh got up. After coordinating our schedules for the day, I jumped in the shower and got ready for my meeting with Lance Hobbs from the search-and-rescue group.

I'd explained over the phone that we'd adopted Coco, and he'd readily agreed to meet with me, as long as I brought Coco along. He lived on several acres of land, and his large, brick home sat nestled beside a couple of giant trees. As I pulled into the drive, I caught sight of a barn and a large corral in the back.

As I opened the car door to let Coco out, he jumped down and took off before I could stop him. He ran toward the back of the house, and my heart lurched. As he disappeared, I started after him, yelling his name. Just then, a man came from the direction Coco had gone and sent me a friendly wave.

"You must be Shelby. I'm Lance Hobbs. Come on back."

He waited for me with a friendly smile meant to put me at ease. He was younger than I'd thought, most likely in his late forties, with short, dark hair. He stood about five-ten, and he had the broad shoulders and muscled arms of a hard worker. In his jeans and white t-shirt, his tanned skin spoke of spending a lot of time outdoors.

I greeted him with a quick hand shake and glanced into the back yard to find Coco playing with another dog. The dog was about the same size as Coco, but with longer, black and white fur.

"That's Scout," Lance began. "He's a border collie. He and I helped train Coco."

"Oh. Now I get why Coco ran off so fast."

"Yeah. They're great friends." He moved toward his back patio, gesturing at me to follow. "Come on over and sit down. I'm anxious to hear how you ended up with Coco."

I sat down in a cushioned chair beside his, surprised at how comfortable it was, and told him the story. "It's like he picked us. Anyway, I took him on a walk, and we ended up at Mack's house. That's where I met Austin and told him I'd look into his father's murder."

Lance nodded, thinking it had been a shock to hear about Mack's death. That someone had murdered him made no sense. He was one of the best men he'd ever met. It still shocked him that Austin had taken Coco to the pound. Why did he do that? It didn't make any sense either. He would have gladly taken Coco if he'd had the chance.

This whole thing was messed up. "Well, if you ever feel like he's too much, I'd be happy to take him off your hands. He's a great dog." He glanced my way, thinking that, if Coco had picked me, I must have done something right. "Or if you need a place for him to stay while you're out of town, he's always welcome here."

"Thanks. That's good to know."

"So, you're a private investigator?"

"Yes. I do consulting work for the police, and I have my own agency. But I wanted to look into Mack's death mostly because of Coco. So what can you tell me about Mack? When did you meet?"

"We met through the K-9 Search and Rescue Team. Mack wanted to get involved, and he contacted me to help him train his dog, so we've known each other for a couple of years."

"Do you know why he wanted to join the team?"

"Yeah." Mack had told him the story in confidence, but now that he was dead, it probably didn't matter if he shared the story. "He had a daughter that went missing when she was about four or five. It sounded like they didn't find her in time to save her. I think joining the rescue team was a way to help him deal with that."

"Oh my gosh. That's terrible."

"Yeah, but, unfortunately, it happens. I wasn't sure it was a good idea for him to get involved. A lot of these searches don't have a happy ending, and I worried it would bring back all the pain and anguish he'd already been through. But he seemed okay with it. I think he just wanted the chance to make a difference, because he'd felt so helpless all those years ago."

"That makes sense. Did he and Coco go on many rescues?"

"Yes. Most of the time, our searches take place during the summer, when kids get lost in the woods. I know Mack and Coco have also searched through the rubble of a couple of tornadoes, and... I think maybe one earthquake. But mostly, he's stayed close to home. I'd say he's been in on about ten to twelve in the last year or so."

"Were any of them happy endings?"

"A few." He smiled. "In fact, recently, there was a little girl who got lost, and he and Coco found her. That was a good day."

The back of my neck tingled. Holy hell. Was it the same search Willow had helped with? Maybe Lance had met her? "Were you there with Scout?"

"No. I was out of town on business, but Mack told me all about it. I think it did his heart good." Lance remembered their conversation and how happy Mack had been. "That little girl was about the same age as his daughter when she disappeared, so you can imagine how it made him feel to find her alive."

"Yeah, I'll bet." This had to be the same little girl. It was too recent to be a coincidence. But hadn't Dimples told me that Willow was the person who'd found the lost child? Was there more to it? Did Willow know Mack, or have something to do with Mack's death? But how could she be involved? And why would she kill Mack? I didn't pick up that vibe from her, but some people hid their dark side really well, even from themselves.

How did Austin fit in with all this? I knew he hadn't killed his dad, but he'd seemed angry about the whole search-and-rescue thing. Was that because he knew about his sister? I remembered him thinking that not all rescues turned out right. There was some definite resentment there. But it could easily be attributed to Austin not wanting his dad to go through that pain again.

"Uh… do you know what Austin thought about all this? He knew about his sister, right?"

Lance nodded. "Yeah, but he never knew her. He was just a toddler when it happened, so he was spared the trauma. I honestly don't know, but the fact that he gave up Coco kind of tells me he wasn't a fan."

"Yeah… but I'm not so sure that's why he did it." It wouldn't hurt to tell Lance Austin's reasons, even if I only knew because I'd read his mind. "You know that Mack put Coco in the back room, right?"

At his nod, I continued. "Well, I think somehow Austin is convinced that his dad did it to protect the dog. He's sure that if Coco had been there, he might have stopped the killer, and Mack would be alive."

Lance considered it. "He's not wrong."

"Yeah, I agree. So why did Mack put Coco in the back room? Whoever killed him had to be someone who didn't like dogs, right? Did Mack ever tell you about anyone who didn't like Coco?"

"Not that I recall, but I guess there are a lot of people who are afraid of dogs, especially dogs like Coco."

"Yeah… afraid… or allergic." Hadn't Reed Gardner mentioned that his wife was allergic to dogs? Had she really taken a sleeping pill? Even so, why would she kill Mack? That didn't make any sense, but, since I hadn't met her, I couldn't rule it out. I glanced at Lance. "Is there anything else you can think of? Maybe someone who held a grudge against him?"

"No. I'm sorry."

"That's okay." I checked my watch. If I left now, I had just enough time to take Coco home and eat a quick lunch before my appointment with Bob Spicer. "I need to go, but thanks for chatting with me."

"I wish I could have been more help."

"Oh, you've helped a lot, and I think Coco's had a great time." We looked at the dogs. They were plopped down next to each other in the grass, and both of them were panting from their play.

"I'd better give them some water before you go." Lance turned on the hose and filled a bucket with water. As they drank, he turned to me. "It was good to meet you. Like I said before, if you need to leave Coco with someone, give me a call."

"I will, thanks." Coco finished drinking and came to my side. "Did you have a good time?" He woofed *yup*. I laughed and patted his head. He barked *stay*. I shook my head. "Nope, sorry bud, but we've got to go home." Coco barked *come back*. I chuckled. "Sure we can come back sometime. I think Scout would like that, right Scout?" Scout barked *yup*. "Okay, I guess it's a date."

I smiled at Lance, and his gaze narrowed. He was thinking *what the hell?* It was like I was talking to the dogs, and they were talking back. He'd only seen something like that once before. No wonder Coco had picked me. I had a real affinity with animals.

Oops.

His gaze narrowed. "Have you ever considered search-and-rescue? You seem to have a knack with animals, and you've got a great dog for it. You'd have to get the training, but Coco's certified and everything."

"Huh... I hadn't thought of that, but it might be worth looking into. I don't have his vest or anything like that. Do you think Austin has them?"

"If he kept them, I'm sure he'd give them to you if you asked. But all the paperwork should be filed with our team. I'll look into it and let you know."

"Okay... sure."

He smiled, thinking that it would be nice for Coco to do what he'd been trained for. The dog was too young and too good at what he did to retire. Plus, I had a real knack with animals. I'd be a real asset for the team, and he hoped I'd agree. "Great. I'll give you a call."

I nodded and started toward my car, with Coco at my heels. Lance watched us go, and I sent him a wave before shutting my door. As I drove away, I let out a sigh. What had just happened? Sure it would be nice for Coco to do the whole search-and-rescue thing, but did I need one more thing on my plate? Not really.

But it would be nice to help find missing children, right? Maybe it was something Josh would be interested in? Of course, he was probably too young, but it wouldn't hurt to check. Still, I wasn't going to cross it off, I mean... it couldn't take that much time to help with a search once in a while.

I made it home with time to spare, and decided to make a sandwich. Before I got started, my phone rang, and I quickly answered. "Hey Shelby, this is Bates. We're bringing in a couple of gang members for questioning in the case we spoke about. Can you come down to the precinct?"

"Uh... sure. Give me about twenty minutes."

"Great. See you then."

With my appointment an hour away, it would be cutting it close, but talking to a few gang members shouldn't take too long. I told my kids I had to go in early, and, instead of a sandwich, I grabbed a granola bar and a soda, and headed out.

I made it to the precinct right on time and found Bates waiting for me outside the interrogation room. He motioned me over and filled me in. "We have two known gang members here, but we'll interview them one at a time. I think we can get this one to talk, so we're starting with him."

"Okay." At my nod, Bates opened the door and led the way inside. The kid sitting at the table looked like he was Josh's age, and it unsettled me that he was so young. Was interrogating him without his parents even legal? The kid wore a graphic t-shirt and shiny gym shorts. His hair was cut short, and his dark eyes held defiance, as well as a healthy dose of fear.

Bates sat down, and motioned to the chair beside him. After I took my seat, he began the questioning.

"So Elijah.... You know why you're here?"

"I didn't do nothin.' You got nothin' on me."

"We know that, stupid. You're not in trouble, but you will be if you don't tell us what we want to know. Got it?"

Elijah stared daggers at Bates before glancing down at the desk. "Whatever, man."

"Look at me," Bates demanded. He didn't speak again until the boy met his gaze. "This is serious. A known drug dealer got popped yesterday, and we think you know something about it. Like I said, you're not in trouble. We're just looking for information about who killed him."

Bates opened the file folder he'd been holding and shoved an eight-by-ten photo in front of Elijah. It showed Tommy lying in a pool of blood, with his eyes wide open in death. Elijah stiffened, but from the dead man's crumpled form, he didn't recognize him as part of his gang. Still, the blood and purple shade of the man's skin, sent shivers up his spine.

"You know that guy?" Bates asked. Elijah shook his head. "Maybe you don't recognize him with all the bullet holes. Here's another photo." Bates shoved a mugshot in front of Elijah. "His name's Tommy Demarco. Now do you recognize him?"

Elijah sat back, barely glancing at the photo and trying to act cool. "I don't know who he is. He doesn't run with my crib."

"Maybe not, but you still get drugs from him." Bates tapped his finger on the bloody photo. "He goes by Slasher."

Recognition leapt into Elijah's eyes. He tried to hide it, but it was too late. "Yeah... maybe I've heard of him, but I don't know who killed him. I wasn't even there when it happened."

He was thinking that Slasher was slangin' keys and smack, so he had a free pass in their hood. Only, that night, Slasher wasn't selling to any of them.

I didn't understand what that meant, but I did pick up that the boy had been there and heard the shots. He'd also seen a car drive away.

Bates glanced my way, so I took over the questioning. "Even if you didn't see who killed him, you were still there. You heard the shots and took off. But wasn't there something else you were interested in? Why don't you tell the detective what it was, so you can get out of here?"

The kid's brows jerked up. Damn. How did I know? "Uh... I don't know what you're talkin' about."

"Oh come on... tell us about the car." He swore in his mind, and I winced. "It won't hurt to tell us something we already know. And... it would help you a lot... but only if you want to leave."

If we already knew, he didn't see the harm in admitting it. "It was a f-in' BMW. Who drives a BMW into our hood?"

"That's a good question," I agreed. "Did you see the driver?"

"No... after the shots, we took a break." But he did see a guy run to the gray BMW. From his fresh face and fancy clothes, he was probably one of those rich kids from the upper east side. The kid had jumped in and peeled out like the devil was chasing him. That kid probably popped Slasher, but, even if he wasn't a homeboy, Elijah wasn't dropping dimes on anyone. He wasn't a snitch.

I figured that meant that he wasn't going to tell us that part. Good thing I picked it up anyway. Now I had to decide if I should tell Bates. I glanced his way and nodded. "I think we're done here."

"You sure?"

Since he didn't think it could be that easy, I had some convincing to do. "Let's chat outside."

"Oh... right."

He followed me into the hall and shut the door. "He's telling the truth. Whoever killed Tommy came from outside his gang. It wasn't one of them."

"That's what I thought." He hadn't thought that at first, but he could see it now because of the car.

"The BMW, right?" Oops. Luckily, Bates just thought we were thinking along the same lines.

"Yeah. A BMW means it was someone with money. I'll have the techs do a sweep of the traffic cameras in the area and see if we can pick up a BMW at that time of night. If we can get a license plate, we'll have our killer." He was thinking it looked more and more like a hit, but tying it to the mob was going to take a miracle... or me.

"Sounds good." I glanced up, catching sight of a man watching me and Bates. He'd come from the observation room and must have listened to our interview of the kid. He studied me with interest, and I picked up that he'd been eavesdropping on our conversation. He noticed me staring and quickly disappeared back into the observation room.

"Who's that?" I asked. Bates glanced up, but the guy had already slid back into the room. "The guy in the observation room. He must have watched the interview."

"Oh right," Bates said. "He's in the gang unit and just wanted to observe. We'd better get back in there."

"I can't. I've got an appointment right now, but let me know if you find something with the car, okay?"

"Yeah... sure." Bates was already thinking about the lead, and eager to find the car. If it belonged to someone in the mob, this was his lucky day.

He hardly noticed me walking away, but I needed to send a text to Ramos and alert him to the BMW, adding the extra tidbit that it was gray. I didn't know who drove what in Uncle Joey's organization, and I had to let him know, just in case. I was probably bending all kinds of rules, or maybe even breaking the law, but I was in too deep to stop now.

I skirted the detectives' desks and took the elevator to the third floor. On the way, I sent the information to Ramos, hoping my phone records never got subpoenaed, or I'd be a goner. Maybe I should get a burner phone for stuff like this?

Just thinking about that sent a wave of guilt over me. Crap. Had I just taken the first step on the long road to hell? Was this what it meant to be Uncle Joey's successor, and that I'd chosen the dark side once and for all?

Bob's door stood open, and he sat at his desk, working on his computer. Seeing me, he stood with a smile. "Shelby. Come on in. I've been looking forward to our chat. How are you doing?"

"I'm good." I closed the door and took a seat in front of his desk. I took a cleansing breath and tried to clear my mind. I sure didn't want Bob to pick up on the guilt I carried.

"Good. I sent a report of our last visit to Leslie Gilman." At my widened eyes, he continued, "Don't worry, it's nothing personal. I just told her you'd been cleared to get back to work. She wanted me to ask if you'd like to take the course on gun safety."

"Oh yeah... I guess."

"Good. It's two days a week for three weeks, or you can go once a week for six. Whatever works best for you."

"Okay... probably once a week would be best." Did I really have to commit to this right now? It was just one more thing on my plate, and it could be enough to push me over the edge. Wasn't coming here supposed to relieve my stress?

Bob turned to his computer and pulled up the schedule. "What night works best? It looks like we've got an opening on Wednesday or Friday."

"Uh... put me down for Wednesday."

"Okay. You're all set for Wednesdays at seven. Do you know where the shooting range is?"

"No."

He explained that it was in the building adjacent to this one, in the basement, and I put it in my phone calendar. With that done, he sat back in his chair and looked me over. "So... did you get a start on a barf journal?"

Oops. I'd forgotten all about that. "No. But I got a pad of paper and a pencil." That wasn't exactly true, but I was sure I could find one in the office at home.

"Well... I guess that's a start. What about the meditation app? Did you try that out?"

Oops. "Uh... I got the app, but I haven't tried it out yet. I guess I had so much on my mind last night that I totally forgot."

He nodded, but couldn't hide his disappointment, thinking that, with so much on my mind; it would have been helpful to use it. Didn't I want to feel less stressed? "Okay... is there anything you want to talk to me about?"

"Uh... yeah, sure. A couple of things... but... actually, I can't think of what they are right now. I guess I should have written them down. Just... let me think for a minute." Damn. I was the worst patient ever.

"It's okay, Shelby. Let's just talk about what's going on in your life right now. Is there anything stressing you out?"

I would have laughed, but I was sure he'd think I was crazy, and want me committed. "Uh... sure, I guess. I mean... right now you made me sign up for that class, and that's just one more thing on my plate, you know?"

"So you've got a lot going on?"

"Uh... yeah." Oops. That came out a little sarcastically.

"Okay. Let's start with that. Out of all those things, what is causing you the most stress?"

Crap. I couldn't exactly tell him I'd just given a mob boss some inside information. Nor could I tell him that Uncle Joey had asked me to be his successor. What about the cases I was working on? I could probably talk about all of them, as long as I left out the drug and mob part. Or maybe I should start with Willow and how I felt about her usurping my place.

On the positive side, getting a dog had actually helped my stress, but now I had to solve Mack's murder. I guess all of it combined could make me a little stressed out... but, if I were honest, it was mostly because of Uncle Joey, and I couldn't talk about that, right?

"I have an uncle who wants me to be... the... uh... executor of his estate. I don't know why that would freak me out so much, but I guess that's the main thing." Damn. Did I really say that out loud? At least I'd kept it simple. I rushed on to cover it up.

"Then there's this psychic person, her name's Willow, and she's kind of taken my spot here at the police department. I have to admit, I'm a little upset about that. I'm also consulting on three different cases for the police, so that might have something to do with it."

Bob narrowed his eyes. That was a lot. No wonder I seemed on edge. "Let's go back to your uncle. What kind of relationship do you have with him?"

"It's pretty good. I mean... it's been strained at times, but, for the most part, it's good."

"Let's talk about the strained times... what made it strained?"

"Uh... well, he's kind of bossy." I cleared my throat to keep from laughing hysterically.

His brows rose. "Bossy? How is he bossy?"

I chuckled out loud this time. I'd sure stepped into that one. "Well... I should mention that I work for him occasionally... and he likes to boss people around, you know? And... he still does, but... it's all good."

Bob nodded, picking up that there was more to this than I was saying. "Why do you think he asked you to be the executor of his estate?"

"Because he trusts me."

My quick answer signaled that our relationship was on solid ground, which also told him a lot about my fears. "So what is it about being the executor of his estate that stresses you out?"

"Uh... well, I guess that it means he won't be around forever."

"So it's his death you're worried about?"

That wasn't quite it, but I decided to go with that explanation and nodded.

"Okay. How old is he? Is he in good health?"

"Uh... I think in his mid-to-late-sixties, and he seems healthy, I mean... he's in really good shape."

Bob nodded. "It sounds to me like your perception of being the executor of his estate means that he's going to die—which we know will happen eventually, but, in reality, he could live a good twenty more years. Does looking at it that way help?"

I nodded. "Yeah. I think so. I guess I just need to remember that he's not that old, so it should be fine."

Bob smiled, thinking that, for the most part, I was a positive person, and that would get me through a lot. "Good. Changing your perspective can help in all kinds of situations. Remember that death is part of life, but it also makes our lives more meaningful." At my nod, he continued, "Now tell me about Willow and that whole situation."

"Sure. Uh... first of all, I don't trust her. Dimples... uh... I mean Harris... is my partner, but now he's working with her instead of me, so I think she's after my job."

"I can see why that would bother you. Is there anything you can do about it?" He wondered if I'd considered changing my attitude, but I had other plans.

"Well... to be honest, I think I'm better at consulting for the police than she could ever be. If I solve the case she's working on, that should do the trick, and they'll show her the door."

He chuckled, thinking that was not quite the answer he'd expected. I had a lot of spunk, and that was another good thing going for me. "I have no doubt you will."

He glanced at his notes. "Okay. I just have one more question. Overall, how do you think you're doing? Have you had any more nightmares or jittery moments?"

My brows rose. "You know what? Now that I think about it, I haven't. I mean... I've been so busy with everything that I've hardly noticed. But... now that you mention it, I think the real key here is my dog. There's something about petting him that is so soothing. Plus, I talk to him a lot, and he's a great listener. It's like he understands me, you know?" Oops, maybe I shouldn't go too far down that road.

Bob nodded, thinking that pet therapy was underrated and I was lucky to get a dog when I did. "That's great."

Relieved he hadn't picked up on anything unusual, I continued. "Yeah. He's been trained in search-and-rescue, so I might take that up. It would be a nice break from everything else I'm doing."

Bob's brows rose. He was thinking that my idea of a break was not the same as most people, but he could see what I meant. I had a lot going on in my life, and we hadn't even touched on my psychic abilities like he'd hoped. But maybe talking about my family would shed some light on it.

"So how are things at home?" He thought if work stressed me out, he hoped I had time to de-stress at home. If not, maybe I needed to talk about it. "I saw in your file that you have two teenagers at home. That could be a cause for stress, right?"

I smiled. "Yeah, but they're great... I mean they have their moments, but what teenager doesn't?"

"And your husband? Does he support you?" He thought that all the close calls I'd had with death could put a strain on anyone's marriage, and I was lying if I told him otherwise.

"Yes... for the most part. I mean... there are times when he's not too happy about all the trouble I get into... and he certainly lets me know about that. Uh... but lately, he's been better. I mean, he seems more accepting. It's not always easy living with me... you know... with my premonitions and all."

Bob nodded his head. Now we were getting somewhere. "How does he deal with your abilities?"

"Probably how most people would. I mean... he's not always happy that I can do what I do, but he's learning to accept it. I mean... sometimes he thinks what I do is pretty impressive."

"That's important." Bob could tell this was a work in progress. "Well, if you'd like to bring him in sometime, I'd be happy to see you both. He might have some questions for me. Or, I can suggest a good family therapist. In the meantime, it sounds like you're doing great under the circumstances, but if anything changes, please don't hesitate to get help. There's no shame in that."

"Sure."

"Good. Is there anything else on your mind?"

"I think I'm good for now. I'll try and be more positive."

"Well... I'm sure you'll do your best. I'd like to meet a couple more times, but let's make it next week, shall we? I want to give you enough time to start on that barf journal and that meditation app. I still think those tasks would be helpful to you. Also... why don't you keep a small notebook handy too, in case you think of anything else you'd like to talk about."

"Sure, that sounds good."

"Great. Then I'll see you one week from today."

CHAPTER 9

I left Bob's office with a much lighter step. Talking to a shrink really did help, and it was nice to know he was there if I needed him. I checked my text messages, finding a text from Ramos saying that no one in Uncle Joey's circle owned a gray BMW.

Relieved, I took the elevator back down to the detectives' offices, grateful that the connection to Uncle Joey through the car was gone, and my chances of getting caught for sending him information weren't so bad. At least for now, I wasn't going to lose my job with the police, or worse, go to jail for obstruction of justice, although hell was still a possibility.

Since I'd told Bob that I wanted to take Willow down, it was time for a more active role in that investigation. Plus, I needed to know more about her involvement in the little girl's rescue, and if she'd known Mack.

Luckily, both Willow and Dimples were sitting at their respective desks. Well... Willow was sitting at my desk, but I decided to be the bigger person and not let it bother me. It helped to know she would be leaving soon, never to come back, if I had anything to do with it.

As I started toward Dimples, he glanced my way, and a big grin broke over his face, showing his dimples to full advantage.

I quickly sat in the chair beside his desk and smiled. "You look happy about something. What's going on?"

"We just got the test results back from Sophie's blood work. It shows she had scopolamine in her system. They call it the zombie drug, or Devil's Breath, on the streets. It's a drug that's like roofies, only worse because it causes amnesia."

"Oh wow... that's it. Did you get the video from the bar too?"

"Yes. There was a man who sat beside her for a few minutes, but we couldn't see his face. It looked like she told him she was waiting for her husband, because he didn't stay long."

"Did you see if he put something in her drink?"

"Not exactly. He could have, but the angle of the camera was off. Right now, we're going through the video footage of the lobby for anyone who had similar clothes to the man in the bar."

I glanced at Willow. "Is that what she's doing?"

"Yeah... divide and conquer, right? We've found a couple of possibilities, and we're going to take the photos to Sophie to see if she recognizes one of them."

"What if she doesn't?"

Dimples shook his head. "I don't know. Willow thinks it's worth a try, and it's the only clue we've got right now."

Willow didn't like being left out of our conversation, so she hurried to Dimples's desk with a brittle smile. "Hey Shelby. What brings you in?"

I took the direct approach. Why mince words at this point? "I wanted to see how your case was going now that Sophie is awake and we know she didn't do it."

Willow sucked in a breath, unhappy I was rubbing it in, and turned to Dimples, totally ignoring me. "I think these three men are the best matches we've got, so I printed out their photos. Why don't we head over to Sophie's house and show them to her?"

"Let me see them," Dimples replied.

She twisted her lips and reluctantly handed them over. Dimples held them out so I could see them too. Willow didn't like that, and I wanted to quote that famous line, "get used to disappointment," but I asked a question instead. "Did you run them through facial recognition?"

"Of course. I've got their names right here. I'm certain it's one of these three. They're the only men that come close to matching the time Sophie was in the bar."

"Any priors?"

"No."

"All right," Dimples said. "Let's see if Sophie recognizes any of them." He turned my way. "Want to come?"

"I don't know. It seems like a waste of time... you know... with Sophie's amnesia and everything, how is she supposed to remember?"

Willow straightened. "I have some tools of the trade to help with that." She was thinking about the crystal she used for clarity, combined with her training in hypnosis. If Sophie was willing, she was confident she could break through the drug-induced fog and get a clear match.

"Hypnosis huh?" I raised my brows. "That's your plan?"

Her eyes widened. That was uncanny... or... no, it was just a good guess—that's all. "Good guess."

I smiled. "Then I wouldn't want to miss it."

She gave me a sideways glance, thinking that she couldn't wait to show me up, and started toward the exit. Dimples met my gaze and shrugged, speaking softly so Willow couldn't hear him. "I'll be so glad when we can get back to normal." He shrugged his suit coat on, and we followed Willow to the car.

She waited for us at the passenger door, relegating me to the back seat, and a smug look on her face. Dimples slowed, realizing this could be a cause for concern. He'd never had to deal with two women who wanted him so badly. He cut his gaze to me with a saucy smile.

I rolled my eyes before climbing in the back seat, picking up that he was happy we could still communicate, even with a third wheel in the car. He chuckled, mentally laughing at his own joke, and I just shook my head.

On the way to Sophie's, I sent Ramos another text about the kid with the BMW, telling him that he was young, like a high school student. Instead of texting me back, Ramos called, and I quickly answered. "Hey."

"Babe, thanks for the tip."

Just hearing his sexy voice sent shivers down my spine. "Sure, anytime."

"You at the station?"

"Not right now, but I'm helping Detective Harris with a case. You need me?"

He chuckled. "Babe... I always need you... but if you're busy, it can wait."

I laughed. "Okay... sure."

"I'll call you later, but you might want to plan on tonight... around nine-thirty at the health-and-nutrition store. Can you come?"

"Uh... yes, that should work."

"Good. See you tonight. And Shelby... try to stay out of trouble."

"Ha, ha." He disconnected on a chuckle, and I put my phone away. As I smiled, I immediately picked up that both Dimples and Willow wondered who I'd been talking to.

Willow thought it must be my husband, because of the warm, flirting tone I'd used.

Dimples wasn't so trusting. His suspicious attitude always ran toward the skeptical side, and he wondered if it was Ramos, and if it had something to do with Manetto.

He thought I needed to put an end to my relationship with both of them before I got in any deeper. It would bring me nothing but heartache and pain... and maybe even death if I wasn't careful. What he wouldn't give to put those two away.

I tried not to roll my eyes again, but this was getting old. It was nice to know he cared, but somehow I needed to tell him that it was too late, and it wasn't ever going to happen. Maybe then he'd quit thinking about it so much.

But what would happen if he ever learned I was Uncle Joey's successor? Yikes. I knew that was a secret I'd have to keep from him. It might just be the one thing that would send him over the edge and ruin our friendship. He might even refuse to work with me anymore, and that would be terrible.

Still, if Uncle Joey managed to get out of the mob-boss side of the business, Dimples would have nothing to complain about. Besides that, it wouldn't happen for a long time... years and years from now, just like Bob said, so I shouldn't worry about it.

Too bad that was easier said than done.

We arrived at the house and knocked at the door. Mrs. Sanchez opened it, surprised to see all three of us there. Willow jumped in, before Dimples could open his mouth, and explained that we were there to show Sophie some photos.

Mrs. Sanchez nodded and ushered us inside. Before we sat down, Sophie joined us, looking like a different person. She wore jeans and a tee, and her hair was washed and clean. Seeing us brought sudden hope to her heart that we'd found Brock's killer.

I hated to disappoint her, especially since she still had that haunted look in her eyes. It brought out the protective side in me, and I hoped Willow's stunt wouldn't set her back.

"We have some photos we'd like you to look at," Willow began. "These men were at the hotel around the same time you were at the bar."

Sophie's brows drew together. She still couldn't remember a thing. Not the bar, not the room, nothing. What made us think she'd recognize a photo? "So you don't know who did this?"

"We're still working on it," Dimples said. "But we're getting closer. On a positive note, we got your blood work back from the lab, and it's confirmed that you were drugged with scopolamine. It causes amnesia. That's why you can't remember anything."

"So it wasn't the shock?" Mrs. Sanchez asked.

"Not entirely, no. Someone drugged Sophie. That's why we want her to look at the photos."

"Please, sit down," Mrs. Sanchez said.

Dimples moved to a chair, and Willow handed Sophie the folder with the photos. She sat beside Sophie on the couch, leaving me to sit on the other chair facing them. I discreetly sniffed the air, but there was no sign of Armani cologne. Maybe Brock was gone? I doubted it, since his murder wasn't solved, but what did I know?

This whole ghost thing was weird. Sure, it had helped Sophie come out of it, but it didn't solve the case. Then there was Mack. Why hadn't I heard from him? Still, I did have Coco, and he'd led me to Mack, so maybe Mack was helping Coco instead of me... if that was even possible. Or maybe I was just going crazy, and I should stop trying to figure it out.

As Sophie opened the folder, anticipation and dread filled her. Would she remember? She studied them one at a time, and tried so hard to pick up anything familiar about them. But it just wasn't there. This was a waste of time.

She shoved the photos back into the folder and glared at Willow, then included Dimples and me, anger glowing in her eyes. "You just told me that the drug I'd been given causes amnesia, and yet you're still here asking if I recognize any of these men? Is this all you've got?"

Embarrassment radiated from Dimples. She was right. Why had he ever let Willow talk him into this? It was stupid and unprofessional. He opened his mouth to apologize, but Willow spoke first.

"No, of course not, but we didn't think it would hurt to try. I'm sure that finding your husband's killer is the most important thing you want to have happen right now. That's why we'd like to try something... as long as you're willing. I'm a certified hypnotist, and I think it's worth a shot. Hypnosis might be the one thing that will bring your memories back."

Mrs. Sanchez shook her head. "But if a drug caused it... she might not have any memories to bring back."

"You're wrong," Willow said. "She has them. She saw what happened, and I think it's worth a try. Besides, what have you got to lose?"

Mrs. Sanchez wasn't convinced. "But seeing that again could hurt her. She just barely came out of this mental fog. What if remembering sends her back into that state? I'm not sure it's worth the risk. Brock is gone, and torturing Sophie with horrible memories of his death won't bring him back. You just need to do your job and find the person who did this without harming my daughter. She's a victim too, and she's been through enough already."

"Mom. It's okay. If it's the only way to find Brock's killer, I'll do it."

I glanced at Dimples. Was it the only way? Was he going to allow Willow to experiment on this poor woman who'd already been through so much? The same questions ran through his mind, but he wasn't as worried about Sophie's mental state as I was.

Concerned about how this could affect her, I had to give her an out. "Sophie, if you're even a little bit unsure about doing this, there might be another way. I haven't personally spoken with any of the people at the hotel, or these three men. Maybe I'll pick up something Willow and Detective Harris haven't. Do you want me to do that first?"

Willow sucked in a breath. What was I implying?

Dimples hung his head, thinking he had to back one of us and it had better be me. "She's right. We can save the hypnosis as a last resort."

Sophie glanced between us. She was scared to remember that night, but if it worked and we found Brock's killer, it would be worth it. "No. That's okay. Let's do it."

Willow's nostrils flared, but she kept a serene expression on her face. Still, inside she was seething. At least she'd prevailed. Now she just had to make sure this worked. Not wanting Sophie to change her mind, she quickly took charge. Opening her big purse, she pulled out a satchel. Loosening the strings, she glanced inside and took out a couple of pale pink rock crystals.

"Hold these in your hands, palms up," she told Sophie. "And rest your hands in your lap like this." She glanced at Mrs. Sanchez. "Could you please pull the curtains, so it's not so bright in here? It will help with her concentration."

While Mrs. Sanchez did that, Willow pulled another crystal from a chain around her neck and held it at eye-level in front of Sophie. It had been polished and cut into a beautiful teardrop pendant. "I want you to concentrate on this crystal and imagine a connection between this crystal and the crystals in your hands. Think of the lines of a triangle connecting them together, and picture that in your mind."

She waited until Sophie nodded and continued. "Inside the triangle is the memory of that night. It can't hurt you while it's inside, and you can close the connection at any time you wish by dropping the crystals from your hands."

Again, she waited for Sophie's nod. "Now look into the crystal and think of that night. Concentrate on what you were doing. You were excited to celebrate your anniversary, but when you got to the hotel, Brock called to say he'd be late.

"You were disappointed and a little upset that he had to stay at work on this special night. Even worse, you couldn't go up to the room without him. You spotted the hotel bar and made your way there to wait.

"The crowd was larger than you anticipated, but you found an empty seat at the bar. The bartender noticed you right away and asked for your order. You gave it to him and glanced around the room while you waited. Is anyone looking at you?"

"No," Sophie said. "But there was a man who sat down beside me. He smiled... I think he asked if I was waiting for someone. I told him my husband was coming... but he was late and I was disappointed. He asked me where Brock was, and I told him he had to stay late to work. I explained that it was our second anniversary, and that's why I was so upset."

"What did he say to that?"

"He said it was too bad... he was really nice. I... I think he was waiting for someone, too, because he mentioned that we had something in common, and that was it. Then his date showed up and he left."

"His date? Was it a woman? Did you see her?"

Sophie shook her head. "I don't know... I don't remember seeing them after that."

"Did your drink arrive while you spoke with him?" Willow knew it had, but she wanted Sophie to remember.

"I'm not sure. Wait... yes... it came. I took a few swallows. It tasted good, so I drank some more." Sophie's eyes began to droop. "So tired. I need to lie down... I... should go to my room."

"Is someone helping you?" Willow prompted.

"Yeah... someone's taking my arm."

"Is it the man you spoke with?"

She shook her head, and her eyes slipped shut. "I... I don't know... maybe."

Willow pursed her lips. "Focus Sophie. Focus on his face. Is it the man at the bar?"

"I don't remember. He held my arm so I wouldn't fall. He opened my door and... and... it was full of roses. Red roses... everywhere... so beautiful." She swallowed, and her brows drew together. "I should have waited... for Brock." Tears began to roll down her cheeks. "I ruined it... I ruined his surprise."

"What happened next? You saw the roses and then what? Did the man take you inside the room?"

She shook her head. "I don't know. Yes.... But it's dark... I can't see very well."

"Open your eyes and look real hard. Are you in your hotel room?"

"I think so... but... I'm so tired... I need to lie down."

"Stay awake Sophie... don't sleep yet. Are you lying down?"

Sophie nodded her head, but didn't speak.

"Is Brock there now? Is he there in the room with you?" Willow pushed harder, hoping to get Sophie past the drug-induced fog. "Can you see him?"

"I don't know. I can't see. It's so dark. Brock? Are you here?" Sophie's eyes were still closed, but she lifted her chin toward the door. The scent of Armani filled the room, and I glanced that way, half expecting to see him walk in. I didn't see him, but I sensed his presence. Sophie must have too, because she dropped her head and began to sob. "Brock. I'm so sorry. It's all my fault."

Willow thought Sophie had lost her focus. She needed to get back into that room. "Sophie... open your eyes. Look into the crystal. Focus. Feel the weight of the stones in your hands. You're safe at home. No one is going to hurt you here." Sophie calmed down a little, but her eyes were still shut.

Willow continued. "Think Sophie. You're in the room at the hotel. There are red roses everywhere. You're sleepy, and you want to lie down. What happens next?"

"I... I don't know... I'm so tired... he's helping me lie down... he's pulling off my shoes... he's... undoing my..." Sophie's breathing quickened, and her eyes squeezed shut. "Wait... no... st...stop." Her head began to move back and forth. "No... please... don't do this...no..." A low keening sound came from her throat like she was trying to scream, but she couldn't get the sound out. It was just like every nightmare I'd ever had.

Stop this. A commanding voice boomed into my mind. *I don't want her to remember. Stop this NOW.*

I jerked upright, and my heart hammered in my chest. I rushed to Sophie's side and grabbed her upper arms. "Sophie. Wake up. It's over. Wake up now."

She began to sob again, and I felt Brock's hot anger like fire breathing down my neck. "Brock's here Sophie. He loves you. He doesn't blame you for what happened, okay? Please don't blame yourself for this. He wants you to know he's okay. He's fine, and he's watching over you. He's here right now. Can you feel him?"

Sophie stopped quivering, and the crystals slid from her palms onto the floor. She opened her confused eyes, and the pain and fear began to clear. A calm feeling flowed over her, and she caught my gaze.

"You're right. I can feel him. He's here." She fell back against the couch and closed her eyes, taking in the warmth of his aura. Her lips moved in a whisper only meant for him. "I love you Brock. I will always love you."

Letting out a long sigh, her head tipped to rest against her mother's shoulder, and she fell asleep.

I glanced at Dimples and Willow. Their mouths had dropped open, and they didn't know what to think. I turned to Mrs. Sanchez and whispered. "We'll let ourselves out." She nodded, overcome by what had just happened.

Willow picked up the crystals from the floor with trembling fingers. She placed everything back in her bag and stood, not daring to glance my way. She'd heard a low, commanding voice, but the words weren't clear. Still... it seemed like I'd heard it too. And what was that scent... was it cologne?

Outside, Dimples led the way to the car, thinking that had been a mistake. It freaked him out that he'd smelled the Armani cologne, and there was no doubt in his mind that Brock had been there. He hadn't heard anything, but... holy hell. The hairs on the back of his neck were still standing up. Worse, we weren't any closer to solving the case. He never should have let Willow talk him into this.

I slid into the back seat and fumbled with my seatbelt, grateful Dimples was driving. Before starting the car, he turned in his seat and glanced my way. "What the hell was that?"

Not wanting to get into it, I asked, "Did the hospital check her for sexual assault?"

That took the wind out of his sails. "I didn't see anything like that in the report." He glanced Willow's way. "Did you?"

She shook her head. "No. It wasn't mentioned."

"Maybe Brock interrupted them and Sophie's assailant killed him." That was the only thing that made sense to me.

"Yeah, I think you might be right." Willow agreed. "We need to find him." She glanced my way. "What did you mean about talking to the people at the hotel? It sounded like you think you'd find the killer, just by talking to them. That doesn't make any sense."

I huffed out a breath. "You're forgetting that I have psychic powers. That's how I do it. Not with hypnosis, but with my abilities. I'll be the first to admit that you know how to hypnotize someone, but, in Sophie's case, it was a bad idea. She's fragile enough, and reliving that experience would have sent her off the deep end. If she hadn't thought Brock was there, it would have."

"What was that all about?" Dimples asked. "Did you make that up? I thought for sure I'd felt something."

Willow silently agreed, but wasn't about to say that out loud.

"Yeah. It seemed like the best thing for her at the moment."

"What should we do now?" Dimples asked, starting the car and pulling out of the driveway.

"I want to talk to the bartender and take a look at the videos. Maybe something will stand out."

Willow stiffened. "But the chief won't like that. I'm on the case. He doesn't need both of us."

"Don't worry. He doesn't have to know I'm helping. And I won't ask to be paid for it either, if that's what you're thinking." I knew that was exactly what she was thinking, and it grated that she was such a mercenary. "All we have to do to solve this case is find the person who sat with her at the bar. If you're convinced it's one of these men, why don't you bring each of them into the precinct and let me help you with the questioning."

Dimples glanced my way through the rear-view mirror. "Yeah... I should have thought of that in the first place."

Willow sucked in a breath, stung that he'd dismissed her so easily. "What in the hell makes you think Shelby will figure it out? Just by questioning these guys, you think she'll know who the killer is? That's absurd."

"Maybe," he said. "But, as she's already explained, it's what she does. And before you say anything else, you'd better think long and hard about it." His message was clear. If she said anything nasty about me, she was crossing a line.

Willow changed tactics. "If you say so. I'm sorry I said anything." She shrugged. "We all want the same thing, so let's not get all worked up over it. I'm sure, with our combined talents, we can figure this out." She glanced over her shoulder at me. "I'm glad you're here if it helps solve the case. We all want justice for Sophie. Let's not forget that. An evil man did this, and he needs to be stopped. That's the most important thing."

She knew we had reached the point where we didn't need her anymore, and she was clinging to whatever she could to stay on. She was even thinking that she'd talk to the chief, before either of us could, and make sure he knew she'd been an asset. Using hypnosis on Sophie had been helpful, and she'd make sure she got credit for that.

Oh please. Listening to Willow was giving me a headache.

Dimples did his best not to roll his eyes, but he wasn't fooled either. "Okay. We'll track these guys down and bring them in for questioning." He glanced at Willow. "Do you have their addresses, and where they work?"

"I'm sure I can get them."

"Okay, good." He glanced at me through the rear-view mirror. "We'll get all that information and set it up for tomorrow. Will that work?"

"Sure. Just let me know."

He nodded, happy that we'd made some progress, even if it would have been much simpler if I'd been helping him. In fact, we'd probably have the killer in jail by now. That brought a smile to my lips, and Dimples did that little head-nod thing.

With that settled, now was my chance to ask Willow about the lost girl. "Hey Willow, remember the search for the little girl that went missing? You helped with that, right?"

Relieved to have something good to talk about, she preened. "Yes, that's right. I'm the one who found her."

"Can you tell me what happened?"

"Of course." She opened her mouth to talk, but quickly shut it, suddenly suspicious. Her eyes narrowed. "Why the sudden interest?"

"I just wondered if there was a search-and-rescue team and their dogs involved."

"Oh. Yeah, they were there too."

"I thought one of them found the little girl."

Her breath caught. "Well... that's not exactly how it happened."

"Oh yeah? Then what was it... exactly?"

"I'm the one who told them where to look, or they never would have found her." At my raised brows, she continued. "The search wasn't going well, and we were losing daylight. That's why my client, Carolyn Brinkley, asked me to help. We've known each other for several years, and it was her granddaughter who'd gone missing."

She was thinking that Carolyn was a regular client, and came to her monthly for tarot readings. Carolyn believed in Willow's psychic gifts, so it was a win-win.

"After I got there, I used my psychic abilities to pinpoint the little girl's location. The search-and-rescue people followed my directions, and that's how they found her."

I nodded, but I wasn't convinced. It probably had more to do with the dogs and their handlers than she let on, and she was taking all the credit. "So how do your psychic abilities work?"

With a pang, it hit me that I was treating her just like most people treated me. Did I want to go down that road? Yes... yes I did. I had to know the truth, and if that meant giving her a hard time, then so be it.

Willow shook her head, suddenly weary. "Of all the people in the world, I thought you'd understand."

I sighed. "I totally do... but you do things differently from me. I just want to know how it works for you."

"Well... most of the time, I give psychic readings. In this case, I used a toy the child loved. Carolyn thought I'd have better success if I went to the last spot little Ava was seen. Once I got there, I held her favorite stuffed animal and... let my senses expand, using the toy as a conduit to find her.

"That's when I felt where she was, and the distance she'd gone, which ended up being much further than anyone had anticipated. After I directed the search-and-rescue team to that area, that's exactly where they found her."

She didn't mention that the dogs sniffed the toy as well, but I picked up that she was telling the truth, and the direction she sent them did, in fact, save them a lot of time. I got the feeling the child had wandered all over the place, so directing them to a specific area had made a big difference.

"Just out of curiosity, do you remember Mack Haywood? I believe he was one of the search-and-rescue people." Willow tried to remember, but the name didn't ring a bell, so I described him. "Mid-fifties, good-looking in a rugged kind of way. He had a German Shepherd named Coco."

"Oh... yes. I remember him. He's the one who found Ava. He was pretty happy about that. I think he carried her all the way back to our group and handed her off to her mother."

"Did you speak with him?"

"No, I didn't." She remembered watching the scene unfold. Carolyn and her daughter, Misti, were so overjoyed to have Ava back that they were hugging everyone who had helped. Thinking back, it had seemed a little odd that Mack had hung around. He'd spoken to both Carolyn and Misti a second time before they left.

Misti had hugged him, but it surprised her that Carolyn did as well, especially since she wasn't a demonstrative person. It irked her that Carolyn had even offered to pay him. Of course, he'd quickly refused, but if Carolyn was paying anyone, it should have been her.

She'd watched them exchange numbers, and she'd wondered what that was about. But she forgot all about it when Carolyn pulled her into the circle and acknowledged that they couldn't have found Ava without her.

Carolyn had offered to pay her as well, but, after Mack's refusal, she couldn't exactly accept any money. Still, Carolyn did send her a two hundred dollar gift card, so it all worked out.

Curious, she glanced my way. "Why do you ask? Do you know him or something?"

"Yes, you might say that." I wasn't sure I wanted to give Willow any information. Who knew what she'd do then? "I might want to speak with Carolyn. Could I get her phone number and address from you?"

"Uh... I guess... but why?" She was thinking that, if I was checking up on her, she'd have to make up some excuse as to why she couldn't give it to me. She wasn't about to let me go behind her back, especially with a well-paying client.

Now I had to tell her. It should be okay as long as she didn't go running to Carolyn. "Well... here's the thing. Mack was murdered last week, and I'd like to ask her a couple of questions."

"What? Are you kidding me? Wait... you think she had something to do with it?"

"No. Not at all. I'd just like to talk to her about the rescue and see if she remembers anything about it that seemed unusual. Mack was murdered only a week later, and that was his last search-and-rescue job. I'm just trying to cover all my bases."

"Is this something you're doing for the police?"

"No. His son, Austin, asked for my help. I have my own consulting agency, so I do a lot of my own work."

"Oh... I didn't know that." She pursed her lips before coming to a decision. "Okay, I'll give you her phone number and address. But you'd better call her first. She hates it when people just drop by."

"Does she live alone, or does her daughter live with her?"

"She's alone. Her husband died when Misti was young, and she raised Misti on her own. Misti lives close by with her husband and Ava, and they're a really tight, close family." Willow found Carolyn's contact info on her phone. "Can I text this to you?"

"Sure." I gave her my number, and she sent it to me. "Got it. Thanks. I really appreciate this."

Willow nodded, but she was wondering if she should call Carolyn and warn her about me.

"Uh... if you call to warn her about me, do you mind not giving her any specifics about my case? Maybe you could just tell her that I'm interested in the search-and-rescue team, and I want her view on how they worked together, or something like that."

Willow sucked in her breath. It was like I'd read her mind. "Okay... I guess."

"Don't worry. I'll be nice."

She shook her head. How did I know she was worried about that? "I... uh... thanks, I appreciate it."

Dimples pulled into the precinct parking lot, which put an end to our conversation. He was thinking that I needed to be careful, or Willow might figure out my secret. Did I want her to know? He sure didn't.

We got out of the car, and he glanced my way. "You coming in?"

I checked my watch, surprised to find it so late. "Uh... no. I need to get going. But you'll call me tomorrow, right? So I can lis... uh... be there to question those guys?"

"Yeah. We'll bring them in, and I'll let you know."

"Okay. I'll see you then."

I headed home during rush hour traffic, so I had lots of time to think. Finding out about Carolyn from Willow had been a huge help, but I wasn't sure how it was tied to Mack's murder. It was obvious she'd been grateful to him, and they'd exchanged numbers, but if she'd sent a gift card to Willow, she probably wanted his information to send something to him, too.

It sounded like another dead end, but it couldn't hurt to talk to her. I briefly considered telling Detective Williams and Clue what I'd found, but decided against it. I'd tell them if I found a connection to his murder, otherwise, I didn't want to waste their time.

Besides, I had tonight to worry about. Ramos hadn't told me much about the meeting at the health-and-nutrition store, but I had to believe that they'd set up a meeting with one of the buyers to sell them drugs, and whoever it was could have killed Tommy.

It made me a little nervous that I'd be part of a drug deal. But if there weren't real drugs involved, it shouldn't be that big of a risk, right? Maybe I should have gone inside with Dimples, just to see if Bates had found the owner of the BMW.

What if Bates had found the kid? And what if they were making a deal with him to catch the ring leader of the drug operation? The kid would be wired and come into the store ready to make a deal that would expose Uncle Joey's organization. Only, instead, he'd find me, and Ramos... and probably Aaron, the store manager. If Vinny showed up with a bunch of drugs to sell... yeah... that would be bad.

But... I'd know before he even said a word, so I shouldn't be so worried, right? I'd make sure nothing bad happened because I was awesome like that, and it would all work out. No one, especially not me, was going to jail for selling drugs. I'd make sure of it.

As much as looking on the positive side helped, it still didn't get rid of the bad feeling in the pit of my stomach.

CHAPTER 10

I walked in the door, ready for a furry body to come rushing to greet me. As I set down my purse and car keys for the onslaught, nothing happened, and disappointment flowed over me. Where was Coco? Where were my kids?

Hearing a bark from the backyard, I hurried to the patio doors and stepped outside onto the deck. Savannah sat on the porch swing with Josh's friend Chloe, both watching Josh and Coco play with the Frisbee.

"Hey mom," Savannah called. Chloe sent me a wave, and I joined them on the swing, asking Chloe how her summer had been so far.

"I guess nothing like you guys," she said, thinking about the story Savannah had told her. It was amazing I was still alive after a mob boss had put a hit on me. How did I do it? It almost sounded like Savannah had exaggerated most of it, because... how could one person get into so much trouble?

I frowned. Not her, too. "Uh yeah... there were a few intense moments, but I hope she told you about all the good stuff."

Chloe nodded, thinking about Savannah's huge crush on Miguel. But she knew Savannah would kill her if she mentioned that little confession that Savannah was in love with him, so she just smiled and nodded.

What? She loved Miguel? I mean... sure she had a crush... but love? What the freak? I swallowed a few times to calm down. She was only thirteen, so it was probably just a passing thing. Nothing to worry about, right?

Chloe blinked, wondering why my eyes had widened in panic. "Uh... yeah she did. It sounded like you had a great time." Since Savannah was staring daggers at her, and I looked like I might faint, she changed the subject. "I love your dog. Josh told me all about him. It's crazy to think his owner was murdered."

"I know, right?" Grateful for the change of subject, I continued. "It's pretty sad, but I'm glad Coco's with us now."

"How's the investigation going?" Savannah asked. She was eager to steer the conversation as far away from Miguel and New York as possible, and questioned why she'd ever confided in Chloe at all. It was dangerous around me, because I seemed to have a sixth sense about things, and she didn't want me to know how deep her feelings went.

"Uh... well, I made some progress today."

Coco bounded over to greet me before getting a drink of water from a bucket Josh had filled. Josh sat on the lawn in the shade beside us, and Coco sat beside him, so I told them about my meeting with Lance Hobbs and his dog, Scout. "He said Coco was an amazing search-and-rescue dog, and he asked if I had any desire to work with him. He even offered to train me."

"Really? That's cool," Josh said, thinking that it made sense to continue with the search-and-rescue team if Coco was that good. "Would you like that, buddy?" Josh ruffled Coco's head, and he barked *yup*.

I smiled. "I think he said yes."

Josh grinned down at Coco, wondering if that was something he and Coco could do together. He might like that. But was he old enough? He may be fifteen now, but he was turning sixteen in the fall. If he could drive, he should be able to join the search-and-rescue team.

"I haven't decided what to do yet, but I know Lance would be happy about it. Josh, would you like to train with me? Maybe we could both learn, and then, once you're old enough, you could do some on your own."

"Really? Yeah. I'd like that." Josh's eyes lit up with excitement. "We could train this summer before school starts. I've got lots of time."

"Okay. I'll call Lance and check it out."

I caught a whiff of jealousy from Chloe, but she thought it was a cool thing for Josh to do, especially with Coco already trained. Savannah didn't care one way or the other, so at least that meant no bickering between them. I'd take that any time.

Josh's stomach growled, and he thought he might be starving to death. Before he could ask me what we were having for dinner, I spoke up. "I'm thinking pizza for dinner. What kind do you guys want?"

Josh glanced at me suspiciously. Was this what Dad had meant last night? Had I read his mind, or was it just my premonitions? It could be either, but he hoped it was just premonitions... having his mind read would suck. He'd never have any privacy, and if I knew his thoughts... shit... he couldn't even imagine it without feeling sick.

Yikes... Now I had to do everything in my power to make sure he never found out. That meant I couldn't call him out on his swearing. But it was a small price to pay, and, since it was in his head, I guess it didn't count anyway.

Savannah's taste in pizza didn't include the toppings Josh liked, so he had to jump in and make sure it didn't all go her way. For once, I didn't mind their bickering, since it took his attention away from me. We settled on the supreme pizza without the olives, even though I liked them. We invited Chloe to stay, but she had to go, so Josh and Coco walked her home.

Half an hour later, Chris and Josh both got home right after the pizza arrived. While we ate, we had a lively discussion about Coco and joining the search-and-rescue team. Chris thought it was too much for me to take on, but, if Josh was interested, he could hardly say no. I told them I'd give Lance a call in a few days, once things had settled down with my workload.

The kids disappeared after dinner, giving Chris and me some time alone. Since I'd been so wrapped up in my work, I asked Chris how his day had gone before telling him about mine. It was nice to hear about a few of his cases, and how the new intern was working out. At least we didn't have to worry about someone spying on him anymore.

"So what about you? Make any progress on your cases?"

"Yeah. It was kind of crazy today." I filled Chris in on Willow and what happened when she'd hypnotized Sophie. "So now we're hoping that they can track down the three suspects from the hotel. Once they do, they'll bring them in for questioning, and I'm planning to be there. That way I'll know which one did it and solve the case. I'm ready for Willow to be done working with Dimples, and I hope she never comes back."

"So let me get this straight. Willow used hypnosis and it worked, but you stopped her because Brock showed up?"

"Hmm... yeah. When you say it like that, it sounds a little nuts, but yes... that's what happened. Brock wasn't too happy."

"So... it looks like Willow has some psychic ability after all."

Why did he have to zero in on that part? What about Brock? That seemed way more interesting. Still, I had to admit there was something to Willow's psychic abilities when he put it that way. "Yeah, and she does astrology and tarot card readings for people. I guess she even has clients. Which reminds me..."

I told Chris about the link between Willow's client, Carolyn, and Mack's involvement in finding Carolyn's missing granddaughter. "I doubt it has anything to do with his murder, but it probably wouldn't hurt to talk to her. I know they exchanged numbers, so maybe they spoke again? If they did, Carolyn might know something that could help."

"Maybe. It's also possible they exchanged numbers because one of them was interested in the other on a romantic level. You never know."

I shrugged. "I guess that's a possibility, but it doesn't seem likely."

"Wouldn't they be close to the same age?" He thought he was onto something, and I wasn't giving him enough credit.

I shook my head. "All right... you might have a point. I'm planning on talking to her tomorrow, so I should be able to figure it out pretty fast. If they spoke to each other between the time Ava was found and Mack's death, she might know something that will help. It's worth a shot anyway."

He nodded, thinking that I had my hands full with both of these cases. It was a good thing Manetto didn't have a lot going on. Well... except for asking me to be his successor. Now that was a doozy. But at least I didn't have to get mixed up in anything like New York, with the local mob and all the drugs. That had been a nightmare.

Crap. How was I going to tell him that I had to leave soon to help Uncle Joey with a drug problem? There was no good way to say it, so I might as well just tell him and get it over with, especially since I needed to leave in about ten minutes.

"About that..." I smiled sweetly to soften the blow. "I have to help Uncle Joey tonight, but it shouldn't be dangerous."

After the initial shock, he closed his eyes and took a deep breath, then slowly let it out. *It shouldn't be dangerous* was something I always said when it turned out to be dangerous. Didn't I know that? "What's going on?"

"It's just a little meeting at the health-and-nutrition store. I thought I told you about that."

He couldn't remember. Had I? "When was this?"

"The other day. I'm sure I told you." At Chris's raised brows, I shrugged, knowing full well I hadn't told him a thing. "It's not a big deal, I just have to listen in on a drug exchange and find out if the buyer thinks that Uncle Joey's still in the business. You know he's not in the drug business anymore, right? So Uncle Joey just wants to make sure he doesn't get caught for something he didn't do."

Chris thought that I was putting it mildly so he wouldn't worry. But, knowing me, I was right in the middle of a dangerous situation... and, of course, there was a lot more to the story than I'd said... probably on purpose.

"Hey... I'm sure it won't be dangerous... and... just so you know, I've said that before when it wasn't, and things worked out just fine. Give me a little credit here."

He shook his head. "I guess so." It always worried him when I left late at night on some errand for Manetto, and, for the life of him, he didn't know if he'd ever get used to it.

"Uh... yeah, I get that, but look on the bright side. Once Uncle Joey gets out of the mob business, you won't have to worry so much."

He snorted. Thinking that I was dreaming if I thought he was really leaving the mob business behind. Manetto might say that, but Chris wouldn't believe it until it actually happened, and I shouldn't either.

"You really think so?" I asked. "But... it's the only way if he wants me to take over, you know?"

"Yeah, I get that. But we've still got some time before all of this happens. I mean... naming you as his successor doesn't mean you're taking over right away. So, maybe someday it could happen, but I don't think we should count on it."

"Yeah, maybe not."

"That's what worries me because, until then, you're still in danger. And it could backfire. If you're caught during a drug deal, you could get arrested. Are you sure you have to go tonight?"

When he said it like that, it was easy to doubt Uncle Joey. I had to face the fact that he was a mob boss today, regardless of his intentions for the future. Damn. "Yeah. I have to go. But I'll be careful. Don't forget my super power. I'll know if something's wrong before it happens. It'll be fine."

"You're sure? What if you don't go? What would happen?"

I shook my head. "It's not that simple. A man was killed, and I need to find out who did it. It will clear Uncle Joey, but it's also the right thing to do."

"What? A man was killed? Someone who worked for Manetto?"

"No, he didn't work for Uncle Joey, but the police think he did, and that's why they're trying to pin it on him. So to clear Uncle Joey, I have to find out who really did it."

"And your meeting tonight will help you do that?"

"That's the plan."

Now he shook his head. Why didn't I ever tell him these things? A man was dead? And I was just telling him now?

"I didn't know it was that important at the time. Look... I've got to go, but I'll tell you everything when I get back." His disappointment cut me to the quick. "I'll try and do better next time. Okay?"

"Yeah... sure."

I could tell he didn't exactly believe me, so I gave him a kiss, and ran up to my room to throw on my black clothes. I still wore my black pants and ankle boots, so I added a black t-shirt and grabbed my black leather jacket. With the temperature in the mid-seventies, I probably didn't need it, but I wanted to look the part.

After slipping my fully charged stun flashlight into my purse, I hurried back to the kitchen. The kids were watching TV, but they'd come up for a snack, so I mentioned that I had to run an errand for Uncle Joey, and I'd be back soon. Chris had followed me in, so I gave him a quick kiss and left with a wave, hearing their worried thoughts that I was headed for trouble.

As the door closed on their thoughts, I couldn't help the tiny bubble of anger, along with a twinge of guilt, that popped in my chest. Didn't they know that this was my job? This was what I did, and I didn't have much of a choice. Geez, give me a break.

I got in my car, but hesitated before starting it up. Was it true? I didn't have a choice, did I? I shook my head and backed out of the driveway. Right now, I didn't want to answer that. I liked what I did, and I didn't want to stop.

Did that mean it was wrong? Not entirely, and this was nothing like New York. The only person in danger this time was me, and I'd be fine. I pursed my lips, knowing from past experience that wasn't entirely true either, but I wasn't about to admit it. Maybe this was something I could talk to Bob about. He was a professional. He could help me figure it out.

On that hopeful note, I drove to the store, listening to some great rock and roll to get me in the mood. It was fully dark as I pulled into the mostly vacant parking lot and stopped the car. In the sudden silence, the emptiness carried a sinister quality, with only a few security lights glowing inside the store.

Had Ramos told me to meet him in the alley behind the store? I couldn't remember. But since his last meeting with the drug dealer was there, it was a pretty good assumption. Glancing around the deserted lot, I climbed out of my car and edged my way to the small alley between the stores.

I hesitated at the entrance. With it too dark to see much, unease flickered down my spine. Good thing I had my fully charged, trusty stun flashlight. I pulled it out and flicked it on. The light didn't penetrate the entire alley, but it was enough for me to see where I was going. Even better, it didn't look like anyone was there waiting to kill me.

Trying to make as little noise as possible, I stepped into the alley. About halfway down, my jaw began to throb from clenching my teeth so hard. Trying to relax, I shook my head and took the last few steps to the back of the building.

Low voices warned me that someone was there, so I switched off the light, and peeked around the corner. Two men, with their backs to me, stood in the bleak yellow light shining over the back entrance. It was hard to make out their faces, but one of them used a key to unlock the door before they vanished inside.

It didn't look like Ramos was one of them, and that worried me, since it wasn't like him to be late. Before I could decide what to do, the sound of a motorcycle reached me. As it came closer, my dread fell away, and I waited for him to arrive.

Instead of parking in the lot, he drove the bike through the back service entrance and stopped in front of the door. He dismounted and pulled off his helmet. Smiling, I stepped from my hiding place and opened my mouth to tell him I was there.

Before I could get a word out, he grabbed his gun from a side holster and aimed it straight at my chest. I let out a yelp and stepped back, knocking into some discarded boxes. Losing my balance, I fell back on my butt, scattering boxes and debris across the alley.

Ramos reached me, his eyes wide with dismay. "What the hell, Shelby. I almost killed you."

"Yeah... I kinda noticed that."

"Are you okay?"

"Um... I think so." My legs were tangled and my butt hurt. I'd caught my fall with my right hand, and my wrist was sore, but I could move it just fine, so I didn't think it was sprained or anything.

"Here, let me help you up." Ramos knelt beside me with enough guilt and fear radiating off him to fuel a small storm. He reached down to help me up, and I winced, cradling my hurting wrist.

"It was my fault. I should have spoken up earlier... I mean... I was going to say something witty, but I couldn't figure anything out, so maybe that was part of it." Ramos helped me to my feet, and I leaned against him until I stopped shaking. His overwhelming guilt that he'd nearly killed me took my breath away.

"Hey... you don't need to feel bad. I mean... look on the bright side... you didn't shoot me after all, right? So it's all good. It's probably because of your great reflexes, you know? I mean... sure I could be dead right now, but I'm not, because you figured it out, you stopped just in—"

"Shelby... shut up." He pulled me close against him and held me tightly until his heart rate began to slow.

"Uh... everything okay back here?" Aaron asked, trying to see what was going on in the dark.

"Yeah," I said, my voice muffled against Ramos's chest. "Everything's fine. We'll be right there." Ramos finally let me go, and I immediately missed his warmth.

"You sure you're okay? You're holding your wrist."

I glanced down to see he was right. "Oh... yeah. It hurts a little, but not too bad. I'm sure it's fine."

He let out a sigh and shook his head. "Let's go in and take a look. I'm sure Aaron's got a first aid kit somewhere."

Not wanting to argue, I nodded and stepped toward the door, then came to an abrupt halt. "Oh wait. I dropped my stun flashlight. It's got to be around here somewhere."

"I'll find it in a minute. Let's go in and look at your wrist first."

"No... I need my flashlight. It might come in handy in there." He opened his mouth to protest, but I wasn't giving up. "I'd just feel better if I had it." I moved a little stiffly and started toward the boxes. It was hard to see in the dark, but Ramos helped me search, and he found it a few seconds later.

"Here you go." As he handed it over, I picked up that his guilt was mostly gone, replaced by profound relief that I was okay.

I was relieved too. I couldn't think of anything worse than getting accidently shot by Ramos. I'd made a stupid mistake. I should have realized the danger. What was I thinking? "How could I be so stupid?"

Ramos's gaze jerked to mine.

"Did I just say that out loud?"

"Yes."

"Well it's true. I'm an idiot."

"Don't beat yourself up. There's enough of that going around."

He was right about that. So I just smiled and nodded. Ramos opened the door, and I stepped inside a small office. He ushered me into a chair at the side of the desk, and I gratefully sat down.

Surprise, and a rush of fear, came from the man standing beside Aaron. I got a good look at him, and my eyes widened. He was the kid who'd stolen the shoe-sized box the other day, and who'd dragged me halfway across the store while I'd clutched his ankle.

After he recognized me, his fear escalated to realize Ramos stood in front of me. He could hardly forget the big guy who'd threatened him with bodily harm. He turned to Aaron. "What's going on? Why are they here? We made a deal. You said we were even."

"My organization doesn't like double-crossers," Ramos said, his face chiseled in stone. "So I'm here to make sure nothing goes wrong this time."

Before the kid could say a word, the back door opened, and Vinny stepped inside. He nodded at everyone, relieved that Nolan had actually shown up. "Good. Everyone's here. Let's get started."

With Aaron and Ramos flanking Nolan, and Vinny in front of the door, he was boxed in, and his nervous tension ratcheted even higher. He thought of grabbing his switchblade, but knew his odds of surviving were pretty slim if he decided to use it. His only option now was to make the deal and get out of there. He swore that, next time, Xavier would just have to get the roids himself.

I picked up that Vinny had worked hard to set this up. He'd promised Nolan that he'd get his drugs, regardless of who he'd been buying from before, and he'd done his best to make sure the kid would show up.

Nolan nervously licked his lips before speaking. "You got the gym candy?"

"Yes I do." Vinny opened his backpack and pulled out a bag full of pills. Seeing it, Nolan sagged with relief and pulled out a wad of bills.

"It's all there." Nolan held out the money, but Vinny didn't move.

"I need something from you first." Vinny held the pills just out of reach. "Slasher was dealing behind my back, and now he's dead. I want to know who killed him."

Nolan hesitated, debating what to say. He'd been sent by Xavier to scope out the new dealer. Giving up Xavier was not an option, especially right now when he was so desperate. With a hard stare of insolence, Nolan spoke. "I don't know, man. It had nothing to do with me."

Vinny shook his head. "You'll have to do better than that if you want to leave in one piece. Try again."

Nolan swallowed. "I swear I don't know anything. All I know is that after Slasher got popped, our supply chain bit the dust. What do you care anyway? As long as you get your money, and we get the roids, everyone's happy."

"That's where you're wrong." Ramos stepped closer, looming over Nolan. Vinny wasn't going to get it out of the kid, so he took over. "We know you're buying steroids for your teammates, Nolan. I can make life hard for you, and your whole team, if you don't help me out. If the coach were to find out what you're doing, how long would it take before you got kicked off the team? Or even worse, suspended from school? While you think about that, I'm going to ask one more time. Who killed Slasher?"

Nolan pursed his lips, thinking this was Xavier's fault. He never should have agreed to help him.

Deciding he needed a little nudge, I spoke. "What does Xavier have to do with it? Did he put you up to this?"

Nolan's mouth dropped open, so I continued. "He did, huh? That's interesting. Why do you think he did that?" Nolan was thinking that Xavier had lost his supplier when Slasher died, so he'd asked Nolan to find another dealer.

"Were Xavier and Slasher partners or something?" I asked.

Nolan wondered how I knew all of this. How did I know about Xavier anyway? He'd never mentioned Xavier's name to anyone outside the team, so how did I know? He glanced at Vinny, and then Ramos, knowing he was in a tight spot.

"You might as well tell us," I said, hoping to encourage him. "No one's coming to your rescue, and there's nowhere to go."

He sent me a glare. "Xavier got the drugs from Slasher, that's all I know."

"Does Xavier drive a gray BMW?"

Nolan's eyes widened. How did I know that? Was I a freakin' cop? "Look, are you selling me the drugs or not?" Nervous, he tensed his muscles, ready to shove Vinny out of the way and run like hell.

I held my hands out, palms up. "Give us Xavier's full name and where he lives. You can buy the drugs, and we'll let you go."

Nolan licked his lips. Could it be that easy? Would we keep our end of the bargain? He didn't trust anyone, but now he had no choice. "Fine. His name's Xavier Bronson. I don't know his address, but he lives in the cove, and he goes to Skyline High School. Can I go now?"

Before I could answer, Ramos stepped in close and grabbed his shirt with his fist. "If you want to live, I'd suggest you keep this conversation to yourself. Your friend, Xavier, doesn't need to know you gave him up. But please be sure to tell him you got the drugs from Vinny, and he's a good supplier. Think you can do that?"

Nolan struggled against Ramos's grasp. "Yeah, whatever, man. Let me go." Ramos released him, and Nolan stepped back, his breathing harsh in the quiet office. He thought there had to be someone else who sold juice, because he wasn't coming back here, no matter what Xavier wanted.

Seemingly unconcerned, Vinny handed him a piece of paper. "I'm not using this place anymore. It's too visible. So next time you need to score, just text that number, and I'll set something up with you."

Nolan nodded, slipping the paper into his pocket. He handed Vinny the wad of cash for the packet of pills and took off so fast it was like he'd never been there.

Vinny scratched his head and glanced at me. "So who's this Xavier person?"

"He killed Tommy... uh... Slasher. I don't know why, but I'm pretty sure he did it."

Aaron didn't know what was going on, or how I knew that, but he was ready for this little scene to be over. "So... is that it?" He didn't like the risk of dealing drugs in his store, especially since he wouldn't get anything out of it.

"Yeah." Ramos caught Aaron's gaze with a hardened stare. "You're done selling drugs here, but I'll make sure Manetto knows that you helped us tonight. He might cut you a break. And if anyone else ever approaches you about the business again, you'll be sure to let me know first. Got it?"

"Yes. Of course."

"Good." Ramos turned to Vinny. "It looks like this was all Slasher's doing, but if it ever comes back to Manetto, you're taking the fall."

At his nod, Ramos continued. "And, in the future—if I hear any more about your drug business infringing on Manetto's organization, there will be no second chances. I will hunt you down and end you, and you'll never see it coming."

Vinny's olive skin turned pale, and he took a step back. He nodded and swallowed. "I get it. I'll make sure it never happens again. You have my word."

Vinny worried whether his word was enough, and he wanted to ask Ramos to give him a chance to explain, if something came up in the future, but he knew that wasn't an option. He'd just have to make sure everyone in his organization knew he'd kill them if they ever tried anything like Tommy had.

That seemed like a good idea to me, and I nodded to show my support. He tried to send me a smile, but couldn't quite make his face move.

Glancing between Vinny and Ramos, I spoke. "Well, if that's all, I guess we can go now."

That seemed to break the ice, and I stood to leave, surprised to find that I could move without too much discomfort, and my wrist was only a little sore. Vinny left without a backward glance. Ramos held the door open for me, and Aaron came out last to lock the door. Done with that, he sent us a wave and hurried away.

I followed Ramos to his bike, and he gave me his sexy grin. "We need to talk, but it's not safe here." He was thinking that the Tiki Tabu bar might be just the spot.

That sounded tempting, but it was already late, and I needed to get home so I could explain everything to Chris.

Noticing my hesitation, his brows drew together. "I need to know what these guys were thinking. We can take the bike." I couldn't hide the gleam in my eyes, and he capitalized on it. "Come on, I almost killed you tonight. Why not do something you'll enjoy that isn't dangerous?"

He had a point, but I didn't want to seem too eager. "Well... I guess, when you put it that way, I might as well go." I shrugged like it was no big deal, but the excitement of heading to the wrong side of town with a hot hitman that was totally off limits flooded me with anticipation. I was going to hell for sure.

Ramos saw right through my nonchalance... thinking that, if I didn't have any scruples, he could think of a much more private place he could take me...

"Uh. The bar's perfect. And it's been a while since I was there, and you know they gave me my very own pool stick... and I've only used it that one time... so yeah... we should totally go there."

He loved how flustered he could make me, and a big grin broke out over his face. "Great. You can wear my helmet." He handed it over, and I almost refused, thinking the wind blowing through my hair would feel amazing. But that also meant it would be a mess once we got to the bar, and I didn't want to look bad.

After fastening the strap under my chin, I eagerly got on behind him. What was it about living a little dangerously that was so alluring? But... it was all part of the job, so no big deal, right?

I'd never ridden behind Ramos so late at night before. But, since it was summer, the cooler air was the perfect temperature, and I enjoyed every minute of it.

The outside of the Tiki Tabu bar was just as I'd remembered it. The neon lights on the sign blinked on and off with that familiar buzzing sound, and all the spots on the street were taken. Ramos pulled around to the parking lot in the back, and we got off. He secured the helmet to the bike, and we walked around to the front doors.

Suddenly nervous, I turned his way. "Do you think they'll be happy to see me? I mean... it's been a few months."

He shook his head. "Of course." He was thinking that I was one of those unforgettable people, and he looked forward to the reception Big Kahuna was sure to give me... although I might not like it.

"Huh?"

Ramos pulled the door open and ushered me inside without answering, thinking I'd find out soon enough. Inside, it was dark and noisy, just like I remembered. As we walked further in, people began to notice us, and the talking slowed and nearly stopped altogether.

They stared at me with my blond hair and thought that I was in the wrong place. A "haole" like me wasn't welcome in this Pacific Islander establishment. As their attention shifted to Ramos, a few sensed his underlying danger, and they immediately stiffened, ready to defend their territory.

"Shelby? Is that you?"

I glanced toward the back, where the pool tables were located, and spotted Big Kahuna straightening from a pool table, and holding his cue stick.

"Hey." I gave him a big smile and a little wave.

He dropped his stick on the table and came toward me with his arms outstretched. Before I knew what was happening, he threw his arms around me and picked me up like a rag doll. He squeezed the breath right out of me and, for a few seconds, I couldn't breathe.

Luckily, he set me down before I blacked out and turned his attention to Ramos. They did some kind of complicated handshake, and Big Kahuna invited us to sit down in an empty booth near the back. I slipped in on one side, and

Ramos slid in close beside me, with Big Kahuna taking the other side. With his big size, he needed the space, and I couldn't complain about sitting so close to Ramos... ever... like... in a million years.

"It's so good to see you," Big Kahuna said. "Everything okay?" He was a little worried that Manetto might have a problem with him. He'd stuck to their agreement... for the most part, but someone could have messed up. If Ramos was here, he might have a problem.

"Oh... no." I rushed to reassure him. "Everything's fine. We just needed a place to talk and thought we'd come here."

"Ah... good choice." He motioned to the bartender. "Bring Shelby a Diet Coke with a... lime." He caught my gaze, and I nodded.

"You remembered. Thanks."

He glanced at Ramos. "And what can I get you, my friend?"

"I'll take the same."

Big Kahuna yelled at the bartender to bring another one, then turned his attention to us. "Well... I should return to my game. If you need anything else, let me know. Come on over if you want to play a round when you get done. Your stick is waiting."

He made it sound like I had a choice, but I knew he'd be offended if I didn't play at least one game of pool with him. "Sure. I'd like that."

His pleased grin sent a little shiver of worry through me. He was someone I'd never want to have as an enemy. He somehow managed to squeeze out of the booth and lumbered back to the pool table.

"He likes you." Ramos caught my gaze and smiled. He enjoyed sitting so close to me, especially when our thighs touched. He knew I liked it too, but he didn't want me to get the wrong idea and get carried away or anything.

"Ha-ha."

With a grin, he slipped from the seat and moved to the other side, thinking that he liked this view too. I felt the heat rise in my cheeks, but it fled as his gaze turned to the entrance, and his face grew cold. "Don't turn around."

"Why? Who is it?"

"Looks like an undercover cop. I think we may have been followed." His gaze flicked to mine. "Don't panic. The gang can smell a cop a mile away. We can sneak out the back before he gets close to our table."

"Has he spotted us?"

"I'm not sure... but... yeah, he just zeroed in on your blond hair."

"Crap. I need to see who it is... I might know him." Would Bates follow me? I didn't think he'd do that, and I knew it wasn't Dimples. So who? I listened to the thoughts of people around me, trying to pick up anything about me and my blond hair, but found nothing.

A wave of distrust rolled through the room, followed by hostility. It included just about every person in the crowd. Oops. That guy was in trouble.

Big Kahuna lumbered by. As he passed our table, he nodded to Ramos, silently telling him to take the back exit. A few others stood to join him, blocking the cop's view of us, and Ramos mentally told me it was time to go.

As we ducked out of view and hurried toward the back, I glanced over my shoulder toward the bar. With a shake of his head, the man turned to talk to Big Kahuna.

I'd seen him before, but it was so brief that I couldn't remember where. Then it hit me. He was the cop from the observation room, the one from the gang unit. But why was he following me? Worse, had he been at the store watching us? Did he know about the drug deal? If he did, I was in so much trouble.

CHAPTER 11

I followed Ramos through a doorway into a back office and storage room. We scurried into the storage room and opened another door that led to the back entrance. With the door closing behind us, we rushed toward the bike.

"Did you see who it was?" he asked me.

"Yes. I know him. He must have followed me to the store, and then here. We've got to get back to my car before he does."

Ramos nodded, not even bothering to hand me the helmet, and we both jumped on the bike. We made it back to the store in no time, and I quickly unlocked my car.

"We need to talk somewhere safe," Ramos said. "Head to Thrasher."

I nodded, following him most of the way. The tension left me as we entered the parking garage. At this time of night, the place was mostly empty, and Ramos pulled into his usual spot by the elevators. I parked next to him, and he joined me, sliding into the front seat of my car.

"Okay. What's going on?" he asked.

Where should I start? I explained the interview with the gang member and that the cop following us had been watching from the observation room the whole time. "I only caught a glimpse of him before I left, so I have no idea what he's thinking, or why he'd follow me."

"But you must have made an impression if you got the kid to tell them about the car. He must have thought you already knew about it, and that's why he followed you."

"So... does that mean he thinks I'm involved in the whole drug thing?"

"Why else would he follow you?" Ramos sighed. "Too bad he's right."

"This is terrible. What do we do now?"

"Do you think he'll go to the detective you're working with and tell him about this?"

I shrugged. "I don't know. Probably. We were in the store for a while. If he was watching, he may have seen all of us. Do you think he took pictures?"

"He could have, but it was too dark to get much of anything. And watching us doesn't prove that anything happened in the store. It's certainly not enough to arrest anyone."

I sighed and laid my head back on the seat. "This sucks. What am I going to do?"

"What were you going to do anyway?" Ramos thought I must have had something planned to tell the police.

"Well, yeah... before the guy followed me, I thought I'd tell them that I had a premonition about the BMW, and that the kid driving it lives in a fancy house with rich parents. For the kid's name, I could say that I keep seeing a big X, like X marks the spot, so it must have something to do with his name.

"I thought I could throw in the name of the high school, only change it up a bit so it's not so obvious, like telling them it's Sky something... like Skyline or Skyview. It's vague, but close enough for them to fill in the blanks with the right information."

His brows rose. "That might work. But what if they're gunning for Manetto?"

"I don't know how they could. Xavier killed Slasher, and it had nothing to do with Uncle Joey."

Ramos nodded. "Yeah, but I doubt the kid will confess without a little coercion from the police. You know how cops are with kids, they could scare him into saying whatever they wanted, especially if they want Manetto."

"Not these cops, especially if I'm there, which I'm planning to be. Once they bring him in, I can pick up what Xavier did with the gun, and maybe even why he killed Slasher. Plus, if we're all out of options, I can always get the police to bring Nolan in. He knows that Xavier killed Slasher. In any case, I think Uncle Joey should be fine."

"But Nolan knows about you. That wouldn't work."

"It might. Nolan wondered if I was an undercover cop, so I could just stick with that."

"But the undercover cop knows you're not an undercover cop."

"Yeah, but Nolan doesn't, and if that cop asks questions, I can tell him I was checking out a lead tonight. I am a private investigator, you know."

His brows rose. "With a license and everything?"

"Uh... no, I kind of skipped that part. But I am a registered police consultant with my own consulting business. What I do, and how I do it, is mostly to help the police. They can't argue with that, right?"

"I guess." Ramos let out a breath. "I hope it's enough for the cop to leave you alone. If he asks you about going to the bar with me, what will you tell him?"

I shook my head. "I don't know. What do you think I should say?"

He grinned. "That I offered you a drink, and you couldn't refuse because I'm so hot."

I smiled, glad that at least one of us wasn't scared to death. "I can just say that I was checking out the Polynesian gangs to see if they knew anything about Tommy's death, and you were my ticket in."

"That might work." Ramos thought this guy complicated things. Even worse, he'd gotten a good look at Ramos at the bar. The cop was sure to look through the police database to find information about him.

That meant he'd see Ramos's file and his connection to Manetto. There was no evidence to tie him to anything, but enough to mark him as someone of interest. He'd have to watch his back for the next little while, and expect some kind of special attention or harassment.

"Wow... would they really do that?"

"It's happened before." He shrugged. "I can take it. It's you I'm worried about. Maybe after this you should take a break from helping the police."

"Yeah... that's probably a good idea." Now might be a great time to let Willow take over for me. I could finally take that break I needed and not have to choose between the police and Uncle Joey. But would I ever do that? Could I resign from helping the police?

My phone vibrated with a text, and I pulled it out. "It's Chris. He's worried. I should go. Is there anything else we need to talk about?"

"Is there anything else you picked up at our meeting that I need to know... about Vinny or Aaron or even that kid Nolan?"

"Uh... Nolan was thinking about buying juice from someone else, Vinny was thinking he'd have to threaten to kill anyone who did what Slasher did, and Aaron just wanted to forget about it all. I'm sure there was more, but that's the gist of it."

"Okay. If you get in trouble with the cops, just remember that Manetto has deep connections. When you talk to the police, don't let them push you around, and don't say more than you need to."

"Don't worry. I won't. And... if it helps you feel better, don't forget that I have my super-power. I'll be fine."

"Right." Ramos smiled and opened the door, but turned back toward me. "There is one more thing."

"What's that?"

"Try not to sneak up on me again."

"Oh... yeah... I've learned my lesson."

"Good. And maybe next time, we can get in a game of pool."

I grinned. "I'd like that."

"Goodnight Shelby."

"Goodnight... Romeo."

He chuckled and closed the door. With a quick wave, I pulled out of the parking space and started home. I kept track of the cars around me, just in case someone was following, and wished I would have done that earlier. I didn't see anyone following me, but keeping watch was exhausting.

Finally pulling into my garage and closing the door, I got out of the car, grateful I'd made it home in one piece. With the time past midnight, everyone had gone to bed, and most of the lights were out, but Chris had left the kitchen light on for me. After locking the door and turning the lights out, I hurried upstairs to find Chris asleep with the bedside lamp on.

As I got ready for bed, he opened his eyes and let out a sigh of relief. "Good. You're home. How did it go?"

"Well... okay, I guess." I finished brushing my teeth and climbed into bed. "Do you want to hear the long version or the short version?" I was hoping for the short, since I could leave most of it out.

"Is there a short one?"

"Well... I could just summarize, so you'd get the gist of it. Since it's so late, it wouldn't take as long."

"Just start at the beginning... like... tell me who died."

"Okay." I explained how Uncle Joey was getting out of the drug business, but the person in charge of it kept selling the drugs anyway, and used Uncle Joey's connections, along with Uncle Joey's name and reputation. "So you can see how that would be bad for him."

Chris shook his head, thinking that getting out of the business had left Uncle Joey open to the incompetence of others, which could get him in more trouble than he'd bargained for. "So what kind of trouble is he in?"

"Someone killed one of his former drug dealers, and the police are hoping to link it back to him. Anyway... Uncle Joey asked me to help the police with the investigation so I could keep him informed."

Chris's eyes widened. Didn't I know how risky that was? If the police found out, they'd never let me work for them again. It would ruin everything I'd worked for. It could also end up with charges against me if they wanted to push it.

"Uh... yeah, I figured as much, but that's not what I'm doing. I'm trying to find the real killer, and I think I figured it out tonight. Now I just need to help the police arrest the right guy. Then Uncle Joey will be off the hook, and the real killer will go to jail."

Chris shook his head, thinking that sounded too easy. "Okay... just be careful. Don't let any of the cops look at your phone. Maybe you should talk to Manetto about getting a burner phone for stuff like that."

He couldn't believe he was advising me on how to avoid getting caught by the police so I could keep my job. I walked a fine line between the cops and Manetto, and it was getting thinner and thinner. If I wasn't careful, it would blow up in my face.

"Yeah... I see that, but I'm being extra careful. And you're right about the burner phone. I thought about it too, but, once this is straightened out, I shouldn't need one. By then, Uncle Joey should be out of the business, and I won't need to be so secretive."

Chris just nodded, hoping it would happen, because staying on this path could have dire consequences, and I could end up in jail.

Just hearing that sent a cold chill down my spine. "There was one other thing that happened... but I'm not sure you'll want to hear it."

He braced for bad news. "What is it? Just tell me and get it over with." His mind raced with all sorts of imagined things, including one where I had succumbed to Ramos's allure and had kissed him or something. It made his stomach queasy just thinking about it.

My brows drew together. "No... it's nothing like that. There was an undercover cop who saw me tonight, so I'm concerned that he'll want to know what I was doing at a drug deal. But... he doesn't have any proof, and he doesn't even know that it was a drug deal, so I should be fine."

"How the hell did that happen?"

I winced at his harsh tone, and my chest tightened. Shouldn't he be relieved that I wasn't having an affair with Romeo... uh Ramos? Guess I was wrong. Not sure I wanted to answer him, I squeezed my lips together and frowned.

Chris closed his eyes and took a breath. "Sorry. I'm not mad... well... that's not exactly true. It just seems crazy that an undercover cop was following you. I mean... this could come back to bite you. So what happened? Did he see you with the drug dealers or what?"

"No, he didn't." I explained that he'd followed me to the health-and-nutrition store, but it was too dark for him to see anything. I sort of left out the part about going to the bar, since Chris was already mad, and finished up.

"I just caught a glimpse of him. So I think I can fix it. At the precinct tomorrow, I'll tell Bates I met up with an informant, and then I'll give him the info about the kid, only I'll say most of it's from a premonition I got while talking to my informant."

Chris nodded, thinking it sounded a little convoluted, but it could work. "Okay, good. Don't tell them any more than you need to."

"I won't." Geez, did both Chris and Ramos think I was an idiot?

"If you're serious about becoming Manetto's successor, maybe you'd better stop helping the police... at least until all this is settled."

"Yeah... you might be right." Hadn't Ramos just told me that? They were both right, but how was I supposed to help people like Sophie and Mack Haywood without the police? Maybe I should just turn Uncle Joey down. But how was that any easier?

Chris could see that I was starting to get stressed out, and he didn't want to add to it, so he pulled me into his arms and held me close. "I'm sorry I got upset... I'm sure it will all work out. Trust yourself. You're amazing. You'll figure this out."

"Thanks, honey."

He kissed the top of my head. "I'm lucky to have you, even if you make me a little crazy sometimes."

I huffed out a breath, but he held me tight, so I couldn't smack him. He chuckled and relaxed his hold. I sighed and snuggled closer to him and the warmth of his love, grateful he'd stuck by my side through it all.

Still, I couldn't stop the worry that kept me awake. Even telling myself that nothing bad was going to happen didn't help, and it was a long time before I fell asleep.

The next morning, I woke to find a wet nose sniffing my face. I opened my eyes to see Coco staring at me. His front paws were perched on the bed, and his tail wagged. He woofed, and I heard, *get up.* "Do I really have to?"

He woofed again. *Yup. Now. We go.*

"Where?"

Walk. Come.

"Okay. I'll take you on a walk, but I have to get dressed first." Coco ran out of the room like he was on a mission, and I wished I had some of his enthusiasm. I slunk out of bed and pulled on some shorts, a t-shirt, and some walking shoes. At least having a dog meant I was actually getting some exercise, so that was positive.

Chris was just leaving for work. He gave me a quick kiss and wished me luck. I picked up his worry about the drug deal last night. He fervently hoped I didn't call him today because I was in trouble and needed a lawyer. But, if I did, at least I had him, and he was damn good. He flashed me a smile before shutting the door.

I just shook my head and waved, grateful he was on my side. Coco and I left right after that, and it was nice to get in a walk and figure out my next move. It was hard with so much on my plate, but taking care of the undercover cop was probably the first place to start.

We returned home, and I put in a call to Dimples.

"Hey Shelby, I was just going to call you. We found all three of the men from the hotel, and they're coming in for questioning. The first guy should be here in about an hour. Will that work for you?"

"Yeah, that's perfect. I'll get ready and come down. In the meantime, can you do me a favor?"

"Sure, what?"

"Will you tell Bates that I had a premonition about the case he's working on, and I'll explain all about it when I get there?"

"Uh... sure. I didn't realize you were helping him. Which case is it?"

"The murdered drug dealer." Dimples didn't respond, so I continued. "I did some digging, and I have a pretty good idea about who did it, but I won't know for sure until they bring him in, so I have to make it sound like a premonition... you know?"

"Oh... yeah, right. Okay... I'll let him know."

"Thanks. See you soon." I hung up before he could ask me any more questions. I could tell from his tone that he wasn't happy I was helping Bates. But seriously? Why should it bother him? Willow was helping him so we were even, right? I knew that wasn't nice of me, but I was done being nice where she was concerned.

I showered and dressed, deciding to look more professional and wear a blue blazer with my dark jeans. I didn't carry a gun, but it looked like I could have one tucked away somewhere, so the blazer was just as effective.

Savannah was awake, so I told her I had to go to the police station, but to call me if she needed anything. It was Josh's day off from lifeguarding, so I decided to let him sleep in. I gave Coco a pat on the head, and hurried out the door.

I arrived at the precinct and headed straight for the detectives' offices. Before I got to Dimples's desk, Bates waved me over. He was hoping that I could clear up something, and it was a good thing I'd already called to volunteer information. It made Grizzo's comments seem less accusatory if I had something to offer.

Grizzo? That had to be the undercover cop, and I picked up that he'd told Bates he wasn't so sure they could trust me. At least it didn't sound like he'd mentioned seeing me last night, but he might bring it up now. Damn. What was I going to tell Bates if he did? I'd just have to stick with my cover story that I was talking to an informant, and hope to keep Ramos out of it.

But with Grizzo's involvement, that might not be a possibility. I was pretty sure Bates already knew I had ties to the mob because of a case involving an escaped convict a few months ago. But if he knew I was still involved with them... I didn't even want to think about it.

Now, I had to make sure I solved the case before Grizzo insisted I might have something to do with passing information to Uncle Joey, and had me fired.

"Hey there," I said. "Did Dim... uh... Harris tell you I called?"

"Yeah. He said you had a premonition about the case."

"I did, and I think it will help."

"Good. I want to hear all about it. Why don't you wait for me in the conference room? I have to make a quick phone call, and I'll be right in." He was thinking that Grizzo wanted to be in on it. Luckily, he was in his office on the fourth floor and could come right down.

Damn. An acute desire to walk past the conference room and right out of the building washed over me. As I neared the room, I took a deep breath and stepped inside. I could handle this. I'd been in a lot worse situations. How bad could this be?

I sat down at the oblong table and Bates hurried in, holding the case file. He had no idea why Grizzo had wanted to be included, but, if he had to guess, he'd say it was because of my awesome psychic ability that he'd witnessed yesterday. Or maybe he had some new information that would be useful?

That calmed me down. At least Grizzo hadn't said anything about last night, but that was probably going to change if I didn't take matters into my own hands. "Are we waiting for someone?"

"Uh... yeah. The guy who works with the gang unit asked me to call him. I think he's got some information for us."

The door opened, and Grizzo walked in.

"There he is," Bates said. "Shelby this is Grizzo. Grizzo, Shelby Nichols."

Grizzo wasn't too happy Bates had told me he was coming to the meeting. He'd wanted to catch me unaware and gauge my reaction, but now I was just sitting there with a congenial smile on my face.

In an effort to be nice, he stuck out his hand. "Hi. It's nice to meet you."

"Likewise," I said, since it seemed we were going with the 'we're pretending we don't know each other' charade. "Is Grizzo a nickname?"

"Uh... yeah."

I picked up that his real name was Greg and, since it didn't fit the persona he liked to project, he never used it. Smiling, I stored that little nugget away for future use.

Bates cleared his throat, thinking we were wasting time. "Shelby called about a premonition she had with the case." He glanced at Grizzo. "You know she's a psychic, right?"

"I'd heard."

"Good. Then let's get right to it." Bates glanced at me with a hopeful smile. "Tell us what you've got."

Grizzo studied me with narrowed eyes, wondering just how much of last night I was willing to share. The Tiki Tabu bar was crawling with some of the baddest gang members in town, and they'd made him the second he'd walked in. In fact, he'd barely made it out of there in one piece.

So what was I doing there? How come they treated me like one of their own? Showing up at the bar right after my visit to that health-and-nutrition store must have something to do with it. And then there was the guy I was with. He'd only caught a glimpse of him, but he knew, in that moment, the guy was one bad dude. And he'd been at the store with me as well. So what was going on?

I didn't sense that he'd told anyone in the department about last night, so at least that was good. Now I just had to convince him I was doing some sleuthing of my own.

"I kept getting little flashes about the case, so I decided to reach out to some of my sources within the gang community last night. After talking with one of my informants, I got some impressions that I think will help us find the killer."

I paused to make sure they were following along. Bates was a little shocked that I had an informant. But... he reasoned that I had my own consulting business, so maybe that had something to do with it. Grizzo was more than a little skeptical.

"Let's start with what we know," I began. "We know that the gray BMW was seen leaving the scene—"

"Gray? No one ever said it was gray," Bates said.

"Huh... then I must have gotten it from my premonitions. I picked up a couple of other things as well. I think the person who killed the drug dealer is male, young, and his name has an X in it. He's young enough to be in high school, and the school he attends is something with sky in it, like Skyline or Skyview. Not sure which one, though."

I shrugged. "Based on that... this is what we need to look for: The person driving the BMW has a name with an X in it, he's young and rich, and he goes to a high school that has sky in the name."

I sat back and waited for Bates to nod. In his search for the BMW, he'd turned up a couple of traffic cam photos that had a partial license plate number. He thought if they could narrow it down to a particular area of residence, they'd have an easier time matching it.

Bates thought the X was interesting, but still too vague to help much. "Is the X part of his first name or last name?"

I closed my eyes and took a breath before answering, hoping they'd think I was using my psychic ability to find the answer. "I think it's his first name. Something like Xavier or Xander. Other names have an X in them, like Jaxon, Max, and Alex, but, to be honest, I'd start with Xavier and Xander first."

"Okay." Bates nodded, completely fascinated and believing every word. "I'll put it into the database and see what comes out."

Grizzo thought I had to be making this up. Or I'd come by it because of my late-night excursion, and I was duping the police into thinking it came from my psychic abilities. Either way, he had to admit that I put on quite a show.

I ignored Grizzo and spoke directly to Bates. "If you get a hit, I'd like to help with the questioning."

"Of course. And if you get any more information... or premonitions, give me a call."

"I will." I stood, hoping to get away before Grizzo asked me about last night. "I've got to go. I'm helping Harris and Willow with their case, and they're waiting for me."

"You're helping them too?" Grizzo asked.

"Yeah, you guys keep me pretty busy. See ya." With a little wave, I stepped out of the room and into the detectives' bullpen. I weaved my way toward Dimples, grateful to have escaped Grizzo. How long would he keep quiet about last night? I wasn't sure, but at least I got away from him this time.

A woman called my name, and I glanced over my shoulder. "Shelby. Do you have a minute?" Spotting Clue, I turned in her direction. She was wondering if I was still working on the Mack Haywood case. She glanced between Bates and Dimples, thinking that, from the looks of things, it seemed like everyone in the department wanted my help. Was I really that good?

I'd forgotten all about Clue and Williams, so it was a good thing she'd called to me. "Hey Clue. How's it going? Find anything new on the case?"

"I was just going to ask you that." She wanted me to go first, since they hadn't found much.

"Why don't you start?" Since I hadn't decided what to tell her, I'd take every advantage I could get.

She flushed. "Well... that's the problem. We're still looking through his financial records. He had quite a nice retirement fund stashed away. I'm talking a couple of million. With him gone, it all goes to his son, Austin."

"Oh wow... I didn't know that. So are you thinking Austin did it?" At her nod, I continued. "Does Austin have an alibi?"

"Not really. I mean, he says he was at home, but he lives alone, and we haven't found anyone who can actually verify that."

"Interesting. But I don't think it's him."

"Why?"

"He was too broken up about losing his father. Plus, he wanted me to look into it. Also, why would Mack put the dog in the other room if it was Austin? Austin and the dog had a good relationship, so that doesn't make any sense. No, I think it has to be someone who doesn't like dogs, or who is allergic to animals."

"Oh... yeah, I guess you're right."

"When I spoke to the neighbor, I found out that his wife is allergic to animals. That neighbor, Reed Gardner, is the one who found Mack and called the police. He told me his wife had gone to bed with a migraine headache earlier, and he'd been downstairs watching TV for a couple of hours. She could have snuck out of the house while Reed was in the basement and killed Mack."

Clue's mouth dropped open. How did I find that out? Damn. I was good. "But why would she do that?"

"Your guess is as good as mine." I shrugged. "But there's always an affair gone wrong scenario... or anger over a neighbor dispute... that sort of thing."

"You know... now that I think about it, we never did talk to her. It was always her husband. I guess we'd better go back and see what she has to say." She thought that was a great lead, and I had proven my worth in her eyes. "Anything else?"

"Yeah, but I've got to do a little more digging before I know if it's going anywhere. If it pans out, I'll let you know."

"Okay. Thanks."

I nodded, feeling a little bad about sending Clue after Reed's wife. But, as much as I liked him, his wife was still a suspect, and I had too much on my plate right now to question her. If this lead with Carolyn and her granddaughter came to nothing, I could still go back to question Reed's wife, and I'd know in an instant if she was the murderer.

Dimples glanced at me, thinking I was sure taking my sweet time getting to him. I grinned and hurried over to his desk. "I can't help it if everyone needs me to solve their cases around here."

He shook his head. "I know... how did we ever manage without you?"

"I seriously have no idea." I glanced around the room. "Is Willow here?"

He glanced back at my desk and grimaced, wondering where Willow was. She should be here by now.

"Maybe you'd better call her?"

"Yeah, maybe." He knew he should call, but right now, he'd like to forget all about her.

A deep sense of satisfaction rolled over me. If nothing else, it was nice to be appreciated.

"Speak of the devil." Dimples caught sight of Willow rushing in. She caught everyone's attention in her colorful clothes, looking more done up than usual. Her arms and neck dripped with jewelry, and she wore a flowing peasant dress, with colorful embroidery, that sported tassels hanging from the sleeves and neck. But the biggest surprise was her floppy hat and big round sunglasses, straight out of the sixties... or was it the seventies?

"Oh good, you haven't started yet. Sorry I'm late. Just let me put these away." She glided to my desk and set her glasses and hat on top, then placed her fringed, leather purse in a big side drawer and locked it up with a key.

Shock flowed over me. What the hell? I didn't even know there was a key to that drawer. She caught everyone staring and smiled, happy for the attention, before rushing back to us. "Are the men here?"

"Yes," Dimples said.

"Good. I hope you don't mind, but I'd like to question them. I have a gut feeling that one of them is responsible, and I think I'll be able to spot him if I ask the right questions."

My breath caught. She was taking a page right out of my playbook. The nerve. Was she trying to copy me? I couldn't get a good read on her mind, but I felt the blossoming thread of conviction that she planned to solve the case without my help. It was her mission to impress Dimples and the whole department, and today was the day.

Hmm... that was a tall order, and I couldn't wait to prove her wrong. With her unfettered confidence, she definitely had something up her sleeve, but I had no idea what it was.

Dimples's brows rose in shock. She wanted to question the suspects? He didn't trust her for one minute, so what was she up to? Had she gone to an outside source? He glanced my way. Had I picked up anything? Did I know her plans?

I shrugged my shoulders, feeling his immediate disappointment. "Shall we get started?"

"Yeah." He opened a folder so I could see it, and Willow crowded to his other side to take a look. "This guy's name is Carver Thomas, and he's a chef at one of the nearby restaurants."

Carver seemed like an unusual name, but it definitely fit for a chef. It fit even better for someone who used a knife and stabbed people.

Dimples closed the file, and we followed him to the interrogation room. He stepped inside, with Willow and me following behind. There were only two chairs in front of the desk, and Willow launched herself into one before I had a chance. Dimples glanced up to the ceiling and shook his head before offering the other chair to me.

I shook my head and moved to the corner, leaning against the wall with my arms folded. With a sigh, Dimples sat down and quickly introduced all of us. "Thanks for coming in. As you know, we're investigating a homicide that happened the night you were at the hotel. This woman..." He placed an eight-by-ten photo of Sophie in front of him. "...was drugged while she had a drink at the bar. A man took her to her room where he planned to rape her. Do you recognize her?"

Carver studied the photo and shook his head. "No. At least not that I remember."

"How about him? This is her husband. He showed up at their room, and this is what happened to him. Did you see him that night?"

Dimples shoved the crime scene photo of Brock next to Sophie's. Brock was covered in blood from multiple stab wounds, and he lay in the red, stained sheets with his eyes wide open. "Take a good look. Someone stabbed him about twenty times."

Carver jerked back, his heart hammering. "I didn't see him. I don't know anything about this. Why are you asking me?" His eyes widened. "Wait. You think I had something to do with this? Are you crazy?"

I opened my mouth to tell Dimples that Carver didn't do it, but Willow jumped in before I could.

"I'm sure this was the last thing you expected when you came in." Willow made an effort to keep her voice soothing and low. "We just want to know if you saw Sophie leave the bar with someone. Just think back to that night. You were at the bar to have a drink after your shift at the restaurant. You needed to unwind after a long day on your feet. After you sat down and ordered your drink, Sophie sat on a stool not far from you. You thought she was beautiful, and she caught your interest—"

"It's not him," I said, cutting her off. She was trying to hypnotize him into confessing, and it wasn't going to work. I glanced at Carver. "Tell them why it couldn't be you."

He glanced from me to Willow and back, finally realizing that I was on his side. "I'm gay. I'm not interested in women. That's why I didn't notice her."

"Thanks Carver," I said. "Sorry about that. You can go now. Thanks for coming in." He gave me a nod of relief, and narrowed his eyes at Dimples and Willow before heading out the door. After he left, Dimples caught my gaze and pursed his lips together to keep from smiling.

"It must be one of the others," Willow said, chagrined that she'd failed. "Where are they?"

"One is in the next interrogation room, and the other guy is waiting in the hall." Dimples was tempted to tell her to wait in the hall, too, but he just pursed his lips together instead.

I liked that idea, but, to be honest, I enjoyed having Willow there so I could show her up. I met Dimples's gaze. "Why don't you bring him in here? We'll wait."

His brows rose. Didn't I like his idea? "Sure. I'll be right back."

The door shut, and Willow sent a furtive glance my way, frustration and insecurity gnawing at her stomach. "How did you know he was gay?" She could usually tell, but this guy didn't fit the bill. Of course, she'd been so busy thinking about her strategy that she'd missed it. She'd have to do better with the next one.

She stared at me, expecting an answer, so I shrugged. "I guess it's my psychic ability."

She inhaled sharply at the dig, then pursed her lips and frowned, trying to come up with a witty comeback. Before she could speak, the door opened, and Dimples ushered another man in.

He was similar in looks to the first guy, but I knew right away that he wasn't gay. Willow looked him over, hoping to pick up a gay vibe from him, but she was baffled, and her confidence took a hit.

Dimples used the same method with showing him the photos, but Willow held back, waiting for my input. I knew right away it wasn't him, but there was a flash of recognition when he saw the photo of Sophie.

I quickly moved to stand beside him. "You saw her at the bar. Did you notice the man who sat by her?"

He shook his head. "No. I mean... I think there was someone who spoke to her for a minute, but it was hardly long enough to lure her away."

"Did you notice when she left? Did she leave by herself?"

"Yeah... I think she did. I remember thinking she was pretty drunk, and I didn't know how she'd make it to her room. But then someone helped her out." From his mind, I caught a mental image of a man who wore a hotel uniform. There was something familiar about him, and it suddenly hit me that I'd seen him in the videos.

"Was it the bartender?"

"Yeah, that's it. He helped her."

Dimples caught my gaze. Was the bartender the killer? I shrugged. I hadn't talked with him yet, but he had ample opportunity to put something in Sophie's drink. Still, if he was working that night, it didn't seem like he could slip away long enough to go through with his nefarious plans, let alone kill Brock.

"I think I need to talk to the bartender."

"Good idea," Dimples agreed.

CHAPTER 12

After leaving the interrogation room, Dimples rushed to his desk to find the number for the hotel bar. Willow left to use the restroom, and I sat down in the chair beside Dimples. While he spoke, I got a text message from Ramos, asking me to call him. Since now seemed like a good time, I strolled to my desk in the corner and put the call through.

"Babe," he answered. "That was quick. Are you in trouble?"

"Ha, ha. What's up?"

"Manetto wants you to stop by. He's got something for you."

"Oh... okay. I'm at the police station right now, but I can come over once I'm done."

"I take it your plan worked?" he asked.

"For the most part."

"Good. I look forward to hearing all about it. See you soon." He disconnected, and I slipped my phone back into my purse. Glancing up, I found Willow glaring at me from across the room. She immediately smoothed her features and jerked her gaze to Dimples, who was just finishing up his call.

After he hung up, Willow asked him what he'd found out, but he was looking for me and didn't answer her. Spotting me at my desk, he hurried over, with Willow trailing behind. "The bartender won't be in until later, so there's a chance he might be at home. I've got his address. Want to go?"

"Yeah, sure." I sent him a warm smile, mostly because he was asking me and not Willow.

"I'll get my purse," Willow said, not about to be left behind. "Could you move?"

Hot anger filled my chest. It was on the tip of my tongue to tell her off. After all, it was my desk, and I'd fought long and hard to earn my place here. Instead, I huffed out a breath and got out of her way, hoping I could contain my rage before I slapped her silly.

Dimples's anger spiked too, and he thought I had a lot more restraint than he would have. Too bad she was there at all, but, no matter what happened, he vowed he'd never work with her again.

That calmed me down a little, and part of me even felt sorry for her. She just wanted to fit in and be part of the group. If that didn't mean taking my job, I might have been nicer. But, after this, I had to make sure she got the boot, no matter what it took.

Sure, both Chris and Ramos thought I should stop working for the police for a while, but I couldn't let her win. Maybe, once she was gone, I could consider cutting back my time here. But until then, this meant war, and she was going down.

Filled with grim determination, I followed Dimples and Willow to his car. Of course, Willow hurried directly to the passenger side, relegating me to the back seat again.

"You know what?" I glanced at Dimples. "I'm going to drive over. I'll meet you there."

"Are you sure?" Disappointment flooded over him. More than anything in the world, he wanted me to be his partner again. But he couldn't fault me for my decision. He'd feel the same way.

"Yeah... I'll follow you. Can you text me the address just in case I get lost?" He nodded and sent the text. "Thanks. See you there."

In my car, I let out a breath and tried to relax my tense shoulders. On top of helping Bates and worrying about Grizzo, this little outing with Dimples and Willow ratcheted the tension even higher, and it was starting to get to me.

Maybe I should talk to Bob sooner than next week? Hadn't he said I could call him anytime? Just knowing that I had a resource like him helped settle me down, and I took a deep, cleansing breath before driving out to follow Dimples.

Several minutes later, he pulled to the curb in front of an apartment complex, and I stopped behind him. We all trooped into the building and up the stairs to the second floor, none of us saying a word. The bartender's room stood at the far end.

Dimples pounded on the door and stepped back to wait for it to open. A few minutes passed with nothing happening, so Dimples knocked again. We waited a little longer, but it was a lost cause, and Dimples stated the obvious. "He must not be home."

"Now what?" Willow asked. She glanced my way, wondering why my premonitions hadn't warned us that he wouldn't be here.

I inhaled sharply and clenched my jaw to keep my mouth shut before I said something I might regret. In that moment, any sympathy I may have had for her totally vanished. Willow's eyes widened. She thought I looked upset, like I might slap her for no reason. What the heck? She hadn't done anything wrong.

"Okay," Dimples said, glancing nervously between us. "We'll just have to meet at the bar tonight and talk to him then. The manager said he had the late shift from seven to closing. Is there a time that works better for either of you?"

Willow was thinking about the reading she had set up for tonight, but she could probably reschedule.

"How about nine?" I glanced her way. "You should be done with your reading by then, right?"

"Uh... uh... yeah, that's... that's true."

"Good." I headed back down the hallway, with Dimples and Willow hurrying to catch up. Dimples mentally applauded me, thinking I was standing up to Willow the best way possible. And, since it was the perfect response without giving away my real secret, he had to admire that I held back my temper.

I wasn't sure if he believed that, or if he was just trying to think encouraging thoughts to help me out. Still, at least he was on my side. I glanced over my shoulder and sent him a grateful smile. He was thinking *we'll get through this... just stick with me, okay?*

Back outside, I turned to him. The sad but hopeful smile pulling up his lips tugged at my heart. In fact, if Willow hadn't been standing there, I might have given him a hug. Instead, I gave him a high five. "You got it... I'll see you tonight."

"Thanks Shelby." His sincere gratitude filled me with warmth, and I smiled in return. Willow felt a little left out... again, but she was happy I was leaving and she was headed back to the department. It gave her more time to cement her position there.

Shaking my head, I hurried to my car, ignoring her and giving Dimples a quick wave. I waited until after they left before I drove onto the street and headed for Thrasher Development. I wasn't sure what Uncle Joey had for me, but I hoped it would be something good. Like a lemon meringue pie or chocolate truffles.

After parking, I climbed out of my car, leaving my police ID badge on the seat, and hurried to the elevators. I exited on the twenty-sixth floor and headed inside. Jackie greeted me with a warm smile. "Hi Shelby. Go on down"

As I passed my office, my heart filled with gratitude that I didn't have to share it with anyone. At least Uncle Joey valued me. I knocked on the closed door before pushing it open.

Uncle Joey looked up from his computer and smiled. "Good. You made it. After Ramos told me about last night, I was a little worried. You want a diet soda?"

"You bet." Sure it wasn't chocolate or pie, but it was better than nothing.

He moved to the liquor cabinet and grabbed a couple of glasses. Opening the small fridge, he filled the glasses with ice, then set one down in front of me, along with a can of diet soda.

"Thanks." I eagerly poured the soda over the ice and took a couple of swallows. "Ah... That's better." As I filled the glass with the remaining soda, the door opened, and Ramos stepped in.

"You want one?" Uncle Joey asked, filling up his glass.

"No. I'm good." Ramos sat beside me, dressed more formally than yesterday in a black blazer and jeans. He smiled, grateful I'd survived the cops, and wondering how I did it. "So what happened with the police?"

With gusto, I explained my encounter with Bates and Grizzo. "So now, I guess they're looking into all the leads I gave them. Bates promised to call me once they find Xavier so I can help with the interview. I sure hope I gave them enough clues to bring him in without being too specific."

Ramos shook his head. "I'd say you handed him over on a silver platter. Now we'll just have to see if they're any good at their jobs."

I smiled, grateful he had my back. "At least it shut Grizzo up. He didn't think about you by name, so I don't think he's figured out who you are yet. Maybe he won't dig around too much if we get Xavier."

Ramos shook his head. "I wouldn't count on it, but, like you said, you can always tell him that I was your way into the Tiki Tabu bar and the Polynesian gang."

"Yeah. We'll just have to wait and see."

"There's something else we need to do," Uncle Joey said. "I got a call from Chris this morning." At my widened eyes, he nodded. "Yeah... it surprised me too. But he wasn't happy that you were passing me information about the case. That's the reason I wanted you to stop by. I've got a burner phone for you. I want you to use it anytime you have sensitive information that you need to give me."

He picked up a box from the top of his desk and handed it to me. "I've already programmed our numbers into the phone, so it's ready to use. It's untraceable, and, unless the police find it on you, there won't be any record that we've spoken. Just remember that if you ever get caught, you need to get rid of it." He was thinking I could destroy the phone pretty easily by breaking it or stomping on it.

"Wow. Just like in the movies, huh? Okay, I can do that." I opened the box and took out the burner phone. It was small and compact, and if it kept me from going to jail, I was all for it. "It looks like one of those old flip phones."

"Yes. That's exactly right, so it shouldn't be inconvenient to carry around. Ramos and I are the only people with that number, so we'll be calling or texting you with sensitive information on that phone from now on."

"Okay."

Uncle Joey was thinking that he should have done this a long time ago, but he'd never had any reason to fear that my phone records could get subpoenaed before now. He'd probably have to go over all of this with me at some point after I became his successor, but, for now, this would have to do.

Why did hearing him call me his successor turn my stomach? In fact, just thinking about it made me a little dizzy. Did I really want to go down that road? Nope. Did it matter? Probably not. It was the road I was on, and it didn't look like I could get off anytime soon. Oh hell.

They both looked at me with concern. Was something wrong? "Uh... no. I'm fine. In fact I'm really glad to have this... mostly." Oops did I just say that out loud? "I mean... not that I'm planning to break the law, or anything... but I guess it's better for all of us, so that's good. And I'll make sure the cops don't get their hands on it either."

I flipped the phone open. "I could probably break the top off if I twisted it, so that should work." Both of them were staring at me with suppressed smiles on their faces. Ramos thought it was great how fast I accepted the whole mob side of things these days. It reminded him of my first day on the job when I wore a wig and glasses. That had been a hoot.

I frowned. He was right. Things had certainly changed. And now I was about to become Uncle Joey's successor. Who would have thought? "Uh... is there anything else?"

"No," Uncle Joey said. "Just call one of us when you hear anything about the case."

"Sure. Hopefully that will be soon."

"Good." He glanced at Ramos, thinking I seemed a little upset. Why was that? "Do you have anything to add?"

"Yeah." Ramos studied me, realizing that the stark reality of my job might be getting to me. Still, he couldn't feel too bad about it. At least it meant that we'd be working together for a long time to come. Maybe I should look at it that way?

I sent him a grin. He had a point. Who wouldn't want to work with him? In fact, if I was honest, it probably made all the rest of it worth it, but I wasn't about to tell him that.

He nodded, happy to put a smile on my face. "There is something I want you to know. If this Grizzo person tries anything, you need to call me." He'd heard of someone with the street name Grizzo. It had to be the same guy. Knowing he was an undercover cop was huge, and he'd be sure and let Vinny and the rest of the crew know.

What? Oh crap. I had leaked privileged information, just like a real informant, and probably broken the law. At least I had a burner phone, so it would be harder to get caught... so that was good. But what about Grizzo? What if my information got him killed? I couldn't live with that. "Uh... just do me a favor, and make sure they don't kill him, okay? I couldn't live with that on my conscience, you know?"

"Don't worry, Shelby," Ramos said. "They know better than to kill a cop... and I'll be sure to remind them."

"Okay good, thanks." I finished off my diet soda and set the glass down. "I guess that's all I've got. Is there anything else you need?"

"No... that should do it," Uncle Joey said, thinking that I was a good person, and he appreciated that I came through for him during this transition. "Thanks for coming in. We'll be in touch."

"Okay... thanks for the soda... and the phone. See you." I slipped the burner phone into my pants pocket. It fit in there easily, unlike my smartphone that I had to lug around in my purse. That should help me keep track of it and make carrying two phones less of a hassle.

I sent them a quick wave and hurried to the door, picking up from Ramos that I shouldn't worry too much about the cops. Manetto would protect me, no matter what happened with them.

As comforting as that sounded, I knew I walked a fine line. Sure I'd want Uncle Joey to step in and help me if I got in trouble with the law, but who would protect the cops from Uncle Joey? Did that mean I'd have to watch out for them too?

I made it to my car and slid inside. Since I didn't want to worry about the cops and Uncle Joey, I pushed those concerns away to concentrate on my next move. I checked my watch to find that it was one-thirty in the afternoon. That meant I had plenty of time for a visit to Carolyn Brinkley, so I might as well head over there.

I didn't know if Willow had called Carolyn about me, but I decided dropping in without a call first might be best. I knew I was taking a chance that she'd be home, but I wanted to get her raw reaction to the news that I was investigating Mack's death. She had to know he'd been killed, but I doubted that anyone had spoken to her about it.

I programed the address into my phone and followed the directions to her house, finding it situated in one of the more expensive neighborhoods. Turning the corner onto her street, I admired the large, stately trees casting their leafy shadows along the road. Lined with identical lampposts and stone-covered mailboxes, the street could have been featured in a catalogue of celebrity homes.

Two stories tall, the homes featured a showcase of the Victorian style, with fancy, wooden doors and curving walkways. The manicured lawns and highly maintained shrubbery spoke of wealth and prosperity. I couldn't see a weed anywhere and not a lot of people either.

I pulled to a stop in front of a large, intimidating house, checking the address one more time. Before leaving the car, I made sure my police ID badge was around my neck so I'd look official. Feeling like an outsider in this ritzy neighborhood, I walked up the steps and rang the doorbell, hearing the gong echo through the house.

I tried not to fidget, and listened for approaching footsteps. Nothing happened, and I reached to ring the bell again. As I touched it, I heard the sounds of footsteps, and jerked my hand away. The beautiful, cut-glass design in the top half of the door distorted the approaching figure, but I caught a splash of red.

As the door opened, it surprised me to find a woman in her late-twenties with shoulder-length, dark brown hair. The woman wore tan capris with a red, sleeveless shirt, and her brown eyes widened with curiosity. "Can I help you?"

"Hi." I smiled, hoping to set her at ease. "I'm Shelby Nichols. I'm a consultant with the police, and I'm here to see Carolyn Brinkley. Is this the right house?"

"Uh... yes, but... she didn't tell me you were coming. I'm afraid now's not a good time. She's resting."

"Oh..."

"What's this about?" The woman's forehead wrinkled, and worry washed over her. Had her mother forgotten about this visit, or was it something she'd forgotten to tell her?

"I know it seems out of the ordinary to come here like this, but I was hoping she could help me with an investigation. You must be her daughter, Misti?"

"Yes."

"It's so nice to meet you. This is actually something that involves you as well. I'm here on behalf of Mack Haywood's son. You might remember Mack from a few weeks ago. He was part of the search-and-rescue team that found your daughter."

"Oh... yes. Of course." She frowned, remembering that he'd been killed recently, and sadness washed over her. "Please come in."

"Thanks."

She ushered me into a spacious sitting room with hardwood floors and an elegant arrangement of matching furniture in mauve and dusty blue. She motioned me toward a chair, and she sat on the couch across from me.

"Did you hear about his death?"

"Yes. It was a real shock." Sorrow lanced through her heart. "How can I help?"

"I'm just trying to gather all the recent information about him that I can find. I'm hoping it will give me more insight into his life and who might have wanted to kill him. Do you remember anything about him? I'm sure you were probably preoccupied with your missing daughter, but I know it meant a lot to him that he helped find her."

"Yes. I think everyone was thrilled to have a happy ending. At the time, I was so frantic that I wasn't sure what was going on. When your child goes missing like that... you always worry she won't come back."

Her eyes teared up. "So it was such a relief to find her, and I think everyone felt that way. I remember Mack handing her to me. I didn't even get a good look at him, but later, he made a point of coming back to talk to Ava and me, which I really appreciated, even more so now that he's gone."

She swallowed, surprised that talking about him made her so emotional. "I owed him a great deal, and now... I'll never be able to thank him properly." She was pretty sure her mother had sent him a gift card or something, but it was hardly enough for what he'd done. "I can't believe someone killed him."

"Yeah. It doesn't make a lot of sense. That's why I've come today. The search for your daughter was the last search-and-rescue he went on. I know you were probably too worried to notice much, but is there anything unusual you remember about that day?"

She blew out a breath. "No... I'm sorry, I was too focused on finding Ava."

I nodded. "I'm sure you were, but maybe your mother noticed something?"

Misti shrugged. "Uh... yeah... she might have. I think they exchanged numbers, so she may have spoken to him again, but right now, I don't want to disturb her. She's not in the best of health, but I'm sure she could talk to you another day."

Misti wasn't about to bother her right now, not after the morning she'd had. Her mother wasn't the easiest person to live with, and lately, she seemed more bad-tempered than usual.

"Would tomorrow work? I could come earlier in the day... say eleven?"

Misti didn't answer right away, not sure she wanted to commit, but what did she have to lose? If her mother had a problem with it, she'd just have to deal with it. "Sure. I'll tell her you'll be stopping by at eleven. Could I get your phone number in case something comes up and she can't make it?"

"Of course. Give me your number and I'll text you." I pulled out my phone and sent the text, grateful that it was a good way to get her number as well. "Perfect. If you remember anything about him that could help, you're welcome to call me, too."

She nodded, thinking that would be a long shot, since she could hardly remember any details from that day except the one that mattered. The patter of little feet reached us, and a little girl came running into the room, holding a piece of paper in her hand. "Mommy! Mommy! See what I drawed."

She bounded to her mother's side, then noticed me and stared with interest. "Who's that?"

"Hi Ava, I'm Shelby." Ava leaned against her mother's legs and studied me. "I was just talking to your mom for a minute. Can I see your drawing?" Suddenly shy, she nodded. I glanced at the blob of black and brown, not knowing what it was. "Wow. That's nice. I like the colors. Can you tell me about it?"

"This is a dawg. He woofs. Woof, woof."

"Do you like dogs?" She pursed her lips and nodded.

Misti glanced at me. "Ever since her rescue, the dog is all she talks about."

I smiled at Ava. "Oh my goodness! I recognize that dog. He's black and tan, and his name is Coco." I leaned in a little closer. "Can I tell you a secret?"

Ava's eyes widened. "Yeah."

"I know Coco. In fact, he lives with me now. He's my dog. Maybe if your mommy's okay with it, you could see him again."

"Yeah. Yeah. Yeah." Ava jumped up and down with excitement.

"Ava, settle down, we don't want to wake up Nana. Remember? You have to use your inside voice."

"Yeah." Ava jumped once more, not using her inside voice at all, and so cute, I wanted to jump up and down along with her.

"Come sit down for a minute." Misti picked Ava up onto her lap, but Ava arched her back and squirmed away. Before Misti could catch her, Ava ran back into the other room.

Misti shook her head and watched her go. "I swear she is always running away. You'd think after getting lost, she'd know better." She caught my gaze. "So you have Coco? How did that happen?"

I told her the story, and she listened with rapt attention. "It's kind of crazy that I ended up with him."

"Wow... no kidding."

"So... if you'd like, I'd be happy to bring Coco with me tomorrow, when I come."

"Oh... I don't know. My mother doesn't like animals, but maybe it would be okay if we stayed in the backyard." At my nod, she continued. "I don't live here. I just stop by when she needs me. My husband and I live a few blocks over."

"I'll bet she's glad to have you so close."

"Yeah." She nodded, thinking that her mother tended to need her more often than she used to, and it was getting tiresome. Now with her illness, it was even worse. She'd always been controlling, but now she was more demanding than ever, and her misgivings about buying a house in the neighborhood were coming true. Add in the money her mother had loaned them, and they were in her debt even more.

Hmm... that didn't sound so great. "Well... I'd better go. But it was nice to meet you."

"You too."

I made my way out the door and glanced over my shoulder. "I'll see you tomorrow."

She nodded, even though she knew her mother wasn't likely to agree to see me. Maybe she wouldn't tell her? Ava would love to see Coco again. So what was wrong with that? "Okay. See you then."

The door closed behind me, and I hurried back to my car, not sure I'd learned anything of value. It sounded like Carolyn was dealing with an illness of some kind, and she wasn't handling it very well. I could understand the pressure the illness put on Misti, but it seemed a little deeper than that. Taking the money into account, there was probably a lot more to it.

If Carolyn and Mack had a thing going like Chris thought, Mack's death could have added to her pain. Maybe that contributed to her unhappiness? Hopefully, I'd see her tomorrow and clear it up, but I didn't have a lot of hope that talking to her would get me any closer to finding Mack's killer.

It meant that I'd have to start over, and that was discouraging, but I couldn't let Coco or Austin down. Still, I'd wait until after talking to Carolyn to worry about that. There was still a possibility she'd know something, and I couldn't give up on her yet.

At home, I walked in the door to find a furry animal running to greet me. Coco seemed so excited to see me that all my worries began to fade away. He followed me through the house, and I told him all about my meeting with Ava. I changed into shorts and a tee, making sure to put the burner phone in my shorts pocket.

Josh was at a friend's house, and Savannah and Ash were in her room. After a short conversation with them, I found my notebook and went outside with Coco to sit on the deck swing. Grateful for the chance to relax a little, I wrote down a couple of my thoughts for Bob. It was time to take my counseling seriously, and that meant that I needed to do my part.

The first thing I wrote was that Willow was driving me crazy, and that I was really starting to hate her guts. Next, I wrote that I was probably breaking the law, but it was for a worthy cause. Last, I wrote that Uncle Joey wanted me to be his successor and it made me sick.

Lastly, I wrote that if I didn't find Mack's killer, I'd be letting my dog down. Of all those things, letting Coco down was probably not the most important. I knew he'd love me no matter what, and that relieved some of the pressure. Still, it was something I needed to do.

I listed all the reasons I felt stressed and noticed a pattern. Most of my worry was based on things that hadn't happened yet, may happen in the future, or may never happen. Still, the fine line I walked between the mob and the cops was starting to weigh on me, and I knew something needed to change, but what?

I wrote down a few ideas, but nothing seemed to answer that question, so I tore the piece of paper from the notebook and ripped it over and over until it was in tiny little pieces. Did it help? Maybe not, but at least now I could focus on something else, like what to make for dinner. I needed some comfort food, and, since I'd been saving my mac and cheese recipe for a day when I had more time, right now was perfect.

After eating one of our favorite dinners together, everyone chipped in to help clean up. Once the dishes were in the dishwasher, the kids took off to do other things, and I had some time to tell Chris about my day.

"And just so you know... I'm also meeting Dimples and Willow at the hotel bar at nine tonight to talk to the bartender." I smiled, proud that I'd told him an hour and a half before I needed to leave. That was real progress.

"Oh." He nodded. "Well, I hope that's the break you need."

"Yeah, me too." I held his gaze, waiting for him to complain. When he didn't, I frowned. "So you're okay with that?"

"Shelby." He put his hands on his hips, his hurt gaze cutting into my heart. "You make me sound like an ogre. Of course I'm fine with it. It's what you do now and part of who you are. I may not always like it, but I've come to accept it."

He was right. Why did I always expect the worst from him? "You're right. I'm sorry. I'll try and do better."

He shook his head. "It's okay. I haven't always been as supportive as I should, but we'll figure this out. I mean... now that you're going to take over the mob, I need to stay on your good side, right?"

I burst out laughing. "Wow... I hadn't even thought of it that way..."

"Yeah... with that much power... don't make me sorry I pointed it out."

I sent him a mischievous smile. "I'll have to get back to you on that. How are all the legal details coming anyway?"

"It's taking some time, but I'm almost done. I haven't forgotten about your stipulation, and I'm going to write it in. I just hope Manetto goes for it."

"I don't know why he wouldn't. But, even with that added, just remember that you still need to stay on my good side."

"Oh... I plan to."

Before leaving for the bar, I decided to change into a sleeveless summer dress. I'd fit in better at the bar, plus I wanted to look good and outshine Willow at the same time. The dress was white, with splashes of bright colors, and I loved the simple yet breezy flow. With dangly earrings and a necklace to dress it up, it was comfortable as well as cool. And with the v-neckline and fitted waist, it was flirty and fun.

I was ready a little early, but decided to leave anyway. Right after I left, my phone buzzed with a text from Dimples, telling me that Willow was running a little late, and would I mind meeting there at nine-thirty?

I replied that I'd see him then and continued on to the hotel. That placed me at the bar about forty minutes early, but it wouldn't hurt to sit there alone for a short time. I could glean some good information from the bartender if he wasn't on the defense. Besides, watching people, and using my secret ability, was highly entertaining, and I didn't get to do it nearly enough.

Entering the hotel bar, I was grateful I'd dressed up a little, since I fit right in. I found a place at the bar closer to the far end, where I could get a better view of the people coming and going. The bartender came right over, and I recognized him immediately.

"What can I get for you?" His friendly smile gave him a youthful charm, meant to put me at ease, but I didn't miss his assessing glance.

Hmm... maybe I should play along? "Oh... uh... I'm waiting for a friend. It looks like she's late, but she should be here any minute now."

"Okay. I'll check back then." He smiled, noticing my big diamond ring, and thought I probably had a load of credit cards in my large purse. Too bad they were taking a break. I looked like the perfect candidate, but, after last time went so wrong, they had to lay low.

Still, it wouldn't hurt to check in with Dex, especially if my friend didn't show up. He sent a quick text about "a perfect target" to him and slipped his phone back in his pocket.

Whoa. So he was part of this... and so was this Dex person? They obviously had a scheme going. It sounded like it had something to do with stealing credit cards from women, and it looked like I was the perfect target.

He pulled a rag from beneath the counter and began wiping it down, keeping an eye on me and his other customers. Maybe I could catch him at his own game? What could it hurt? He might be more willing to implicate his friend if he got caught.

It was now or never, so I pulled out my phone, looking at it like I'd gotten a text, and let out a sigh. "Damn."

He glanced my way. "What is it?"

"She's not coming." I looked up at him. "This is the second time we've set something up, and now she's saying she can't come... again. I'm starting to get a complex."

"That's too bad."

"Yeah."

"Well... you could still get that drink. What do you like?"

I let out a discouraged breath, knowing I had to play along. "Uh... maybe a Daiquiri. I'm in the mood for something citrusy."

"Sounds perfect." While he left to mix my drink, he sent another text, telling Dex that it looked like my friend had ditched me, and I was ripe for the taking. The response came right away, saying that he'd just arrived to check me out.

Whoa. That was fast, and my heart rate picked up. I fought the urge to look around the room to spot him and checked my watch instead. I still had nearly thirty minutes before Dimples was supposed to get here, but maybe that was perfect timing to pull this off.

A man slid into the chair beside me, and I tried to stay calm. He held up his hand to get the bartender's attention, using a predesignated hand signal that the job was a go.

"I'll be right with you." The bartender finished mixing my drink and brought it over. "There you go."

"Thanks."

"What can I get you sir?"

"That looks pretty good." He motioned toward my drink and sent me a smile. "How is it?"

I took a couple of small sips and nodded. "Mmm... it's really good." Just to be safe, I made sure it was too far away for him to put anything in it.

"Then I guess that's what I'll have."

The bartender nodded. "Right away sir." He hurried to mix the drink, thinking it was a good thing he'd already added the drug, since Dex would never have gotten the chance to do it himself.

Oh crap. I'd just taken a few sips. This was bad.

"Are you waiting for someone?" Dex asked.

Knowing I still had a part to play, I frowned. "I was, but she bailed at the last minute."

The bartender set Dex's drink in front of him, and Dex picked it up and turned to me. I caught the gleam of excitement in his dark eyes. His brown hair was slicked back, and he wore a goatee and glasses that looked a little off. Was it a disguise? He looked nothing like the men Willow and Dimples had picked out, but, if it was a disguise, maybe that explained it.

"Then I propose a toast. To making the best of a disappointing night out."

I smiled, but I wasn't as enthusiastic as him, and I picked up my drink to clink it against his. He took a swallow, watching me while I raised the glass to my lips. Keeping my lips closed, I tipped my head back and made swallowing motions, so it would look like I'd taken a drink. A little of the liquid managed to enter my mouth, but not enough to matter... I hoped.

Setting the glass back down, I licked my lips to keep the drink from dribbling down my chin and swallowed. Crap.

I'd just swallowed a little more, but it shouldn't be too bad. In all, I'd taken maybe a couple of spoonfuls, maybe less. Surely that wouldn't be enough to affect me.

Dex had been watching me closely, and he'd enjoyed the sight of my tongue licking my lips. It excited him, and he could hardly wait for the next ten minutes to pass while the drug took effect. Then I'd be his for the next half an hour or so, and he could hardly wait.

Yikes. This might not have been the best idea. I still had twenty minutes before Dimples arrived. Maybe I'd better send him a text. I reached for my phone, but it wasn't on the counter. I must have put it away.

"Do you come here often?" Dex asked.

"Uh... no. This is actually the first time."

He nodded, thinking that I needed to drink a little more. "Well, it looks like my friend is here. I hope you have a good evening."

"Uh. Thanks. You too."

He held up his glass, so I grabbed mine, sloshing it a little, and tapped his. He took another drink, so I pretended to as well. He walked away, and relief filled my chest. I rummaged through my purse for my phone and couldn't find it.

Did I put it somewhere else? The last time I'd used it, I'd pretended to get a text. Had I left it on the counter? It wasn't there either. Damn. Had it fallen on the floor? I glanced toward my feet, and a wave of dizziness washed over me. Crap. I had to get out of there. But where could I go?

Wait. I had a burner phone in my pocket. I could call Ramos. As another wave of dizziness washed over me, I pulled the phone from my pocket and concentrated on flipping it open. It had been a long time since I'd used a phone like this, and I couldn't remember how to find the numbers.

I pushed a few buttons and a number came up. Taking deep breaths, I held it to my ear and heard it ring. Yay. It worked. "Babe. What's up?"

"Hey... I'm... I think I'm in... troub... trou...uble." I knew I was slurring the words, but I couldn't help it.

"Where are you?"

"A bar... hotel.. my... dr.. drink.. spik...spiked. I feel... fun... funny." I took a deep breath and waited for him to talk, but the line was dead. Had he hung up on me? I swallowed, leaning against the counter with my head in my hands. "Damn, damn, damn."

"Miss? Are you all right?"

I glanced up to see the bartender hovering over me. "Yes. I'm... fi... fine."

"You don't look so good. Would you like to lie down? There's a couch in the back." He came around the end of the bar and put his arm around my waist to help me stand.

"No. Don't... don.. touchme."

Startled at my outburst, he backed away.

"I need..." What did I need? Oh yeah. "Wa..ter. I nee.. som.. wat..er."

"Sure. But you look like you're about to fall over. At least sit in a booth. There's an empty one right over there."

I glanced where he pointed, but it just made me dizzy. He put his arm around me and helped me stand, then began to walk, taking most of my weight along for the ride. I couldn't seem to pull away and, before long, someone else took his place.

Was it Dex? I fought against the man's grip, but his arm tightened around me like a steel vise. I moved my eyes, since I couldn't seem to move my head, and caught sight of a goatee and glasses.

CHAPTER 13

Knowing my time was running out, I concentrated on slipping my hand into my purse. I felt for my stun flashlight, my fingers drifting over the pill bottle, a pack of gum and my notebook. Finally, in the bottom of the bag, my fingers touched the cold handle of the flashlight, and I gripped it tightly.

Now I just had to get it out of my purse. Everything around me was slightly blurry, and I knew we weren't in the bar anymore. We stopped walking, and I felt movement, like we were in an elevator. Then we were walking again, only slowing in front of a door, where he used a key card to pull it open.

Part of me knew that, if I went inside, it was over. Hearing the click of the door shutting behind me sent terror and panic into my heart, clearing my mind. With sudden strength, I pulled my stun flashlight out of my purse and swung it toward the man. Growling with determination, I hit him in the groin and pushed the button.

He yelped and doubled over in pain, clutching his groin and dropping his hold. I stumbled against the wall and slipped to the floor. He continued to fall to the ground and jerked a few times before going still.

Elated, I tried to get up, but my legs just didn't want to move. A lone light from a lamp across the room left most of the room in darkness, and I fought to keep my eyes open. Dex wasn't going to stay quiet forever, so now was my last chance to get out of there.

I did everything I could to move my legs and wake up, but nothing worked. At least I could still think. In desperation, I started to bang my head against the wall. It kept me from blacking out, and soon, I began to feel the strength return to my arms and legs. Thank goodness I'd only had a couple of sips, and the drug was wearing off. A small ray of hope that I could make it out of there washed over me.

A groan came from Dex, and his arms began to move. Damn. I just needed a few more minutes. I struggled to move my arms, but could barely lift them. As panic filled me, Dex pushed into a sitting position. Even a little dazed, he stared at me with hate-filled eyes.

"You little bitch."

He slowly climbed to his feet, wobbling a bit. Finding his balance, he stepped toward me until he stood over me like a hulking monster. With a glare, he reached down to grab my arm.

I managed to move sideways, but it wasn't far enough. As his hand closed around my arm, the door burst open. Startled, Dex jerked back, tripping over his feet and falling onto his butt. Light from the hallway cast the man in shadows, but I'd know him anywhere. "Ramos?"

"Are you hurt?" He knelt beside me.

"No... jus... drugg... drugged."

Dex rose to his feet, ready to lay Ramos flat and charge out of the room. Dex was a big guy, but he'd underestimated Ramos. Before Dex could move, Ramos stepped over me and sent a couple of punches into his gut before landing a right hook to smash into his nose. I heard the crunch and grimaced.

The momentum pushed Dex back and Ramos followed, sending another one-two punch to the gut, before landing another right hook into Dex's jaw, spinning him around and knocking him out cold. He went down hard, and I wasn't sure he'd ever get back up.

"Whoa. Is he... dead?"

Ramos came back to kneel by my side and studied my eyes. "Unfortunately... no. Your pupils are dilated. Do you know what he gave you?"

"Somethin like zom..bie ... or maybe it's the devil... but I only had one... two... swallows... so I'm feeling better now. See? I can even move my... yarms." I lifted my arms slightly, then let them drop since it took a lot out of me. "I'm hardly... even slurr..ing words."

His mouth twisted, and he shook his head. "What the hell, Shelby?"

I frowned. "Did you jus.. say that out loud?" I couldn't tell. Had his lips moved?

"No."

"Oops."

"What's going on? Tell me why you're here."

"Sure. There was a murder... and... that guy over there..." I pointed to the prone figure. "Did it. He tried it on me... but I messed up... the bartender... had the stuff... but Dimples... should be here soon... at the bar...he's late... prob..ly because of Willow... she is the bane of my exis...exist...ance."

"Right. So Dimples knows you're here? Is he downstairs?"

I tried to nod, but only managed to hit my head on the wall. "Ouch."

We both heard a groan, and Ramos glanced toward Dex, who was lying on the floor with blood all over his face. With an effort, Dex moved to his side, and then pushed into a sitting position, holding his face with one hand.

"Guess I'd better take care of him. Sit tight. I'll be right back."

He went back over and punched Dex in the face again. Dex went down hard, hitting the back of his head on the floor, and Ramos nodded in satisfaction.

"That should do it." He came to my side and helped me stand, but my feet still wouldn't hold my weight. "Maybe you'd better lie down." He maneuvered me to the bed, then stacked the pillows for my head and lifted my legs, so I was lying down.

"I'll be right back."

"Hmm...kay." Now that he was taking care of things, I could relax. Phew. That was close. But everything was fine now, and it was okay to let my eyes drift shut.

"Shelby?"

I opened my eyes to find Dimples standing over me. "Hey Dimps. Wass-up?"

"Damn."

I shook my head and felt a stabbing pain. "Ouch. That hurts."

"Here. Drink this." He propped me up with his arm and handed me a can. Suddenly thirsty, I drank it down. I wasn't sure what it was, but it sure tasted good. A few seconds later, my vision cleared, and I felt more like myself. "What is this?"

"An energy drink. Feel better?"

"Yes. Thanks." Dimples helped me sit up on the edge of the bed and held me until I was steady.

He stayed by my side, and I glanced around the room. A couple of police officers pulled Dex to his feet and cuffed his hands behind his back. As he muttered obscenities, they read him his rights and led him from the room.

"Where's—"

Dimples put a finger to his lips, and I froze. He was thinking that I shouldn't say anything about Ramos if I wanted to keep him out of this. I nodded to let him know I heard that, and he dropped his hand. "Do you remember anything?"

I nodded. "I remember it all. That Dex guy they just took out? He's the killer."

"Yes. I got that." He was thinking that it had been a shock to see Ramos motioning to him at the bar. Then, to find me and that murderer in the hotel room nearly gave him a heart attack. What was I thinking?

"Uh... I can explain."

"It's okay... I'm not mad. I'm just glad you're all right."

"Did you get the bartender too?"

"Not yet. Why don't you tell me the whole story?"

"Sure." It took longer than I liked, but I told him everything that happened. "I didn't realize it was the bartender who put the drug in my drink, or I never would have had any. I'm surprised it did anything. I only had about one swallow."

"That must be why you remember what happened. It's a good thing Ramos came. How did you manage that?"

Since I didn't want to tell him about the burner phone, I explained it another way. "There's a tracker in my watch. I managed to tell him I was in trouble and he found me."

"Oh. That's handy." As much as he didn't like my relationship with a hitman or a mob boss, he couldn't possibly be mad about it... at least not right now. "We'd better get the bartender before he skips town."

"Yeah." I glanced around the room. "Where's Willow?"

He shook his head. "She had car trouble and wanted me to pick her up. Since I was already late meeting you, I told her I couldn't do it. But she was stranded on the highway, so I had to find someone to help her out before I could get here."

I nodded, catching his thoughts that he was done with that woman, and the chief could stuff it up his... he stopped to catch my gaze, and I smiled. "I'll be back. Don't go anywhere." He left my side and told the remaining officer to go with him to arrest the bartender, leaving another officer with me.

"Dimples... wait!" He turned back. "I think the bartender took my phone. Will you see if he's got it?"

"Yeah sure." With a scowl, he hurried out the door.

I noticed my purse on the bedside table and checked inside to find my stun flashlight, grateful I still had it. What about my burner phone? I patted the pocket in my dress and felt the bulge. How had I managed that? I couldn't remember putting it there, but I must have.

Now that I felt better, I tested my legs and slowly stood, putting a little weight on them. Standing without too much trouble, I let out a breath, and crossed to the bathroom, needing to splash some cold water on my face.

My hair was more than a little mussed, and my cheeks were flushed, but I didn't look too bad. After finger combing my hair, I rinsed my mouth with water and wiped my face with a towel. I did feel a lot better, but I wasn't sure I could drive home.

A strange ringing sound echoed through the bathroom, and I realized it was coming from my pocket. I quickly pulled the phone out and flipped it open. "Hello?"

"Babe. Sorry I had to leave. Are you okay?"

"Yes. So much better. Dimples gave me an energy drink. It really helped."

"Good. When can you leave?"

"I'm not sure. Dimples left to arrest the bartender, so I think I'll head down there and see if he found my phone."

"Okay. Just make sure you get a ride home. You shouldn't drive."

"Yeah... you're right. I will. And... Ramos... thanks for coming tonight. That was a little scary."

He didn't answer for a moment. "Yes, it was."

"Good thing that tracker is still working, right?"

"Uh-huh."

"Uh... I'll have to make you some cookies or something. I know that's hardly enough, but—"

He snorted. "Shelby... don't worry about it. I'm just glad you're okay. I'll see you tomorrow." The line went dead before I could reply. I couldn't tell if he was mad at me, or if he was just worried. Either way, I was more than grateful.

I stepped out of the bathroom, and Dimples came through the door. He caught my gaze and smiled. "Got him. He's keeping his mouth shut, but I found your phone behind the counter." He held it up. "I should keep it for evidence, but I think we have enough on him without it."

"Thank you. I was just about to go down there and look for it." I slipped the cell phone into my purse. "Do you need me for anything else, or can I go?"

"You can go. I've got enough to write up your statement, but you'll need to come in sometime tomorrow so we can go over it."

"Sure. I can do that."

"Good. I'll have an officer drive you home. His partner can follow in your car."

"Oh that's great. Thanks so much."

He nodded, and his brows drew down over his eyes. "Just... Shelby, that was..." He thought about saying stupid, or crazy, or scary, but none of those words were right. "You solved the case, but... I don't like thinking about what could have happened."

"Yeah... I get that. I wasn't expecting things to happen like that either." I caught his gaze. "Or that you'd be so late."

He winced. "Yeah... no kidding. I just don't like you taking such a risk..."

"I know... I don't either. But it kind of fell into my lap, and I went for it. You would have done the same thing."

He nodded, thinking that was his job... and I was the one who took the risk and caught the killer. He'd feel like a failure if I wasn't so nice about it. "You show me up all the time." He smiled. "Just don't tell the chief."

"I won't, and... just because I'm so nice... I'll let you tell Willow all about it. Oh... and since we're leaving Ramos out of it... you're taking his place in the story, right? Because I totally think you'd better."

His lips turned down. As much as he didn't want to, it was the only way to explain it all without involving the hitman. "Fine." He shook his head and caught my gaze. His lips turned up in a big smile, bringing out the dimples in his cheeks. "You know what? Willow's going to be so upset."

I snorted. "Yup... and based on that, it was totally worth it."

I got home close to midnight. I'd sent Chris a text after I got my phone back, telling him that we'd captured the killer, and it was a huge success. That had a nice positive spin to it, and I hoped it would make telling him the rest of it easier.

As I climbed into bed, he woke up and pulled me into his arms. I cuddled against him, grateful to feel safe and secure. "So you got the guy," he said, kissing the top of my head. "That's great. I'm so proud of you."

My heart melted. "Thanks honey."

"You want to tell me about it?" He was thinking that it was late, and he had an early morning, but he didn't mind staying awake a little longer.

"How about this? It was great taking that murderer down and solving the case, but the details can wait until tomorrow."

"You're sure?"

"Yeah."

"Okay. Thanks honey... you're my wonder woman." After another squeeze, he relaxed and began to drift off...but a stray thought jarred him awake. Usually, when I didn't tell him things, it meant that I'd been in trouble. Was that the case this time?

With an effort, he pushed the thought away. I was home safe and snuggled in his arms. Right now... that was all that mattered.

Chris was gone before I got up. I didn't know if that was good or bad, but, since it meant I could put off telling him about my close call, it was probably for the best. Coco barked that he needed to go out, so I opened the door. He came back a few minutes later and barked to be let in, and I knew it was past time to get that doggy door.

While eating a bowl of cereal, I checked places to get one on my cell phone. Coco ate his food at the same time, but scarfed it down pretty fast. Before I finished, Coco sat at my feet and woofed *walk.*

"Sure... just let me finish my cereal." It was early enough that I could fit in a walk before my eleven o'clock appointment with Carolyn. A moment later, Coco returned, carrying his leash in his mouth. *Walk. Go. Now.*

I laughed. "Okay... just let me put on my shoes." He woofed *Yup* and sat at attention at the door to wait for me. As I slipped on my walking shoes, my phone rang. It was Misti, and I quickly answered. "Hello."

"Hey Shelby, sorry to bother you, but I'm afraid we're going to have to cancel today."

"Oh darn. That's too bad."

"Yeah. My mother's not feeling the best. Can we try for another day?"

"Yes. Of course."

"Okay. Let me talk to her, and I'll get back to you."

Since that sounded like it may never happen, I quickly spoke. "Why don't we say tomorrow at the same time? Even if she isn't up for it, at least let me bring Coco over so Ava can see him again? We could just meet in the back yard, so we wouldn't disturb her. That way, if she's feeling well enough, she could join us."

Misti didn't answer for a moment. "Okay... sure. Let's do that. Ava really wants to see the dog, and I hate to disappoint her, so it should be fine."

"Great. I'll see you tomorrow." It frustrated me to put it off another day, but at least I'd managed to set it up again. Hopefully she wouldn't bail on me a second time.

Since both Savannah and Josh were still asleep, I checked my calendar for their schedules. Seeing nothing important this morning, I left a note that I'd taken Coco on a walk, and snapped the leash onto his collar.

A few blocks away from home, my phone rang again. I checked the number, but it wasn't familiar. "Hello?"

"Shelby? This is Austin Haywood. Did you send the police over to talk to me?"

"What? No. Why? Are they there?"

He huffed out a breath, clearly upset. "Not right now. I'm at my dad's house. They were next door, so they came over. They just left, but they practically accused me of killing my own father. Why would they do that? Please tell me you have something."

"I do have something, but I'm still looking into it. You know what? I'm not too far from your dad's place. I can be there in about fifteen minutes. Why don't I stop by and we can talk. Will that work?"

"Yeah... sure. I'll probably be here most of the day."

"Okay, I'll see you soon." I could hardly believe that Williams and Clue would accuse Austin of his father's murder. I'd told them he didn't do it. Had they spoken with Reed Gardner's wife next door and found out something about Austin?

Several minutes later, I stepped onto the porch, and knocked on the door. Coco stood quietly beside me, but he didn't seem too happy about being there. "It's okay buddy, we're just stopping by to talk to Austin for a minute. Then we'll go home."

Home?

It sounded like a question. Was that because this used to be his home, and now he thought I was bringing him back here? "We're just staying for a minute. Okay?"

He sat down on his haunches and woofed. *Yup.*

Austin opened the door, and Coco dashed inside. It was like he was looking for Mack all over again, and it broke my heart. It broke Austin's heart too. Guilt tore into his chest. He didn't know I'd have Coco with me, or he might not have wanted me to come.

"Hey, Coco's doing great with us, so you don't have to feel guilty. I think he just wants to look around for a minute, but he'll come back. So... what happened with the police?"

"I guess the detectives were next door talking to the Gardners and saw me over here, so they stopped by to chat. But the woman detective started asking me about my inheritance and basically said that having all that money would sure help me out."

He clenched his jaw. "She was insinuating that I'd kill my own father for money. Why would she do that? I've got a good job. I don't need the money. I can take care of myself."

"Of course you can. I know you had nothing to do with it, so try not to let them get to you. They're just grasping at straws, you know?"

He sighed and nodded, grateful for my comforting words. Burying his father had been the hardest thing he'd ever gone through, and it hurt every day. He wasn't sure he'd ever feel whole again. Now he was an orphan, all alone, with no family left to belong to. Even his girlfriend didn't get it.

His sorrow lanced through my heart, and I wondered if there was anything I could do to help him. Coco came back and sat down beside me. Austin ran his fingers through his hair, thinking that even the dog didn't want anything to do with him.

He could hardly blame Coco after he'd left him at the shelter. Now he was thinking it had been a huge mistake. Even if he didn't have his father, he could have had his dog. Now he had nothing.

I pulled away from his thoughts, and my gaze landed on a box of photos. One of the binders was opened to a page of Austin as a small child. "Is that you?"

"Yeah." He nodded. "My parents were so young there." His father held Austin's hands, while Austin took a few steps. "I'm just learning to walk in that one." He turned the page, and a large photo of Austin, his parents, and a little girl took up the space. "That's the last photo of all of us before my sister was killed."

I took a good look at the photo, feeling a hint of déjà vu. Had I seen her before? Then it hit me. She looked a lot like Ava, Misti's daughter. My stomach twisted, and the room swam. I swallowed and it came back into focus. "Do you have any other photos of your sister?"

"Sure. There's a whole binder full of them." He rummaged through the box and pulled out a pink binder. "Everything's on a disc now, but there are several photos in here."

I took the folder and opened it up. The photos of his sister began as a newborn at the hospital and continued through the years until she disappeared. Several had Austin in them as a baby, with his sister holding him and smiling, along with both his parents. His sister looked so much like Ava that my breath caught.

"Are you sure your sister's dead? I mean... did they find a body?"

He shrugged. "I honestly don't know. I don't even remember her. She was four or five then, and I'm three years younger. My parents never spoke to me about the details, probably to protect me."

"What was her name?"

"Macie."

A shiver ran up my spine, and my heart raced. Macie was close enough to Misti that it was easily interchangeable.

Everyone had assumed she was dead, but what if she wasn't? Could this be Mack's missing daughter and Austin's sister? Had Mack recognized something about Ava and confronted Carolyn?

If Carolyn had taken Misti, and Mack had even hinted that he suspected Misti was his daughter, it would have threatened everything Carolyn had worked for. Before confronting her, Mack could have invited Carolyn to the house with the intent to disclose what he knew.

Carolyn could have told Mack any number of stories, but if he'd threatened to tell Misti what he suspected, Carolyn would lose everything. It gave Carolyn the perfect motive to kill Mack.

I shook my head in wonder. This had to be the connection. "Can I take one of these? I'll bring it back. I just want to check something out." I wasn't ready to tell Austin any of this until I was certain it was true.

He shrugged. "Sure. Go ahead." Although he was curious, he'd thought of Macie as being dead for so long that it didn't even cross his mind that she could still be alive.

"Thanks." I took the best photo that closely resembled Ava, and slipped it into my purse. Even if I didn't get a chance to talk to Carolyn tomorrow, I could show it to Misti and tell her what I'd found. She might not believe me at first, but she deserved to know it was a possibility. And if she still doubted, DNA tests would confirm it. Still... it would change her life.

I smiled at Austin. It would change Austin's life too. He'd have a sister... a brother-in-law, and a niece. A whole family to help fill that empty place in his heart. "I have a lead that looks pretty good, so hang in there. By tomorrow, I should know who killed your father."

His brows rose in shock. "Really?"

"Yes. That's all I can say for now, but I'll be in touch." I glanced at Coco. "Coco. Ready to go?"

He jumped to his feet and woofed. *Home?*

"Yup. Let's go home."

At home, I found Josh and Savannah eating breakfast. We spoke about our schedules for the day, and I hurried upstairs to take a quick shower. I emerged to find that I'd missed a call from Dimples. I quickly called him back, and he picked right up.

"Shelby... I need you at the station. Can you come?"

"Uh... sure. What's going on?"

"The charges against Dex and the bartender are being questioned. I need you to come in and verify what happened last night."

"Oh." I sighed with relief. "Sure. I can do that."

"Good. And... just so you know, Willow's on her way in as well. Word is she's called the chief a few times to complain. I think she might throw something at you... and maybe include me as well. I think it's about what happened last night."

"What do you mean? She wasn't even there."

"I don't know that for sure."

"You think she might have come late and seen Ramos?"

"It's a possibility, but your guess is as good as mine. All I know is that she's got something up her sleeve. At least you'll know what is it, and we can figure it out after you get here."

"Damn. Okay. Thanks for the warning. I'll be there soon."

Wanting to look good, I took some extra time with my makeup and hair. Because things were heating up at the station, I slipped on my navy jeans, pairing them with a purple shirt and my navy blazer, making me look pretty darn sassy.

It didn't hurt that I wanted to look good in case I managed to fit in a motorcycle ride after it was all over. By then, I might need something to help with my stress levels, and I was sure Bob would agree.

Feeling confident, I left after a quick goodbye to my kids and Coco.

I strode into the precinct with my badge around my neck and a confident swagger, although I had to admit to a case of nerves. What did Willow have on me? Was it just jealousy, or was there more to it? I guess I'd find out soon enough. Still, it couldn't be anything serious. If only my stomach would stop churning, I might believe that.

Stepping into the detectives' office, I looked for Willow, wanting to hear her thoughts before she pounced on me. Dimples caught sight of me and waved me over, thinking that Willow had just arrived and was entrenched in the chief's office. He didn't like it.

I sat beside him. "Really? And you have no idea what she's saying?"

"Not a clue."

"Damn."

"Since you're here though, we can go over what happened last night."

"Okay... and we put you in Ramos's spot, right?"

He grimaced. "Yeah... we'll say you called me instead of him. I was late, so I missed you at the bar. Everything else is the same."

"Okay... got it."

He let out a sigh and leaned his elbows on the desk. "Your testimony works for last night, but not for Brock's murder and what they did to Sophie."

"Oh... so what do we need?"

"Well... the murder weapon would be nice. But, beyond a confession, which neither of them will give, I think the only way for this to work is to get them to turn on each other. With your help, we might be able to do that."

"Right. Sounds like I need to talk to them."

Dimples glanced at the chief's office, wondering what Willow could be saying to keep him in there for so long. "It might be good to do that before they're done in there." He picked up his phone. "I'll have them bring Dex up to the interrogation room."

After Dimples finished his call, we had to wait for Dex. Each second we waited I worried that the chief's door would open, and I'd get the boot. Finally, we got the signal that Dex was ready, and I leapt up to follow Dimples into the interrogation room.

Dex sat with his wrists in handcuffs, locking him to the table. His swollen and bandaged nose, along with the black-and-blue swelling around his eyes, made him look like he'd been in a fight and lost. The goatee he'd been wearing was gone, so it must have been a disguise, and there was no sign of his glasses.

Seeing me, his eyes glittered with malice. "What's she doing here?"

Dimples motioned me into a chair across from Dex. I wasn't sure I wanted to sit that close, but I sat down anyway, hoping I didn't look as uncomfortable as I felt. Dimples sat next to me, and I relaxed.

"Didn't you know? Shelby works for us. We've got you for kidnapping, attempted rape, and murder."

He jerked. "Murder? I didn't kill anyone." Realizing his mistake, he continued. "And I didn't kidnap or rape her. She came willingly, and there was no sex involved. You've got nothing."

"That's where you're wrong," Dimples said. "Your little friend... your partner in crime... has taken a plea deal. He didn't like getting charged with murder so he told us all about your scheme. He also told us all about Brock Blackwell and what you did to his wife, Sophie."

Dex shook his head in denial. "I don't believe you. You're bluffing. Randy would never rat me out." He was thinking Randy was the perfect partner because he was so afraid of his secret getting out, that he'd never talk.

I huffed out a derisive breath. "You think keeping his secret is worth more to him than going to jail? If you believe that, you don't know him very well."

He went still and glanced between us, knowing that, if Randy talked, it was over. "I'm not saying another word."

I picked up his thoughts of the murder and how it happened. Angry and appalled, I threw them back at him. "We know you drugged Sophie and took her to her room. Things were going fine until her husband showed up. He couldn't believe what was happening at first. His surprise gave you just enough time to attack him. You were in such a panic, that you stabbed him again and again.

"As he lay dying, you had an idea to make it look like a lover's quarrel so Sophie would get the blame. You positioned him on the bed and left Sophie lying next to him in a drugged stupor. You even cleaned yourself up in the bathroom before you left."

My hands curled into fists, and my voice shook with emotion. "Did you know it was their anniversary? They loved each other so much, and you took that away from them. You took their whole lives from them." I swallowed, regaining some control. "But there's something you don't know…"

He had listened with a stone cold face. Now his gaze jerked to mine. Still, he didn't speak, thinking he wouldn't let me get under his skin.

I leaned forward and spoke softly. "Brock is still here." I was telling the truth. I'd felt Brock's presence and it was scaring the crap out of me.

Dex jerked slightly before shaking his head. The man was dead. He'd made sure of that himself.

"Oh... he's dead all right. But that doesn't mean he's gone, and he's more than upset with you. His dying wish was to see you pay for what you did. And, one way or another, that's exactly what you'll do."

Dex sneered, thinking that shit wasn't going to work on him. How gullible did I think he was?

The lights flickered a few times. Then the table began to shake. It got worse, with our chairs shaking so badly that they literally danced across the floor. Dex's chair slipped out from under him and spun across the room. The only thing holding Dex in place were the handcuffs on his wrists attached to the table.

The shaking stopped, and Dimples and I exchanged a surprised glance. He opened his mouth to speak, and the lights went out.

CHAPTER 14

The complete darkness sent my heart racing. I reached for Dimples. Finding his arm, I clutched it tightly. A grunting sound came from across the room, turning into a gut wrenching groan, and the hairs on the back of my neck stood on end.

The chains holding Dex to the table began to clank together, like he was trying to get loose. As he jerked against his bonds, the sound came faster and faster, until I feared he'd break free. Another moan came, higher pitched and increasingly desperate.

Freaking out, I gripped Dimples even harder. Without even thinking about it, we jumped to our feet and backed away from the awful sounds. Our backs hit the wall, but that didn't stop me from clutching Dimples and trying to squeeze into a non-existent space behind him.

We heard another desperate jerk, and Dex began to yell frantically, screaming at something to get away from him. He kept saying the word, no, over and over. Chills ran down my spine, and my legs barely held me up. I wanted nothing more than to get out of that room.

"Let's move to the door so we can get out of here," Dimples said, over the din. He let go of me, and I plastered myself against his back, wrapping my arms tightly around him. He took one step toward the door, dragging me behind.

The noises coming from the area where Dex sat suddenly stopped. What had happened to him? It sounded like someone had tortured and killed him. Was he dead? The silence was almost as frightening as the screaming.

Before Dimples took another step, the lights flashed on.

We froze in place. My breath came fast and my heart pounded, but I wasn't about to let go of Dimples. With apprehension, I turned my gaze toward Dex, hoping I wouldn't find a bloody mess. His hands were still attached to the cuffs, but the rest of him was under the desk, like he'd tried to hide. He poked his head up and glanced around the room, his eyes darting from side to side.

"He's alive." After all that noise he'd made, I could hardly believe it. Dimples straightened, and I reluctantly dropped my arms from around him.

As Dimples moved back toward the table, I followed closely behind. Dex leaned his arms on the table to relieve the pressure on his wrists and licked his lips. He knelt on his knees in front of the desk, breathing heavily.

Dimples surveyed the room for a threat. Finding none, he grabbed Dex's chair and pulled it toward the kneeling man. Dex could barely get his legs under him, and gratefully sat, still out of breath, with his fists clenched and his wrists bruised and bleeding.

His dark eyes were filled with terror and panic. All of his previous cockiness was gone, replaced by shock and fear. His gaze landed on Dimples, and a surge of anticipation filled him. "I'll do it," Dex said. "I'll confess. I did it all. Just like you said. I'll even put it in writing. Just. Get. Me. The Hell. Out of here."

Dimples glanced my way, wondering if this was for real. I nodded, and he stepped toward our chairs, bringing them both back to the desk. I didn't want to get too close to Dex, so I stayed in the back corner, closer to the door.

Dimples stooped to gather the scattered paperwork off the floor and slid a piece of paper toward Dex. Reaching into his suit coat, he pulled out a pen and set it on the paper. "Go ahead. Write it down, and sign it."

Exhaling with relief, Dex eagerly grabbed the pen and began to write. I wasn't sure how legible it would be, since his hand shook so badly.

"And be sure to include what your friend, Randy, did as well," Dimples said. "Since he put the drugs in the drinks."

Dex didn't look up, but gave a slight nod and kept writing. Every so often, his body jerked like he'd been slapped, and his eyes darted to look around the room or at the ceiling. At one point, he glanced into the corner where I stood, and I lurched back to my chair.

With shaking legs, I pulled the chair a little behind Dimples and sat down. Every time Dex jerked, I did too. I even followed his gaze to the corners, but I couldn't see a thing. That didn't mean something wasn't there, especially from what I picked up from Dex's mind. I'd never felt such fear coming from anyone in my life.

Finally reaching the bottom of the page, Dex signed his name. He sat hunched over the table, and his gaze kept darting around the room. "There. It's done." To the ceiling, he said, "Now leave me alone."

Dimples' brow scrunched together. "I didn't make you—"

Dex slammed his fists on the table. "Just get me out of here! Get me the hell out!"

I jerked to my feet and stepped back to my corner, not sure who scared me the most, Dex or the ghost.

Dimples stood. "Take it easy man." He stepped to the door and cracked it open. An officer stood outside, and Dimples motioned to him, pulling the door completely open. "We're done here. Take this guy back to his cell."

The officer came in and unlocked the chain, then took Dex by the arm and led him out. Dex could barely stand, but he shuffled out of the room faster than I could imagine, no longer the confident jerk he was when he entered.

After he left, Dimples turned to me, his eyes wide and mouth slightly ajar. "What just happened?"

Before I could answer, a detective poked his head inside. "Are you guys okay?" Dimples and I exchanged glances before we both nodded. "That was some earthquake. It must have been close. I've never felt anything like it."

"Oh..." Dimples said. "Yeah... crazy." He caught my gaze, thinking there was a lot more going on than that, right?

I nodded. Before I could speak, the scent of Armani drifted through the air. Wafting through the room, like a purifying cleanse. Then it was gone. Dimples caught the scent, and his eyes widened. "That was him?" At my nod, he continued. "When Dex was saying to leave him alone, he wasn't talking about us, was he?"

"Nope."

"But the shaking... that was an earthquake, right?"

"I guess so... but it's kind of strange that the earthquake came right at that precise moment, you know?"

Dimples huffed out a breath and nodded, thinking that experience was way beyond his pay grade, and he hoped nothing like that ever happened to him again. "Come on. Let's get out of here."

It didn't take much to convince me to step from my corner and follow him out of the room. "That was intense."

"No kidding. I'm going to file the report, but I'm putting you down as the driving force behind his arrest. I don't care what Willow or the chief has to say about it."

"Sure, that's fine." I was still a little shaky after the ordeal, and it was hard not to grab his arm, but I managed, and followed closely behind him back into the bullpen. The chief was busy inspecting the building for damage, while everyone else looked a little shocked.

The room didn't seem any worse for wear. No cracks on the ceiling or fallen artwork with broken glass on the floor. The only damage of significance seemed to be a few paper files lying on the floor, which people quickly picked up.

Willow stood by the chief. Catching sight of us, she hurried in our direction. As Dimples continued on to his desk, Willow stopped beside me, placing her hand on my arm. She drew me toward the filing cases where no one could hear us.

Dropping her hand, she leaned toward me like she was sharing a secret. "Wasn't that earthquake insane? I was in the chief's office when it hit. It shook everything up for a few seconds before it quit." She shook her head, thinking it was a sign. One of the clearest signs she'd ever received.

I picked up an image of tarot cards, and my eyes widened. "Were you giving the chief a card reading?" Her face slackened with shock, but she gave me a slight nod. "What did they say?"

She shook her head. "That's just for him, but I tell you... it was the strangest reading I've ever given. I'd just pulled out the reversed Tower card when the earthquake hit. Isn't that crazy?"

I shrugged. "I don't know. What does that mean?"

"When it's reversed like that, it can mean that there's a breakdown or a crisis looming. And just after I pulled it, the earthquake hit."

"Oh... wow... that is interesting."

"Yes, and with the Wheel of Fortune and the Justice cards both reversed as well... it's troubling."

Since I had no idea what that meant, I just nodded. She caught my gaze and came to a decision. "I think my work here is done." She thought, with the turmoil surrounding me, and the pull of chaos it brought, she finally understood that this wasn't the place for her. Not if I was going to stay.

She realized that she'd been caught up in my circle of influence, and now she was thankful she hadn't gone through with her plans to tell the chief about my two-faced nature. I must be a Gemini to work for both sides at once. Add that to my ties with the underworld, and it didn't bode well.

Her use of the word underworld shocked me at first, but then I picked up that she was mostly thinking of it metaphorically as the mob, since underworld encompassed that whole dark-side thing.

She glanced my way, thinking that she had to hand it to me... amid the chaos, I was the great equalizer. I brought the balance. It didn't make sense to her, but it worked, and she knew better than to interfere, especially after the sign of the earthquake. It didn't get more powerful than that.

Holy hell. I wasn't sure what all of that meant, but it sounded like the earthquake had done more for me than I knew. If she was going to accuse me of helping Uncle Joey during the police investigation targeting him, I'd just dodged a bullet.

She met my gaze with a tentative smile, wanting to leave on good terms. "It was nice meeting you, Shelby."

"Uh... yeah. You too."

"You're one of a kind, but I have to warn you..." She glanced around before speaking. "There's a black cloud of trouble that seems to follow you, so be careful, okay? I think you're a force for good, but you're walking a fine line. One false move and it could come back to haunt you."

Why did she have to say haunt? I'd had enough haunting for one day to last a lifetime. I nodded. "Uh... sure. Thanks for the warning."

She nodded, and her gaze fell on Dimples. "It looks like Drew is busy. Do you mind telling him goodbye for me?" A heavy urgency to leave washed over her, and she couldn't wait to get out of the building. Maybe there was an aftershock coming? Whatever it was... she didn't want to be here when it happened.

"Yes... of course."

"Thanks." She turned on her heel and headed straight for the exit.

Whoa. An aftershock? Should I leave too? Dimples sat at his computer, busy writing his report. It didn't look like he needed me for anything else, so I might as well go.

I stepped toward his desk, but a commotion in the hallway caught my attention. I heard Bates before I saw him. He was arguing with a young man and dragging him into the room by the crook of his arm. As he continued toward the interrogation room, he caught sight of me. "Shelby. We got him. Why don't you come with me so we can sort this out?"

Crap. It was Xavier. Was this the disaster Willow was worried about? "Uh... sure."

Filled with misgiving, I followed Bates back into the same room I'd just left. Knowing Brock was gone gave me the courage to go in there, but I still didn't like it.

Bates shoved the young man into the chair Dex had sat in, and took a seat in front of him, motioning me to do the same. "So Xavier," Bates began. "Why did you run?"

Xavier shook his head. "You're a cop. What'd you expect? You have no reason to bring me in. You have no reason at all."

"Whatever, smartass. What were you doing in the park?"

"Duh. Skateboarding."

"Fine, but before we're through, you're going to tell me about the drugs. More important, you're going to tell me why you killed Slasher."

Xavier's eyes widened, but he smirked to hide it. "I didn't kill nobody. I don't even know who that is."

"Oh yeah? Well that's too bad, because we have witnesses. Your car... that gray BMW, was seen leaving the scene of the crime right after Slasher was shot. Does any of that ring a bell in that little piece of gray matter you call a brain?"

Xavier sat back in his chair and folded his arms. "I want a lawyer." He was trying to look tough, but inside, he was scared to death. How had they found him? No one had seen him shoot Slasher, he was sure of it. Why would the cops even care about a low-life drug dealer anyway? Bates didn't respond, so he spoke louder. "Get me my lawyer."

"All right kid. You want a lawyer? We'll get you a lawyer. But it still doesn't change the fact that you murdered someone. You're going away for a long time."

Unable to sit still, Xavier rubbed his hands through his hair. Pursing his lips, he railed against the fact that no one should care so much about a stupid drug-dealer. "I didn't do it."

"I tell you what. We'll go easy on you. Just tell us who put you up to it. Who do you sell for? I'm sure we can get you a deal... maybe even a reduced sentence."

"Put me up to what? I didn't do anything." Then the words hit him. Did the cop want him to rat out the person

Slasher got the drugs from? Slasher had told him he used to work for the mob. Was that what the cop wanted?

He could give up the health-and-nutrition store, since he and Slasher had set up the operation there. He could say that Slasher worked for the mob, but he didn't know any names. Would that help him?

He opened his mouth to speak, but hesitated. How did he know the cops would follow through? He knew they said stuff like that all the time to get confessions, but it didn't do shit. Still, it gave him a small hope that he had a bargaining chip.

Before Bates could push the issue, I jumped in. "So tell me Xavier." I leaned forward. "If you're running a drug operation, why kill Slasher? If he was your supplier, you'd have to get someone else. Did he threaten you or something?"

"I didn't kill him." His thoughts turned to the night Slasher told him he had to lay low for a while. It made him so angry, he could hardly stand it. They had a deal, and this ruined everything. His business would go down the toilet, and the people he sold to would find someone else. Laying low was for sissies.

He remembered how the gun felt, tucked into the back of his pants. The rage burning inside him had to go somewhere, so he'd pulled the gun and shot Slasher. He'd expected to feel elation that he'd gotten rid of the jerk, but it just made him feel sick instead. What the hell had he done?

He had to figure a way out of this before his parents found out. His dad was gonna kill him. This had turned into the worst nightmare. He closed his eyes and tugged at his hair. Who had ratted him out? It had to be someone on his crew... no one else knew anything about it. At least he was high right now, or he'd really be freaking out.

I glanced at Bates. "He's high."

"Yeah." Bates shook his head. "Tell me something I don't know."

I knew it was a rhetorical question, but I answered anyway. "Uh... okay. This is what I've picked up. Slasher was Xavier's supplier, but they were partners in this. When Slasher told Xavier he was taking some time off, Xavier got angry and killed him. It wasn't premeditated... so I think you could go for a lesser sentence."

"What?" Xavier asked, his eyes widening. "That's not what happened. You don't know what you're talking about."

"Yes I do. I just don't know what you did with the gun."

Xavier's thoughts immediately went to the box under his bed. He should have hidden it better, but once he got out of here, he'd see if he could leave it at someone else's house until all this blew over.

"Are you charging me with something?" He'd seen enough on TV to know that we couldn't hold him without bringing charges against him.

Bates glanced my way, thinking he couldn't get away with putting words into the kid's mouth with me there, but he sure wished he could say something about the mob. He thought for sure this Slasher person worked for the mob, but the kid hadn't taken the bait.

"Just tell us who Slasher's supplier is, and we'll go easy on you," Bates said.

"I don't know. Probably the..." He quit talking, realizing he'd almost given away his one bargaining tool. "No. I'm not talking."

"Look Xavier... we don't care so much about who killed Slasher," Bates continued. "We care more about stopping the drug deals in the first place. You give us some names, and we bump the charges down... maybe you'll only serve a couple of years.

"But if you don't help us, we'll throw the book at you. Second-degree murder could put you away for the rest of your life. You want to spend your best years in jail over a low-life drug dealer?"

Alarm tightened my stomach. Bates wanted Uncle Joey so badly that he was willing to tell this kid anything, but none of it was true. Bates wasn't about to go easy on the kid, no matter what he told him. I wasn't sure what to do, but I couldn't let Bates bully this kid into pointing a finger at Uncle Joey.

"Just tell us the truth," I said, hoping to steer Xavier in the right direction.

Xavier started to sweat. No way did he want to go to jail, now or ever. Should he confess? Give the cop something? Yeah... maybe that would work. "I don't know, but I think Slasher worked for the mob."

Crap, crap, crap. How could I stop this?

Bates leaned forward. "Do you have a name?"

Xavier shrugged. "He set up the drug drop at a health-and-nutrition store. I don't know any more than that." He rubbed his face with his hands. What was he doing? This was all too much. He shouldn't be talking to the cops.

"I want my dad. He's a lawyer. I'm not saying another word without him here." His dad would kill him, but at least he wouldn't lie to him and, right now, he was the only person he could trust.

I swallowed my panic. Having the name of the health-and-nutrition store wouldn't necessarily implicate Uncle Joey, right? They weren't selling drugs there anymore, so it wouldn't lead anywhere. And Vinny had promised he'd take the fall if it did. I hoped Uncle Joey was still safe.

Bates huffed out a breath and looked at me. Did I have anything? I tried not to show my nervousness and shrugged. He pursed his lips and shot Xavier a disgusted look. "This is your last chance. It's now or never."

"Never." I had to give it to the kid. He didn't even flinch. That didn't mean this was over. But it was over for now. Bates stood, his chair screeching on the floor. He stomped out, and I glanced at Xavier with sorrow. What a waste. He was only seventeen, and his life was ruined.

"What are you lookin at?" He knew he was in trouble. I had that same look in my eyes as his mother. Damn... why did he shoot Slasher? Why did he take the gun? It was a stupid mistake.

A chill swept over me, and I glanced at the mirror. Was Grizzo watching? Damn. If so, that meant he'd heard about the store—the same store where he'd seen me and Ramos. What was I going to tell him?

This was just getting worse and worse. Suddenly apprehensive, I left the room. Sure enough, Grizzo stepped out of the door down the hall. He'd seen the whole thing and wondered if the scenario I put forward was correct. The health store had been a surprise though. And I had been there. Why? Had I warned them?

With more confidence than I felt, I pinned Grizzo with a hard stare. "I was following a lead at that store. That's how I found out about the kid."

"So you knew about the drug operation?"

"No."

He folded his arms and leaned against the wall. "What about the Tiki Tabu bar? Why did you go there?"

"Like I said, following a lead. Everything I've picked up points to Xavier as the mastermind behind selling the drugs. I don't know where he got them, but I do know that he killed Slasher."

Grizzo nodded. He had his own contacts and agreed with me. Xavier sold the juice to all of his school mates, and

Slasher was just the poor sop who got played. That kid had no conscience, and if I had any information that would put him away, it couldn't come soon enough.

I stepped toward Grizzo. "Tell me something. If that kid goes to jail, what's going to happen to him? Is he going to get rehabilitated? Or is he just a lost cause?"

"That's not my concern. If he broke the law, he pays the consequences, especially for murder."

"I think it should be your concern. It should concern all of us. He's only seventeen."

Grizzo's lips quirked. "That's the mother in you talking. Most of these kids will never change. Once on that path, they never get off."

"So you've never seen anyone turn their life around? Not even once?"

He shrugged, thinking about the gang members he knew. They treated each other like family and, for the most part, it was the only family they had. When they got out of prison, they went right back. It was all they knew. Sure, it wore on him, but there was nothing he could do about it.

I knew it was time to tell him about the gun, especially if it kept Uncle Joey out of it. I just hated sealing that kid's fate. With his dad's help, would he get a second chance? I wasn't sure.

"I picked up something from the kid. He still has the gun. You might want to get a search warrant and check under his bed. It's in a box."

Grizzo's eyes widened. "And you got this from your premonitions?"

"Yeah. But you'd better move fast. Once he tells his father, it's bound to disappear."

He nodded and pulled out his phone to make the call.

I let out a breath and headed back into the office. That was close, and it wasn't over. At least I could warn Uncle

Joey about the store, and he could do damage control. I headed toward Dimples, ready to tell him I was done for the day. He sat at his desk, so I plopped down next to him.

He glanced up and smiled. "Did you notice that Willow left?"

"Yes. She wanted me to tell you goodbye and that she wasn't coming back." His eyes widened. "Yeah... it's true. She couldn't wait to get out of here. I think it was the earthquake. She said something about a crumbling tower on one of her tarot cards and decided this wasn't the place for her."

He lifted his hand for a high-five. "That's the best news I've heard all day."

"Yeah." Smiling, I high-fived him, grateful it was over. "I'm heading out too."

He nodded, thinking I looked a little frazzled. But, after that earthquake and the ghost out for revenge, he could totally understand. "Good idea. You did great today. You and that... other guy."

I huffed out a breath and nodded. "That's for sure."

He wasn't comfortable saying Brock's name out loud, and I didn't blame him. "He really followed through on his dying wish, didn't he? He scared that poor SOB nearly to death. Do you think he's going to haunt Dex for the rest of his sorry life?"

I shrugged. "I have no idea. But I hope not. I hope he moves on to whatever place we go after we die. Or at least that he watches over Sophie for a while until she can stand on her own."

"Yeah... me too. You want to come with me to tell Sophie the news?"

"Uh... I don't know. When are you going?"

"Not for a couple of hours. I've got to get this report done and file it with the DA's office so they can bring charges."

"I think I'll pass. But you can tell me about it."

"Okay." He smiled real big so his dimples twirled, knowing how much I liked them. "Thanks Shelby. I have to admit it's a day I'll never forget."

I chuckled. "Yeah. Me neither."

I left the office feeling totally spent. I'd solved two murders today, but it hadn't brought me any joy. Well... maybe it was nice for Brock to get his revenge, but it had scared me to death. I got the chills just thinking about it.

I also felt bad for Xavier and his family, but at least Uncle Joey should be fine. And... it looked like my job with the police was secure... for now.

Since I'd dressed for a motorcycle ride, I headed over to Thrasher Development. Uncle Joey was sure to be happy that I'd found the killer, and I could warn him about the store. Plus, after all my hard work, he'd be happy to reward me with a motorcycle ride. I just hoped Ramos wasn't too far away for it to happen.

I stepped off the elevator and entered Thrasher to find Ricky sitting at Jackie's desk. "Hey. I just stopped by to talk to Uncle Joey. Is he here?"

"No. I don't know what happened, but Jackie asked me to cover for her."

"Why?"

"She had to take him to the emergency room at the hospital."

My heart stopped, then began to gallop. My lips seemed frozen, and it took a minute to get the words out. "Do you know why?"

He shook his head. "Not exactly. But she didn't sound too concerned. She told me she'd check back in a few hours, but there wasn't a lot on the schedule. I did cancel a couple of appointments for him though."

"What hospital?"

"Uh... she didn't say." He hadn't been too concerned until I'd showed up. Although my tone was even, my face had gone white, and I sounded a little breathless. It made him worried. Did I know something he didn't know? Was Manetto having health issues?

"Okay. I'll give her a call."

"Good. Let me know what's going on."

"Sure."

I stepped into my office and took a couple of deep breaths to calm down. It couldn't be too bad, right? With a heavy heart, I practically dragged myself over to my chair. Sitting, I pulled out my cell and tried Uncle Joey's phone first.

It rang forever before going to voice mail. I left a short message to call me, and tried Jackie. Her phone rang forever too. With my voice pitched a little high, I left another message before disconnecting.

Maybe Ramos would know something? I put the call through to him and held my breath. Come on... pick up, pick up. It went to voice mail, and I nearly sobbed. I swallowed and left another message, which I was sure sounded frantic, even though I tried to hold it together... but seriously? What the freak?

If it wasn't a big deal, then why hadn't she told Ricky? It had to be an emergency of some sort to take him to the hospital. Did that mean he'd had a heart attack, or a stroke, or something horrible like that? If she'd driven him, rather than call an ambulance, maybe it wasn't as serious, but that still didn't mean it wasn't bad.

The picture of my family, along with all the Manettos in New York, caught my gaze. I zeroed in on Uncle Joey's face.

His usually hard, mob-boss expression had transformed into a smile of happiness. He stood beside Miguel, beaming with pride.

I swallowed, noticing a wooden plaque with gold engraving beside the photo. When had this been added to my desk? I picked it up and read the inscription. "No good deed goes unpunished."

My breath hitched, and tears filled my eyes. I blinked rapidly to hold them back, remembering the exact day he'd threatened to put that on my door, and there it was. I wiped the tears from my cheeks and caught sight of the beautiful painting hanging on my wall.

He'd bought that just for me, and had placed it in this office so I could enjoy it. I remembered him saying that it reminded him of me. What had he said exactly? That I was like a burst of color rising out of the darkness? That sounded about right. He'd also told me that I'd made a difference in his life.

Well... he'd certainly made a difference in my life too. Who would have thought I'd be worrying over a mob boss? Still, I couldn't imagine my life without him. What would I do if he died? I closed my eyes and swallowed past the lump in my throat, and tried not to cry. But I couldn't stop the worry. I didn't want him to die. I wasn't ready to lose him.

Time stretched on. I tried to wait more than five minutes, but I just couldn't do it. I picked up my phone, ready to call them all again. Before I pressed the numbers, a knock sounded at my door. It opened, and Ramos poked his head in. I sprang from my chair and rushed toward him.

"What's going on? Is Uncle Joey okay?"

"Yeah... he's okay."

My breath whooshed out, and I threw my arms around him, needing the support. "I was so worried. What happened?" He held me tight, enjoying the feel of me in his arms. He understood my worry and was sorry he hadn't been able to answer his phone.

I pulled away, but he didn't want to let go of me just yet. So I gave in and relaxed against him. He held me tightly, like he needed that contact. After a few seconds passed, worry tightened my stomach. I listened to his mind, but his thoughts were blocked. Did that mean Uncle Joey was okay for now, but Ramos still had bad news to tell me?

I pulled away, and this time, Ramos let me go. A crooked grin broke over his face. "That was nice."

I smacked his arm. "What's going on? Is Uncle Joey okay or not?"

"Yes. He's fine."

"Then what happened?"

He huffed out a breath and shook his head. "Did you feel that earthquake?"

My brows drew together. "Yes, but what has that got to do with it?"

"Well... Manetto was... playing... with his knife. You know how he carries them around. He likes to get them out once in a while and flip them like this." He made a motion with his hand.

I shook my head. "I've never seen him do that."

Ramos shrugged. "Well... when the earthquake struck, he'd just flipped the knife. With all the shaking, he missed catching it, and it fell straight into his foot."

"Oh... ow... I bet that hurt."

"Yeah, it went right through his shoe." Ramos was there when it happened, and I picked up his memory of seeing that knife standing straight up in Uncle Joey's foot. "He pulled it out, but Jackie insisted on taking him to the hospital. After the x-ray, they decided that he didn't need surgery to reattach anything, so they're stitching him up and sending him home. I got your call on my way back here."

I snapped my jaw shut, and shook my head. "That's a relief." I let out a breath and pushed my hair away from my face. "I kept thinking the worst... you know? I mean... he kept talking about me being his successor... and I thought it meant something was wrong with him."

"Yeah... I know what you mean." Taking pity on me, he took my elbow and guided me into a chair. "Well... at the hospital they said nothing else is wrong with him, so we don't need to worry about that."

"Oh... that's a relief."

He nodded. "Yeah... I'm sorry I didn't answer the phone when you called, but I was on the road and couldn't pick up. After I got on the elevator, I listened to your message. You sounded a little frantic, and I felt bad you went through that."

I huffed. "Me? frantic? Why would I be frantic?"

He grinned, then raised his brow. "Want a soda?"

"You know it." I followed him down the hall to his apartment, stopping to let Ricky know that it was just a flesh wound and not to worry. I mentioned the knife and the earthquake and caught a hint of surprise from him, which was soon followed by a grin.

As Ramos handed me a glass of ice and a diet soda, I let out a chuckle. "It is kind of funny, you know? Joey "The Knife" Manetto stabbed himself. I'd laugh more if it hadn't scared me so much, and I've had enough of being scared today."

"Why? What happened?"

He grabbed a drink, and I followed him into the living room. We both slouched on his white couch and enjoyed the view of the city below. Since Ramos knew all about my other secret, that I could hear dead people, I told him the whole story.

He already knew about my brush with Dex from his encounter last night. But he relished hearing that the ghost had kicked his ass, even if it was hard to believe. "He confessed?"

"Yup."

"So the earthquake... you think that was the ghost too?"

"Nah." I shook my head. "It couldn't be... right?" I took the last swallow of my drink and set the glass on the coffee table. "Oh... and we caught Xavier... the kid who killed Slasher? There might be a problem."

I filled him in on the health-and-nutrition store, and he promptly called Vinny, telling him to put the word out that the cops were onto the store and to stay away from it. He also called to warn the store manager in case the police showed up.

Finished, he turned his gaze my way. "There's nothing there for the cops to find, so that should take care of it."

"There's one more thing. Grizzo might check you out. Do I need to worry?"

He shrugged. "He can try, but I've got it under control." He was thinking that he had his own connections and he'd be fine, but it pleased him to know I had his back. He raised his brow. "Want to go for a ride?"

My heart soared. "I thought you'd never ask."

CHAPTER 15

Nothing beat a motorcycle ride with Ramos to make me feel better. It ended sooner than I liked, but I'd take what I could get. Still, even after the ride with Ramos, I drove into my garage feeling totally drained. How was that possible? Of course, I'd had more than one scare for the day, so that probably accounted for it.

Since we'd already had pizza this week, I'd stopped at a sandwich shop on the way home for our dinner. My kids weren't nearly as happy to see me as Coco, but it was nice to catch up and relax. With the earthquake the major focus, it surprised me that my kids had hardly felt it. I checked the Internet and found that it had been a minor magnitude quake of about 3.5 on the Richter scale.

To find that the epicenter of the quake was just a few yards east of the police station made a lot of sense. Most of the downtown buildings felt the quake, but the only damage at the station was an ornamental vase that had broken in half.

Then there was Uncle Joey. He'd had his moment with the quake that hadn't turned out so well, but at least it wasn't life-threatening. I still couldn't believe he'd gone to the emergency room, and that it had scared me to death. Sure, I didn't want him to die, but I also wasn't ready to be his successor. I wished there was a way out of it, but I didn't see how it was possible. He was counting on me. How could I let him down?

That left the earthquake. I couldn't decide if there was a connection between the quake and Brock's dying wish. It seemed crazy that it was just a coincidence, but I didn't want to think about that too hard. I was just grateful that Dex had confessed and was going away for a long time.

Chris was grateful too, especially after he found out what had happened to me last night at the hotel bar. He didn't like hearing about my drink getting spiked, or that I'd put myself in danger without Dimples to back me up. But he held it all in and didn't criticize me once. In fact, he only interrupted me when I brought up Ramos.

"Wait... so... you called Ramos?" That was the part he liked the least.

"Uh... yeah. My cell phone was missing, but luckily, I had the burner phone with his number already programmed in. It was a good thing you called Uncle Joey and talked him into getting one for me, otherwise, I don't know what would have happened."

"Yeah." He reluctantly agreed, especially since looking at it that way didn't leave him much room to complain. "You're right."

"But it all turned out okay. And you should have seen Dex. Ramos punched him a couple of times, and I think he even broke his nose. At least he got what he deserved. Then Dimples took over and covered for Ramos, even taking his spot in the narrative. I thought that was pretty nice of him."

Chris nodded. "Yeah... I suppose so."

"Then there was the earthquake today. Did you feel it?"

"Yeah, but nothing really shook... mostly, the building just swayed a bit."

"Well, it happened right as Dimples and I were questioning Dex, who refused to cooperate. He sure changed his tune after that." I filled him in, including how scared I'd been, and how badly it had terrified Dex. "He wrote down his confession and signed it so he could get out of that room. After they took him away, I smelled the Armani cologne, then it was gone too. I hope that means Brock is done, but honestly, I have no idea."

"That's crazy... you think Brock made the earthquake happen?"

"No way. That's... I just can't believe that. Still, there was another benefit because it convinced Willow that working for the police wasn't for her." I filled him in on what happened, and he was surprised she'd given up so easily.

"I guess if she took the earthquake as a sign, it makes sense."

"True. But after she left, Bates brought in Xavier." I explained that whole deal and Chris could hardly believe so much had happened.

"But there's more." I told him about visiting Thrasher, only to find that Uncle Joey had been taken to the emergency room. "It all turned out okay, but it scared me to death, too."

"What happened?" I explained Uncle Joey's accident with his knife during the earthquake, and Chris got a chuckle out of that.

"It's been a weird day. I mean, the ghost was bad enough, but thinking that Uncle Joey might be dying just about did me in."

"No doubt." He thought my fear probably had a lot to do with being named Uncle Joey's successor. He still wasn't sure how he felt about that. "You've certainly been busy."

"You can say that again."

We were in our room getting ready for bed, and Chris began to pull off my shoes. He started rubbing my foot, and it felt so good that I flopped back on the bed and groaned. He moved to the other foot, paying special attention to the pad and joints. Next, he traveled from my ankle and on up my leg, rubbing my calves with his magic hands.

Happy and relaxed, he helped me out of my clothes, and I kissed him tenderly. "You sure know how to help me feel better." I unbuttoned his shirt.

He sent me a sexy smile. "It's a job I take rather seriously."

I laughed. "And you're very good at it, too."

"Oh baby, oh baby."

I woke the next morning at eight, surprised that I'd slept so well. In fact, I hadn't had one nightmare, even after the ghostly visit at the precinct. Maybe things were looking up. Of course, it helped that I'd solved a couple of cases yesterday. Now, I had one more to go... only this case seemed the most difficult.

I hadn't heard a thing from Misti, so I hoped my appointment to meet with her and her mother today would actually happen. Still, each time my phone rang, I held my breath, worried that they'd cancel. At ten-thirty, with no call, I was ready to go. I gathered some treats and a couple of dog toys for Coco, and we were off.

I pulled up in front of the imposing house and called Misti. She told me to come to the side of the house opposite the driveway, and she would let me in the gate to the back yard. Coco followed me with his ears up, curious about where we were going.

Misti stood at the gate, waiting. She pulled it open and we stepped inside, catching sight of Ava standing behind her mother. Seeing the little girl excited Coco. He dropped his head, and his tail wagged furiously. Ava squealed, and he trotted straight to her side, sniffing her, like he was making sure she was all right.

He held perfectly still while she put her arms around his neck and kissed him. She patted him and hugged him, all while talking a mile a minute. Coco licked her a few times, and she giggled.

"Let's move into the backyard," Misti said.

We walked around the house into a beautifully manicured yard, lined with shade trees and a covered deck, connected to the house by a set of patio doors. In the back corner, a small stream flowed down a rocky path and into a shallow pond. Another small patio set, with cushioned chairs and a table, were arranged by the water feature, making it private and lovely.

Misti led me to the patio by the pond, and the sound of the trickling water played pleasantly in the background. On the table, a pitcher of lemonade, along with a plate of fruit, awaited us. I opened the small backpack that contained Coco's toys and treats, and showed them to Ava and Misti so they could play with Coco.

I picked up that Misti had never had a dog before, and she was a little nervous around them, but, with Coco, she let go of her fear and began to enjoy his company. After playing for a while, Misti sat down and poured the lemonade.

I took a swallow, enjoying the fresh-squeezed tartness. "Is your mother going to join us?"

"I'm not sure." Misti shouldn't have been surprised by her mother's vitriolic response to my visit, but it still upset her. It got worse after she'd found out I was bringing a dog. Apparently, she hated dogs, even the one who'd found Ava. That stung even more, but her mother was like that.

I glanced up at the windows in the house. At a second-story window, I caught sight of a woman watching us. She was thin, with a patrician nose and a scowl on her face. Her short, white hair poked up in a few places. She caught me staring, and the curtain dropped.

"I take it she doesn't like dogs?"

Misti shrugged. "I guess not." She smiled, hoping to soothe any hurt feelings that might have caused me. "But I'm really glad you're here. Ava's having a blast." Coco lay on the grass, and Ava sat beside him, showing him a flower she'd picked.

"Ava's adorable. How old is she?"

"Five."

"How did she get lost?" I listened while Misti spoke about that day, looking up at the window every so often, in case Carolyn watched us. After hearing the story, along with the happy ending, I was pretty sure Carolyn wasn't going to come down. I picked up that Misti didn't think so either.

Without talking to Carolyn first, I wasn't sure if telling Misti about my suspicions was a good idea. I mean... what if I was wrong? On the other hand, if I asked Misti what she thought about the picture, maybe she'd get her mother to see me.

It was now or never, so I reached into my purse and pulled out Misti's photograph. "I thought you might want to see this." I handed it to her, and her eyes widened with surprise.

"It's Ava. But I don't recognize it. Where did you get this?"

"That's the thing. It's not Ava. I think it might be... you."

"Me? But... I've never seen this before. How can it be me?" She studied it, thinking it looked exactly like her, but the age was wrong. In this photo she was two or three. "My mother doesn't have pictures of me at this age. She told me all my baby pictures were destroyed in a fire. Did someone give this to you?"

I nodded, not quite sure how to continue. "Yes. Mack Haywood had a whole album full of pictures just like this one, including baby pictures."

She caught my gaze. Was I trying to pull something over on her? "What are you saying?"

"I was hoping to talk to your mother, so she could explain. I don't know exactly what this means, but I have a pretty good idea, and it involves Mack Haywood. Do you want to hear it from me, or shall we ask her?"

Misti sat back in her chair, her breath coming out in short little gasps. Did this mean that something had happened to her? When she was a child? "So if this is me... what do you think happened?"

"I think... you were taken away from your family... and raised by someone else."

Misti's breath caught. "You mean kidnapped? And you think..." Her gaze swiveled up to her mother's room. How could it be possible? If I was right... did this mean her mother wasn't really her mother, and she'd... kidnapped her? What the hell? That was insane. Still... in a place where she'd never admitted it... she'd known there had been something missing... something wrong... all her life.

In the first place, she didn't look a thing like her mother, and she never had. Her hair and eye coloring were completely different. They had different body types. In fact, nothing about them matched, and it had always bothered her.

Then there was her father. She'd always believed that she must have taken after him, but her mother had refused to talk about him. There were no pictures of him, or any of his possessions that remained behind after he left. When she did mention him, the story seemed to change every time her mother spoke. But, most of the time, the subject was strictly forbidden.

If this was true, it made sense that her mother had been so secretive. She'd made up the story that her father had left her right after Misti had been born. It meant that her mother's reticence to talk wasn't because he'd broken her heart... it was because he'd never existed.

Misti inhaled sharply, thinking that it explained her mother's constant neediness. She'd tried to escape her mother's controlling will all her life, even finding a college far away. But nothing really changed. Her mother had always found a way to weasel back into her life. It usually involved money that came with conditions attached.

Even after she'd found a husband, and had a child of her own, her mother had managed to insinuate herself into her life. Look at her. Here she was, right back with her mother where she started.

But this... could it be true? "Tell me everything. I want to know."

I opened my mouth to speak, but the sound of her mother's voice calling from the house stopped me.

"Misti? Misti!"

My gaze jerked to the window, finding that Carolyn had pulled it open and was leaning her head out. "Can you come up here for a minute? I'm ready to meet your friend, but I need your help first."

Misti frowned, unhappy to put me off, but years of dealing with Carolyn kicked in, and she couldn't turn her down. "Will you watch Ava for a minute?"

"Of course."

With a nod, she hurried inside. I glanced back at the window, but Carolyn had disappeared. Had she heard us talking? It sure seemed like it. So what was she planning to tell Misti? I noticed the photograph sitting on the table and picked it up.

As far as proof went, this was kind of flimsy. Could Carolyn convince Misti that I was wrong without promising to look into it? From what I'd picked up, Misti wanted to know, but would she defy her mother to find out? Her mother held something over her, but what? Her fortune? I had no doubt that Carolyn had a lot of money; maybe that was part of it.

Several tense minutes later, Misti emerged from the house, her face flushed and angry. I picked up that her mother had used her illness as leverage to keep Misty from upsetting her and had denied the whole thing. The reprimand from Carolyn accusing Misti of being taken in by me still stung.

Misti held my gaze, wondering if I was the gold-digger her mother had insinuated. Had I made it all up for a piece of her fortune? I didn't seem the type. Then there was the photo. Was it a fake? But what about Mack and the dog? Something was going on... and she needed to know the truth. "Mother will see you now."

"Okay. Good." Facing Carolyn was the only way to settle this. I just hoped Misti wasn't swayed, especially if her mother accused me of lying. I stood, clutching the photograph in my hand, and took a few steps toward the house before glancing over my shoulder. "Aren't you coming?"

"No. She wants to see you alone."

A chill ran down my spine. "Oh... don't you want to hear what she has to say?"

"Yes but... she insisted on talking to you first. I'll come up when you're done."

"Uh... I don't think that's a good idea. You should be there too."

Misti shook her head. "It's fine. Besides, her health isn't the best, and I don't want to upset her too much. After she's spoken to you is soon enough. Her room is on the second floor. Just go inside and take the staircase. Her room is on the far end. The door's open, and she's sitting in a chair by the window."

I nodded, picking up that Misti was slightly embarrassed, but, if I had ulterior motives like her mother claimed, she was best suited to deal with it.

Ulterior motives? Crap. If she'd convinced Misti to doubt me so quickly, she was a force to be reckoned with. But I was up for it. I could read her mind, so I had a huge advantage. If I was wrong then fine, but if she was a murderer, she needed to pay.

I stepped toward the house, and Coco immediately followed. "Oh, hey boy... you need to stay here. I'm just going inside for a minute, but I'll be right back. Okay?" Coco sat on his haunches and stared at me. I ruffled the fur around his ears and gave him a pat. "Stay."

He woofed, but this time it wasn't *yup* like I expected. It sounded almost like a growl. *Watch out.* Hearing that took me by surprise. "Watch out?"

Yup.

I nodded and smiled. "I'll be careful."

Yup.

I entered the house, glancing over my shoulder to see Coco in the exact spot that I'd told him to stay. He hadn't moved an inch. He was lying down on his stomach with his head up and his ears standing tall. Wow. That was impressive, and it was nice to know I had backup if I needed it.

I passed through the kitchen and into the big, open floor of the main house. To my left, a large staircase, with a heavy, wooden balustrade, went up to the second floor. It seemed to take forever to get to the top, but that was probably just my nerves.

At the top, I continued to the end of the hall, where a door leading into a bedroom stood open. I stepped inside and found Carolyn sitting in a plush, scarlet-colored, wingback chair. She sat straight and tall, as if the chair was her throne, and I'd been granted an audience.

Her sharp eyes were gray and cold, matching her silver hair. She was a little pale, but she looked pretty spry to me, and I wondered how sick she really was. She wore a yellow blouse over white capri pants, and the sandals on her feet showed off her red painted toenails.

"Shelby Nichols." She tilted her head to study me. "You've certainly made a nuisance of yourself. Why are you filling my daughter's mind with lies? What do you want?" Her piercing gaze caught mine with glittering accusation.

"I'm investigating Mack Haywood's murder, and I want the truth."

"That has nothing to do with me."

"That's where you're wrong. It must have been a surprise to see Mack after all these years. You probably didn't recognize him at first. When did you figure it out?"

"I don't know what you're talking about."

Ignoring her, I continued. "Was it after he called you on the phone and mentioned that he'd lost his daughter all those years ago?"

She swallowed. "He didn't tell me anything about that."

"Is that why you agreed to meet him at his house? So you could convince him that Misti wasn't his missing daughter?"

"Stop it. You don't know what you're talking about. We never spoke about that."

My brows rose. "But he did invite you to his house... maybe to look at some of his old photos? Like this one?" I held the photo out to her. "Go ahead. Take a good look and tell me that's not Misti... or should I say... Macie?"

She twitched, but otherwise held onto her regal demeanor. She stared at the photo and hesitated before snatching it from my hands. "This means nothing. You can do all kinds of things on the computer these days."

Guilt and fear tore into her. She couldn't believe I had come to ruin all of her carefully laid plans. This couldn't be happening. Not right now. Why had Mack ever found them? If only Ava hadn't run away. She thought she'd taken care of it by killing Mack, but now I was there. Me and that damn dog.

She turned her head to gaze out the window, and I could see that she had a perfect view of the back yard. With the window open, the sounds of Ava and Misti talking were easy to pick up, and I knew she'd heard every word of my conversation with Misti. Coco sat in the same spot, and I realized he hadn't moved, even with Ava trying to distract him.

Glancing back at me, she gave in to her anger and ripped the photo in half. "You don't know what you're talking about. You have no proof. And now you're trying to spread these horrible lies. Misti doesn't believe you. She won't believe that I'm not her mother. I've been a good mother, and I've taken care of her all her life. She won't throw that away."

I shook my head. "It's too late for that. She's seen the photo. She wants to know the truth. You can't keep it from her anymore. It's time she found out who her real family is, and what you did all those years ago."

"I don't know what you mean, but if you're looking for a payout, I might consider it, as long as you take your dog and get out. Otherwise, I'm calling the police."

My brows rose. "You think I want to blackmail you?"

"You're here and you're upsetting my daughter. What else is there?"

My eyes widened. "I don't want your money. You've just... you've gotten away with this for a long time, but you crossed the line when you killed Mack Haywood. When Misti finds out that you kidnapped her and killed her father, do you think she'll stand by you?

"This won't have a happy ending, but there's a chance you could still salvage something if you tell Misti your side of things. If she hears it from you, it might make a difference, but, once you go to jail, you know it will be too late. She'll never want to talk to you again."

I knew that appealing to her sense of right and wrong was a long shot, but it was worth a try.

Carolyn shook her head, and slumped in her chair. "You think you have this all figured out, but you're wrong. When she was little, she got lost in the woods. Her parents were negligent and careless. They lost her. It was their fault, and they didn't deserve a child."

I picked up her thoughts that Mack was a horrible parent because he'd let Misti wander away. Her memory of that day came through loud and clear. Misti had wandered off while Mack had his back turned, and Carolyn had seen an opportunity and followed the child. She'd scooped up the little girl and taken her home, and she'd done it for the child's own good.

"When did Mack figure it out?"

She sighed and closed her eyes, remembering how shocked she'd been to see him with the search party. After the elation of finding Ava had died down, Mack had approached her. He'd marveled at how much Ava looked like his missing daughter.

Carolyn had feigned ignorance, and agreed to keep in touch, knowing he was a danger to her if he ever figured it out. Only a few days had gone by before he invited her to his house, telling her he wanted to show her something. She knew right then that he had to go.

He'd been so trusting, even putting the dog in the other room, and when he turned his back, she didn't hesitate to kill him. She had to do it to protect Misti and Ava. It was her duty.

Whoa. Hearing that chilled my blood, and the hairs on my arms stood on end. How was I going to get her to confess? She seemed half crazy. I needed Misti to hear all of this, but how could I get her up here?

Carolyn straightened and caught my gaze. "I'm not letting her go."

I shook my head. "I'm going to tell Misti the truth, but I'll make one concession; I'll bring her up here and you can tell her your side of it first, before I tell her mine. Then we'll let her decide who to believe."

"No. No... you can't tell her. She can't know anything about it. She'll leave me. I... I need her." Her regal bearing disappeared and desperation filled her voice. "You don't understand. She's all I've got. I'm an old woman. I'm not going to last much longer. I have congestive heart failure... and the doctor told me that I only have a few months left. You can't do this to me."

She hadn't started begging yet, so I shook my head, not about to be taken in by her act. She picked up on that and continued, sounding even more desperate. "Think about Misti... and Ava. This will devastate them both. Misti... might never get over it. She'll never what to see me again."

I took a deep breath and shook my head. "I'm sorry, but I can't do that."

Her eyes filled with tears. "But... can't you see that I'm dying? I can't face my death without my daughter. The one person I love more than anything in this world. I need her by my side. I don't want to die alone. Please... can't you wait?"

She picked up my reticence, and tried a different tactic. "I'll give you money... whatever you want. Just give me a little more time with her. Please... it's my only wish before I die, the only thing that I want. It's the only thing I have left. Please... I'm sorry for everything that happened. But you... have to understand... please... don't tell her... just wait until I'm gone."

I didn't know if she was telling the truth about dying or not, but I wasn't about to agree with her. She'd taken a little girl from her family and killed her father to keep it a secret. She didn't deserve my compassion... but I had to give her an out. "You might not have to die alone if you tell Misti the truth and ask for her forgiveness. But that's the only way this is happening. I'm going to tell her. Do you want to tell her your side of it, or not?"

She shrank into herself with grief. I would have felt sorry for her if I hadn't picked up the barely controlled rage that simmered just below the surface. She was thinking that I was heartless and cruel, making her go through this right before the end.

"All right," she said, her voice shaking. Tears fell from her eyes. "I'll agree. Just let me talk to her alone first. Then you can join us." She glanced up and met my gaze. Beneath all those tears, her eyes glittered with rage.

Yikes. A need to run washed over me, and I quickly agreed with her. "Good. I'll get her."

I turned on my heel and stepped into the hallway, relieved to get out of there. Nearing the head of the stairs, I heard a rustling noise. Glancing over my shoulder, I caught sight of her right behind me. Holding a hammer in a tight grip, she raised her arm above her head, and swung with all her might.

With a yelp, I dodged the blow and rushed toward the stairs. She followed closely behind, surprising me with her speed. Before I could put any distance between us, she swung again. I jerked to the side and stumbled on the top stair.

I managed to stop my fall, but a shove from behind sent me tumbling down the staircase. I hit my shoulder hard and began to roll, sending pain into my hips and arms with every turn. I managed to raise my arms protectively around my head and kept rolling to the bottom. Coming to an abrupt stop, I took in a shaky breath, dazed and disoriented.

Dizziness engulfed me, and I wasn't sure I could move without something hurting. I lay flat on my back and had a clear view of Carolyn gasping at the top of the staircase. Her eyes widened to see me looking at her, and her face turned dark and vicious.

She slowly made her way down the stairs, her focus laser sharp and her eyes full of contempt. In one hand, she held the hammer; and with the other, she clung to the railing. As she descended, her breath came in little gasps, but her eyes held an angry gleam. She could hardly wait to kill me.

I got my arms under me and pushed to a sitting position. Pain exploded in my shoulder, but I fought through it. As I tried to stand, another sharp pain burst from my ankle. With no time to lose, I scooted backwards on my butt, looking for anything I could use as a weapon to stop her.

Coco began barking frantically at the patio door, his paws scratching against the glass. I kept backing up, reaching a small round table with a lamp on top. I grabbed the table leg, hoping to knock it into Carolyn's path and slow her down.

Seeing this, Carolyn rushed down the last few steps, desperate to finish me off. She raised the hammer with both hands, her face a mask of rage.

The patio door burst open, and Coco charged into the room. Without hesitation, he rushed at Carolyn, his bark sounding more menacing than I'd ever heard it. She screamed, and he knocked her down with his front legs. The hammer fell from her hand, and he stood over her with his teeth bared and his growl deep.

I felt his readiness to rip her throat out. He recognized her smell, and knew at once that she was the one who'd killed his master. His bark turned deadly, and I thought for sure he was going to kill her.

"Coco. Stop. Stop."

He kept barking, but a part of him heard me, so I continued to talk to him, telling him to stop. After a tense moment, his barking turned into a low growl, and I let out a breath, finding Carolyn cowering against the wall at the bottom of the stairs. Other than quivering with fright, she wasn't harmed.

Coco stood over her, continuing to growl with his teeth bared and his jaws inches from her face. Carolyn whimpered under him. She tucked her face into her chest and raised her arms to cover her head.

"Coco. That's enough. Come here. Come. Now." I got to my knees and managed to push into a standing position. I tested my ankle and found that I could put a little weight on it to keep my balance. I carefully moved toward Coco, needing to grab him if he didn't retreat. I couldn't let him hurt her. They'd have him killed for it.

From the corner of my eye, I caught sight of Misti and Ava watching, horror and fear on their faces. They didn't understand what was going on, but Coco's menacing growl and bared teeth frightened them.

Coco's growling slowed, and he sensed the person under him was no longer a threat. Listening to my direction, he backed a few steps away, never taking his eyes off Carolyn. As soon as he reached my side, I took a knee and wrapped my arms around his neck. "Good boy, Coco. Good boy."

"What happened?" Misti asked. "Mother, what's going on?"

Carolyn scooted closer against the wall, hiding the hammer under her, thinking she'd hit the dog if he got close again. Seeing Misti's confused gaze, she spoke. "That woman tried to kill me. She pushed me down the stairs when I wouldn't give in to her demands. You need to call the police." She glanced my way. "And get that dog out of my house."

Coco lowered his head and bared his teeth, his low growl rumbled through the room. Instinctively, Carolyn raised the hammer in front of her, surprising Misti that she had a weapon and was strong enough to hold it.

Carolyn opened her mouth to yell, but Coco barked with menace and took a step toward her. Carolyn snapped her mouth shut and cowered against the wall, still holding the hammer in front of her.

I glanced at Misti. "I'll call the police." In my tumble down the stairs, my purse had come off my shoulder and landed on the floor a few steps away. As I limped toward it, I groaned with pain.

Coco turned his head to glance my way and whined. "I'm okay, boy. You're doing great. Stay right there."

That brought Misti out of her shock, and she turned to me with a whisper. "Did she push you?"

"Yes."

Misti glanced Carolyn's way, noticing the sheen of sweat on her face, and unsure about what to do.

Carolyn caught Misti's gaze and spoke. "What are you waiting for? Get that dog away from me and call the police."

At her outburst, Coco lowered his head and growled again. It shut Carolyn up, and I finally got my phone out of my purse. Misti had been holding Ava in her arms and now took her into the kitchen to call her husband, needing his help to get this sorted out.

Since I didn't have Williams's or Clue's numbers in my contacts list, I called Dimples. He answered right away. "Hey Shelby. How's it going?"

"Um… okay, but… I'm in kind of a tight spot." I quickly explained where I was and asked him to send a car and the detectives. "She attacked me. Coco's guarding her, so we're good for now, but I need help."

"Right… got it. Hang on." I heard him talking, and then he came back on. "Are you okay?"

"Oh… I'm a little banged up. She pushed me down some stairs, but I'll survive."

"Damn. I'm coming too."

"You don't—" He'd already hung up, so I slipped the phone back into my purse. Needing to sit down, I sat on the rug and leaned against the back of the couch, close to the stairs, while Coco kept guard over Carolyn.

A few minutes later, Misti came out, still holding Ava on her hip. She wasn't sure what to do about Carolyn. With her mother sitting at the bottom of the steps, and holding a hammer like she knew how to use it, Misti decided to let the cops handle it.

"The police are on their way," I said, hoping to sound reassuring. I even tried to smile, but it hurt my cheek where I'd hit the stairs a few times.

Misti nodded. "My husband's coming too. I'm worried about Ava." The little girl was sucking her thumb and resting her head against Misti's shoulder. Her eyes drooped, like she was ready for a nap. "Is it okay if I take her outside and wait for the police out there?"

"Sure."

As Misti opened the door, Carolyn perked up. "Where do you think you're going? You come back here. You can't leave me with that dog." Coco put his head down, bared his teeth, and growled. That shut her up and she cowered back into her corner. With a shiver, Misti slipped out, grateful to be away from Carolyn.

The minutes slowly ticked by. Carolyn tried to get up a couple of times, but Coco growled to keep her there. She yelled at me once, threatening to sue me if I didn't get my dog away from her, but Coco snapped at her and she shut up.

Eight minutes later, the police showed up. Misti had left the door open, and I heard them asking her to explain what was going on. Upon hearing a dog was involved, one of them suggested they call animal control.

At that, Carolyn started yelling. "Help. That dog's trying to kill me."

The officer rushed in, took one look at the dog standing over her, and assumed she told the truth. As she continued to yell, Coco barked and stepped closer until she shut up. Worried the dog was ready to attack, the cop fingered his gun, thinking he might have to shoot Coco.

Alarm rippled over me. "Dude. Don't you dare pull your weapon. I'm Shelby Nichols. I work for the police, and this is my dog. I swear, if anything happens to him, I'll have your badge."

He didn't back away, but he didn't pull his gun either. My name rang a bell, but the old lady looked like she was scared to death. How could she even hold that hammer up, let alone threaten anyone with it?

Clue came through the door, followed by Williams. They took in the scene, and Clue spoke. "Hey Shelby. What's going on here?"

I thought about standing, but couldn't muster the strength. "Guys, this is Carolyn Brinkley. She killed Mack Haywood, and I can prove it. See that hammer she's holding? That's the murder weapon. And she just tried to kill me with it. If it wasn't for my dog, she might have succeeded."

Williams nodded. "Okay. Why don't you call off your dog, and we'll get this sorted out."

"Uh... right." Part of me enjoyed having Coco terrify her, but all good things must come to an end, right? "Coco. Come." He didn't budge. Oh great, now what? The police officer was thinking of the word release, so I tried that. "Coco. Release. Come."

That did the trick, and Coco rushed to my side. He whined and licked my face, letting out little yips that sounded like *you safe, you safe.* "Yup. I'm good, thanks to you." After a few more licks, I gave him some reassuring pats, and he sat down beside me.

Released from Coco's vigil, Carolyn didn't waste any time telling Clue and Williams that I was lying. Through her tirade, they had the officer bag the hammer, and Clue read Carolyn her rights while Williams handcuffed her.

"You can't do this to me. I did nothing wrong. That woman attacked me. I was just defending myself." Out on the porch, she caught sight of Misti and started all over again. "Misti... help me. I didn't push her. This is all a mistake. You've got to stop this."

I managed to get to my feet, and followed them out. Leaning against the doorjamb, I watched the police load her into the back of the car. With her screaming and yelling, I felt a little sorry for them, but it was a big relief to have her gone.

As they drove away, Dimples drove up. He jumped out of his car and hurried to my side. "You okay?" He examined me, thinking my hair was mussed, and my cheek was scraped and bruised.

I automatically touched my cheek, finding it more swollen than I liked. "I hope this doesn't give me a black eye."

Dimples smiled, remembering the two black eyes I'd had after the shootout in Uncle Joey's office. The dimples in his cheeks swirled, and I had to smile back, even though it hurt my cheek.

"Anything else hurt?"

"Well... I hit my shoulder, but it's not too bad." I moved my shoulder and only felt a little pain. "And I must have twisted my ankle, because it hurts to walk."

He wondered if I needed a doctor, and I quickly shook my head. "No. I'm not hurt that bad. Just a few bumps and bruises." It warmed my heart to have him there to look after me, just like we were partners again.

"Okay. Let's get you back inside so you can sit down." He slid an arm around my waist and helped me limp to the couch. Williams and Clue followed, and I picked up their worry that they'd just arrested an old woman, whom I'd said was a killer. I'd better be right or they were in deep shit.

I sat down and rolled my eyes. They were worried about her? Of course, they didn't know the whole story, so I began with the search for Ava a few weeks ago. "Mack and Coco," I indicated the dog lying at my feet, "found Ava safe and sound."

Misti and her husband entered the house, catching that part, so they quickly sat down to listen. Ava had fallen asleep in Misti's arms, but she woke up and squirmed off her lap. Ava stepped beside Coco and lay down next to him, quickly falling back asleep.

I explained how I'd ended up with Coco, which had led me to find Austin. I caught Misti's gasp to realize she might have a brother. She was still shocked to think her mother had kidnapped her and she wasn't her mother at all.

I continued, telling them of Carolyn's meeting with Mack, and how she'd planned to kill him all along.

Misti could hardly believe that her mother had killed the man who might be her father. It left her so bereft and shaken that she couldn't stop the tears from flowing down her cheeks. Could this really be happening?

Part of her could hardly believe that her mother had kidnapped her, and another part of her was relieved that Carolyn wasn't her mother. It was going to take her a long time to get over the betrayal.

"So," Clue said. "She admitted to you that she killed Mack?"

She hadn't said the words out loud, but I'd heard them just the same. "Yes. And she didn't want Misti to know. That's why she tried to kill me."

"Okay. We'll get forensics to take a look at the hammer for evidence. Even if she washed it, there might be something there to link it to Mack's murder." She stood, signaling that they were done. "We might need you back at the station later, but I'll call you first."

"Sure."

Clue glanced at Misti. "I'm sure this has been a shock to you. Is there anything we can do to help?"

She shook her head. "Not right now. I need some time."

"Of course. We'll be in touch. Here's my card if you need anything."

Clue and Williams left, leaving Dimples behind. "Can I walk you to your car?"

Misti glanced my way, overcome with a sudden need to talk to me. I glanced at Dimples and smiled. "I think I'll stay a little longer. But thanks for coming."

"You bet."

After he left, Misti sat down in his place. "So she really admitted it? She took me from my real family?"

I nodded, and explained what I'd picked up from Carolyn's mind as if she'd said it all out loud. "She rationalized it... to make it all okay in her mind. I guess she really wanted a daughter."

"So my real last name was Haywood?" At my nod, she continued, "What about my first name?"

"It's Macie... with an ie... Macie Haywood."

Misti sighed and shook her head. "It's hard to believe this is for real. What if it's a mistake, and he's not my father after all?"

"I'm sure you can do a blood test to confirm, but Carolyn admitted it. I don't think it's a mistake."

"I still might want a blood test... just to make sure." She chewed on her bottom lip, reminding me so much of Austin that my breath caught.

"Your brother, Austin, is my client. I have to tell him what happened to his dad... your dad. When you're ready, I'd be happy to arrange a meeting between the two of you. I'm sure he'll want to meet you."

Her hopeful gaze caught mine. "He's younger, right?"

"Yes, about three years younger."

She had so many questions about him... about her whole family. Her dad was gone, but what about her mom? A deep foreboding overcame her. "You haven't mentioned my real mother. Is that because she's ... gone?"

"Yes... I'm afraid so."

"They're both gone?" Tears coursed down her cheeks. "Now I'll never know them."

My eyes clouded with tears for her loss. Her grief was so new and real, it broke my heart. I slipped my arm around her shoulders. "They're not completely gone. You have a brother. He can tell you all about them."

She nodded, and I sat back. We both wiped tears from our cheeks. "I should go." I glanced at Misti's husband, realizing we hadn't met. "Hi, I'm Shelby."

"Oh... I'm so sorry." Misti quickly introduced her husband to me. Beneath his calm exterior, he was almost as shocked as Misti, but a part of him felt profound relief. He'd never liked Carolyn, and now he knew why. If this was all true, they would finally be finished with her meddling and manipulative ways. Their lives could be so much better.

At my request, he happily gathered Coco's toys and treats from the back yard. He even offered to walk me to my car. Since I needed the help, I took him up on it. We ushered Coco into the back seat. After I got settled behind the wheel, he told me they'd be in touch and closed the door.

As I drove home, I counted my blessings. I'd survived a fall down the stairs that could have killed me. I had an amazing dog who had saved me from serious damage by a hammer-wielding crazy lady, and, since it was my left ankle that was sprained, I could still drive my car.

Now all I needed were a couple of pain pills and a diet soda. That, along with nothing to do for the rest of the day, and I'd be set, which, of course, wasn't going to happen. I needed to let Austin know I'd found his father's killer. I should probably do it in person, but I was too banged up to track him down, and I hoped a phone call would do.

I hobbled into the house and found a note from my kids that they were both gone to friends' houses, and to check my text messages. Oops. Guess I'd missed them. I made it up the stairs to my bedroom and changed my clothes, finding several bruises all over my body, with the worst on my shoulder.

I took an ace bandage from the first aid kit and wrapped my ankle. With the extra support, it felt a lot better. After downing some pills, I carried my diet soda, along with a couple of ice packs, onto the deck and got comfortable on the swing with a few pillows to prop up my foot.

Coco had followed me around, and I gave him a chew treat while I put the call through to Austin. I explained the whole story and heard his shock and surprise to find out his sister was alive. "I want to see her."

"I'm sure you do, but she needs a couple of days to sort this all out. Can you give her that?"

"Yes, yes, of course. It's just that... well... this is huge. I never thought... if only Dad... he would have been..."

I heard the catch in his voice, and sorrow lanced through my heart. "Yeah... your sister's devastated about this too... as I'm sure you can imagine. I mean... finding out the woman who raised her had actually kidnapped her is bad enough, but add in that this same woman just killed her father... and now she'll never know him... well...you get the picture.

I heard his sniffles and continued. "You're going to have to help her through this, Austin. She's lost so much, but there is something good about it. She has you. You can help her know your parents, even though they're gone. And you'll have each other to lean on."

He cleared his throat and swallowed. "You're right. She's lost a lot, and she knows how I feel about losing our dad. We can share that."

"Yes... that, and so much more. She has a husband and a daughter. You're an uncle. Your niece's name is Ava." I told him what I could about Misti and her family and promised to call him in a few days.

"Thanks Shelby. I owe you so much, and I'm happy to pay you. I'm sure you went beyond anything I ever expected and—"

"No. No way. I didn't do it for the money. We figured it out... and now you have a sister. That's the best payment I could get." After disconnecting, I closed my eyes and let the rocking motion of the swing lull me into sleep.

Much later, I jerked awake to the sound of the patio door opening.

"I thought you might be out here," Chris said. "Whoa. What happened to you?"

"I fell down some stairs... well, actually, I was pushed." I shifted, so he could sit down with my legs in his lap, and told him the whole story.

"And here I thought working for Manetto would be the most dangerous part of your life." He shook his head. "Well, at least you solved the case." He scratched his chin, wondering if he should tell me now or wait until later.

"Tell me what?"

"Oh... geez... yeah. Uh... I finished up with Manetto's will and all the legal documents for handing the business over to you. I managed to get that condition inserted that you wanted about not actually running the business. I went over it with him this afternoon. He wanted me to go over it with you tonight. Are you up for it?"

"Why not go over it at his office?"

Chris shrugged. "I think he wants you and me to have the time alone to look it over and think about it before you sign it. He said he'd give us a day or two."

I nodded. "Okay. I guess I'd better get started on dinner, and we can do it after that." I struggled to get up, but Chris stopped me.

"You stay put. I'll make dinner tonight."

I smiled. "Thanks honey. While you're at it, could you get me another diet soda?"

He chuckled, then leaned over to pet Coco, knowing that he'd saved me today. "What a good dog you are."

He barked. *Yup.*

"What did he say?"

"I think he wants another treat." Sure it wasn't what he said, but after saving me today, he deserved it.

"Okay... one Diet Coke and a doggy treat coming up."

CHAPTER 16

Two days later, I got a phone call from Uncle Joey asking me to come in so we could discuss the will. My shoulder didn't hurt unless I moved it the wrong way, and I was back to walking normally, if a little slower. So that meant I had no excuse.

I looked into my closet and pulled out my black jeans. On a whim, I picked out a black, scoop-neck tee and tucked it in, wearing a black-and-silver belt as an accent. I slipped on a black necklace that I borrowed from Savannah. It consisted of black leather and chains and had the whole Goth look going for it.

I finished the ensemble by slipping on my black ankle boots. The boots helped support my ankle, but the rest of the outfit also seemed appropriate for the occasion. Hmmm... what would Bob say about that? Did I equate this with going to a funeral... which happened to be my own?

The bruise on my cheek had faded, but I wasn't about to hide it with makeup. Besides, it fit right in with my black outfit, so I might as well leave it alone. At least I didn't have a black eye, although I did add a little dark gray eyeshadow to my eyelids. I kept it to a minimum since I didn't want my eyes to look like Hella from *Thor Ragnarok*. I may be signing my life away, but it didn't mean I was a bad person.

I walked into Thrasher, and Jackie greeted me with a smile that turned into a frown. "Whoa, what happened to you?"

"I was working a case and got pushed down a flight of stairs by a crazy person."

Her eyes widened, and she wondered if I was telling the truth. "Seriously?" At my nod, she continued. "Wow, that's nuts. But you're okay?"

"Yeah. Just some bumps and bruises. How's Uncle Joey's foot?"

She rolled her eyes and shook her head. "Better. I think he's more embarrassed than anything, so I have to keep reminding him it wasn't his fault. Did you feel that earthquake?"

"Yes, I certainly did. I'm glad it wasn't any worse."

"That's for sure. Well, go on down, he's waiting for you."

I thanked her and began the long walk to his office, realizing I hadn't felt this much trepidation for a while. Going to Uncle Joey's office used to make me sick to my stomach, and today was just like that. Standing outside the door, I hesitated. I still had a choice. I didn't have to sign it if I didn't want to, right?

I sucked in a breath and knocked, then pushed the door open and stepped inside.

"Shelby, you made it. Come on in." He stood, noticing my all-black outfit and wondering if I'd done it to please him, since black was his favorite color. Other than the bruise on my cheek, it relieved him that I looked so good. "Chris told me about your incident with the stairs. You doing all right?"

"Yes, I'm fine. How about you? How's the foot?"

"It's good. Luckily, the knife didn't go all the way through, but it ruined my good shoes."

He motioned for me to sit down in front of his desk, thinking that he'd saved the voice mail I'd left on his phone from that day, mostly because I sounded so worried. It warmed his heart. That's why it was important to get this taken care of right away.

"Did you go over all the documents with Chris and have him explain everything to you?"

"Yes."

"Good." He opened the folder with the documents, then studied me before he spoke, noticing the anxious way I chewed on my bottom lip. He let out a big sigh, and fingered the paperwork before raising his gaze to mine. "I've had second thoughts about this, and I wanted to pass something by you before you sign anything."

He'd blocked his thoughts from me, so I just nodded and hoped for the best. "Uh... okay, sure."

"Good. Here's the deal." He leaned forward, resting his arms on his desk, with his fingers clasped together. His eyes held deep intensity. This was important to him, and he wanted to make sure I understood.

"After the whole drug fiasco, I started to wonder if getting out of the business was a good idea. If I'd been in charge, nothing like that would have happened, because I know what I'm doing." He shook his head and sat back in his chair.

"Those amateurs sullied my good name and implicated me for something I didn't even do. It made me think that the same thing could happen with any number of my other businesses. You know what I mean?"

"Yeah... sure. I can see that." Did that mean he was keeping the mob part and still wanted me to be his successor anyway? Crap.

"So... after further consideration, you'll be happy to know that I've decided to forego the plan to leave it all to you." He caught my gaze and smiled. "In other words, Shelby, I've changed my mind. I'm keeping the business the way it is. I'm good at what I do, and I'll figure out a way to divide it up if and when I ever get to that point."

"What?" I sat up straight. "So... you're not leaving it to me?"

"That's right. I hope you're okay with that." Given how unhappy I'd been with the whole idea, he thought I'd be ecstatic. Instead, I sounded disappointed. Or was it shock?

"I'm not your successor?"

"No."

My breath whooshed out of me, and I flopped back in my chair. "Holy hell."

His lips twisted in a sardonic smile. "I still want you to be the executor of my estate after I'm gone, but that's all." He was thinking he'd leave me with a nice chunk of real estate too, but we could discuss that another time.

"Okay... sure. I can do that." I sounded way too cheerful, but I couldn't help it. A big weight had just lifted off my shoulders, and I could finally breathe again.

"Good. So, now that things are back to normal, I was hoping you could help me out with something."

I smiled. "Of course. What do you need?"

His grin turned devilish. "First off, I need you and Ramos to take a message to Vinny." He was thinking that Vinny had messed up and he needed Ramos to remind him of who was in charge. I was mostly going along for the ride, but I might learn something valuable.

I grinned so hard that my bruised cheek started to hurt, but I didn't mind in the least. "Sounds good to me."

Uncle Joey put the call through. Ramos said he was just finishing up a job, and he'd meet me downstairs in the parking garage.

I took the elevator with a lighter step and it dawned on me that Uncle Joey wasn't leaving his life of crime behind after all. I'd been pleased about that, but now I didn't mind so much. In fact, if it kept me from running the business, I was all for it. I shook my head, hoping that didn't mean I was a hypocrite.

Exiting the elevator, I heard the approaching roar of Ramos's motorcycle, and a little thrill went through me. He pulled up next to his car, and I met him there. After popping the trunk, he took out my helmet and handed it over.

He couldn't help noticing that I wore all black, and I looked sassy as hell. Had I finally accepted my fate and come over to the dark side? Or... did I know I'd be going on a ride with him? His gaze landed on my face, and his brows puckered. "Whoa. Where'd you get the bruise?"

A satisfied smile from his compliment twerked my lips. "Did you mean sassy or sexy?"

He shrugged. "Is there a difference?"

I grinned. It was nice to know he drooled over me once in a while, although... looking sassy, or sexy... wasn't exactly in the same category as his full-blown and complete hotness, but it was still gratifying.

"Your bruise?"

"Oh, right." I explained the stairs and the crazy person, watching his face darken with each word. "The dog saved me."

He shook his head. "I swear, you get into the worst situations." He blew out a breath. "Just tell me you're keeping the dog?"

In true dog-like fashion I answered. "Yup." Snickering to myself, I slipped on the helmet. After climbing on behind Ramos, I clutched his waist and we were off. I didn't even know where we were going, so it surprised me to pull into the back parking lot of the Tiki Tabu.

I pulled off my helmet. "Is this for real?" I wouldn't put it past Uncle Joey to rig this.

"What? You think I have ulterior motives?"

"That wasn't an answer... and yes... always."

He grinned and motioned with his head. "Come on. We've got work to do."

"So did Uncle Joey tell you I was off the hook?"

He nodded. "If you want to know the truth, you have me to thank for it." At my widened eyes, he continued. "I may have told him he needed to stay in control of the business, so stupid things like this drug incident wouldn't happen again." He was thinking that Manetto had already come to the same conclusion, but it didn't hurt to tell me he'd also done his part. "So how does it feel?"

"Ah... so... so great."

Smiling, he pulled the door open, and we entered the dark bar. It took a minute for my eyes to adjust, but, since it was just after noon, there wasn't the big crowd I was used to. Ramos spotted Vinny at the bar and motioned him to join us at a back booth.

Vinny sat on one side, and Ramos slid into the other next to me, our thighs touching in the small space. I could have scooted further into the corner, so he'd have more room, but why on earth would I do that?

"Here's the deal," Ramos began. "Manetto and Shelby have straightened out the mess you made. Shelby used her position as a police consultant to help them find the kid who killed Slasher. She had to explain to the cops that her information came from an informant, in order to keep her association with Manetto under the radar. It put her in a compromising situation. You understand?"

Ramos waited for Vinny to nod before continuing. "So... from now on, you are going to take the role as her informant. Anytime she gets information from me, or Manetto, or whoever... it's you who gets the credit. That way, if anything ever comes back to her, or she has to give up a name to stay in good with the cops, it's your name she'll be using. Is that clear?"

"Uh... yeah... sure." He didn't like it much, but it was better than being dead.

"And one more thing... Manetto's back in the game. Your incompetence proved to him that if he wants to stay out of jail, he's got to be running things. He also doesn't want his reputation ruined by some upstart wannabes. Lucky for you, he's trusting Vic to take care of all the loose ends... which includes you. But this is a warning. Your days are numbered if anything like this ever happens again."

"So... it's up to Vic what happens to me?" Vinny thought he was getting off easy if that were the case. At Ramos's nod, he continued. "And I need to pass information to Shelby if she needs it? But Shelby's on Manetto's side, right?"

They both glanced my way, and I quickly nodded. "Yeah... sure."

"Okay, I'll do it." He thought I seemed too nice to turn him in, so he'd take what he could get.

A man stepped beside our table, his large bulk casting a shadow over us. "Hey... you're back."

"Oh... hi." I smiled up at Big Kahuna. "Thanks for the interference the other night."

"Ah... no problem, but I was disappointed you couldn't stay and use your cue."

"I could play now. Would that work?" I glanced at Ramos. "Uh... you don't need me anymore, right?"

He leaned toward me, his lips tantalizingly close. "Not at the moment." I froze, unable to move until he smiled and slid out of the booth. Embarrassed, I hurried out behind him, following Big Kahuna to the pool tables.

It had been a couple of months since I'd played, but I knew right where my cue stick was. I took it down and chalked the end while Big Kahuna racked the balls.

He glanced my way. "You wanna break the rack?" He was thinking that I should go first to make it fairer, since I wasn't as good as him.

I was terrible at breaking the balls, but his reasoning made sense, so I nodded and got in position. He thought I should set the white ball more to the left and not hit the first ball head-on, so I moved slightly and leaned over to line up the ball with my stick.

Hearing nothing from him, I figured it was a good placement and, after moving the cue stick back and forth a few times, I concentrated on hitting the white ball dead center. Ready, I held my breath and hit the ball as hard as I could.

The ball basically went where I wanted, and one of the striped balls hit the corner pocket. Surprised, I grinned and pumped my fist in the air.

"Yay. Guess I'm stripes." I studied the table, listening closely for what ball he thought I should go for. Following his advice, I lined up the shot and leaned over to take it.

His mind went blank again, which puzzled me, but I took the shot anyway. Unfortunately, I missed and it was his turn. I straightened and glanced his way with a frown. He sent me a smile, thinking that he'd take a couple of shots, but he might have to miss so that I could have another turn.

His thoughtfulness surprised me, since I knew he didn't like to lose to anyone, but this was my lucky day. I mean... I was off the hook with Uncle Joey, so it could happen.

Ramos and Vinny finished their conversation, and both of them came over to watch the game. They stood behind Big Kahuna, and Ramos leaned casually against one of the unused pool tables. He looked so hot that it was hard to take my gaze away.

I heard Big Kahuna take his shot, and watched the ball miss the pocket, just like he'd planned. Hmm... did that mean if I won, it was rigged and didn't count? Maybe... but I'd still take it. Big Kahuna thought about the shot I should take, so I got into position.

Leaning over the table, I lined up the shot. I caught a strangled sigh from someone in front of me, but concentrated hard to block out everyone's thoughts, and took the shot.

The ball hit the corner pocket and I glanced up with a smile, catching Ramos's gaze. "See that?"

Swallowing, he nodded, and I calculated my next shot. The best one was on the other side of the table, so I moved into position. Everyone shifted to watch me take the shot, so I listened carefully to Big Kahuna's mind for advice on how to line up the ball.

Leaning over, I listened again, hoping he'd have more to say, but all I heard was *take your time, take your time*, which he kept repeating over and over.

After moving my stick back and forth a few times, his mantra was starting to make me nervous. Knowing I'd taken way too much time by this point, I took the shot. The cue ball hit the striped ball, but, instead of going into the pocket, it hit one of Big Kahuna's balls and sent it into the side pocket. Oops.

"Does that mean I get another shot, even if it was your ball I hit in?" I knew that wasn't right, but what the heck? Today was my lucky day, so it didn't hurt to ask.

"Uh... sure. I'll give it to you."

"Really? Okay." It was a shameless move, but I didn't care. I listened to him for my next shot, and moved around the table to line it up. As I set up the shot, leaning over to size it up, I picked up a thought from Ramos. Only it was more of a groan... in his mind. I'd never heard him groan like that before.

As I leaned over to take the shot, it dawned on me. My scoop-neck tee gaped open, showing a lot more than I wanted, every time I leaned over.

Damn. I hit the ball so hard, it missed the one I aimed for and hit a grouping of balls behind instead, sending one of mine into the pocket by pure luck. With my mouth open, I glanced up at all three men and shook my head.

Holy hell. Big Kahuna wasn't being nice to take it easy on me. He was being nice because of the view he got every time I leaned over. I gave them my best stare, but not one of them looked a bit sorry.

I narrowed my eyes at Ramos and lifted my brow. Why hadn't he told me? His lips twitched, but he wasn't about to apologize. It wasn't his fault I'd worn that shirt, and I could hardly blame him for enjoying the view.

I rolled my eyes, grateful that I'd worn my black bra... but still.

"It's still your turn. You gonna take the shot?" Impervious to my stare, Big Kahuna dismissed my antics, and smiled with encouragement. "How about you go for the blue four? It's in a good place."

Yeah... a good spot for him. I took a breath. How was I going to finish this game now? I didn't want to disappoint

Big Kahuna. I glanced at Ramos, and he raised his brow in a challenge, thinking *your move, Babe.*

I stepped to the cue ball, which left me facing all three men... of course. I felt their anticipation and shook my head. Before leaning over, I twisted my arm behind me and pulled the back of my shirt down at the waist, tightening it just enough that the front didn't gape open so far. Quickly letting go, I got in position and took the shot, totally missing the ball.

I heard their collective sighs that I was on to them. Exhaling with disappointment, Big Kahuna figured he might as well finish the game. He sunk every single shot after that, ending the game with the eight ball in the corner pocket.

He glanced my way. "Wanna play again?" He could always hope.

"Uh... I need to go. But good game. You're the best."

That made him smile. "Don't wait so long to come back next time."

"I won't." I slipped my stick back into its slot, and both Ramos and I said our goodbyes.

Ramos followed me out of the bar, walking by my side to the bike. "It looks like you've got a real informant now. It should help your job with the police."

"Yeah. I didn't expect that. But it's a good move."

He smiled, thinking I'd made some good moves back there too. It was enough to keep him happy for a while. He looked forward to bringing me back to play pool again, as long as I wore that shirt.

"Ha ha. How about this? I'll wear it as long as you play without one."

He chuckled. "Babe. You've got yourself a deal." He meant every word.

Oops... me and my big mouth. "Uh... yeah, right. As if..."

He turned to face me, standing close, without any part of our bodies touching. "I don't make deals I don't keep."

"We'll see."

"So you're not taking me up on it?"

"Would you really take your shirt off?"

"I guess you'll never know."

"Ugh. I can't win. Remind me that I shouldn't play games with you."

He chuckled. "Now what would be the fun in that?"

I shook my head and smacked him in the arm because he was right. I enjoyed this banter with him way too much, and I wasn't sure I could stop. No, that wasn't right. I could probably stop, but did I want to? Nope. Still, I vowed to do better in the future.

That worked until I got on the motorcycle behind him, and all I could think about was playing pool with a bare-chested Ramos. My cheeks flushed just thinking about it. Sure... it was tempting... but, of course, it was never going to happen. Even so... I could still dream about it, right?

The next morning, I left home to take Coco on a walk. But this wasn't just any walk. We were headed over to Mack Haywood's house. Today, Misti and Austin were meeting at Mack's house for the first time, and since they'd both wanted me and Coco there, I was happy to oblige.

They'd decided to meet at Mack's house because it was common ground, and Austin had asked me to come a little early.

I was excited to be included, but I didn't plan on staying too long. I had other things to do today, one of which was finally getting that doggy door installed. I'd had to order a

whole new pane of glass with the door in it. That meant
they had to take the old pane out to make the exchange. But
I was excited that Coco wouldn't have to wait for one of us
to let him out whenever he needed to go.

I'd also had a chat with Lance Hobbs about getting the
training for the search-and-rescue team. He'd been thrilled,
especially when I'd asked if Josh could come with me. I told
him I'd solved Mack's murder, but I was waiting to tell him
all the details until our first training session at one this
afternoon.

I knew he'd be proud of Coco when he heard that the
dog had come to my rescue when I needed it.

As we neared Mack's house, I told Coco we were going
for a visit. "It's just for a little while, then we're going home.
Okay?"

Yup.

I didn't know how dogs dealt with death, but Coco
seemed like he'd moved on.

I knocked on the door, and Austin pulled it open with a
big grin on his face. "Hey there." He leaned over and ruffled
Coco's fur. "Come on in. Look Coco, I put everything back.
See?"

Inside, everything had changed. The furniture was back
in place, and pictures hung on the walls. All the boxes were
gone, and it looked like someone was living there.

"Do you like it?" Austin asked me. At my nod, he
continued. "I decided to move in. I mean... why live in an
apartment when you have a house, right? Some of the
furniture is mine, but I kept most of my Dad's stuff."

"That's great. What made you change your mind?"

"I think I finally accepted what happened to him... and
that he's gone. He'd want me to be happy and live a good
life. I had to let go of the anger. A lot of it is because of you.
It made a difference to find out what happened to him and

why. Now I have a sister. I just thought she'd want to see this place and the things that made us a family."

I nodded. "That makes sense."

Austin stuffed his hands in his pockets, and I picked up an underlying worry. He wanted to ask me something, but he didn't know how. Glancing at the dog, he spoke. "Hey Coco... I got your bowls out. Want a drink?"

Coco woofed and ran into the kitchen. He knew right where his bowls were and lapped up the water. Finished, he sniffed around and trotted over to a shaggy dog bed that sat in a special place by the back door. "See your bed? I found that too."

Coco sniffed it first, then turned around in a circle a few times and plopped down. He rested his head over the edge, like all was right with the world, and closed his eyes. My stomach tightened, and I suddenly knew what Austin wanted.

"Wow," I said, my heart breaking. "He looks comfy."

"Yeah. Uh... there's something I wanted to ask you." He rubbed a hand over his face. "You have to understand that when I found my dad..." he motioned to the spot where his father had died, "like that, I wasn't thinking straight. I blamed Coco, and I shouldn't have. It wasn't his fault. I took him to the pound, and that was wrong. I shouldn't have done that to him. He was all I had left, and it was a stupid thing to do.

"I know this isn't fair for me to ask, and I'll totally get it if you don't want to agree... but I was hoping that maybe... just maybe... there was a slight chance you'd let me keep him?"

I couldn't seem to breathe. "Oh... uh... I don't know what to say. He's... uh... a great dog, and we've ... my family... we've all gotten pretty attached to him."

Austin nodded. "Of course. I just... I just wondered if you'd give me a second chance. But if it's too much, I understand."

My heart broke for him. If Mack had died any other way, Austin would have taken Coco and been happy to have him. He was right. His emotions had gotten the best of him, and he'd made a mistake. Did that mean he'd lost his chance? He'd lost his dad. That was huge. Coco would probably help him through his grief. Coco had lost Mack too. Was it right for me to keep them apart?

"How about this," I said. "Let's leave it up to Coco. If he wants to stay, I'm not going to fight it. But if he wants to go with me, will you let him leave?"

Austin nodded, thinking that was better than nothing. With Coco's bed and his bowls back in place, Austin hoped the dog would choose him. "Yeah, sure. I think that's a great solution. Thanks for giving me a chance."

"Sure." I nodded, but I couldn't exactly smile. This visit was breaking my heart. How could I give up the dog who'd saved my life? Who'd become so important to me? What would I tell my kids? I glanced at Coco. He seemed content, but that didn't mean he'd stay, right?

The sound of a car door shutting drew both of us to the living room. Misti stood uncertainly beside the car before stepping toward the house. I went outside onto the porch while Austin hung back, awash with sudden nerves.

Misti waved and smiled. She'd wanted this first meeting to be without her husband and daughter, but she was grateful I was there to break the ice. As she stepped toward the house, Austin came out on the porch. Catching sight of him, she stopped.

"Macie?"

Hearing Austin use her real name triggered something inside of her. A flash of a dark head on a swing danced in her mind, and she knew it was him. Her brother. All those years ago, and it was still there in her memory. "Aussie?"

With tears in her eyes, she stepped toward him, and he met her in a tight embrace. Coco came to the door to see what was going on, and I let him out. He ran to them and barked, jumping up with excitement.

"Hey Coco," Misti said, patting his head.

Coco barked and ran around them a couple of times. Laughing, they hugged again. With their arms around each other's waists, they came to the porch where I stood. I let Coco inside, and Misti gave me a hug. "Thanks for being here, Shelby."

"Of course. How are you doing?"

"I'm doing pretty good actually. I feel so free, and I'm a lot happier now." She was thinking that she hadn't seen Carolyn since she'd been arrested, and she'd probably never see her again.

"That's great."

I followed them into the living room, and Misti took in the furnishings. Her gaze landed on a picture that hung on the wall, and her breath caught. She rushed forward to examine the family photo of her parents with her and Austin sitting on their laps.

As tears ran down her face, Austin came to her side and put his arm over her shoulder.

"There's so much that I missed... it's breaking my heart. I don't know if I can handle it."

"We both missed a lot," Austin said. "But you're here now. We can start over." She sniffed and nodded. "I don't know what to call you. You've always been Macie to me, so I might mess up."

"It's okay, as long as I can call you Aussie once in a while."

He chuckled. "You want something to drink? I've got coffee, tea, soda, juice, or beer. I didn't know what you liked, so I got a lot of different things."

"Uh... I don't know... how about juice?"

"You want something, Shelby?"

"No... I'm fine, thanks."

He rushed into the kitchen, and Misti turned to me. "This might sound crazy, but, being here... it feels like home."

Austin came back with a can of juice for her. "Here you go. I hope you like peach."

"Oh my gosh... it's my favorite."

"Mine too." Joy brightened Austin's smile, and I knew he'd be just fine.

That was my cue to leave, even though it was killing me. "I think it's time for me to go. Is that all right? You guys okay here?"

"Yes. Of course," Misti said.

"Thanks so much." Austin gave me a quick hug, meaning it with all his heart.

I glanced into the kitchen. Coco lay curled up in his bed, just like he belonged there. I swallowed and turned toward the door. "All right. Let's keep in touch."

"You can count on it," Austin said.

I hurried out the door, blinking back the tears that blinded me. My mind knew it was right that Coco belonged with Austin, but my heart didn't agree. Mack would have wanted Austin to take Coco... and Coco would be fine there in his own house. Austin would take good care of him. He'd probably even join the search-and-rescue team in honor of his dad.

How could I stand in the way of that? Still, leaving Coco behind hurt more than I'd imagined, and I had to bite my tongue to keep from calling him to my side. Somehow, I managed to keep walking all the way to the corner of the street before I stopped.

I took one last look back at the house. A part of me had hoped Coco would notice that I wasn't there and come running after me. Or at least bark to be let out. But all I got was silence. After waiting several seconds, I turned away and began the long walk home.

The tears came fast, practically blinding me. I had to keep wiping my eyes so I could see where I was going. I realized that I still held Coco's leash in my hand, but there was no way I could take it back to Austin. I turned another corner and started down the next street.

A car passed, and I ducked my head, turning slightly away, so they wouldn't see me crying and wonder what was wrong. I shook my head and tried to calm down. It was just a dog. It wasn't like someone had died. I could get through this. I'd been through a lot worse.

As much as I'd hoped that would help, it didn't make a dent. No matter what I'd been through... this was still hard. I stopped to pull a tissue out of my pocket and blew my nose. I stuffed the tissue away and tried to calm down. Taking a couple of deep breaths, I closed my eyes and pushed the tears away.

A bark sounded behind me. My breath caught, and I whipped around. A flash of black and tan darted toward me. He'd come. As he bounded my way, I knelt on one knee to catch him in my arms. He licked my face and whined. His woof caught me off guard. *Why you leave?*

"I'm sorry, but I thought you wanted to stay with Austin."

Stay you. You mine.

"You're mine too." Tears ran down my face, but this time they were happy tears. "I promise I'll never leave you again."

Don't cry. I here. I here.

"I know. I'm so glad you came."

You mine.

"Yes." My phone rang, and I dug it out of my pocket. "Hello?"

"Shelby, it's Austin. Is Coco with you? He just ran off, and I couldn't stop him."

"Yeah. I've got him. He's with me."

He sighed. "Okay... good. I guess that means he picked you."

"Yes. I think it does."

"Take good care of him."

"I will."

I tucked my phone away and gave Coco another rub and kiss on the nose. In the excitement, I'd dropped his leash, so I leaned down to pick it up and fastened it to his collar. "You ready to go home?"

Home. You.

"That's right."

Yup.

I wiped my eyes, and we started off, Coco beside me and my heart full. He'd chosen me, and I'd promised to take care of him. Of course, he'd helped me more than I could say in the short time he'd been in my life, and I vowed that, no matter what the future held, we'd face it together.

The last few weeks had challenged me, but a lot of good had happened as well. A ghost had helped me put a killer away. Misti and Austin had been reunited. A psychic was out of my hair, and, best of all, I didn't have to worry about being Uncle Joey's successor. There was plenty of work to do, but I had a great family, a faithful dog, and special friends to depend on.

Sure, I got into some crazy stuff that I couldn't always explain, but that's what made life interesting. Maybe that's what Bob Spicer meant when he talked about keeping a barf journal.

I'd learned that it's important to acknowledge that a lot of things are upsetting and out of my control, but it's just as important to let them go, so they can't hurt me anymore.

I'd also learned that it's equally essential to focus on the positive side of things. So... even after everything I'd gone through lately, I needed to remember that I had a good life. Full of ups and downs, scary earthquakes, and wet doggy kisses. But, in the end, my life was awesome, and from now on, I'd do my best to appreciate every last minute of it.

Thank you for reading **Dying Wishes: A Shelby Nichols Adventure**. I am currently hard at work on Shelby's next adventure and promise to do my best for another thrilling ride!

If you enjoyed this book, please consider leaving a review on Amazon. It's a great way to thank an author and keep her writing! **Dying Wishes** is also available on Kindle and Audible!

Want to know more about Ramos? **Devil in a Black Suit**, a book about Ramos and his mysterious past from his point of view is available in paperback, ebook, and audible formats. Get your copy today!

A Midsummer Night's Murder: A Shelby Nichols Novella is available for just .99 on Amazon Kindle. It's also available on Audible. Don't miss this fun novella!

NEWSLETTER SIGNUP For news, updates, and special offers, please sign up for my newsletter on my website: www.colleenhelme.com. To thank you for subscribing you will receive a FREE ebook.

SHELBY NICHOLS CONSULTING Don't miss Shelby's blog posts about her everyday life! Be sure to visit shelbynicholsconsulting.com.

ABOUT THE AUTHOR

USA TODAY AND WALL STREET JOURNAL
BESTSLLING AUTHOR

As the author of the Shelby Nichols Adventure Series, Colleen is often asked if Shelby Nichols is her alter-ego. "Definitely," she says. "Shelby is the epitome of everything I wish I dared to be." Known for her laugh since she was a kid, Colleen has always tried to find the humor in every situation and continues to enjoy writing about Shelby's adventures. "I love getting Shelby into trouble... I just don't always know how to get her out of it!" Besides writing, she loves a good book, biking, hiking, and playing board and card games with family and friends. She loves to connect with readers and admits that fans of the series keep her writing.

Connect with Colleen at www.colleenhelme.com